II0700735

# Charity's Cross

Charles Towne Belles 4

*MaryLu*
# Tyndall

CALGARY PUBLIC LIBRARY

OCT     2016

# Charity's Cross

## Charles Towne Belles 4

© 2016 by MaryLu Tyndall

Published by Ransom Press
San Jose, CA 95123

ISBN: 978-0-9971671-1-5
E-Version ISBN: 978-0-9971671-0-8

All rights reserved. No part of this publication may be reproduced, stored in a retrieval system, or transmitted in any form or by any means without the written permission of the author, MaryLu Tyndall.

Library of Congress Cataloging-in-Publication Data is on file at the Library of Congress, Washington, DC.

This book is a work of fiction. Names, characters, places, incidents, and dialogues are either products of the author's imagination or used fictitiously. Any similarity to actual people, organizations, and/or events is purely coincidental

**Cover Design** by Ravven
**Editors:** Lora Doncea

Ransom Press
San Jose, CA

## Dedication

To anyone who believes God has forgotten them

*He has not dealt with us according to our sins; Nor*
*punished us according to our iniquities.*
*For as the heavens are high above the earth, so great is*
*His mercy toward those who fear Him*
*Psalm 103: 10-11*

## Acknowledgments

All praise to my Father in Heaven, who opens my mind, stirs my creativity, and gives me great story ideas. I only hope and pray I do them justice.

I'm so grateful for my friend Debbie Mitchell, who always reads my manuscript in its raw and unpolished form. And she still loves it! She also creates great Memes and helps me market my books. You are a rare gem, Chappy.

Many thanks to Michelle Griep, an author far better than I am, who blesses me by exchanging manuscripts so we can nitpick on each other's work. All in fun, of course!

I so appreciate my online friends, too many to name, who offer ideas and support. And I especially am grateful to all my readers. Without you, my books would be so lonely.

Thank you!

But most of all, to God be the glory!

# Chapter 1

Charity killed her husband. She knew it the minute the pistol fired. She knew it the minute he froze and his eyes widened in horror. His grip on the barrel of the gun remained strong as he stared at her, the life spilling from those eyes like water from a glass tipped over. She trembled and sought her breath, but only gun smoke filled her lungs. She couldn't cough ... couldn't move. And still he stood there, frozen in time, as if unwilling to accept his fate.

Jerking the pistol from his grip, she nudged him back before he used his remaining energy to strike her again. Her mind spun as she rubbed the bruise forming on her cheek. The gun clattered to the floor, though she barely heard it...or her husband's moan as he stumbled backward, clutching his chest. He toppled to the Persian rug he loved so much and breathed out his last words, "I'll see you in hell."

'Twas the only truthful thing the man had said in their two years of marriage.

Blood bubbled over his cherished gold-embroidered waistcoat, but all she could think about was the way the fading sunlight streaming in through the parlor windows danced on the settee beside which he lay. Steam from the silver teapot swirled upward in a vaporous dance that defied the evil tidings of the day. Outside, the clomp of horses and clank of carriages blended with the distant bells of ships in Portsmouth harbor.

Charity blinked. Her lungs dense as iron, her mind awhirl. Was she free? Was he *truly* dead? Or would he rise any minute, mock her with his usual caustic tone, and then finish what he had started?

A drop of blood trickled from her lips, the metallic taste all too familiar.

"Milady, milady!" The hysterical voice preceded a scream that would no doubt alert the entire staff. Sophie, her lady's maid, halted in the center of the parlor, her eyes wide as biscuits, her screech loud enough to raise the dead. Her tray crashed to the floor in a jangling mass of biscuits and teacups. "Holy mother of … Wha' 'ave you done?"

Taking a deep breath, Charity swallowed, stretched out her neck, and replied with more calmness than she felt. "I've killed Lord Villemont, as you can see."

Clutching her skirts, she moved to the buffet, poured herself some of her husband's precious *Brandy de Jerez* from Spain, and flipped it to the back of her throat. The spicy liquor burned her tongue and slithered down to her stomach like a searing serpent. She coughed and held a hand over a belly that was threatening to dislodge what remained of her dinner.

"Milady." The quiver in her maid's voice turned Charity around to see poor Sophie, her face a sheet of white, her mobcap askew, and every inch of her plump body trembling. Still, she remained, didn't dash out as Charity would have expected, abandoning her like everyone else. "Wha' are we to do?"

A very good question. The answer to which escaped Charity at the moment. She must think … think …

Footsteps alerted her to Jenson, their butler, bursting into the room faster than she'd ever seen him move. "I heard a shot, milady. Is everything—" His gaze landed on his lordship lying on the floor in a pool of blood. He darted for him.

Dropping to her knees, Sophie pretended to minister to Lord Villemont as she blocked Jenson's sight of his master.

Charity lifted her chin. "Lord Villemont has had an accident, Jenson. Please send for the physician straight away." She heard the quiver in her own voice and hoped the butler was not so astute.

"But he looks ..."

"Jenson, do you wish him to die while you are dawdling?"

"Yes, milady. I mean, no milady." Turning, he rushed away, blubbering to himself.

Though Sophie still shook like a tree under a gale, she placed her fingers on Lord Villemont's throat as the front door slammed shut.

"Is he dead?"

"Yes, milady."

Charity finally found the courage to look at the man who had caused her more pain than she'd thought humanly possible. Lying there, he seemed so small, so powerless, like a fire deprived of its flames, a ship its sails. Remorse, followed by a tinge of sorrow, dared to burn in her throat. But she swallowed them down. There was no time for either.

Sophie rose. "I know you didn't do it on purpose." Tears slipped down her cheeks as she picked up biscuits and broken tea cups. The pieces of china clattered in her hands.

Kneeling beside her, Charity touched her arm. "Never mind about the mess, Sophie. I need you to calm yourself. Can you do that?"

The maid swallowed, but finally nodded and wiped her face with her sleeve. Charity grabbed her hand and all but dragged her out the parlor doors and up the staircase to her bedchamber.

Flinging open her wardrobe, she grabbed her valise and stuffed it with her underthings, a skirt, bodice, an extra pair of shoes, cloak, anything she might need.

"You mean to leave, milady?" Sophie whimpered.

"Sophie, my jewels. Gather them."

"Which ones?"

Charity turned to see her maid wringing her hands and staring at her with a look of horror.

"*All* of them."

Wiping tears once again from her face, Sophie stepped toward the dresser and began opening drawers.

Now, for the money. The eight pounds, ten shillings Charity had managed to pilfer from the funds Lord Villemont had given her to run the estate. She lifted the painting from the wall above her dressing table, laid it face down on her bed, grabbed a letter opener, and snapped open one of the wooden slats forming the back of the frame. *Still there.* She breathed a sigh of relief, then withdrew the notes and coins.

Sophie approached and gasped at the sight, her hands full of velvet pouches.

"Where did you get all tha' money?"

"Never mind that. Put the jewels in my valise." Grabbing the case, Charity tossed in the money then held it open for the maid. She complied, but tears once again streamed down her cheeks.

"You're bleedin', milady." She reached toward Charity's face, but Charity swatted her hand away with all the force of her anger. Her husband's opal ring had left its mark for the last time.

"Forgive me, Sophie. I must leave at once. There's no time." Slamming the case shut, Charity took one final glance over her bedchamber, the crimson velvet curtains with gold-braided trim, her ivory-topped dressing table with gilded mirror, four-poster bed covered in silk embroidered hangings, her mahogany wardrobe full of London's latest fashions. Lord Villemont had kept her in luxury. *Kept* being the appropriate term. Though she had not shared the chamber with his lordship, neither had it been a haven, for he'd often crashed through the door in a drunken rage and forced himself upon her. Taking a deep breath, she nodded at Sophie and headed toward the door.

The maid leapt in front of her. Anxious, pleading eyes pierced hers.

"But it were self-defense, I'll attest to tha' milady."

"You and you alone. They won't believe us, Sophie. They'll hang me." Charity took the maid's hand and squeezed it. Sweet, innocent Sophie.

"But where will you go?"

"I have no idea." Charity had no family nearby. No friends that weren't first Lord Villemont's. She was completely and utterly alone. Tearing out the door, she sped down the stairs.

"I'm comin' with you, milady." The *tap tap* of Sophie's footsteps followed her.

"Nay, Sophie. I cannot allow it. You'll be branded a murderer right alongside me."

"Do you think I care about tha'?"

Swallowing her emotion at Sophie's loyalty, Charity stopped at the parlor door and stared at the man who had been her husband. She fully expected him to rise, laugh at her stupidity, and advance on her with the full force of his rage. But he remained still, not a breath stirring his chest, not a snarl on his lips, not a twitch from those hands that had been so cruel.

"Now, you can never hurt me"—she placed a hand on her belly—"*us* ever again."

Shadows passed over the windows, and she glanced up to see men approaching.

Sophie tugged on her arm. "Hurry, out the back, milady."

They rushed through the back hallway, past the servants' stairs, warming room, and the kitchen, past staring servants, footmen, and kitchen maids who were cleaning up after supper and already preparing for the morning meal. Hemsley House boasted a housekeeper, butler, cook, two kitchen maids, a valet, lady's maid, and four housemaids. Servants—a luxury Charity would never have again.

Nor would she have a carriage and footman, ready at her command. Flinging open the back door, she halted and turned.

"I'll always remember you, dear, sweet Sophie." Charity kissed the maid on the cheek.

"Of course you will, because I'm comin' with you, milady." Sophie grabbed her coat from a hook by the wall.

"I order you to remain." Charity shot back over her shoulder as she crossed the small yard and ducked into the shadow of a tree. From there, she spotted the physician and none other than her brother-in-law, Charles, following an hysterical Jenson through the front door.

Sophie appeared beside her. With no time or energy to argue with the stubborn maid, Charity grabbed her valise with one hand, her skirts with the other, and slipped into the encroaching night.

Minutes that seemed like hours later, she slid beside an old warehouse on Broad Street and scanned the ships anchored at port. Though darkness had descended, goods were still being loaded and unloaded onto vessels tied to long wharfs and others anchored in the bay. Laughter and music blared from pubs and brothels just coming to life and opening doors to sailors who'd been long at sea.

Sophie inched beside her, breathless. Charity shifted her shoes over the rough gravel, seeking a comfortable position for her aching feet. A chilled mist drifted in from the bay, smelling of fish and brine and cooling the perspiration on Charity's neck.

Clanging bells joined the lap of waves as eerie music from a pianoforte snaked around the bricks of the warehouse.

*Think ... think...* She bit her lip as the reality of her situation finally took hold. By now, Charles had gathered the Constable and they'd be scouring the city for her.

And the port would be the first place they'd look.

She closed her eyes. *Sing a song of sixpence, pocket full of rye, four-and-twenty back birds baked in a pie* ... She continued the song in her thoughts, longing for it to draw her deep into the safe place in her mind where there was no fear, no fury—where no one could do her harm.

But it wasn't working.

Setting down her valise, she clutched Sophie's trembling hand. "You shouldn't have come, Sophie." Though in truth, Charity was touched that she had. Despite that the maid's skills at cinching up a stay and coiffing Charity's hair were of little use to her on the run, she was glad for the company. For the care.

"I couldn't 'ave left you, milady."

Charity squeezed her hand. "Well, we must find our way onto one of those ships. I bid you pray to God for a miracle."

Sophie would have to be the one doing the praying, for Charity had given up on that useless endeavor years ago.

"I don't take passengers, Miss...Miss..." The rotund, balding captain turned to issue more orders to his men then spit to the side as he eyed her suspiciously.

"Ald...Aldsworth. And this is my maid, Miss Carrol." Charity gestured toward Sophie, whose gaze skittered about like a bird trapped in a cage. "Please, Captain. I beg you. The dock master said you are the only ship sailing out tonight."

"Aye, that be true. If my rattlepated purser hadn't gotten the shipment wrong, I wouldn't be late on me delivery. As it be, I can't wait till mornin'."

"I'm willing to pay."

He scanned her with brazen impudence. "Miss Aldsworth, were it? I don't want no trouble, an' bringin' a woman aboard without benefit o' escort will bring me plenty of that."

*Impudent man.* Charity ground her teeth. "I promise we will keep to our cabin. I beg you, Sir, 'tis a life and death situation."

"Humph. Here or in Nassau?"

Footsteps and shouting sounded behind her.

Sophie tugged on her sleeve.

*Nassau?* Charity swallowed. She hadn't even thought to ask where the ship was going. The dock master said it sailed to the colonies. Still, she had hoped for a more northerly port—somewhere near Charles Towne where her father and sisters had moved.

"I have family in Nassau. They are ill."

The captain scratched his bald head. "All o' them?"

The footsteps grew louder. Sophie's grip tightened. One glance over her shoulder revealed several men pushing their way through the throng toward them. Panic froze her in place. She took a deep breath and pushed it back. *When the pie was opened, the birds began to sing...*

The captain followed her gaze and narrowed his eyes. "Sorry, Miss ... I smells something fishy an' it ain't from the sea." He turned, shouted further orders to the sailors in the boat, then started for the plank.

"How does two pounds sound?"

The captain spun about and cocked his head.

Reaching into her valise, she pulled out the notes. "I'll pay you double if you take us to the ship right now and don't tell a soul."

"Lady, I'll take ye to the moon for that sum." He chuckled and held his hand open.

"You'll have half when I'm standing on your deck and the other half when we arrive in Nassau."

His smile revealed teeth that matched the muddy water of the bay. "Yer a shrewd one, I'll grant ye that. But 'tis a deal ye have. My men'll help ye aboard."

At their captain's command, two slovenly-looking fellows assisted Charity and Sophie down into a small boat. Within minutes—and after awkwardly climbing a rope ladder—they stood on the deck of the *Neptune,* or so it said on the hull, a rather large ship that looked as though rust and tar alone held it together.

The commotion ashore had turned into a full-fledged ruckus with whistles blowing and men pushing through crowds and darting down docks to search every boat tied to pilings.

The captain climbed aboard, and winked their way before bellowing a string of orders to his crew to weigh anchor and raise sails. Sailors jerked their attention from the women and darted across the deck.

Putting an arm around Sophie's waist, Charity gazed over the town that had been her home for the entire five and twenty years of her life. But there was no time for nostalgia as a familiar face poked through the mob. She drew in a breath. 'Twas Lord Villemont's brother, Charles. She'd know him anywhere—that light hair that stuck out like a porcupine, those dark pointed eyes, and the slight limp on his right side. The first wave of guilt struck her. Charles and Herbert had been closer than two brothers could be, so close she'd often wondered if Charles knew what sort of man his brother was—what he was doing to her—and, if so, had merely turned the other way.

Canvas rumbled, then snapped as the sails caught the wind, and the ship began to glide through the dark waters. Grabbing Sophie, Charity moved out of the light of a lantern into the shadows beside the quarterdeck. But it was too late. Charles marched down the wharf and halted.

His eyes, like spears, stabbed straight into her.

# Chapter 2

Eight weeks on a ship at sea felt more like a year in hell. The endless leaping and vaulting, plunging and careening—worse than riding on a country road in a carriage without springs—was bad enough, but add to it the stench of mold, sweat, and something foul that seemed to have died below decks, and Charity doubted she would ever get the odor out of her nose. Or feel cool again in the stifling heat. She spent her days with naught else to do but pace a cabin no bigger than a crawl space. In her haste, she'd brought no books, no pen and parchment, few toiletries, and no ginger or peppermint to ease her stomach—though she knew tossing her accounts into the chamber pot each morning had naught to do with the voyage.

Sophie was a grand companion. A true friend, indeed. Never failing to cheer Charity up when her mood dipped to the bottom of the sea, nor scold her gently when anger and complaining got the best of her. To help pass the time, she told Charity stories of what went on below stairs with the servants, and they laughed together at the antics Charity had never suspected.

Neither spoke of Lord Villemont.

Nor did they speak of what awaited them in Nassau, though Charity thought of it often. Her plan was to charter the first ship to Charles Towne, where her sisters and father had recently moved. Their last post said they'd settled in nicely and were enjoying the fresh wildness of Carolina. If they knew what she had done, would they welcome her home? In her condition? Her sisters perhaps, her father—her stern admiral father—may banish her to the streets without a second thought. Or worse, alert the authorities. Not that she could stay with them long, anyway. If her brother-in-law Charles had seen her board the ship, he would more than likely use his influence and money to send a posse after her.

And Charles Towne would be the first place they would look.

However, she hoped her family would lend her money to start her own printing business as she'd always wanted to do. Then she could move north, perhaps Boston, change her name, and live out her days in peace. Lord Villemont had told her that women possessed neither the brains for business nor the ability to take care of themselves without a man's provision and protection. She intended to prove him wrong on both counts.

But she wouldn't think of that now … *couldn't* think of that now.

Though the crew leered at her and Sophie when—unable to tolerate the heat and smell any longer—they went on deck for air, they left them alone. Charity guessed 'twas the captain's doing, for he wanted the rest of his money when they arrived in Nassau. Twice they dined with him in his cabin, but found the experience so unpleasant in both conversation and manners, that they begged illness and took the rest of their meals alone. A young lad no more than fifteen delivered their food and removed their chamber pot, but offered nary a word to either of them.

Time ceased to exist in the endless monotony of each day, and Charity began to believe that she'd died and gone to hell for her crime. Only Sophie's presence convinced her otherwise, for the sweet Godly maid had never done anything to deserve such a fate.

Finally, shouts from above—different sorts of shouts, excited shouts—snapped Charity's eyes open as she dozed on her cot in the afternoon heat. An unfamiliar shift of sail, stomp of sailors' feet, and the softening of water rushing against the hull added to her hope.

Dragging a chair to the tiny window, Sophie leapt upon it and peered outside. "Milady, I see land!"

Jumping up, Charity joined her on top of the chair, both ladies hugging and giggling and nearly toppling over as they stared at the lump of green interrupting the endless span of blue that had made up their view for months.

Within an hour, the *Neptune* lowered sail and eased into Nassau Harbor. Charity and Sophie bid good riddance to their cabin and ascended to stand on the main deck where wind tore curls from Charity's bun, bringing with it the smells of smoke, fish, and horses. Pig squeals drew her gaze to an uninhabited strip of land to her left where wild boars grazed without restriction. On her right, the town of Nassau spread out from the docks in rows of brick and wooden structures that rose from sandy streets. Wagons, carriages, horses, and people bustled to and fro, weaving around bands of chickens that strutted like kings through the city. Certainly not as civilized as Portsmouth, but compared to life aboard this ship, it might as well be London itself.

The sailors aboard the *Neptune* were less interested in the women as they furled sail and dropped the anchor just a few yards off shore, their gazes seeking the new object of their desire—the pubs and brothels ashore that waited with open hands to rob them of their hard-earned pay.

The captain approached and offered a clumsy bow. "Ladies. I trust ye enjoyed yer journey." He doffed his hat and wiped sweat from his shiny scalp with a handkerchief.

"Thank you, Captain, for delivering us safely to Nassau."

"My men are lowering a boat as we speak an' shall have ye ashore"—he leaned toward Charity and winked—"to yer *ill* family before ye knows it." He held out his calloused hand. "Now to the matter of my payment."

Forcing a smile, Charity opened her valise, withdrew a pouch, and handed him the remainder of what she owed. His hand closed around the coins like a snake's mouth around a mouse.

"'Tis been a pleasure, Miss."

Over his shoulder, Charity spotted a small boat shoving off from the longest wharf and heading their way. An odd sense of dread caused a shiver, though the day was hot.

"Captain, who is that heading toward us?"

Plunking his hat back atop his head, he turned, hesitated a moment, then shrugged. "More' en likely some merchant sellin' his wares." With that, he ambled away.

But it wasn't a merchant, for as the craft drew closer, Charity saw no goods aboard. Just men. The more she stared, the more her heart clambered up her throat.

"Wha' is it, milady?" Sophie laid a hand on her arm.

Charity's legs turned to mush, and she leaned against the railing. "How did he? How ... How...?" Perspiration trickled down her back as dark clouds drifted in from the sea, swallowing up the sun.

"Milady?" Alarm blared in Sophie's tone. "Who is it?"

"'Tis Charles Gregson," Charity managed, breathless. "Or should I say the new Lord Villemont."

Sophie slapped a hand to her chest and glanced at the boat. "His lordship's brother?"

Charity scanned the deck of the *Neptune*, then gazed over the docks reaching into the turquoise waters from the city like spindly fingers ready to grab her. If only she could leap atop one of them from here.

The boat was within ten yards now.

"How is he 'ere, milady?" Sophie continued staring at the boat in disbelief.

"I saw him in Portsmouth after we boarded the *Neptune*. He must have seen me, taken a faster ship." Blood rushed to Charity's head, and she blinked to clear it, lest she faint. "He's here to arrest me and bring me back for trial. Or worse, take justice into his own hands."

"Come, milady, we'll hide in the hold." Sophie's plump features twisted in panic as she tugged on Charity's sleeve.

"Nay. He will find us."

Five yards away now. "Ahoy there, Neptune! Permission to board!"

*Think...think...Charity, think.* Grabbing the railing she leaned over the side. Water caressed the ship at least twenty feet below.

The boat struck the hull on the other side, and men called up for a rope ladder. Kneeling, Charity attempted to open her valise, but her trembling hands betrayed her. *The king was in his counting house, counting out his money...* She closed her eyes momentarily, continuing the song she'd sang when her husband was on his way up the stairs to beat her. Finally, she opened the case, gathered a pouch of jewels, then lifted her skirts and stuffed them in the pocket dangling from her waist.

Sophie began to sob.

Rising, Charity gripped her shoulders. "Sophie, take what is left of my money and buy passage back to England. You have an aunt in Dover, right?"

The maid nodded, her lip trembling. "Wha' are you saying, milady?"

Charity glanced over the maid's shoulders where most of the crew was engaged helping the strangers aboard. "When they ask you where I am, tell them I went below. Will you do that?"

"Aye, milady. But where are you going? I don't understand."

Charity looked over the side again.

Sophie grabbed her arm. "Nay! You will drown. I could not bear it!"

"You'll have to, or else you'll bear watching me hang. Besides, I can swim. My father taught me when I was young." She hugged the woman, storing her kindness deep in her soul. "Thank you, Sophie, for everything. Now, do as I say."

"But wha' about you, milady?" Tears streamed down her face.

Charity didn't respond. Instead she moved toward the back of the ship away from the commotion, slipped over the railing, and dropped into the bay.

Elias Dutton leapt onto the dock and stared out over Nassau Harbor. *The Caribbean.* It was good to be home among the emerald waters and warm breezes, swaying palms and fresh tropical fruit. Though his father's family originally came from England, and some still resided there, every time Elias returned for a visit, the dreary, cold weather reminded him how blessed he was to call these West Indies home. He drew in a deep breath of the briny air and swept a gaze over the boats at anchor—several fishing trawlers, merchantmen, an East Indiaman, various schooners, brigs, and passenger ships, along with a Royal Navy frigate.

The dock wobbled as men disembarked behind him. Bells clanged. An egret screeched overhead, and he withdrew his hat and glanced at the dark clouds forming above. His sister would be married now. Yesterday, in fact, if his calculations were correct. He hoped—no, prayed—that the ceremony and celebrations had gone off splendidly. He regretted having to leave early, but the post his parents had received from his other sister, Rose, had them concerned. And with her husband Duncan in London with them and unable to leave, they'd sent Elias to her rescue. He only hoped that his parents, along with Uncle Alex's influence at court, would be able to procure a letter for Duncan from the King and stop this madness on Barbados. In the meantime, that they trusted him to ensure Rose's wellbeing meant the world to Elias. Especially after what had happened three years ago to Caleigh. Had it been three years?

Guilt slammed his shoulders, weighing them down.

Thank God, the captain of the ship had made the crossing in record time. Now, to procure passage on another ship heading to Barbados. *Stay safe, Rose, I'm coming.* One more week and he'd be there to protect her, and then he could send word to his mother, or rather his father, that all was well. 'Twas Rowan Dutton who tended to fret over everything, while his mother Morgan trusted God.

Elias would show them both that—despite his past mistakes—they could trust their eldest to take care of their other seven children.

He withdrew the wooden cross hanging beneath his shirt and fingered the smooth oak carving. "Never again," he whispered into the wind. "As God is my witness, never again will I allow tragedy to strike my family."

A sailor bumped into him from behind. "Hey, ye gonna stand here all day? We needs t' offload these goods."

Elias nodded and started down the wharf when a flash of rose fabric caught his eye. A woman dangled off the railing of a ship anchored several yards off shore. He stepped to the edge of the dock, heart pinching, praying someone from the ship would come to her aid. But she fell—a parasol of skirts catching the air before she disappeared beneath a bubbling splash. Without hesitation, Elias dove headfirst into the water, his one thought—his only thought—to reach her before she drowned.

# Chapter 3

Charity realized far too late that it would have been more prudent to have removed her shoes before leaping into the water, in addition to one or two petticoats. Not to mention her stays. Which at the moment felt like an anchor wrapped around her middle, squeezing the life from her. 'Twas said they were made with whale bones, but at the moment this particular whale had forgotten how to swim.

Water gurgled around her, muting sounds of life above and forcing her down ... down ... down into the darkness where all was peaceful ... serene ...happy... But no! She couldn't die. Not after all she'd endured. Not after her years of suffering. God wouldn't be that cruel, would He? Or perhaps He would. He had certainly not proven Himself to be anything but a harsh overseer. In truth, she'd lost hope of any happiness in life and would gladly succumb to a watery grave—

If not for the life growing within her. A reason to go on. The *only* reason.

She attempted to untie her stays but couldn't reach them. She kicked her feet, yet they tangled among her skirts. Anger rose, not fear, not panic, but full-fledged rage at the injustice! It took over every limb and muscle as she shoved her arms through the water and thrashed her legs with all her might. Lungs near to bursting, she broke the surface and sucked in a huge breath.

A man grabbed her waist.

"Hold on, Miss. I've got you."

Wiping water from her eyes, she pushed against him. "I don't want you to have me!" she heaved out between breaths. "Leave me alone!"

But the man only strengthened his grip and swam backward with his other arm, drawing her alongside him.

Charity glanced up at the *Neptune*, fully expecting to see her brother-in-law pointing over the railing at her, shouting for his men to give chase. But no one was in sight, save for a few sailors handling the rigging.

What *was* in sight was her, apparently, as a crowd formed on the closest dock, gasping and pointing in her direction. No, no, no! They would alert Charles to her location! She tried to pry the man's hands from her waist. "Let me go, you brute!"

"Never fear, Miss. Try not to panic." He breathed out in a harried tone. "I won't let you go."

The man's clumsy efforts forced her head below the surface. Choking on a mouthful of salty water, she struggled as he jerked her upward into the air again, coughing, hacking, and spitting out the sea. "Vapors! You daft loon. You're going to drown the both of us!"

Only then did she notice that her struggling and shouting drew more people to the edge of the wharf as well as a few sailors aboard the *Neptune*. Perhaps 'twas best to keep calm and allow the man to complete his gallant rescue.

Several hands reached down to her from the dock. She grabbed one and her rescuer pushed her from behind as another man pulled her to stand on the wobbling wood—an aged sailor whose face looked more weathered than the planks he stood on.

"Miss, are ye all righ'?" He leaned to study her face—so close she could smell his fishy breath.

"Yes, yes, I'm quite all right. Thank you, kindly." She attempted a smile as she peered through the mob toward the

*Neptune* where her brother-in-law and several men were now staring over the water. It wouldn't take them long to figure out where she was.

Ducking further into the crowd, she laid the back of her hand on her forehead and stumbled as if she were going to faint. "I nearly drowned. How frightening."

"If not fer this gentleman, Miss." Another sailor steadied her with a touch to her elbow, and she turned to see the man who had rescued her—or so he thought—hoist himself onto the wharf with minimal effort. His sodden shirt left nothing to modesty as it clung to a broad chest rippling with muscles and rounded arms, sturdy as table posts. Hair the color of chestnut escaped his queue and dripped onto wide shoulders. A day's stubble shadowed his chin and jaw, as stark blue eyes assessed her with more clarity and kindness than she'd seen in years. He smiled, a sincere, pleased-to-meet-you sort of smile that sent her mind spiraling and her body heating.

If she hadn't written off men altogether, she would have swooned at his feet.

But she *had* written off men. They were not to be trusted. Not even dashing heroes.

"You gave me quite a scare, Miss," he said, raking back his wet hair. Which only made him more handsome. "Elias Dutton at your service."

Mumbling, the crowd dispersed, and Charity cast a quick glance toward the *Neptune*. Though it was too far to see clearly, Charles' gaze was definitely pointed her way. She must hide. She must endure the touch of these men, though everything within her told her to run. Clutching one of the sailors beside her, she reached for her rescuer, moaning, "I feel faint." Both men gripped her, one by the waist, the other by her elbow, and escorted her down the wharf into town.

Thankfully some of the crowd followed, then scattered to whatever they were doing before her leap in the bay provided their only excitement of the day. "Thank you, gentlemen, I feel much better now," she said when they reached the crowded street. Yanking from their grips, she straightened her saturated skirts and proceeded on her way. To where, she had no idea, but at the moment, anywhere where Charles couldn't see her.

The sailor ambled away, grumbling. The gallant rescuer followed her. Thunder rumbled in the distance as wind blew the spice of rain past her nose and chilled her sodden gown.

"Miss ...Miss, allow me to aid you in getting back on your ship."

Ducking behind a parked wagon, she faced him. "What ship, Sir?"

"The one you fell from." His brow wrinkled.

"Oh, that. Nay. I was to come ashore anyway." She waved him off and started across the street, weaving around carriages, people, and chickens, while doing her best to avoid attracting attention. An impossible task since she looked like a mermaid risen from the sea. People gaped at her as if she were, indeed, a mermaid, casting glances over their shoulders at her in passing. She attempted to rectify her appearance as best she could, but her skirts swished and rubbed against her legs like sheets of iron, and any effort to pin up her wet hair ended in futility.

The man's sarcastic tone grated on her from behind. "Most people take a boat to shore."

"I am not most people. Now, if you don't mind." *Would the man never leave?* Dark clouds hovered overhead, portending doom, as a wind whipped the dust off the street and sent a chill through her again.

"May I at least escort you to your destination?"

She should be flattered by the handsome man's attention, but she knew better. He wanted something. They *all* wanted something.

"Sir." She faced him, pasting on a smile. "Mr. Dutton, was it? I thank you for your attempted rescue but—"

"Attempted?" He snorted. "Bah! If not for me, you'd be at the bottom of the bay."

"You are mistaken. I was merely swimming ashore."

He chuckled. "Swimming was it?"

She raised a brow. "Did I not demand that you release me?"

"You were panicked, Miss. People say all sorts of foolish things when they are panicked."

"I assure you, I was no more panicked than you." She planted hands at her waist.

His smile lit up the gloomy day, straight white teeth with a dimple creasing the right side of his mouth. She averted her gaze from it. "As I said, I am in your debt, Mr. Dutton, but I have business in town and must be going."

"Business? In your soaked gown? What of your luggage? Or does a mermaid not require luggage?" His chuckle grated on her.

"Business that is *my* business, Sir," she ground out.

"Miss, though Governor Rogers has done much to rid the city of pirates, I daresay, 'twill not be safe for you wandering about town alone."

There it was again, that concern in his eyes, as if he truly cared. Ah, this man was good. Most likely a villain who tricked innocent women out of their fortunes.

"I can take care of myself." Even as she said it, she bit her lip, knowing it was more of a dream than a reality. Still, she was determined to never need a man's support or protection again. And she might as well start now. She set her jaw and stared him down.

"Very well." He shrugged. "I shan't press it. Good afternoon to you."

She faced forward and heard his footsteps fade. *Finally.* Now, first things first. She would sell some of her jewelry, seek out a ready-made gown or at least a dry overskirt, then inquire about the next ship heading to Charles Towne. If need be, she'd rent a room for the night in a reputable tavern.

Nay. She huffed. She had no need of anyone—especially a man—to take care of her.

Clutching her skirts, she made her way down a row of buildings, only then noticing a group of men in colorful attire, strapped with swords and pistols, drinking from mugs outside a pub. No doubt the nefarious sorts of which Mr. Dutton had warned her. Ignoring their whistles and grins, she hurried past a lady dressed in fine embroidered taffeta holding a silk parasol over her head, her hand on the arm of a gentleman who was equally well-dressed—both turning their noses up at Charity. *Humph.* Pompous clods! If they only knew she bore a title, Lady Villemont, wife of Lord Villemont!

Or at least she had.

A group of slaves marched by, burdened with crates and boxes, and Charity's heart broke at the sight. Turning away, she nearly ran into a man who scowled and gave her wide berth as if she had the pox. It was then that she saw the sign. A piece of parchment tacked onto a post. She rubbed her eyes, not believing what she was seeing, but as she drew closer, her heart nearly froze. 'Twas a drawing of her, a rather good one sitting above the words:

WANTED FOR MUDERING HER HUSBAND,
CHARITY GREGSON, LADY VILLEMONT
REWARD FOR INFORMATION LEADING TO
CAPTURE, 40 POUNDS. CONTACT LORD VILLEMONT
THROUGH CONSTABLE WILSON

Lowering her head, Charity darted into a narrow alley between two buildings and backed against the cold brick wall. Her breath galloped. Her pulse raced. She clutched her throat. How could Charles have alerted the authorities so quickly? No doubt every greedy sot in town was on the lookout for her.

*The Queen was in the parlor, eating bread and honey ...* She needed dry attire. Yes. And a large hat to hide her face. *The maid was in the garden, hanging out the clothes.* Terror pricked her skin, causing it to itch. Then she must either find a ship leaving today or a place to hide for the night. Reaching through a slit in her skirts, she searched for her hanging pocket. Nothing but wet petticoats met her hand. Terror rising, she slid her fingers over her waist. The rope that held the pocket was gone.

Which only meant one thing. Her jewels were at the bottom of Nassau Bay.

Thunder growled and a blast of rain-scented wind struck her.

Her legs gave way and she leaned against the wall, wondering if things could get any worse. A man's voice drew her gaze onto the street.

Her brother-in-law was heading straight for her, five men on his heels.

Elias stomped away from the ungrateful woman, chastising himself for playing the fool yet again. Why was he always drawn to defenseless, distressed women? Surely some of it was his calling to be a missionary, for God commanded His people to come to the aid of widows and orphans. But it went deeper than that. Elias was the eldest of eight children, and ever since he could remember, he felt responsible for their safety and wellbeing. Perhaps he was a protector at heart, a misplaced Knight of the Realm from ages past. Or mayhap 'twas part of God's protective nature given in extra measure to him. Protect and save. Principals he lived by. The protecting from evil and want, and the saving of the soul from hell.

Yet his zeal had gotten him into trouble on more than one occasion. Particularly with the ladies. The comely ones. As was Miss … Miss … she'd never given him her name.

Just as well. He hoped he'd never see her again. He prayed Godspeed to her and her biting tongue. A rather lovely tongue set among pearly white teeth and lips as pink and full as hibiscus petals…and most likely just as soft. He changed the direction of his thoughts before they got him in trouble. Such a wisp of a lady for so much spitfire. The top of her head stood no farther than his shoulders, and she was as thin as a ship's mouse. Saturated hair the color of coffee flattened around a comely round face. And something in those large, honey-colored eyes, fringed in a wild thicket of black lashes, told him she needed help, despite her insistence otherwise.

He shook her memory away as the swish of his boots reminded him he needed to get his luggage from the docks, change into some dry attire, and seek out a ship heading for Barbados. Mayhap God would smile on him and there'd be one setting sail before dark.

Shops, taverns, punch houses, stables, and warehouses lined the street. No doubt they'd moved the brothels to another part of town. Such a change from a year ago when Nassau had been a haven of pirates, boasting the likes of Benjamin Hornigold, Stede Bonnet, and Calico Jack Rackham. Unwanted memories skittered out from hiding of a time when Elias had joined such villainous sorts—first to save their sorry souls. But in his weakened condition, he'd been trapped in their quicksand and sank into the mire alongside them.

'Twas a short time in his life of which he was not proud, but enough time spent in the darkest of worlds to know that he never wanted to go back.

Thankfully, Woodes Rogers, a reformed pirate himself, became governor of Nassau and chased most of the freebooters out to sea.

A fiddle and pianoforte joined in a discordant ditty. Thunder rumbled yet again, and a drop of rain struck his forehead. He passed a punch house and stepped off the walkway onto the sandy street, weaving around a lone horseman, a wagon, and a woman and her children, who eyed his soaked attire with curiosity. Once at the dock, he found his dunnage and then located the port master who told him that there was, indeed, a ship heading for Barbados within the hour.

Silently thanking God, Elias made his way to the dock in question and found a weathered man with a gray beard who looked to be in charge, ordering sailors to load crates into the waiting boat.

"Captain Littleman?" Elias inquired.

"Aye." The thick chested man with the bulbous nose withdrew a pipe from his mouth and looked up from the parchment he was holding. "Who might ye be?"

"Elias Dutton." He glanced at the brig anchored just offshore, a worthy craft by all appearances. "I seek passage aboard your brig, Captain. Do you have room for a paying customer? I'm proficient at handling sails."

"Ye there!" The captain shouted at one of his sailors. "Ye brainless lout! Move that crate to the other side or we'll sink." He shook his head and returned to his parchment. "We're all full up, Mr. Dutton. Don't need more deck hands neither."

Elias growled silently. "I'll work, won't eat much, and will sleep anywhere."

"Be that right?" The captain snorted. "The last passenger I took aboard—a big strapping fellow like yerself—was a pirate who sabotaged me brig and allowed his fellow marauders to board and rob us blind. Stole me ship as well and left me crew to rot on some island." His eyes became slits as he pointed his pipe toward Elias. "An' ye *do* look like a pirate, Mr. Dutton, if I do says so meself. Why are yer clothes all wet?"

Frustration rumbled in Elias' belly. "I rescued a lady who fell in the bay."

"Humph." Turning, the captain shouted obscenities to his men, before facing Elias again. "Sorry, can't help ye."

If Elias had a choice, he'd rather not sail with this man who seemed intent on insulting his crew every chance he got. But he must get to Barbados. His sister's safety depended on it. And there wasn't another ship heading out for two days. "If you would but—"

"*There* you are." A female voice danced around Elias' ears before a woman appeared by his side. "I've been looking everywhere for you, darling."

*Darling?* The mermaid vixen smiled up at him as if they'd been friends forever.

Captain Littleman's drooping eyes suddenly came to life as he spread back his shoulders and attempted to stand taller. He perused her wet attire—that for all the undergarments women wore—clung to her curves rather nicely.

The men in the boat stopped loading and gaped.

"Be this the lady ye fished from the bay?"

"One and the same." The mermaid held out her hand for the man to kiss. Which he happily did. "What a man won't do for his wife." She winked at Elias.

*Wife?* Elias swallowed, attempting to make sense of her words. "What are you talking—"

"Well," the captain started, still staring at the lady. "I suppose a man wit' such a wife wouldn't be a pirate."

"A pirate?" The mermaid vixen chuckled. "My husband a pirate? Why he's as gentle as a lamb. Oh my, you have made my day, Mr...Mr..."

"Littleman, Captain Littleman at yer service." He adjusted his lapels and brushed a hand through his scraggly hair.

"A captain?" she cooed. "Oh, my. Such a pleasure."

Captain Littleman grinned. "On second thought, I'm sure we can find a berth for ye both on board. I'll enjoy the company o' such a lovely lady." His smile faded as he turned to Elias, hand extended. "That'll be one pound, three shillings."

The lady glanced up at him with a smile. "What are you waiting for, darling, pay the man."

# Chapter 4

M r. Dutton begged a moment from Captain Littleman, then dragged Charity aside. "Just what do you think you're doing?" He spat, his jaw a steel line, his eyes aflame.

Charity dropped her smile. It had been an effort to keep it up, anyway, a bigger effort to flirt with the captain—not something she enjoyed doing or had perfected like her sister, Hope. And a *major* effort to allow this man to touch her. She jerked from his grip and stepped back.

"I'm getting you on the ship. Isn't that what you want?" she whispered curtly as she glanced over her shoulder and scanned the crowded street, her heart galloping. Charles and his henchmen were nowhere in sight. She'd managed to evade them by slipping through the back door of a mercantile, then taking the alleyways onto the main street several blocks away. She'd spent an hour searching for Sophie, but to no avail, until finally, running out of time and options, she'd spotted Mr. Dutton at the end of a long wharf, looking as though he was bartering passage on another ship. Which was exactly what she needed. As she approached, she'd overheard the entire conversation, and a glorious idea had occurred to her.

Now if the buffoon wouldn't ruin it for them both! She inched in front of him, using his large body to block her from sight.

"This is absurd!" he all but growled. "I will not deceive these people into believing we are married."

"Do you wish to get to Barbados or not, Mr. Dutton?"

He huffed and ran a hand through his hair. "I thought it was *darling*." A hint of a smile peeked at her from beneath his scowl. A rather handsome scowl, if she were to admit. Not at all like Lord Villemont's depraved grimace that had sent the staff, and even the rats, scurrying.

Raindrops tapped on Charity's head and gown and absorbed into the already sodden fabric.

The captain's open palm thrust toward Mr. Dutton. "Are ye gonna pay or not?"

Mr. Dutton huffed and puffed like a bellows for several minutes, staring out at the bay, then shifted angry eyes toward her.

*Please,* she mouthed, gazing up at him with a pleading look that she hoped conveyed her desperation.

His lips flattened and he let out one last sigh before he tugged a pouch from his breeches and counted out the amount. *Ching ching ching*, it chimed in Captain Littleman's rough-like-rope hand, sounding out her salvation. Yet, by the frown on Mr. Dutton's face, one would think it sealed his doom.

Thunder quivered the dock as if God Himself were angry at the deal just made. Wiping rain from her eyes, Charity glanced over the harbor, a blue canvas of dots where rain pummeled the water. Back on the crowded street, parasols bobbed above ladies as gentlefolk ran for cover from the storm.

*Storm, indeed.* A more threatening one came her way if they didn't hurry! *Hurry...*time ticked by interminably.

"Wilson, make room for two passengers! Is this yer luggage?" The captain's voice sounded hollow in the rain as he pointed to Mr. Dutton's case." And where be yours, Mrs. Dutton?"

"I'm afraid I lost it in the harbor."

Mr. Dutton stared at her again with that benumbed look as if she'd spoken in Chinese.

"Come, darling," she said. "Do assist me into the boat. Forgive him, Captain, the poor man is still in shock after nearly losing me in the bay."

Captain Littleman nodded his understanding.

As if waking up from a stupor, Mr. Dutton tossed his luggage to a man waiting in the boat, then leapt in himself as if he'd done it a thousand times. Charity started carefully down the rope ladder, hoping she didn't fall and make a spectacle of herself, but the wind wrapped her damp skirts around her ankles and sent the rope swaying. She started to trip. Strong hands gripped her waist. Uncontrolled fear sped through her at the man's touch, her first thought to slap him away, but he lowered her into the boat and released her. 'Twas Mr. Dutton, his concerned look filling her vision.

She averted her gaze only to find five sailors ogling her. Clearing his throat, Mr. Dutton led her to sit on the only empty spot in the craft beside an old sailor, whose one remaining eye never left Charity as she settled on the thwart.

Vapors, but she was far too close to Mr. Dutton. His thigh rubbed against hers with every jostle of the boat, sending her pulse racing. Not in a good way, either. She doubted she'd ever feel delight at a man's touch again. Still, Mr. Dutton didn't seem to notice, just dropped his head into his hands and stared at the water sloshing about the bottom of the boat as if he'd lost a bet with the devil himself.

Within minutes, they arrived at the ship, and, ignoring her protests, Mr. Dutton assisted her up another much larger rope ladder. At the top, she swung her legs over the railing as modestly as possible and found herself assaulted further with ribald stares and a bull of a man—with more hair sprouting from the collar of his shirt than his head—storming toward her.

The rain ceased, and Mr. Dutton leapt on deck and immediately stood in front of her.

"Who are ye? No passengers allowed on board!" the man bellowed, spittle flying from his mouth.

"Stand down, Bates!" Captain Littleman swung over the railing and fisted hands at his waist. "These be payin' passengers an' they'll be treated as such. "

"But women is bad luck. Ye said so before."

"I'll be sayin' somethin' different now. Get these crates on board, then ready the ship to set sail."

Casting seething looks at Charity, Bates turned and shouted orders to the crew.

"I'll have your cabin prepared," Captain Littleman said, and off he went, leaving Charity alone with the man she'd just tricked into paying for her trip to Barbados.

He gripped the railing and stared at Nassau. "Married?" He grimaced. "What kind of woman are you to forge such a lie?"

"A desperate one, I'm afraid. Thank you for indulging my deception."

"Don't thank me. I'm not altogether sure why I didn't reveal your treachery." Icy blue eyes speared her.

"Because you wanted to get to Barbados quickly is my guess," she returned, a bit too sharply.

"That I did. But now I fear the cost." His mouth tightened as he stared at the water slapping the hull.

Feeling a twinge of guilt, Charity stepped away from him. What else could she have done? Face the noose? Besides, she would pay him back once she established herself, of that she was sure, for she never wanted to be indebted to any man again.

The last crate was brought aboard, the boatman paid, and men leapt into the tops to lower sails. Rays of sunlight speared through the parting clouds, glistening over buildings and turning puddles into sparkling pools. And ... *No!*

Charles marched down the wharf from which they'd just left, his henchmen behind him, his eyes scanning the bay.

Charity dropped to the deck.

The Honorable Mr. Charles Gregson, now Lord Villemont upon his brother's death, could only stare at the woman who murdered his beloved sibling—his only brother, his *only* living relation. Even if he had a pistol, the bullet would never hit her from the wharf. *Damnation, where were his men?* He turned to see the five brutes he'd hired charging up behind him. *Imbeciles.* But then again, he hadn't hired them for their brains. He'd hired them because the Constable had recommended them as good trackers, good with weapons, and the type who would look the other way if need be.

Charles wouldn't need that last quality. He intended to do things honorably. He intended to capture and bring his sister-in-law back to Portsmouth for trial. He'd heard enough from Jensen, his brother's butler, along with several servants in the house, to convince him that Charity had shot and killed Herbert.

Sorrow clamped his throat. Poor Herbert. He'd always been there for Charles, ever since they were innocent children, bearing the rod of their father's cruelty. And by God, Charles would be there for him. He owed Herbert at least that for the many times Herbert had taken the blame and received a beating for something Charles had done.

He slammed the tip of his cane onto the wooden dock. Yes, the woman would pay!

A breeze flapped his cravat, and he tucked it inside his velvet coat as Charity spotted him and ducked behind the railing.

"You can't hide from me, little hell-cat," he seethed into the wind.

His men crowded behind him.

"Is that her?" one of them asked.

"Yes, and if you'd been here sooner, you might have captured her before the crew rowed her out. You there!" Charles yelled to a dock worker on the wharf beside theirs. "What ship is that?"

The boy looked up and wiped rain from his eyes, then followed the point of Charles' finger. "That be the *Enmity*, Sir."

Charles withdrew a coin from the pouch at his hip. "And would you know where she is heading?"

Spotting the money, the lad licked his lips. "Barbados, Sir."

Charles flipped the coin over the watery stretch between them, and the boy caught it with a smile.

*Barbados, it is.*

So many emotions rioted within Elias, he didn't know which one to deal with first. Shame for his stupidity, anger at being tricked, fury at being used, fear he'd allied himself to a mad woman, and pity for whatever situation she found herself in that would cause such a desperate act. He decided to embrace anger and turned to inquire the reason for her bewildering actions ...when she suddenly disappeared. A thump and an ouch drew his gaze down to a circle of damp fabric ballooning around the woman as she crouched behind the bulwarks.

"For the love of ... what are you doing, Miss?" He reached down to assist her. "Are you hurt?"

"Shhh." She kept her head down. "Don't look at me."

Elias returned his gaze to the city, convinced even more that this poor creature was two masts short of a three-masted ship. Six men stood at the edge of the wharf staring their way. The one in front pounded his cane on the wood as if he could break through the dock itself. Odd. Perhaps they were in need of passage to Barbados as much as he was.

Captain Littleman gave the men a cursory glance as he continued to issue orders to raise tacks and sheets and haul in the anchor. As the anchor crew heaved on the capstan and topmen inched across yards unfurling sail, Elias itched to join them. If only to get away from the mad mermaid and keep his mind off the alarming situation he found himself in—the *immoral* situation he found himself in. *Father, I'm sorry.* He breathed out a quick repentance for his rash actions. But what else could he have done? The lady was obviously in trouble. The desperate look on her face had done him in. He'd never been able to resist a woman in need, much to his own dismay—and ofttimes despair. What would God have done? Abandoned her?

He gazed down at the puddle of wet skirts and brown hair and wondered what to do with her, when the purser, a Mr. Lawrence, approached and offered to lead them to their cabin. The man stared curiously at the lady slumped on the deck as the sails caught the wind and the ship jerked forward.

It occurred to Elias he had no idea how to address her, so he grabbed her elbow and attempted to help her to her feet. She yanked from his touch, cast him a fiery gaze, then peered over the railing toward the city.

"Mayhap you could hide better in your cabin." Elias gave a tight smile to which she frowned and rose slightly, keeping her body bent. Once amidships, she stood to her full height—which only came to Elias' chest—stuck her little nose in the air, and followed the purser.

"'Tis the third mate's berth," Mr. Lawrence said as he led them down a narrow ladder below deck. "Not much, but it'll do ye nice." He halted before a door and flung it open. "Captain requests yer presence at dinner. Until then, 'tis best ye stay here."

Clutching her skirts, the lady sashayed into a cabin no bigger than a necessary room and promptly plopped onto the only wooden chair. Elias followed and tossed his case onto the cot, keeping the door ajar. Something he would have to do constantly. What in God's name was he doing? He couldn't share a cabin with this woman. Or with *any* woman! He was just a man, a young man with a young man's passions. And he'd already proven his inability to control them.

"I must inform you, Mr. Dutton," the lady began. "That although the crew assumes we are man and wife, you will not lay so much as a finger on me." She held her jaw firm, but her voice trembled, and Elias spotted fear streaking across her eyes.

Even with skirts caked in mud and her hair a tangled mass about her face, she presented a lovely vision. Though her gown was modest, the heave of her chest drew his gaze to the swell of her bosom, rising and falling beneath the fabric. He looked away as the ship heaved and picked up speed. "Mayhap you should have thought of the consequences before you fabricated this lie. You don't know me. Yet you put yourself completely at my mercy on board a ship full of men, most of whom would love to have their way with you."

The lady clutched her throat. "How dare you say such an inappropriate thing!"

"'Twill be even more inappropriate should it come to pass." Elias watched as the anger on her face transformed to fear. "So, why do it?"

"Believe me when I tell you the alternative was far worse."

He ran a hand through his wet hair. "Worse than being ravished? Indeed, you must be in a great deal of trouble."

She didn't answer, simply dropped her gaze to the deck and laid a hand on her stomach, reminding him of a kitten, a wet kitten, lost and alone.

"Which are you then, mermaid vixen? Foolish, mad, or desperate?"

She grabbed a tangle of hair and tugged on it, eyes narrow and defensive as if she feared he'd assault her any moment. "I'll admit to all three, Sir." Her gaze lowered to the knife sheathed at his belt. "In truth, because you rescued me from the bay, I assumed you might be a decent man."

"You certainly didn't treat me as such in town."

"I am sorry for that."

Feet pounded above as shouts echoed over the ship.

Elias leaned back against the bulkhead and crossed arms over his chest. "You mean you don't always jump over the railings of perfectly good ships? And you don't always pretend to be married to a man so he'll pay for your passage?"

She gave a sarcastic huff, a slight tilt to her lips. "Only on Sundays."

He wanted to smile but didn't. "You've nothing to fear from me, Miss."

"Then why agree to my charade? There must be something you want."

He shrugged. "You seemed terrified, in need of help."

"Nobody helps someone for nothing."

Her hopeless, defeated tone saddened him. Yet, if she truly believed that, then why put herself in harm's way?

The creak and groan of wood filled the silence as water purled against the hull.

She picked at the lace drooping at her cuff. "My father has land in Charles Towne. He's an admiral in the Royal navy. He will pay you for your help."

"Hmm. You are aware that you boarded a ship to Barbados?"

She made no reply.

Elias pushed from the bulkhead. "I have no desire nor need of your money, mermaid."

"Stop calling me that." She wrapped arms around her belly, her eyes aflame. "'Tis all I have to give you, Mr.

Dutton." Her gaze traveled to the knife at his hip again, and he wondered if she intended to stab him with it. Ludicrous. This frightened mermaid wouldn't be so daring. Though she *was* plenty foolish. Elias had seen enough foolish women to last a lifetime—trusting women, naïve women who threw themselves into dangerous situations. Two of his sisters still paid for such careless behavior.

The deck canted. She gripped the edge of the cot and seemed about to fall. Elias headed toward her, but she jumped to her feet and backed away, glancing around the room as if just noticing where they were. "You can't stay in here with me."

"Miss, if I do not stay in here, our ruse will be forfeit, and the crew will assume you are ripe for the plucking."

"Surely not!"

"You don't know sailors, Miss."

"And you do?"

He did. More than she realized. "I know men," he responded.

She looked away, her cheeks reddening. "Well, you needn't worry, Mr. Dutton. I can take care of myself."

"Apparently not or we wouldn't be in this situation."

She frowned and narrowed her eyes.

Elias sighed. Surely, God must be testing him—testing his patience, his resolve to control his urges, to do the right thing, to help a woman in need and protect her from whomever or whatever she was running from.

He took another step toward her, hands raised. "I call a truce, Miss Mermaid. Why don't we—"

She plucked the knife from his belt and held the sharp tip to his chest. "Touch me and I'll gut you."

The mermaid had transformed into a shark.

# Chapter 5

Charity pressed the blade. A red dot blossomed on Mr. Dutton's shirt. She would never allow another man to hurt her. Or her child! She had more than proven that.

Fear made no appearance in the man's eyes. Rather the amusement twinkling within them set her nerves on fire. Not a malicious amusement like her husband, but a genuine, warm amusement. Air heated between them as a bead of perspiration slid down her neck.

He had the knife in his hand before she even felt his grip on her wrist. Spinning it in the air, he caught it by the handle and replaced it at his belt. "I wasn't going to hurt you, Miss. In truth, quite the opposite."

Who was this man with the kind blue eyes and the sharp wit? And reflexes of a cat? His speech and mannerisms revealed education and status, but his clothes were those of a common sailor. One minute she spotted desire in his gaze, the next they were filled with concern...then annoyance...and then curiosity, like now.

"A lady cannot be too careful," she retorted.

"Rarely has anyone, especially a lady, been able to relieve me of my knife." Suspicion filled his gaze, even as a smile curved his lips. "Forsooth, I do believe the mermaid has claws."

"'Twas merely luck and the desire to protect myself." She backed against the bulkhead. Though necessity had forced her to learn how to handle a knife, she wouldn't admit that to this man.

He studied her. "You'll do well not to threaten the only man protecting you."

The ship leapt, and she stumbled and gripped the edge of a table attached to the wall. "If you refer to yourself, Sir, you would do well not to advance on a lady in private."

His jaw worked as if he restrained his anger. "Why don't we start over, Miss...Miss..."

She avoided his gaze. "Charity ... Charity Vi...Westcott."

He quirked a brow. "Well, Miss Charity Viwestcott, mayhap I can help you if you but tell me from what or whom you are running?"

"Just Westcott, if you please, and I'm not running from anything." *Stupid. Stupid.* She shouldn't have given him her real name.

"Miss Westcott, I can tolerate many things, but never lying. If you speak the truth, regardless of what it is, I will understand. But you will make a quick enemy of me should you lie. Now, those men on the docks. They were after you, were they not?" He sat on the cot and stretched out his legs. Rather long muscular legs encased in leather boots to the knee.

"I suppose so."

"What do they want with you?"

Water rushed against the hull as the ship creaked over another wave. It gave her time to think of an answer. "If you must know, I broke off my engagement to the man's brother. I fear he intends to drag me back and force me to marry him."

"And where is back?"

"Ports... London."

"PortsLondon? You seem to have trouble with names, Miss Viwestcott." He grinned.

"I have a stutter, Sir." She huffed. "Are you so cruel as to taunt me?"

His grin reached his eyes in a twinkle of disbelief. "Is that the reason you took a swim in the bay?"

"Why would I jump overboard because of a stutter?"

He groaned and leaned forward on his knees. "Miss Mermaid, we are going nowhere if you continue to patronize me."

Charity hugged herself, though 'twas hotter than an oven in the cabin. Several strands of chestnut hair had escaped the man's queue and hung about his face—a strong face with firm lines and noble cheekbones. His scent filled the air between them—a mixture of man and spice, and her nerves pricked at being so closely confined with him.

Finally, he stood with a sigh. "Are you saying this man followed you all the way from England to Nassau just to force you to marry his brother?" One brow lifted tauntingly. "Do you have a large estate, an enormous dowry, perhaps? Are you the daughter of a duke? Or mayhap a close relation of the king?" He blew out a sigh and shook his head. "And why, pray tell, did you not simply seek the protection of your family?"

"My family is in the colonies. Carolina, to be exact." She flattened her lips.

"Surely they did not leave you alone in PortsLondon?"

*Impudent man.* "'Tis none of your business."

"'Tis very much my business to know the reason I am suddenly burdened with your care."

"Mayhap you have trouble understanding me, Mr. Dutton," she seethed out through a forced smile. "I free you from any further *burden*."

"You may free me, Miss, but my conscience bears no such liberty."

She gave an incredulous snort. "Your conscience, Sir? Do people still possess such things?"

Again he studied her with those penetrating blue eyes as a doctor would a patient, mayhap seeking the cure for whatever ailed her.

She should save him the trouble and tell him there was no cure for her malady. And never would be.

A sailor appeared at the door, a basin of water in hand. "Cap'n sends his regards and says ye can use this t' clean up before supper." He purposely brushed against Charity as he passed, dousing her with his stench of body oder.

After setting the basin on the table, he turned and made no pretense of scanning her with his gaze. "I'll be back to escort ye to the cap'n's cabin at sundown."

"Thank you." Mr. Dutton assisted him out the door, shut it, and turned to face her. "Perhaps you should ..." He gestured toward her wet skirts and then looked away as if embarrassed. "Attempt to dry."

Charity found herself amused at his discomfort. "Remove my skirts to air them out? Is that what you are trying to suggest? I will do so after you leave."

"Believe me, I have no desire to remain."

She almost *did* believe him, so filled with disgust was his tone. "What is it you do, Mr. Dutton?"

"I'm a preacher," he said proudly.

*Preacher?* A sour taste filled her mouth as she closed her eyes and breathed a sigh. She'd had more than her fill of clergy. Vapors, they were often worse than common laymen, preaching one thing, and then doing the opposite themselves.

"Do you have something against preachers?"

His playful tone brought her gaze to him. "I have everything against so-called men of God."

"Hmm." He eyed her curiously. "We shall have to rectify that."

"Unless you like to fail, I urge you to forsake that desire. I didn't take you for a preacher, Mr. Dutton." He seemed too strong, confident, commanding, not mealy-mouthed, meek,

and feeble like most rectors. "And just how, *Mr. Preacher,*
will you protect me from the crew when your God demands
you turn the other cheek when attacked?"

At this he smiled. Almost a mischievous smile that defied
his occupation. "You better get cleaned up and prepare for a
grand performance, Miss. Viwestcott. For tonight you must
pretend you are happily married to this preacher or I fear you
will find out."

Then exiting the door, he shut it behind him.

Charity dropped into the chair. He was right, of course.
She *did* need him. She needed his protection and she hated
herself for it. She had escaped one prison only to fling herself
into another—begging the favor of a man just to live, just to
survive.

Of all the luck! She struck the chair arm. A preacher! A
good-looking one at that. Regardless, she'd not allow him—
or his God—to worm their way into her heart with kind,
merciful words, only to stab her in the back the minute they
gained her trust. Never again!

For a lady who had no maid, a single damp gown, salt
encrusted hair, and only a basin of water, Miss Charity
Westcott presented quite the vision of beauty when Elias
returned to escort her to dinner. She'd even managed to pin
her hair up into a bounty of coffee-colored curls at the back
of her head. Refusing his arm, she followed the sailor as he
led them through a maze of underground hallways to the
Captain's quarters. No bigger than a ship's mouse in
comparison to Elias and the other sailor, she seemed so
vulnerable as the teetering brig tossed her back against him
more than once. Each time, he felt her tremble. Did she still
fear him, even after he'd told her he was a preacher? Or
mayhap 'twas *because* he was a preacher.

The sailor whistled a tune as he strolled in front of them
before halting at the end of a corridor, tapping lightly on the

door, and swinging it open. Elias stretched back his shoulders, tight from his day's exertion. Captain Littleman had no compunction putting Elias to work—hauling in and loosening sheets, polishing brass, repairing ropes and sails, holystoning the deck—even though Elias had paid for the voyage. Regardless, he welcomed the distraction from the baffling woman and hoped it would give him time to formulate a plan of how to handle spending the night in the same cabin with her. But, all he achieved was sweat, sore muscles, and thoughts focused on places they ought not venture.

Now, he faced an even bigger challenge. Making these sailors believe he and Miss Westcott were married without actually lying. But wasn't the pretense itself a lie? If so, surely God understood the reasons for it and wouldn't add it to Elias' long list of failings.

He led her into the cabin. "Did I mention you look lovely tonight, darling," he said as all eyes embraced them from the dining table that centered the room.

"No, you didn't, *darling*," she returned with a tight smile.

"Ah, do come in." Captain Littleman rose from his seat and gestured toward two empty chairs on either side of him. "Our guests, gentlemen, Mr. and Mrs. Dutton." He made quick introductions of the three men who also rose at the sight of Miss Westcott. Rigley, his second mate, whose head appeared far too large for his small body, Bates, his quartermaster, a balding, barrel-chested man with a perpetual scowl on his face. But it was Nelson, his first mate, a man with a pock-marked face, greasy light hair, and angry eyes, who reacted quite oddly at the sight of Miss Westcott— brows leaping, eyes widening, and a smile stretching his mouth so wide Elias thought his jaw would crack.

The Captain took no note of it. "An' yer husband's right, Mrs. Dutton, if I do say so meself. Ye look lovely."

"Thank you, Captain," she said as Elias pulled out her chair, then took his own seat across the table.

She sat with all the grace and poise of a true lady, defying what her lack of possessions, suspicious flight from her past, and deceptions indicated.

The ship rolled and platters skidded over the rough-hewn table laden with all manner of steaming food, baskets of fruit, decanters of wine, and several candles whose dripping wax formed chaotic shapes down the holders. The cabin was like most captains' quarters Elias had seen, save a bit more disorderly. A wooden desk, covered with charts and navigation instruments, had been shoved against the bulkhead to make room for the table. Chests overflowing with clothing and trinkets sat at the foot of a small cot, a pile of weapons lay haphazardly in a corner, and heavy, dark-blue-and-gold brocade curtains hung down each side of the stern lights. Beyond the windows, a starlit night dappled silver on the dark sea.

Platters and bowls were passed containing rice, boiled pig, sweet potatoes, and carrot pudding. The men dove in without thanks to God, and despite their mouths stuffed with food, proceeded to engage in lively conversation. If one could call it conversation. Elias cringed more than once at the coarse language used in the presence of a lady. Spending most of his time among sailors, he was accustomed to it, but he could tell by the lowering of her lashes, the shifting in her seat, and how she gazed out the stern windows that Miss Westcott was not. Which spoke well of her character. Of which he was strangely glad.

"How long before we reach Barbados, Captain?" She took the opportunity of a lull in the discussion to ask.

Captain Littleman lit his pipe from a candle and leaned back in his chair. "With fair winds and clear skies, no more than a week, my dear. What be yer business there, might I ask?" His gaze shifted to Elias.

"Visiting family," Elias said between mouthfuls.

"Just visitin'? Seemed ye were in a bit more of a hurry than a simple visit would warrant."

Elias forced back a grimace. "There's trouble with the family business that only I can address. And my sister is expecting her first child."

"My wife just popped out our fourth wee one," Rigley announced. "After so many, they just come sliding out like butter."

The other men chuckled. Miss Westcott blushed.

Captain Littleman finally noticed her discomfort and chastised his men, but they only shrugged and took to more drink.

"Why have ye not eaten, Mrs. Dutton?" Nelson, the first mate pointed at her plate with his fork where barely a few bites were missing.

Only then did Elias notice that her face was pale and her hand was pressed to her stomach.

"D'ye not like the food?" The captain's tone was incredulous.

"Nay, Captain, the food is quite good. I'm just not feeling well."

"Ye aren't in a family way, are ye?" Nelson laughed and slapped Elias on the back.

Miss Westcott seemed to be having trouble breathing.

"Nelson, ye fish-brained oaf!" Captain Littleman's shout caused Miss Westcott to jump in her seat. "Ye've the manners of a barnacle. Apologize t' the lady at once."

Nelson only snorted and returned to his meal.

Elias braced himself for the Captain's fury and the punishment that would surely follow for the man's insubordination, but only the creak and groan of wood filled the air as the captain returned to his drink. Deciding 'twas best to change the subject, Elias said, "Captain, how long have you been a merchantman?"

"Aye, do regale us wi' yer tales o' bravery, Cap'n." Bates sneered at his captain and chuckled.

Either not noticing or ignoring the sarcasm in the quartermaster's voice, Captain Littleman puffed on his pipe and raised his shoulders. "Thirty years at sea I've been. Since I was a boy helpin' me father on his ship."

"'Tis a family business, then?" Elias asked.

"Aye, an' a good one. Took over from me father when he was murdered at sea five years back. Pirates it was." He scowled. "It weren't enough they stole his ship an' all its goods, but when he wouldn't sign on wit' them, the vile curs stripped him naked, gut an' quartered him, and hung his—"

"I'm sorry to hear of it," Elias interrupted and gestured toward Miss Westcott, who stared at the captain in horror.

"Sorry, mam." Littleman nodded toward her. "I'm not used to havin' a lady around."

Sails thundered above as the ship rolled over a wave, and men held onto their plates and mugs.

"Is this your father's ship?" Elias set down his spoon.

"This old bucket? Nay. Me father's ship *Red Hawk*—God rest her wooden hull—was a sleek-lined, three-masted, square-rigged beauty, swift as her name, and armed with thirty guns."

"Where is she now, Captain?"

"He ran her aground." Nelson snorted and the other men shared a chuckle.

"I did no such thing!" Spit flew from the captain's mouth. "I should have you flogged fer such an insult."

Nelson poured himself more wine.

Elias' heart coiled tight. The lack of respect—or even fear—for their captain made the crew much more dangerous, especially to Miss Westcott.

"'Twas a storm that ended her fair life, one of them wicked hurricanes," Captain Littleman continued. "No captain an' no ship coulda survived that monster. Straight from the Kraken's lair, says I, all blusterin' and blastin' wi' seas eruptin' like volcanoes. Only due to me skill did I save the entire crew, 'cept one. The ole *Red Hawk*, well, the winds drove her into the rocks an' she broke up."

His men chuckled.

Oddly, Miss Westcott cast a scolding glance at them before she faced the captain. "Sounds terrifying, Captain. How fortuitous you survived."

"'Twas by me own skill, Mrs. Dutton," he announced, proudly. "That's why ye've naught to fear on board this ship wit' me in command."

She smiled. "That brings me great comfort."

Nelson snickered.

The deck canted over a rising swell, sending one of the platters crashing to the deck as if in defiance of the captain's boasting.

Miss Westcott laid a hand at her throat, skin still white and perspiration gleaming on her forehead.

"Darling, allow me to take you on deck for some fresh air. Mayhap that will help?" Elias scooted out his chair and stood.

"So soon?" Rigley sat back in his chair and belched. "Don't take her away so soon! We hardly ever entertain a decent lady."

"Indeed? I hadn't noticed." Elias teased, but the insult floated past the man and never made a landing.

"Some air would be nice." Miss Westcott slowly rose. "I thank you for your hospitality, Captain."

Captain Littleman stood, staggered a bit, and reached up to swat a fly that buzzed between them.

Shrieking, Miss Westcott ducked as if the man intended to strike her.

Elias darted toward her, but the Captain grabbed her arm, a look of dismay on his face. "I wasn't goin' t' hit ye, mam."

Miss Westcott groaned and hugged her waist, her face turning as white as a sail in full sun. She covered her mouth and seemed to be having trouble breathing, wide eyes skittering about the cabin. Finally, she leaned over and spewed what little she had eaten all over the Captain's boots.

Howls of laughter rose from the three sailors as Littleman's face grew red and a string of curses shot from his mouth.

Offering his apologies, Elias quickly escorted Miss Westcott out the door, through the hallway, and back to their cabin before the captain's temper got the best of him and he tossed them both overboard. "I'm sorry for their crude behavior, Miss," he said after he shut the door and lit a lantern.

"Why should *you* be sorry?" She sounded breathless, embarrassed, as she dabbed her mouth with a cloth.

"I'm sorry any time a lady is made uncomfortable."

She looked at him as if he'd said he was growing another head. "Many things make me uncomfortable, Mr. Dutton. Few I can avoid."

He frowned. "Are you truly ill or was it the company that made you so?"

"My stomach is unsettled." She lowered her gaze to the deck.

"No need for shame, Miss. The food wasn't good and the company worse. In truth, I'm rather enjoyed watching you toss your accounts on the captain's boots."

His comment brought the first smile he'd seen on her lips, a glorious smile that lifted her cheeks and sparkled in her eyes and made her twice as beautiful, if that were possible.

A giggle broke through her smile. "I can't believe I did that." Then another giggle and another, and in moments they were both laughing so hard, it drown out the rush of water against the hull.

Oddly, the musical sound of her laughter soothed his soul and unwound nerves far too tight.

Finally, she lowered into a chair. "Were you telling the truth about why you are traveling to Barbados?"

Unsure of where to stand in the tiny cabin, he leaned against the bulkhead. "You'll find I'm an honest man."

"Except for telling the captain we are married."

"'Twas you who told him. I merely refused to correct the error."

Her smile disappeared. "So like a man of God, twisting the rules to suit your conscience."

"I thought you didn't believe in consciences." He gave her a sideways smile. "However, if you have changed your mind, I'll be happy to appease mine and go correct the error right now." He nodded toward the door.

Silence filled the room, and she lowered her gaze. "'Tis commendable that you care so much for your sister."

"I am close with all my siblings."

"All?"

"I'm the eldest of eight. Three sisters and four brothers."

"I am the oldest of four, all girls."

Elias huffed. "I trust they are not as troublesome as my siblings."

At this, the mermaid smiled again. "I would not venture such a wager, Sir."

Shrugging off his coat, he began unbuttoning his vest, causing the expected look of horror on the mermaid's face.

"What are you doing?" she shrieked.

"I'm tired and wish to sleep. 'Twill be a long day tomorrow."

"Surely you know that you can't stay here." She stood and scratched her arm as if an itch suddenly rose.

"I assure you, *darling*. I can and I will." Tossing his waistcoat and coat on the table, he grabbed his case, dropped it to the deck, and laid down with his head atop it.

Several minutes passed, filled with the lady's sighs and groans and the sound of water dashing and wood creaking. Finally she said, "How am I to undress with you here?"

"Blow out the lantern. I can't see you in the dark."

But he *could* see her in the dark. Especially in the moonlight sifting through the salt-encrusted window. He squeezed his eyes tighter, filling his thoughts with his sister's wedding, his parents, Scripture, God help him! ... anything to keep his mind off the beautiful woman disrobing just a few feet away. But the swish and swash of her gown and her tiny sighs and moans drove him to distraction.

This was going to be a very long night.

# Chapter 6

Lord Villemont's fist came down on Charity so fast, she hadn't time to leap aside. *Crunch!* The eerie sound of bone snapping was followed by his hate-filled voice. "I told you not to entertain Lady Beverly and that baseborn companion of hers! Why must you always disobey me?"

"I didn't disobey ... I ... I ..." Charity sank to the floor, hand over her aching jaw.

"I ... I ..." he mocked and shoved her down on her side with his boot. "I *what?*"

She curled into a ball, protecting the babe growing within. "She came to the door," she sobbed. "Hysterical and upset. I couldn't...I couldn't turn her away."

"More lies!" His boots pounded on the wooden floor, and she braced herself for another kick.

Instead, he grabbed her hair and yanked her up. Pain burned through her scalp and down her neck as he thrust his face into hers.

"What did we learn in church only yesterday about lying?" Rage ignited his eyes as breath, hot and stale, blasted over her. "Apparently you weren't listening, as usual."

"I'm *not* lying." The words slipped out, though she knew better than to contradict him. Every muscle within her tightened. *Please, God. No!*

He dragged her to the bed and tossed her down. She slammed her eyes shut, trying not to cry, trying not to give him the satisfaction, but tears spilled down her cheeks anyway.

The clip of his knife sheath, the scrap of metal on leather—sounds she knew all too well. *Not again!* Pushing off the quilt, she bolted for the door, screaming for help she knew wouldn't come. He snagged her by the waist, hoisted her off the ground, and shoved her onto the bed again.

Hovering over her like a bird of prey, his knife dripped silver in the lantern light. Squeezing her eyes shut, Charity went to her secret place.

*Sing a song of sixpence, a pocket full of rye. Four and twenty blackbirds baked in a...*

No!

She jerked up. Chest heaving, her eyes darted over the room, expecting Lord Villemont to leap out at her. But instead of her four-poster oak bed, she lay on a cot. Instead of her spacious room, four walls closed in on her. And instead of his raspy voice, creaks, groans, and rushing water flooded her ears. A predawn glow filtered in through the small window and alighted on a man sleeping on the floor.

Pulse rising again, she laid back down on her pillow and covered her mouth. Had she screamed? When had she fallen asleep? She'd spent most of the night listening to the man's snores, wondering whether he would transform into a beast and pounce on her. She'd learned long ago to keep one eye closed and one open during the long reaches of the night, for she never knew what mood Lord Villemont would find himself in or what infraction of hers he would invent that deserved punishment.

Scattering the morbid memories, she listened to the gentle creak and grind of the ship as it rocked like a baby's cradle, and she slipped a hand beneath the coverlet to touch her belly. She smiled and took a deep breath to calm her nerves.

Lord Villemont was gone. He couldn't hurt her anymore.

A ray of sun penetrated the window and speared hope into the gloomy room. Shouts, feet thumping, and sails flapping joined other sounds above. The man stirred.

Charity closed her eyes and kept still. He groaned, rustled, and must have risen due to the creaking floor. A flap of cloth, a few sighs, and the door opened and shut. Mayhap he was a preacher, after all. A good one. One who actually abided by what he taught. Not like the many rectors she'd run to for help who'd either chastised her for being a bad wife or offered to assist her—but at a price she would not pay.

Rising, she swung her feet over the edge of the cot and pried the knife she'd gripped all night from her sore hand—the knife she'd taken from Elias' things while he slept. Slipping it into her garter, she lowered her chemise, grabbed a damp cloth, and attempted to wipe salt out of her petticoats and skirts. She missed Sophie. For more reasons than one. Having a lady's maid was a luxury she'd never enjoyed until she'd married Villemont, at least not a single maid dedicated solely to her needs. Having one who was also a friend was a special privilege, and she hoped Sophie had found safe passage home. However, that left Charity with no one to lace up her stays, so she finally abandoned them and hoped her multiple petticoats would suffice for modesty's sake. That shouldn't be a problem since her bodice rose up to her neck, which was how Villemont demanded she dress.

"No woman of mine is going to dress like a trollop for all men's eyes to see!" he had said. When in truth, he'd forbidden her to go out enough for anyone to see her at all.

Odd that she felt like thanking him at the moment for that particular restriction since she found herself on a ship full of men.

Something foul brewed in her stomach, and she sat for a moment and tried to level her light head, wondering when this nausea would stop. Fresh air. She needed fresh air.

After splashing water on her face and pinning her hair up as best she could, Charity headed above deck. Sunlight blinded her as she took the final step onto the teetering planks. A blast of tropical wind struck her with more force than she'd been expecting, flapping her skirts and sending her hair flailing like an octopus.

Whistles and catcalls bombarded her as she stumbled to the starboard railing and gripped the wood, praying she didn't toss her accounts yet again in front of these men. Below, the sea churned and sloshed as sunlight flamed the tips of rising swells as far as the eye could see.

"Sheet home. Lower Top Sails!" The captain's voice bellowed behind her, and she glanced over her shoulder to see him nod in her direction. At least he wasn't angry at her for ruining his boots. She wondered where Elias was but didn't dare glance across the ship where she felt dozens of eyes boring into her. But then the captain shouted his name, something about bracing and bluntlines, and Charity couldn't help but glance in the direction of the reply.

Shielding her eyes from the sun, she spotted him balancing precariously on a topyard, adjusting sail alongside four other men. Stripped to the waist, wind tossed his tawny hair while sweat glistened on a chest far too bronze for a preacher.

He yelled something to the captain, who cursed in return before shouting another order up to him. With the ease of a hardened sailor, Elias slid down the shrouds and landed on the deck to assist a group of men who were tugging a line.

Why was the captain working him so hard when he'd paid for their trip? More importantly, why was Elias allowing it? Either he was a fool or he was too weak to stand up to the captain.

*No. Not weak.* At least not physically. Muscles rippled up his biceps and across his back with each heave of the rope like powerful waves of liquid steel glistening in the sunlight.

Mesmerized, Charity couldn't help but stare—continued to stare when he finished his task and headed toward her. *Oh, my.* Lord Villemont's chest had never looked like that, rounded and firm in all the right places. The only deterrent to Elias' Adonis appearance was the wooden cross hanging around his neck—a reminder of his vocation.

When she lifted her gaze, his blue eyes absorbed her, twinkling with mischief. Half a day's stubble peppered his jaw, making him look more rogue than rector. And she hated the blush that burned her face.

"Good day to you, Mermaid Darling." He slid beside her. "How did you sleep?"

She frowned at his nickname for her. "Well enough," she lied, still not looking at him as she took a step away.

He glanced down at his chest. "Forgive my appearance. The captain keeps me busy."

"As I see. Why do you let him order you about?"

He shrugged and leaned on the railing. "He needs the help. I need the fresh air. Besides, it gives me a chance to get to know the crew."

"And why would you want to do that?" Clearly they were beneath him in education and status.

"Mayhap 'twould give me a chance to speak to them of God."

"Ah, yes, ever the preacher." Charity huffed as the ship rose over a swell. She gripped the railing and eyed him. "Mayhap the men would listen to your proselytizing if they didn't deem you a ninny for groveling at the captain's feet."

He laughed. "My, my, the mermaid has a bite." He rubbed his jaw, studying her. "And where, may I ask, has your stutter run off to? Blown away in the trade winds, perhaps?"

She narrowed her eyes. Her intention with the affront was to dissuade any interest he had in her. But the blasted man kept smiling her way.

"It comes and goes, if you must know." she said. "Why are you not insulted by my remark?"

"Do you wish me to be?" He grinned.

"I wish you to have a backbone. Though I shouldn't expect it of a preacher. 'Let every soul be subject unto the higher powers. For there is no power but of God: the powers that be are ordained of God. Whosoever therefore resisteth the power, resisteth the ordinance of God: and they that resist shall receive to themselves damnation.' "

"Ah, impressive! The lady knows Scripture."

"Enough to know that God asks us to bend our backs to the taskmaster's whip, to submit to the authority He places over us, to allow a thief to take the shirt off our back and then give him another. Following God creates weak men." She curled her fists. *Weak men who beat their wives.*

The wind blew hair in his face, and he snapped it aside. "An interesting interpretation, Miss Westcott."

"And yet you demonstrate the truth of it before my very eyes." Grrr. Why was he still smiling at her? "How did you learn to handle sails, Mr. Dutton?"

His smile remained—white teeth, all straight save one that was slightly crooked on his upper right side. "Here and there."

"Ah." She raised a brow. "The preacher has secrets."

"No more than you."

"I have no secrets, Preacher. I told you why I'm here."

He leaned on the railing and cocked his head. "Have you?"

Sails snapped overhead, startling her. "Are you really a preacher, Mr. Dutton?"

"Is it so hard to believe?"

"Who on earth do you preach to? Do you have a church hidden on one of these islands?"

"The world is my church, Miss. I speak the truth to whoever will listen, sailors, natives, pirates ..."

"Pirates?"

He glanced over the glistening sea. "It might surprise you to know many are quite receptive to the Gospel."

"It *would* surprise me. I have rarely seen such interest among the finest of gentlemen."

"Mayhap you've been associating with the *wrong* gentlemen."

"On that I will agree." Her stomach gurgled and she placed a hand atop it.

"You look pale. Have you broken your fast this morning? The ship's biscuits are barely edible, but they are better than nothing."

"Thank you, but I doubt I can eat anything."

"Mayhap the captain has some ginger for your *mal-de-mer*?"

"A preacher *and* an apothecary." She bit her lip, finding herself more than curious about this preacher. "Do tell, is your goal to save the entire world from hellfire?"

"Something like that."

"Mr. Rigley!" Captain Littleman shouted. "Mr. Nelson! Shorten sail! Stand by to take in main course!" His gaze found Mr. Dutton. "Mr. Dutton, quit dawdling an' get back to work!"

But instead of complying, Mr. Dutton stared up at the sails, his expression one of bewilderment and alarm.

"What is it?" she asked him.

He shoved his hair back. "For all his supposed years at sea, Captain Littleman has very little understanding of wind, currents, and sails. With the direction and force of our present wind, hauling in the main before the topsails could cause excessive heeling and weaken the upper spars."

"Are we in danger?"

"Some of his men know what they are doing." He glanced over the sea. "But the Windward Passage is not the safest place in the world. Filled with pirates, smugglers and the like. Ships are easy prey sailing between Cuba and Saint Dominique."

Charity hadn't considered such dangers.

She must have looked worried, for he added, "Forgive me. I shouldn't have said anything." He reached to touch her hand.

She instantly pulled it from the railing and leapt back.

"If you keep acting like your husband has the pox, people will start to suspect."

Releasing a sigh of frustration, she studied him. "You seem like an honorable man, Mr. Dutton. I appreciate that you behaved the gentleman last night, and I pray your honor continues. But there is no need to pander, protect, nor pamper me further."

"Mermaid darling, I rarely pander or pamper, though protect I'll own up to. And I've been known to preach on occasion."

She gave a tight smile and gazed out to sea. "I forbid you to do that as well."

Captain Littleman yelled once again for Elias to return to work, but he wasn't ready yet to leave the elusive Miss Westcott. Elusive and baffling. One minute her courage astounded him, the next, she shrank from his touch like a skittish mouse. And where did her mistrust of God come from—the bitterness and anger that sharpened her eyes and barbed every word when she spoke of the Almighty and preachers, in particular? Equally baffling was her nightmare, screams that had woken him and nearly sent him to her bedside. But not wanting to add to her fright, he remained still, lying on the deck, listening to her cries for mercy, her whimpers of pain, and then a song ... a nursery rhyme whispered on a distant prayer.

Before she woke with a shout of agony.

The man in him longed to take her in his arms and protect and comfort her. The preacher longed to open her eyes to a God who was both Father and Friend. But Elias did nothing. He'd merely said a prayer for her then. And another one now as she lifted her face to the wind and closed her eyes.

"Mr. Dutton!" Captain Littleman's shout intruded on his chance to admire her beauty without her notice.

Wind fluttered her brown hair, dark and rich like mahogany, the sun luring out reddish-gold streaks he'd never noticed before. Unbidden, his thoughts drifted to another lady with lustrous dark hair. *Rachel.* Yet Miss Westcott was nothing like her. Miss Westcott comported herself like a lady, modest in her attire, adhering to strict morals. Nary a flirtatious bone existed within her, repulsed even by the attentions of men. She was an Admiral's daughter who cared about her family and longed to be with them again. Just like Elias.

Such wit and banter! She never failed to surprise him. Regardless of why God had brought her into his life, Elias must change her mind about the Almighty.

Another shout from the captain, and Elias sighed in frustration. He bid Miss Westcott good day and headed for the ratlines when "A sail! A sail!" blared from above.

Leaping into the shrouds, Elias made his way to the tops where he hoped to borrow the glass and study the advancing ship. Thankfully the sailor complied, and while bracing himself against wind and wave, Elias leveled it on the sails, seeking the ensign that would identify the nationality. There. The red blue and white of England flapped from the masthead.

But something was wrong.

Elias had been at sea his entire life. From the moment he could stand without falling, his father Rowan had assigned him duties on board his ship, *The Reckoning.* Then as Elias grew, his father taught him how to tie lines, climb the ratlines, furl and raise sail, tack, heel to, navigate shoals, man the wheel, the pumps and a host of other tasks. But most of all he taught him to trust his gut, his instinct, and the Spirit of God within him. And at the moment, that Spirit was twisting his stomach into a knot. One more glance through the glass confirmed his suspicions. He knew that ship. 'Twas the twenty-gun French ship of the infamous pirate Charles Vane.

# Chapter 7

Cupping his hands, Elias shouted "pirate!" down to the captain, but the man merely stood there, feet spread apart, hands fisted at his waist, and ever-present pipe stuck in his mouth. Finally, he grabbed the telescope from his first mate Nelson and leveled it on the horizon.

Elias made quick work of the shrouds and ratlines back down to the deck, and—noting the fear on Miss Westcott's face in passing—dashed to Captain Littleman.

"Captain, 'tis Charles Vane. I know his ship."

He plucked the cold pipe from his mouth. "Ye do, d'ye, and how d'ye know that?"

"I've sailed these seas many years, Captain. My father has done battle with the man."

"Yer father?" The captain chuckled. "An' who might that be?"

"Captain, we are wasting time." Elias glanced over his shoulder at the advancing ship, foam curling up her bow and sails heavy with wind. "Rowan Dutton. My father is Rowan Dutton."

The ship pitched over a wave, and Captain Littleman gripped the binnacle, a snarl on his lips. "The pirate turned preacher? Joined up wit' those Hyde missionaries, if I remember. Ye be his brat, eh?"

Elias bristled at the term. "Captain, please. The madman gains."

Perching the scope on his eye again, the captain shook his head. "I don't see nothin' suspicious. Just a British merchantman same as us."

Elias groaned. "Then why is he fast on our heels?"

"I'm guessing because he's not got a hold full o' goods same as us. Oh, very well, ye nag me more than me own wife." He turned to Nelson who exchanged a harried gaze with Elias. "Ready the guns just in case."

"Aye aye, Captain. Sakin!" Nelson leapt down the quarterdeck ladder. "Load the guns!" Several men darted across the deck, some dropping below.

Wind blasted over them, thundering sails above and whipping Elias' hair against his face. He shoved it aside. "I would raise all sail to the wind if I were you, Captain. With luck we can outrun him."

Captain Littleman's chest expanded as if it would burst open at any moment. "I'm Captain here, and I'll do as I see fit! Now, off with ye. Back to work!"

Elias grimaced, standing his ground. The man was naught but a toad, a toad full of hot air—a toad that would get them all killed.

"Captain, if I'm right and this *is* Vane, you have no doubt heard of his cruelty to captured sailors."

"Leave me quarterdeck at once, Mr. Dutton!" Spit flew from the captain's mouth. "One more word an' I'll chain ye to the keel. I'll thank ye to remember that ye are but a passenger on board me ship. " He pointed his pipe toward the main deck. "Go tend yer lovely wife. She looks a bit distressed."

Nelson returned, gave Elias another glance that said he agreed with him, then took up a spot beside his captain.

"Clew up the main topsail!" Captain Littleman shouted across the deck.

Elias could hardly believe his ears. "But Captain, that will slow us and give him the weather edge!"

"What did I say about one more disrepectin' word from you!"

Elias knew he meant it. *Blasted Fool!* He stomped down to the main deck, glancing back at Nelson and then over the hustling crew. Why did they obey the man when 'twas obvious they bore him no respect? If only Elias could get them on his side. *Mutiny.* He shook his head. What was he thinking? Yet, how could he protect Miss Westcott and the crew if he had no power to do so? Frustration mounting, he slipped beside the lady and studied the ship approaching fast off their starboard side.

"You must get below at once, Miss Westcott."

"Why?" Her voice bore the tremble of fear. "What is the matter?"

"We are about to be attacked by pirates."

*Pirates?* Did he say pirates? Charity stared after Elias as he leapt back into the ratlines and climbed to the tops as if he'd been doing it all his life. Swerving her gaze to the advancing ship, she shielded her eyes from the sun and studied it more carefully. Not that she would know a pirate ship from any other, but weren't they supposed to have black flags with scary things like bones and knives and hourglasses on them? And what about cannons? Shouldn't there be a row of them pointed their way and a host of scary-looking men mobbing the deck. She saw none of those things as the details of the ship came into view. Just a few sailors attending their duties and a man with a floppy hat standing at the wheel.

The sun's rays spired down upon her. She rubbed the back of her neck as perspiration slid beneath her gown.

How would a preacher know such a thing anyway? Surely Captain Littleman had more experience in these matters. She'd heard—in fact, the entire crew had heard—their argument of only moments before. Drawing a deep breath, she gripped the rail as the ship plunged over a wave yet again, spraying her with salty mist—a welcoming cool mist. Sails hammered above, and she glanced up to see several canvases flapping lifeless. The ship veered to larboard and more canvas sagged, slowing their progress.

The captain cursed, and the crew hurried to haul lines and adjust yards.

The advancing ship gained.

Perhaps she *should* go below. She started to do just that when Elias sped down the ropes again, and the first mate shouted, "They've run out their guns, Cap'n!"

Charity heard the words, but either the wind or her good reason tore them from her mind. Everything...slowed...down...as if the world moved through molasses—the rise and fall of the ship, the movements of the sailors, the flap of sails. Even the shouting became muffled ... distant. 'Twas like a dreamworld that one watched from afar. Certainly not reality, for she couldn't possibly be standing on the deck of a ship that was about to be blasted to bits. She gazed over the starboard railing and noted with curiosity that the advancing ship had doubled in size. The dark muzzles of more cannons than she could count stared at her like vacant eye sockets of death from the underworld.

"All hands down!" The voice was Elias', muted yet strong. The hands were also strong as she felt herself forced to the deck and his body cover her like an iron blanket.

Thunder quivered the sky. An eerie whine sounded overhead, followed by an explosion that trembled the ship like an earthquake.

Smoke and charred oakum filled her nose, burned her lungs. She coughed. Time sped up now. Her iron shield abandoned her, and she found him leaning over the side and cursing under his breath.

He helped her to her feet, his blue eyes stark with fear. "Get below!" He didn't wait to see if she complied as he stormed up onto the quarterdeck and charged the captain.

But Charity couldn't move. She glanced at the ship, finally spotting the black flag she'd been seeking, flapping in the breeze complete with skull and a dagger dripping blood. At least fifty men armed with cutlass and pistol and wicked grins covered the deck like flies on horse manure.

Her blood turned to ice. Had she rid herself of one monster only to be captured by dozens more? Tales of horror had made their way to Portsmouth of the tortures inflicted by these pirates. Especially the unthinkable things they did to women. And what of her child? She pressed a hand to her stomach and fought back tears. Fought back nausea. Terror. She'd spent the past two years a victim of brutality, and she'd be dead in her grave before she'd endure that again.

Angry shouts drew her gaze to the quarterdeck where the captain and Elias were engaged in another verbal battle. Sailors dashed chaotically back and forth across the deck, cursing and grunting, their expressions stiff with fear. The captain's face had gone completely white. Shoving Elias to the side, he howled orders that scattered the crew.

She leaned over the side and saw a charred hole in the hull sinking below the water line with each sway of the ship.

They were taking on water.

Above them, two sails were ripped clean through. How could they possibly outrun the pirates now?

"Lay aloft, loose the main!" Captain Littleman shouted to his men.

"Belay that!" Storming onto the main deck, Elias spouted orders, different orders, something about swivels and gunpowder and pumps.

The crew halted, their gazes shifting between the two men and finally landing on the first mate Nelson.

Captain Littleman gripped the quarterdeck railing and glared at his crew. "I am the captain and ye will obey me orders or face execution!"

"If you obey this man you will all die!" Elias shouted with enough conviction to convince Charity, though she wondered how he knew what he was doing. Vapors! He was a mere preacher. Had he ever commanded a ship in battle?

"What!" Captain Littleman drew his sword. "I'll have your heart on a pla—!"

The world suddenly exploded above them, and Charity's heart with it. Ducking, she covered her head as the ship splintered all around and screams shot into the air. Face down, she stared at the wooden planks of the deck, heart pounding in her ears, mind reeling, afraid to stand up, afraid to breathe. A stream of blood trickled down the deck beneath her and pooled in a cleft of the wood.

She finally lost the contents of her stomach.

"The captain! The captain!" someone yelled.

Batting away smoke, Charity looked up to see Captain Littleton lying on the quarterdeck.

Without hesitation, Elias pointed to two men. "You, you! Bring the Captain to his quarters and alert the surgeon. You, Myson, was it? Get two more men and take the rest of the wounded below."

He marched toward her. "Miss Westcott, below!" There was something different in his eyes. Not fear, as she would expect. Nay, 'twas a sense of justice, of power and command, of control. And it stirred within her a desire to trust this man, a sense that she was safe with him. She shook the betraying feeling away.

"Give me a gun." She held out her hand. "If we are to be boarded, give me a gun so I can defend myself." And her child. Or, if need be, end their lives before falling into the hands of pirates.

Elias didn't have time to argue with the surprising woman. "Do you know how to use it?"

She nodded and snatched it from his hands as another volcano of fire charged the air.

A plume of gray smoke thrust from the pirate ship. The whiz and whine of shot scraped past his ears, and shielding Miss Westcott, Elias forced her to the deck once again. Explosions rippled through the ship. The sting of gun smoke and blood filled his nostrils.

Rising, he motioned for her to remain where she was, then he took charge like he'd been taught to do his entire life. Like he'd done many times before.

Only he'd never faced an enemy with a ship so crippled before. Or a crew that wasn't his. Would they even obey him? Instead of waiting to find out, Elias took stock of the situation and fired off orders.

Nelson, jaw stiff, and eyes shifting, charged Elias as if he intended to challenge him. But his gaze shifted to the approaching pirate ship and then to the crew awaiting orders. Fear blazed in his eyes.

Giving a nod to Elias, he faced the men. "You heard him! Do what he says!"

As the sailors scrambled to their tasks, Elias studied their oncoming enemy. He had but one chance to save Captain Littleman's brig, and one chance only, before Charles Vane sunk them to the depths.

# Chapter 8

Charity knew she should go below, if only to get out of the crew's way. But she couldn't tear her eyes off Elias. Or off the pirate ship advancing fast off their starboard beam—black flag taunting in the breeze, foam spewing from her bow. Gray smoke hovered over her, a cloud of haunting specters, as her guns were reloaded and run out like tongues salivating for meat.

She knew enough about ships from her father to know that the *Enmity* was badly damaged. With two sails ripped and a hole in the hull, she listed to starboard and moved as if she sailed through a sea of mud.

Curses and threats fired at them from the pirate ship, and every inch of Charity screamed in terror. She had assumed God had abandoned her years ago. Now, if she was to be tortured and ravished by pirates, there would be no doubt.

Crouching against the quarterdeck, she gripped the gun tightly to her chest and awaited her fate.

Elias, on the other hand, was the epitome of calm assurance as he marched across the deck issuing orders like he commanded a ship at battle every day.

"Watch your luft! Watch your luft! Ready about! Bring her into the wind. Steady now."

Captain Littleman's officers, Nelson, Rigley, and Bates, repeated Elias' orders as if there hadn't been a change in command at all. One by one, the crew also scrambled to do his bidding, some leaping in the tops, some jumping down hatches below.

She couldn't blame them. Something about Elias' tone, his fearlessness, evoked a confidence and hope that made one want to obey his every word. He came into view then, the wind flapping his shirt and tossing his hair behind him, his jaw a steel rod, his eyes locked on the pirates. He had strapped on a sword and two pistols and looked more pirate than preacher, for not a speck of fear emanated from him as he gripped the pummel of his blade.

The pirate ship belched another fiery round, and Charity shielded her head with her hands. A death whine filled the air. Wood snapped. Then a splash. Charity looked up to see that the cannonball had chipped a piece of the mainmast below the sails then dropped into the sea off the larboard railing.

Elias, who had not ducked at all, continued shouting orders as if nothing had happened. Water gushed against the hull. Sails roared above, some flapping impotently, others bloated with wind. The *Enmity* leapt over a rising swell. Black squalls swept back over the deck, foaming around Charity's shoes and leaping up to douse her skirts with seawater.

Elias barreled down the quarterdeck ladder onto the main deck and shouted something Charity couldn't make out to Nelson.

"Hot shot?" The first mate stared up at him, balancing on the heaving deck. "With musket shot, ye say?"

"Aye, and now!"

"But the galley fire's been put out for battle."

"Stoke it."

"'Tis dangerous."

"And being captured by Vane isn't?" Elias yelled. "Do it now!"

Nodding, Nelson dropped blow.

"Bates!" Elias turned to the quartermaster. "We'll tack to starboard and come along her stern."

"Aye, Cap'n," the man said without question, then brayed further orders to the men.

The ship turned and slowed a bit then turned again. Sails floundered like fish out of water, and for a moment it seemed they had lost all momentum. Charity gripped the gun tighter. Her pulse pounded so hard she thought her veins would burst. One peek beyond the quarterdeck ladder showed her the pirates were gaining fast and making a turn for a broadside. *A broadside!* Ten guns fired at once at such close range would be the end of them.

Minutes went by like hours as the two ships made quick maneuvers, counteracting the other's in some eerie dance of death. Silence invaded, save for creak of block and tackle and rush of wind, which only increased Charity's terror. Sun slashed her from above. Perspiration trickled down her neck beneath her gown.

Elias paced, shouted orders, then paced some more, his hawk-like eyes ever on the pirates. And she found herself almost believing he *could* save them, that he could defeat these pirates, these expert warriors of the sea. She forced down the admiration rising within her. She didn't want to admire him. For admiration led to affection and affection led to trust. And trust is something she would never give to another man.

Finally Elias cupped his hands and shouted, "Brace in the mainyard! Up helm! Shift over the headsheets!"

The wind came around on their starboard quarter, catching the sails in a thunderous snap.

Palms on the rough deck, Charity braced herself as the ship tilted high and veered to starboard. Elias must have anticipated the pirates' move, for he was making a sharp turn away from them. Or was it away? Sunlight blinded her as the *Enmity* angled so high, she thought it would overturn.

Splinters dug into her palms. She tumbled to the right and braced against the quarterdeck, breath heaving.

When the ship finally righted, she dared a glance and discovered they had actually veered closer to the pirate ship, not farther away, and were coming around on the pirate's stern.

"Haul out! Brace up!" Bates shouted.

The *Enmity* jerked forward and picked up speed. Struggling against the galloping deck, Charity stood and backed against the quarterdeck, pistol tight in her grip.

No doubt caught off guard at Elias' quick maneuver, the pirates attempted to follow the tack and protect their stern, but the wind vacated their canvas.

"They are all aback!" one sailor shouted with glee.

Charity had no idea what that meant, but from the sounds of "huzzahs" coming from the men, it was something good.

Elias stooped and shouted down the companionway. "Get me that hot musket shot, Nelson!"

"Ready, Sir. Loaded and primed!" came the bellowing answer.

"Bear off, haul your braces, ease sheets!" Elias shouted. "Starboard guns standby. Fire as you bear!"

Within minutes, the air quivered with the roar of guns. The *Enmity* shuddered from bow to stern, matching the one coursing through Charity. Black smoke swept over the deck and engulfed her. She gasped for air, her lungs stinging.

Then all was silent. A ghostly silence, as if they were all dead and drifting through a portal to the afterlife.

Finally men shuffled to the starboard railing. Coughing, Charity rose and crept behind them, fearing that if she were dead, she'd be stuck with these men for all eternity.

But then a distant crackle sounded, followed by horrified shouts, and some of the crew laughed. Stepping up on the quarterdeck ladder, she peered above the crowd to the pirate ship. Shattered glass and splintered wood was all that remained of the stern as flames reached for the sky through gaping holes. Black smoke obscured the stern railing along with the guns mounted there. Pirates darted across the deck in a frenzy, buckets in hand and curses flying. A few pirates fired muskets at them from the tops, but they were already too far away. A large man wearing a multi-colored vest that glistened in the sunlight and a cocked hat with a bright blue feather approached the railing and gripped it hard.

"Let's hear it for Captain Dutton! Hip hip hurray!" Bates shouted.

"Hip hip hurray!" the men chanted as they punched fists in the air.

"Make all possible sail, gentlemen!" Elias ordered before leaping onto the bulwarks and bowing toward the pirates. "Another time, perhaps, Vane!" His shout echoed over the water.

Charles Vane, the infamous pirate, glared at Elias as if his eyes could fire cannon balls. Charity shuddered at the sight.

But thankfully, the *Enmity*, with most canvas spread to the wind, tacked aweather and soon sped on her way.

Charity rubbed her eyes and tried to settle her heart, not yet fully able to believe they were out of danger. Yet with each passing minute, 'twas obvious they were.

All due to Elias.

But how? It made no sense. Holding the gun to her bosom, she watched the sailors congratulate themselves as Elias ordered them to task. Then before he noticed her, she quietly slipped below to their cabin and sat in the chair, her mind reeling, her nerves a tangled lump. She settled the gun in her lap and tried to slow her breathing, but her racing heart refused to calm. It wasn't only from witnessing a battle with pirates. Nay, it had more to do with witnessing *Elias* battling pirates. Her suspicion only grew as hours passed and she waited, pondering the hopelessness of her situation and plotting her next move.

Just when she'd decided Elias wasn't going to join her, the door creaked open and in he walked, his skin flush with exertion, his hair tousled, a smile on his face, and his presence larger than life.

Jumping to her feet, she pointed the pistol at his chest.

One brow cocked. "Not exactly the thanks I was expecting."

"Who are you?" She cocked the gun. "You are no preacher, Sir, for no preacher I know could have commanded this ship and beaten those pirates against such overwhelming odds."

Elias would laugh if he didn't know the pistol was loaded—and waving across his chest in hands that were trembling far too much.

"Your low opinion of preachers cuts me to the quick, Miss Westcott." He took another step toward her, his intent to snatch the weapon.

But she only tightened her grip on the handle and raised it to point at his head.

What a treasure this lady was! Like a frightened forest sprite—and no bigger than one—with those large honey-colored eyes, her brown hair tumbling in disarray to her waist, her lips quivering … chest heaving. What prompted her to do such a thing? Such bravery, such spunk. Such *foolishness!*

Her lips pinched. "Not another move! Not until you tell me who you are."

"Elias Dutton, as I have said."

She narrowed her eyes. "What do you want with me?"

"If I recall 'twas you who created the facade of our wedded bliss and insisted I take you on board." He drew his sword from its sheath.

The cold barrel of the gun pressed on his temple. "I *will* shoot you."

Her unique scent, so feminine and sweet spiraled around him. He laid the blade on the table and raised his hands. "Just removing my sword. Unless you wish me to remain armed?"

She took a step back and gestured with the gun. "Remove your pistols as well, then."

Slowly slipping the baldric over his head, he laid it beside his sword and eased into the chair, his taut muscles screaming. "You've had a frightening experience today, Miss Westcott. Any woman would be distraught. But I am not your enemy."

"And you are no preacher, either. Of that I am sure. Besides, what happened to 'thou shalt not kill'? Or do you only choose those commandments that suit you?"

Elias leaned forward, elbows on his knees and gazed up at the crazed woman. "You know many Scriptures, my little mermaid, yet you fail to understand their meaning."

Frowning, she braced herself as the deck slanted. "Then tell me this, how did you learn to command a ship during battle?"

"I grew up on a ship. A brig to be exact. My father's, the *Reckoning*."

"And did your father make a habit of engaging in battle?" She smirked.

"More often than he would have liked, I'm afraid." Elias shoved his hair back, the exhaustion of the day finding its way into his bones. If he could but lie down and rest, only for a moment. "Give me the pistol, Miss. I have no intention of harming you." He held out his hand. "If I did, I would have taken what I wanted already."

"Not if you are one of Charles' henchmen."

He studied her. "I suppose this Charles is your would-be brother-in-law?" He huffed. "I fail to see how I could be allied with him. I don't even know the man."

"So you say."

A spiral of hair dangled over her cheek, and he longed to touch it, to move it out of the way and see if it was as soft as it looked. As well as the skin beneath it. "So what are you to do now? Shoot me and toss me overboard?"

"If I have to."

He smiled at her boldness. "Then you'd be left at the mercy of the crew."

"I told you, I don't need your ..." The ship pitched over a wave. Miss Westcott wobbled. In one swift move, Elias jumped up, swiped the weapon from her hands, shoved it behind his back, and steadied her.

Startled, she shrieked and jerked from his touch, then backed away, eyes wide, breath coming fast. Finally, she deflated like a sail losing wind and sank onto the cot, dropping her head in her hands.

"Miss Westcott, 'tis been a trying day. I don't know of many women who could have faced a battle at sea and possible capture by pirates with such courage." 'Twas true. She'd stayed above, clutching her pistol, witnessing the entire bloody business. He knew of only a few women who wouldn't have fainted on the spot. His mother for one, along with his Aunt Juliana. But those two ladies were rare finds, indeed.

As this woman seemed to be.

"Mayhap I can find Bates and have some food brought for you."

She pressed a hand to her stomach and raised glassy eyes to him, the fight gone from them, replaced by a sorrow so deep, he felt it in his gut. "I'm not hungry."

He longed to kneel before her, take her in his arms and comfort the tears from those eyes. "What has made you so brave, dear lady?"

She looked away. "I've had no other choice."

Elias gulped, wanting to ask more, but dared not. How on earth could he gain the trust of such a woman? And what sort of beast had stolen every ounce of it from her? Mayhap she did the right thing in fleeing from this fiancé of hers.

A rap sounded on the door.

He opened it to Rigley, blood splattered on his shirt, and a hesitancy in his droopy eyes. "The captain's dead," he said without emotion. "Nelson requests yer presence on the quarterdeck. The crew voted to make ye actin' cap'n 'til we make port." He turned to go, but halted. "Oh, an' we're takin' on water faster than we can pump it out."

Elias made no reply, merely stared after the man as he left. He already knew about the water. He could feel the sluggishness, sense the brig lowering in the sea. What he hadn't realized was how badly injured the captain had been. But Elias, acting captain? That he also hadn't expected.

Miss Westcott hugged herself. "Dead. How horrible."

Elias stuffed the pistol in his belt and went to retrieve his other weapons. "Life at sea can be brutal, Miss."

"Life anywhere is brutal," she returned. "What are you going to do?"

"First thing, give him a proper burial. Then take command of the ship and head for the nearest port. In this condition, we won't make it to Barbados."

# Chapter 9

"**O** death, where is thy sting? O grave, where is thy victory?

The sting of death is sin; and the strength of sin is the law.

But thanks be to God, which giveth us the victory through our Lord Jesus Christ."

Charity stood beside Elias as he read from the Holy Scripture. Around them mobbed the sailors of the *Enmity* while in the middle of the crowd—and within reach of Charity—lay the body of Captain Littleman, shrouded in white sailcloth.

Oblivious to the sorrowful occasion, the sun danced toward the horizon in a festive array of brilliant saffron and gold, flinging hot spires upon them until it felt as though they would enter hell along with the captain. Charity bit her lip. She shouldn't even think such a thing. If there was a hell, she wouldn't wish it on anyone. *Well, perhaps Lord Villemont.* Nay, not even him.

Perspiration dampened her gown as Elias droned on with more Scripture. The men wiped sweat from their brows and shifted their feet, appearing no more interested in this final salute to their captain than she was. Besides, she hated funerals. She'd only attended two in her life. Both times she'd left a piece of her heart buried deep beneath the ground, never to be retrieved.

Her mother's funeral was nothing like this one. The day had been dismal and gray, cloaked in fog and a mist that chilled to the bone, as if the world itself mourned the loss of such a sweet soul. The other funeral had taken place in the pouring rain, dark skies weeping along with Charity. Hundreds had swarmed to pay their respects to her mother, while only Charity grieved at the second funeral for the life that had never been.

"Ashes to ashes, dust to dust, we commend your spirit, Captain Herman Littleman to the deep and into the hands of God." Elias' voice brought Charity back to the present, and she shuddered despite the heat.

He nodded to two men holding the plank on which Littleman lay, and they tipped it until the body slid over the railing and splashed into the sea. The end of a life. Just like that. What did it all matter? She swallowed as memories of Lord Villemont came crashing down.

*The good Book says your life is but a vapor, woman! Naught but a cloud, a shadow that 'appeareth for a little time and then vanisheth away.* He thrust the Bible in her face, then tossed it to the table. *No one will remember you when you're gone. Egad, I hardly remember that you are here now!*

Except, no matter how much she tried to stay out of his way, he *did* remember she was there. Far too often.

"Miss Westcott ... Miss Westcott." Elias' handsome face appeared in her vision, looking concerned. He lifted a hand toward her. Heart pinching, she jumped back and flailed her arms in front of her in defense. She struck him, but he gripped her hands and clasped them within his. Warmth and strength enfolded them and settled the fear that rose at his touch.

"Calm yourself, my little mermaid. I was merely brushing hair from your face."

She jerked to attention and glanced around to see most of the crew had returned to their duties. Those who weren't staring at them.

"Forgive me." Holding a hand to her mouth, she grabbed her skirts, dashed down the companionway to her cabin, and fell onto the cot, sobbing. Why did her husband haunt her even from the grave? Would she never be free of him? She pressed a hand to her belly. Nay, she would not, for this child would be a constant reminder. Yet...she would love him or her with all of her heart. If only God would give her a chance.

Hours passed, her tears finally spent, she rose, lit a lantern, and washed her face with day-old dirty water. Dabbing her puffy eyes, she tried to convince herself 'twas the terrifying events of the day that had caused such a childish outpouring of tears and not a past she'd just as soon forget.

The ever-present swoosh of water filled the room, along with muffled shouts and footsteps from above, but darkness prevented her from seeing anything through the porthole. Now that Elias was captain, would he stay in the captain's quarters and leave her be? Mayhap after her performance on deck, he'd be glad to be rid of her.

Her stomach grumbled, and she laid a hand over it and smiled. "I know, precious one, I must find food soon." She'd eaten so little in the past few months and kept so little of it down that she worried for the babe's health. Still, she could hardly wander about the ship at night in search of food.

She sighed. 'Twould seem she had no choice. For all his espousing of Christian values and offers of protection, Elias certainly didn't seem overly concerned with her basic needs. *Typical preacher.*

Stuffing wayward hair into her bun, she started for the door, when it swung open on creaking hinges and in walked Elias, carrying a tray of food. If she wasn't so terrified of a man's touch, she'd hug him right there.

"Your dinner, milady." He grinned and set it on the table. "'Tis not much." He lifted his baldric over his head, then glanced at her cautiously. "Just taking these off, no need to point a pistol at me." He placed his cutlass down beside the belt and gestured toward the food. "As I was saying, 'tis not much, but we have salted fish, biscuits, yams, half-rotted mangoes, and rum-tainted lemon water."

Savory scents, both sweet and sour, wafted over Charity, and her mouth watered. Perhaps she was past the early sickness of her condition. Which also meant she would not be able to hide that condition for long.

She wanted to tell Elias how much she appreciated his thoughtfulness. Instead she pasted on a smirk. "I thought you'd be in the captain's quarters."

"Without my wife?" He winked and shut the door.

Which sent a spike of alarm through her, though she knew she had no cause. "There is no longer need for pretense. The captain is dead."

"The crew is not, however. Now, sit." He pulled up a chair. "You must be famished."

She bristled at the way he ordered her about, but for the sake of her babe, she complied and quickly piled food onto her plate.

He also filled a plate and then lowered to the cot and bowed his head. "Bless this food, our Lord. We thank you for it and also for the victory today. Amen."

"Amen," she said, trying to hide the bite of fish in her mouth.

At first, they both sat quietly eating, but as her stomach filled, Charity took a sip of rum water and sat back in her chair. "So, *Captain*, are we to sink or have you found a port nearby?"

He tossed a piece of biscuit into his mouth. "Aye, Kingston."

"Jamaica?"

"'Tis the closest anchorage, and I know people there."

Stories of Jamaica had made their way to Portsmouth, fables of pirate havens and cities so wicked, God sank them into the sea. Surely those were merely embellished stories. "When will we arrive?"

"Tomorrow, if the holes we patched in the hull remain intact."

She watched how the muscles in his jaw bunched as he ate, shifting an errant strand of hair that had settled on his cheek. "And if they don't?"

"Then we'll arrive later." He smiled and took another bite of fish. "But never fear we *will* arrive."

There was that confident tone again that made her believe everything he said.

He set his plate aside. "Drink your water, Miss Westcott. I had cook put an extra ration of rum into it. Lord knows your nerves could use it after the day's events."

"Your nerves never seem in need of soothing, Mr. Dutton." Oh my, had she just complimented him? She quickly corrected the mistake by adding, "I thought preachers weren't allowed to drink spirits."

"Another misconception of yours, my little mermaid."

"Please stop calling me that! Besides, what makes you think I need calming? Am I shrieking hysterically? Fainting in your arms?"

He studied her, eyes twinkling. "Nay, but I wouldn't fault you if you did."

"I am not some weak-kneed female swooning at every danger."

"Yet you seemed quite distraught after the funeral." It was a statement, a question, and a look of concern all in one.

Charity gazed out the dark porthole. "I was thinking of something else."

"Something that frightened you."

"It doesn't matter." She gulped down her water, wincing at the strong taste, but enjoying the warmth spiraling down her throat. Perhaps the rum was a good idea, after all.

Thankfully Elias asked no further questions. She'd give him credit for discretion if she were tallying his good qualities. Which she wasn't.

Minutes passed as she finished her meal and then together they stacked their dirty plates on the tray. Though she tried to avoid the man—all six foot and more of him—each tilt of the deck sent her bumbling into his body, a rather firm body that, against her will, caused something to stir within her that she hadn't felt in years. Certainly not the fear she expected.

Finally, she settled onto the cot, and tried to focus on anything but the man whose presence took up the entire cabin.

"Would you like me to read from the Bible? It may bring you peace and help you sleep." He sat on the chair, pulled a book from his case, and opened it in his lap.

"Nay. I sleep well enough."

"Not by my account." He said it so matter-of-factly with neither accusation nor surprise. Or even embarrassment that he pried into such intimacies. The embarrassment was all hers, apparently, as heat flooded her face.

Lantern light flickered over his shadowed jaw and lit the sun-bleached strands of his hair as he gazed at the Bible with the reverence of a monk. But he *wasn't* a monk. A preacher, perhaps, but most likely a pirate. A pirate who shared a cabin with her.

Vapors, if word got out, what little remained of her reputation would be tossed to the wind. She nearly laughed. What was she thinking? She had no reputation left, save that of a murderess.

"How dare you spy on me whilst I'm asleep," she snapped.

He raised his gaze to her, those dark blue eyes sparkling. "I can hardly do otherwise, Miss, since I find myself in the same cabin."

"You can remedy that by sleeping elsewhere tonight."

"Nay." He returned his glance to the Bible. "I'll not leave you to the mercies of this crew."

Charity's jaw tightened as memories of another man intruded—a man equally as kind and protective. During their courtship, Lord Villemont had expressed nothing but care for Charity as if she were the most important thing in the world. Over and over, he lavished her with promises of protection and happiness. And just like this man before her, he also quoted Scripture.

*I will not be duped again!* She was no longer a naïve maiden who longed for the love and protection of a man to fill the void left by a distant father. Stupid, stupid girl, so easily swayed by good looks and kind words, so quick to fall in love. Never again!

"Mr. Dutton," she began. "You need not pretend to care about my welfare—either my physical or spiritual. I relieve you of any false sense of obligation you may feel toward me as well as any hope you have to receive something from me in return."

Oddly, he smiled at her, scratched his head, then shook it as if she babbled nonsense. "Miss Westcott, I bear neither pretense, expectation, nor obligation. It pains me you think otherwise. Regardless, I still intend to sleep in this cabin with you."

Charity crossed arms over her stomach and forced back what was sure to be an unladylike growl.

"Good night to you, Miss." Closing the Bible, he gave her a grin that she longed to smack off his face. But then he blew out the lantern and it was gone. She heard him settle on the deck and quickly fall asleep. *Infuriating man!* She lay back on the cot with a huff and listened to the creak and groan of the ship, a constant lullaby that finally lulled her to sleep, despite her conflicted thoughts.

Sometime in the middle of the night, the dreams returned. Charity ran through a forest, batting aside leaves and branches, following the light of a pale moonlit path. Tall spindly trees clawed their way through the moist earth and reached upward, limbs sprouting, twisting and turning, blocking her path. She darted the other way. Fog curled over the ground, slithering like misty snakes up tree trunks, over boughs, spinning around leaves. Cold. Why was it so cold? Her bare feet sank into chilled mud as she struggled forward, seeking a way out. Trees burst through the dirt ahead of her, growing in maniacal shapes and forms, branches like skeleton fingers reaching for her. Panicked, she turned left. More trees blocked her path. To her right, more wooden limbs crisscrossed into a tangled web. She was trapped.

She awoke encased in strong arms, a hand caressing her back and words of comfort whispered in her ears. Alarm pricked each nerve and she jerked away, but the arms tightened, pressed her closer, the words grew softer and more intimate.

"'Tis all right, little mermaid. You are safe. Naught to fear. Nothing will harm you. Safe and warm and ... loved ..."

The tears came then, pouring down her cheeks in abandon, dripping off her chin onto the man's shirt. Elias' shirt. In her sleep-clouded mind, she knew it was him. But it felt so good to cry—to cry and be held, to feel safe...if only for a moment.

He continued caressing her, combing fingers through her hair, whispering that all was well ... and she found all her fear spilling out along with her tears. He smelled of man and sweat, salt and wood, and she breathed him in, desperate for his touch, sensing no evil intent within it. Within him.

She must have fallen asleep in his arms for the next thing she knew, sunlight rocked in golden bands across her eyelids, back and forth, back and forth with the sway of the ship, awakening her thoughts to the night's events. And in those precious moments of semi-conscious bliss, before reality and fear brought her fully awake, she felt an unintended smile form on her lips. She attempted to stretch. But her hand was caught. Not caught. Held. She opened her eyes to find Elias lying on the deck beside the cot holding her hand.

Horrified, she slammed her eyes shut and lay as still as possible. He groaned, sat, and then did the sweetest thing. He kissed her hand, laid it beside her, then grabbed his weapons and left.

She couldn't move for the longest time, trying to sort the traitorous feelings invading her heart and jumbling her thoughts.

*No, no, no!* He wanted something from her. No one was that kind and thoughtful without an ulterior motive.

*Foolish, foolish woman!* How could she be so gullible after what she'd endured?

She knew one thing. When they arrived at Kingston, she must get as far away from Mr. Elias Dutton as she could.

# Chapter 10

Kingston. *Home*. Or the only home Elias had truly known. Though his parents had built a lovely house here on his Uncle Alex and Aunt Juliana's land—a beautiful cliff side field of flowers and fruit trees overlooking the sea—they were rarely home. In truth, Elias felt more at home on board his ship, *Restoration*. Still, as he navigated the *Enmity* through the narrow channel beside Old Port Royal and into Kingston Harbor, he couldn't help but feel a sense of joy seeing the familiar landscape of ramshackle buildings making up Kingston.

Adding to his joy were thoughts of the mermaid below. Not since Rachel had a woman both intrigued him and stirred his heart into mush. Indeed, Miss Westcott was quite the enigma. So dainty and feminine on the one hand, but staunchly independent and courageous on the other. Beautiful and alluring, yet not flirtatious in the slightest way. So unlike Rachel. Which is precisely what he wanted—a chaste woman, a proper lady, someone who challenged him instead of tricked him. Someone who didn't lie to him. *Oh, how he hated lies!* Someone who valued family and loyalty and honor. He'd seen evidence of all those within Miss Westcott. And, much to his great relief, last night she'd finally trusted him, allowed him to comfort her. It was a small step. But a step nonetheless.

Now, if only she would accept his offer to transport her to Barbados and then Charles Towne.

"Steady now, Bates!" Elias shouted. "Haul taut! Shorten sail! In jib, royals, and studding sails!"

Nelson repeated the orders before taking a stand beside him. "She's a sluggish one. She'll have t' be patched soon or she'll meet her fate wit' Port Royal's ships at the bottom o' the bay."

Elias nodded, though it was not his problem anymore. "Did Captain Littleman have any relatives?"

"Not that I know of."

"I suppose the ship is yours, then." Elias clapped him on the back.

"This ole bucket of tar?" Nelson laughed, rubbed a hand over his hooked nose, and squinted up toward Elias. "I was hopin' ye could use me on yer ship. I don't have t' be first mate. I can do anything."

Elias blinked. "How did you know I have a ship?"

"I heard o' ye before, Captain Dutton. Jist didn't put the two together till I saw the way ye commanded the *Enmity*."

The ship slowed as the topmen lowered sail, and Elias took a deep breath of sea air, tainted with odor of human habitation—horse manure, wood smoke, and sweat. Even in the heat of the noonday sun, Kingston was abustle with activity. Carriages, wagons, mules, and people of every class and color hurried down Harbor Street. Smoke rose from a few of the taverns, and the scent of roast pork drifted past Elias' nose. His stomach grumbled as his gaze swept beyond the town. Were there a few more houses perched in the hills than the last time he'd been here?

Nelson cleared his throat.

A breeze struck Elias, cooling the sweat on his neck. Aye, Nelson would be a good addition to his crew. Though he was as wiry as a vine, he had more than proven his physical strength. Plus, he had a good knowledge of seas and sailing. Why, just an hour ago, he'd spotted a ship following them that no one else had seen. Thankfully, after close inspection, it turned out to be a British merchantmen and nothing to worry about.

He faced the first mate. Besides, mayhap God was sending Elias another soul that needed saving. "I don't see why not, Mr. Nelson. I could use another man of your caliber. As long as you don't mind that, along with transporting goods, I have also been known to preach and privateer."

"I don't mind at all, Cap'n. Thank ye." He touched his hat as if he'd once been in the navy and turned to leave but halted at the sight of Miss Westcott emerging from below.

Elias thought he saw the man grin from ear to ear before he sped off. He couldn't blame him. Even with her soiled skirts and unkempt hair fluttering about her in the wind, she was lovely. Her eyes met his and his heart leapt in hope she'd given up her mistrust of him after last night. But instead, she lifted her chin and strode to the railing, yards from where he stood.

Ignoring the pinch to his heart, he ordered the remainder of the sails furled and the anchor dropped, and soon the *Enmity* slowed to a halt as close as they could get to land without grounding her.

"Mr. Rigley." He called the second mate over to him. "The ship is yours."

The second mate's eyes widened along with his gap-toothed smile. "Aye aye, Sir. Thank ye Sir. I'll fix her up an' get her sailing quick as a wench can—"

"I know you will," Elias interrupted and nodded toward Miss Westcott, instantly silencing the man. "Godspeed to you, Rigley. Miss...my wife and I will be taking a boat ashore."

"Aye, Sir, I'll have one lowered."

Within minutes, Elias found himself in a jolly boat alongside Nelson, Miss Westcott, and two sailors.

She spoke not a word to him as they rowed to shore. Nor when he assisted her onto the wharf. In fact, the baffling woman uttered a simple, "Thank you, Mr. Dutton," before clutching her skirts and proceeding down the dock toward town. *Thank you!* That was all he received for the trouble she caused him—the lies he'd told, the sacrifice of sleep to keep her safe, last night when he'd held her during her nightmare. *Thank you?*

He followed her down the dock onto the street and grabbed her arm. "Miss Dutton, I know you have no money for passage on another ship. I will happily take you to Charles Towne, but I must stop at Barbados first."

He waited for her quick agreement. After all, what choice did she have?

"And just how will you take me there? As your wife again, I suppose?" Spite stung in her tone, and he had no idea what he'd done to deserve it.

So, he attempted humor. "Was it such a bad experience?" His grin only caused her scowl to deepen. He rubbed the back of his neck and studied her, perplexed as usual. "Nay, as my guest this time."

She laughed and glanced over the city. "Guest? Vapors. You are captain for a few days and you act like you have your own ship to command."

He quirked a brow, too angry to correct her. "Miss Westcott, Kingston is no place for a lady alone."

"It looks harmless enough." She shielded her eyes from the sun as a pig chased two chickens not a yard from where they stood.

"'Tis not like Portsmouth. Kingston is a wolf in sheep's clothing."

"Hmm. Another Biblical reference, Preacher?" She started on her way. "I can take care of myself," she shouted over her shoulder with a wave of her hand.

Elias resisted the urge to fling her over his shoulder and take her to his ship. He was no longer a pirate and even when he was, he'd never stooped to kidnapping ladies.

Though, in truth, he'd never been tempted so strongly to do so.

However, he wasn't a man to beg. And he seemed to be doing a lot of begging with this lady. After all, he still had some pride left, the good kind, the male kind. Though the thought of never seeing her again was slicing a rent in that pride at the moment. But what could he do?

"You can find me on the *Restoration* when you change your mind," he yelled after her. "But I'm leaving first thing tomorrow."

She didn't respond, just kept walking. An innocent dove strolling into a lion's den.

Whispering a prayer for her safety, Elias headed to his ship. He hadn't time for this. His sister Rose could be in a great deal of danger by now, and every minute was a delay in coming to her aid. His parents would never forgive him should tragedy befall another of his sisters on his watch. He would never forgive himself. He'd already been delayed enough by Captain Littleman's incompetence.

He cast one last glance at Miss Westcott, but the crowd had swallowed her whole.

It wouldn't take her long. She'd speak to the wrong person, enter the wrong building, and she'd be running back to him, begging him to take her with him.

Or so he hoped.

With every step Charity took away from Elias, her nerves cinched tighter. Half of her—the foolish, gullible half—longed to run back to him and take him up on his offer to bring her home. Two years ago she would have done just that. She *had* done just that. With another man equally as kind, gentlemanly, and pious. And look where that had gotten her. Men were not to be trusted. Especially religious men who were too good to be believed. No one was kind. Everyone was out for themselves. If only she could get that through the ridiculous romantic half of her that still dreamed of happy endings.

At least she had other choices now. Truth be told, she never thought she'd *had* other choices. At first she'd been too humiliated to leave her husband, too worried she'd bring irreparable shame to her family. Then after her family left for the colonies, she'd been too frightened to leave Lord Villemont and wander the streets of Portsmouth penniless. Yet here she was in a place far worse. What had changed? Had she grown stronger? Or had her fear of being enslaved again overcome her fear of starvation? Either way, she was at the mercy of the fates.

Or of God—if He bothered to take notice.

*For my babe, God. For my babe.* The innocent growing within her.

Weaving around a peddler hawking some kind of fruit, she started across the street and stepped in a pile of horse manure. Warmth sludged over her foot as flies buzzed up her legs. A man passed her and chuckled.

Precisely her point. No happy endings here.

Extracting her shoe from the smelly muck, she forged ahead and drew a deep breath. Now, what was she to do? On the rare occasions her father had been home, he'd taught her to be strong, independent-minded—though she was a female—and resourceful. Tears were not allowed. Shows of weakness were scoffed at. Though still mere girls, she and her sisters had run the house in the absence of her mother and had run it like a tight ship.

Gathering her resolve, Charity stepped onto the porch of a chandler's. She needed money. Women had few opportunities to make a living in this world, most of which were too immoral to mention and even now caused a blush to heat her cheeks. Ignoring the strange looks by passersby, she shielded her eyes from the sun and scanned the harbor—a turquoise sea of silver-tipped waves, upon which over a dozen ships rocked. Perhaps she could sign on with one of them heading to Charles Towne as cook or cabin steward. Nay. They would never accept a single woman aboard for anything but ... well, she'd already gone there.

She wondered which ship was the *Restoration*. Perhaps Elias was even now booking passage aboard her. But what did it matter?

Putting the thought out of her mind, she started down the street and came upon the *Skinny Goat* Tavern. One peek through the glassless window revealed a clean, well-lit place that served both drink and food. Several women ate with their husbands and even a few children wandered about. Charity could certainly serve food or even sweep the floors if necessary. She cringed at how far she'd fallen from the wife of a Viscount with a healthy fortune and a bevy of servants. But she wouldn't trade a lifetime of servitude for one more day trapped in Lord Villemont's clutches. Besides, it would only be for a short while until she could procure passage home.

Lifting her head high, she entered through the open door and searched the room for the person in charge. That must be him, the well-dressed man standing by the back table shouting at a group of workers. Of course she had no way of really knowing. She'd never been in such an establishment, nor in a pub or punch house—all places her father had warned her never to enter. Then after her marriage, Lord Villemont rarely allowed her to leave the house. Perhaps she *was* naïve, but how hard could it be to walk up and ask for work from the proprietor?

She stopped before the man and waited for him to finish shouting orders. But they weren't orders. The man told a vile joke which Charity was glad she hadn't heard from the beginning. The three men surrounding him—who suddenly didn't look like workers at all—bent over laughing when suddenly their eyes latched upon her and widened in desire. The man telling the joke faced her, his brows lifting.

"Are you the proprietor of this place, Sir?" she asked.

Which sent the men, including the joke-teller, into another bout of hysterics.

"Ole Jamaica Jim ain't the proprietor o' nothin' 'cept his next mug o' rum!" one of the men slurred out, eliciting further chuckles.

Only then did the foul odor of stale spirits reach her nose. She started to leave, but the man clutched her arm and drew her back. The perspiration on her neck turned to ice as she stared into cold, foggy eyes, brimming with malevolence.

"I'll be whate'er ye want, Missy." He wiped drool from his mouth with his sleeve.

*Keep calm, Charity. Keep calm. Never show your fear.* "I'm looking for employment. If you're not the proprietor, would you be so kind as to point out who is."

Again the laughing.

"I'll be happy t' put ye to work, Missy." The man ran fingers through his slick, dark hair, then adjusted a rather lavish silk cravat, the posh attire defying his unschooled speech. "How's about comin' upstairs wit' me. I'll compensate ye fairly."

Fury boiled, devouring her fear. Just because men were physically stronger, they thought they could rule the world and everything in it. Charity jerked from his grip and lifted her nose. "I would rather be dragged over the bottom of the sea than be touched by the likes of you. You are a pig, Sir. A foul-mouthed, drunken beast of a man who preys on innocent women. You should be ashamed of yourself."

Music ground to a halt, along with the hum of chatter as patrons glanced their way. But Charity didn't care. Spinning on her heels, she marched from the tavern into a gust of wind and a blazing sun.

Amidst the crowd, a familiar face sprinted across her vision. The first mate, Nelson. But then he was gone.

Music picked up behind her, along with voices, as she stormed down the street, searching for some way to make money.

There! A picture of a printing press engraved on a signpost above the door. A printing shop! Perfect.

Peace settled on her instantly once she stepped inside and breathed in the smell of ink and wood and parchment— familiar, happy smells from a time long ago when on occasion her father allowed her to assist in her uncle's shop, and she had fallen in love with the printed word.

"May I help you, Miss?" A kind-faced man wearing an ink-stained apron and a genuine smile looked up from setting type into a form.

"Yes, I—"

The door crashed open and before she could stop them, the four men from the *Skinny Goat* entered. The one called Jamaica Jim pinched her arm and dragged her from the shop.

"Ye'll be comin' wit' us, Missy! No one insults Jamaica Jim an' gets away with it!"

Heart crashing through her chest, she fought against his grip as he dragged her down the street, his men following behind, laughing and cursing.

"Help! Help me please!" she cried out, but people scattered when they saw who held her in his grip.

Perspiration slid into her eyes. She blinked it away and dragged her feet. A cloud of dust rose that nearly blinded her as she continued appealing for help. Surely there was *one* honorable man willing to stand up to this fiend. Even as the thought crossed her mind, she chastised herself for needing a man at all. She was smart and she was strong. There must be something she could do.

Jamaica Jim flung an arm around her waist and attempted to hoist her up. Before he could, Charity shoved all her weight against him. Instead of causing him to lose his balance, pain thundered up her arm and the beast chuckled and spit to the side.

"Where are you taking me?" she demanded.

"Some place quiet where ye can pay off yer debt, Missy."

His friends grunted like pigs in heat.

Terror clamped every nerve. *This can't be happening.* She would not be abused by another man. She would not!

Hoisting her up beside him, he hauled her down the street, laughing and joking with his friends.

*The maid was in the garden, hanging out the clothes.* Charity drew a deep breath. *When down came a blackbird and pecked off her nose...*

Up ahead a mare was tethered to a post. Her big brown eyes met Charity's, soft and kind as if the horse sympathized with her predicament. And a thought occurred to her. A fleeting thought that she wouldn't allow to settle into reason, for if she did, she doubted she'd attempt it.

Forcing her body to go limp, she pretended to faint.

"Blast it all!" The man halted, released her for a moment, then reached down to jerk her upright.

She jumped up and kicked him in the groin.

Growling in pain, he bent over. In that split second before his men reacted, she charged toward the horse, put her foot in the stirrup and swung herself up. Then grabbing the reins, she kicked the mare into motion.

"Thief! Thief!" was the last thing she heard as she galloped down the street.

Blood rushed so fast through her, she could hardly think, hardly breathe. All she could do was keep her head low and keep the horse moving as fast as she could. The street narrowed and inclined. Buildings gave way to gated properties with cultured gardens leading to wooden homes in the distance.

Vapors! What had she done? More importantly, what was she to do now? She hadn't time to think about it when the sound of horse hooves pounded behind her.

One quick glance showed her two men were following. And gaining!

*No!*

"Stop or I'll shoot!" It was not the voice of Jamaica Jim. Whether that was a good or bad thing, she didn't know.

Pressing her body against the rolling muscles of the horse beneath her, she nudged the beast faster.

The crack of a pistol sounded. The whine sped past her ears.

"No more warnings, Miss! The next one goes in your gut."

*Vapors!* Could her life get any worse? Tugging on the reins, Charity brought the mare to a stop.

"Hands in the air!"

She complied.

Above the pulse thrumming in her head, she heard someone dismounting, the neigh of a horse … and oddly, the warble of colorful birds above her staring down upon her misfortune.

Rough hands grabbed her waist and dragged her from her perch.

A tall man, neatly dressed, with tiny eyes, and a bushy mustache stared down at her. "I'm Constable Clemmins, Miss. And you are under arrest for horse thievin'."

# Chapter 11

"She *what?*" Elias tossed down his quill pen and rose from behind his desk.

"Aye, Cap'n, I swears." Nelson fumbled with his hat. "I saw it wit' me own eyes. She's locked up in Braysworth Prison as we speak."

"For horse thieving?" Elias circled the desk, positive he'd heard the man wrong.

"That's wha' the Constable be sayin'. He's given her a choice. Hang on the morrow or be sold as an indentured servant t' the horse's owner."

"This is madness!" Elias swung his baldric over his head and stuffed pistols into the clips.

His first mate, Josiah entered and glanced between them, his dark skin gleaming in the rays of a setting sun through the stern windows.

"They say it were Jamaica Jim that's started it," Nelson continued. "He were draggin' her through the city, intent on makin' her his own."

*Jamaica Jim.* Elias knew the man. Worthless bedeviled pirate. But how did she get mixed up with him? More importantly, now what was he to do? He must leave at first light. His sister's life depended on him. But how could he allow Miss Westcott to become a slave? Or worse, hanged. He sheathed his sword.

"Josiah, this is Nelson. He'll be our new bosun. See that he gets settled."

"Looks to me you be the one needin' settlin', Cap'n. Or an extra blade by your side?" The large black man gripped the pommel of his sword as he stepped forward.

"Nay. Stay here and ready the ship. I must do this alone." He opened a desk drawer, pulled out a pouch, and tied it to his belt beneath his coat. "I'll return soon."

Everyone had a price. He only prayed he had enough to pay this particular one.

Drawing her knees up to her chest, Charity wrapped her arms around them and stared at the flies swarming over the bowl of slop they'd served her for supper—hovering and buzzing, but never landing as if the food was too grotesque *even* for them. A ray of fading sunlight from a barred window barely lit the dark prison cell that was encased in cold stone, save for the door made of rusty iron bars. It had only taken her two hours to get used to a smell so foul, it seemed to have a life of its own. She'd also grown accustomed to the cursing, shouts, and howls of agony from her fellow prisoners echoing down the long corridor. What she hadn't gotten used to was the terror etching its way through every bone and fiber of her body, leaving a benumbed death wish in its wake. She laid a hand over her belly.

"Seems I've failed you, little one." If it weren't for the life growing within her, she'd break her bowl of slop and use the sharp edge to slit her throat. Better that than end up enslaved to yet another man.

She dabbed the sweat on her forehead with her sleeve and released a heavy sigh. Why, when she did everything in her power to fend for herself, did she always end up under someone else's control? 'Twas as if God Himself had foreordained that she would never be free, and no matter how hard she tried, nothing she did could ever change that.

A cockroach the size of her thumb scampered to her supper and dove into the foul porridge. Cringing, Charity hugged herself tighter, trying to focus on plans of escape and not allow her mind to sink into despair.

The jangle of keys, grate of metal, and voices sounded in the distance. Footfalls headed her way. No doubt the guard came to collect the empty bowls. The brawny man with a hawk nose and four missing front teeth had stared at her far too long when he'd brought her meal. Mayhap she could use his lust to her advantage, play the coquette and lure him into distraction while she stole his keys and made a dash for it.

But it wasn't the same man. It was the Constable. He unlocked her door and swung it open on rusty hinges that squealed like the mice scampering away. "'Tis your lucky day, Miss."

She was about to offer a clever retort when another man stepped in behind him. *Elias Dutton.*

Against her every attempt to stop it, overwhelming relief flooded her. Especially when she saw naught but concern and affection in those sea-blue eyes of his.

"What are *you* doing here?" she asked him in a curt tone that belied her joy.

"Unchain her at once," Elias ordered as if he were the king himself.

The Constable grumbled a few choice words then knelt to remove Charity's irons. "This man here worked out a deal with Mr. Bolton, the owner of the horse you stole. He paid him double the horse's value to forget the entire incident." He snorted as if the mere thought were ludicrous.

Charity rubbed her sore wrists. Elias' hand appeared in her vision, his smile at the end of it, more comforting than she wanted to admit.

She was free? She could hardly believe it. "You did what?" She took his hand, and he grabbed her arm with his other one and helped her to stand.

"Well, Mr. Dutton," the Constable said. "For the large sum of ten pounds, you've purchased a horse thief. Seems you got the bad end of the deal, if you ask me."

"I didn't ask you, and I'll thank you to keep your opinions to yourself." Elias proffered his elbow as if they were attending a soiree. "Miss Westcott."

Her legs wobbled with the shock of so drastic a change in her fate. Placing her hand on his arm, she allowed him to lead her out of her cell and down the gauntlet of ribald suggestions and grimy hands that reached for her from the rows of cells.

She must be dreaming. No man would sacrifice so large a sum for her, especially when she'd been naught but ungrateful and disrespectful. They exited the prison to a dusty wind and a glorious sunset of crimson and gold spinning atop the horizon. 'Twas as if God Himself was happy to see her freed. But that couldn't be.

She drew a deep breath, refusing to look at Elias for fear—in her emotional state—she'd crumble in his arms at the kindness in his eyes.

A horse and wagon bore down on them, and Elias took her arm and pulled her out of the way. Vapors! *Rescued yet again.*

Freeing from his grasp, she put distance between them. "I cannot fathom why you paid so large a sum to set me free, Mr. Dutton, but—"

"You cannot?" His loving, playful tone sent a warm spire through her. Now, she really wasn't going to look at him. Instead, she glanced both ways down the street, sensing a malevolence slinking out from the byways with the descending darkness. A chill iced over her, though the air was thick with heat and humidity.

The sounds of a pianoforte and a fiddle rose on the shifting wind.

"Where does a poor preacher get such a sum, anyway?" She eyed him suspiciously.

"Who said I was poor?"

"Don't you take a vow of poverty or something?"

"You have me confused with monks, my little mermaid."

Groaning, she clutched her skirts and started down the street. She should thank him. She should at least do him the favor of looking in his eyes, offering him a smile. But his unfathomable kindness only increased her suspicions. "I intend to repay you every shilling, Mr. Dutton."

He kept pace with her. "Your debt grows, Miss Westcott. By the time our trip is over, you'll no doubt be indentured to me for life."

"That's not at all amusing after what I nearly endured."

"Yes, forgive me." He frowned. "What I meant to say is you owe me nothing. Money means little when it comes to a life."

*Who was this man?* And why was he always following her? "You play the preacher well."

"As you do the damsel in distress."

"I am not"—she halted and finally met his gaze—"and there is no *our* trip. There is your trip and there is my trip."

A band of sailors cut in front of her on their way to a punch house from which doxies lured them with smiles and low bodices. Upon seeing Charity, they lifted hats and grinned at her, and she suddenly found herself glad Elias was by her side.

"Did you truly steal a horse?" he asked, taking her arm and leading her away from the men.

She pulled from his grip. "Yes."

"Hmm. I find that hard to believe. I feel as though I've come to know you the past three days."

"You don't know me at all, Mr. Dutton."

"Then, pray tell, help me to do so and explain what possessed you to commit a hanging offense?"

She hated that she cared what this man thought. Even so, if he thought her a thief, perhaps he would leave her be. "If you must know, I found myself in need of quick transportation." A gust of wind brought the scent of fish and salt to her nose as the sun sank into the bay.

"Ah yes, Jamaica Jim."

She halted yet again. "You know?"

"Nelson told me."

So, she *had* seen him amongst the crowd. A carriage ambled by, stirring up dust as a young lad just ahead climbed a ladder to light a street lamp. "You!" Charity pointed at Elias. "You sent him to spy on me." She started on her way again, weaving around a wagon and two slaves carrying crates atop their heads.

"I did no such thing, Miss Westcott. What were you doing with the likes of Jamaica Jim?"

"Seeking employment." She heard the disdain in her voice over something she never thought she'd lower herself to do.

"Hmm. I can think of only one type of employment that man would offer you."

"Which is precisely why…oh, vapors, why am I talking to you?" She hurried her pace.

He appeared beside her. "Mayhap, because I saved your life once again."

"Speaking of that." She stopped and faced him, clinging onto her suspicion and anger and forcing away her gratitude. "Stop doing that!"

"Do you have a death wish, my little mermaid?"

"I have a wish to be free, Mr. Dutton."

"Then you can be free in Charles Towne. I told you I would take you there as soon as my business in Barbados is concluded. Owe me if you want. I have no care. But why do you insist on putting yourself in harm's way?"

He stared at her with more concern than she'd ever seen from her own father. Another blast of wind swept hair the

DO NOT REMOVE SLIP FROM ITEM

SHIPPING SLIP

13-SEP-2018

Ship To:

**Delivery Point:**

**Requesting Library:**

Medicine Hat Public Library

**ID:** AMP

**Address:** Medicine Hat Public Library, ILL
Dept
414 1st Street SE
Medicine Hat, AB
T1A 0A8

**Phone:** (403) 502-8538

Medicine Hat Public Library

**ID:** AMP

**Address:** Medicine Hat Public Library, ILL
Dept
414 1st Street SE
Medicine Hat, AB
T1A 0A8

**Phone:** (403) 502-8538

Ship From:

Calgary Public Library

**ID:** AC

**Address:** Calgary Public Library, Central
Library 5th Fl. ILL
616 Macleod Tr. SE
Calgary, AB
T2G 2M2

**Phone:** (403) 260-2722

**Responder Req.**1830252
**No.:**

**Item Barcode:** 39065138839822

**Title:** Charity's cross

Pickup Point:

Medicine Hat Public Library

**ID:** AMP

**Address:** Medicine Hat Public Library, ILL
Dept
414 1st Street SE
Medicine Hat, AB
T1A 0A8

**Phone:**

**Requester Req.**1829770
**No.:**

DO NOT REMOVE SLIP FROM ITEM
DUE DATE: (25-OCT-2018)

color of wheat over shoulders too broad to be legal. The
infuriating man was as handsome as he was tall. A good foot
above her. A towering bastion of strength clad in linen and
leather, offering her the two things she wanted most in the
world—love and security.

She snapped her gaze from him. "I will not allow you to
pay for my passage again."

"Yet you allow me to pay for the horse you stole."

Grrr. The man did have a point. "Without my permission,
Sir. Please, leave me be." She took off, this time at a faster
pace.

He clutched her arm, halting her. "What if I promise not to
pay for your passage?"

Confusion spun her mind into annoyance. "Then how...?"
The darkening sky churned above her, and she raised a hand
to her head, feeling as though she could float away on the
next gust of wind.

"When was the last time you ate?" he asked.

Gathering herself, she took a step back, feeling her resolve
weakening beneath the man's persistence. But it was a trap. It
had to be. A way to gain control over her for some reason she
could not fathom. "Mr. Dutton, I owe you my life yet again,
and I thank you. Truly. But 'tis here our ways must part.
Surely, I've caused you enough trouble." *More than most
men would tolerate.* "I can take care of myself."

"And yet evidence to the contrary is mounting." He gave
her that half-arrogant, half-irresistible smile again.

She pursed her lips. "Good eve to you, Mr. Dutton."
Clutching her soiled skirts, she started down the street toward
the print shop, where mayhap the proprietor had not closed
for the day. With her experience, surely the man would hire
her for a week or two.

When no footsteps sounded behind her, her traitorous
heart sank into the brew that was her stomach. But that
couldn't be helped.

To avoid thinking of Elias, she pondered where she might stay the night. Perhaps the printer had a spare room in the back. Or mayhap she'd convince the owner of a boardinghouse she spotted on the outskirts of town that she'd clean and cook in exchange for a cot. She was thinking on these things when someone grabbed her by the waist and flung her over his shoulder.

Alarm screeched through her until Elias' back bobbed into view.

"Sorry to do this, Miss Westcott, but I haven't time to rescue you again. You're coming aboard the *Restoration*."

Nelson's grin nearly cracked his sun-baked cheeks. It wasn't the buxom wench cooing in his ear that made him so happy, nor was it the third mug of ale foaming in his hand as he stood on the porch of the *Crowne and Shilling* punch house, staring out over Harbor street—though both were pleasurable enough. Nay, 'twas the vision of the high-and-mighty preacher tossin' Miss Westcott over his shoulder and haulin' her away that caused his overwhelming joy. There'd be no chance Nelson would collect a reward if they'd hanged the lady or even sold her as a slave.

He knew his luck was turnin' as soon as he'd seen her enter Captain Littleman's—the devil take his soul—cabin for dinner. Not even a fish-brained fool woulda missed the signs posted all over Nassau offerin' a reward for the lovely Lady Villemont's capture. An' Nelson weren't no fool. O' course, he had no way to get off the ship by then, but he determined from that point on, he wouldn't let the murderous vixen out o' his sight.

Handing his mug to the doxy, he pushed her aside and barreled down the steps onto the street, ignorin' her slurrin' protests. He must make it to the print shop and leave a message for Lord Villemont before they sailed on the morrow. Of course he couldn't be sure the man was followin' them, but he'd spotted the same ship twice since they'd left Nassau—a merchantman with orange sails, keepin' pace off their larboard quarter. And, though he hadn't realized the lady was on board when they'd set sail from Nassau, Nelson had also seen the angry man pointin' at the *Enmity* from the docks just before they'd left. That *had* to be Villemont!

As he pushed open the door to the printer's shop, Nelson couldn't help but smile as he thought of the reward he would receive for the doltish lady's capture.

# Chapter 12

"Unhand me at once!" Charity pounded her fists against Elias' back—dough against rock—but it only made her hands sore and her frustration rise to near boiling. She screamed for help but received only jests and insults from the men strolling the streets of Kingston. Some even cheered Elias on as if he were a gladiator hauling off his prize.

"Be still, woman. 'Tis for your own good," Elias murmured in a voice stiff with conviction and a bit of annoyance.

*Vapors!* Why did everyone think they knew what was good for her? She struggled against the steely arms holding her legs to his chest as the vision of sand beneath her head transformed to pebbles and then to the aged wood of a wharf.

Another vision intruded. *This is for your own good, my dear.* Her husband's sharp features—pointed chin, thick eyebrows, and cold, heartless eyes—peered at her from above the stool over which she leaned. He puffed on his thick cigar, igniting the tip in a glowing ember. Charity buried her face in the stool's cushion and whispered the rhyme that would take her away...far, far away from the pain and the heartache.

"Sing a song of sixpence—" Searing pain struck her bare back. "Pocket full of—" Another strike, lower this time.

"Four and twenty—" Another iron-hot brand, and she smelled her own flesh burning. "Baked in a pie ..."

She had lost consciousness then. Now, she was fully awake as Elias leapt into a waiting boat and lowered her to sit on the thwarts. She sprang to her feet and pushed him with all her might. He toppled backward. Shoving past him, she hobbled through the teetering craft toward the ladder leading back to the wharf.

The other men in the boat laughed but made no effort to stop her. Gripping the ladder rung, she started to climb. Elias grabbed her by the waist again and hoisted her backward, legs flailing and skirts flapping.

"Preachers don't kidnap innocent women!" she shouted.

"I'm not kidnapping you, Mermaid Vixen. I'm rescuing you." He growled as he forced her back down, wrapped an arm around her and pressed her so close, she could barely move. He smelled of dampness and danger, and his warmth seeped through her, offering comfort she didn't want. He ordered the men to row as if he owned the craft then lowered his eyes to hers. He must have sensed her fear, for he brushed hair from her face ever so gently. "What has you so frightened, little one?"

Tearing her gaze away to the choppy black water gurgling past the boat, Charity bided her time. Surely the captain of this *Restoration* would not allow a woman to be kidnapped before his very eyes. Unless he was a pirate—in which case her predicament was far worse. But even if he wasn't a kindly sort, he certainly wouldn't want any trouble on board his ship.

Yet once Elias set Charity's feet upon the deck of said ship, she found no man looking like a captain ready to greet them. Nevertheless, she charged to the center and shouted, "Where is the captain? I wish to see him at once! This man"—she pointed to Elias— "has kidnapped me! I am an innocent woman and no one's slave or concubine!" Placing hands on her hips, she stomped her foot for emphasis and glowered at Elias, waiting for at least one or two of the sailors to come to her rescue, or at the very least escort her to the captain.

Instead, laughter filled the air as if she'd told a joke or performed a comedy scene in a play.

"Stow the cockboat! First watch to task. The rest of you get some rest. We set sail at first light." The voice was Elias', the commanding tone spinning her around to see him ordering sailors about.

"Aye, Cap'n." A large black man approached and shouted further orders to the men.

"How many still ashore?" Elias asked him, fists at his waist, gaze traveling to the city.

*He* was the captain? This preacher, this missionary, captained his own ship?

"Ten, Cap'n. But they know to return before mornin' watch."

Dumbfounded, she merely stared at him. Dumb was more like it. She should have known he was a seaman—a leader of seamen—from his performance on board the *Enmity*. But now seeing it with her own eyes, her suspicions ratcheted to near bursting. A missionary who captains a ship and pays ten pounds to free a troublesome woman who doesn't wish to be freed. She might be a murderer, but she was no fool. *Charles!* 'Twas the only explanation. Her brother-in-law must be paying Elias to bring her to him!

She backed to the railing and glanced down at the dark water frothing against the hull. If she jumped, she'd have to do it quietly or this preacher, missionary, pirate—whatever he was—would no doubt jump in after her.

She hadn't time to implement her plan before Elias' shout of "Mr. Ballard!" brought a tall man with brown wavy hair to his side. "Take the lady below to Hendricks' cabin. Remove his belongings and lock her inside."

*Lock?* Heart exploding, Charity swung her leg over the railing, every instinct screaming to flee, but the man—this Mr. Ballard—clutched her arm and yanked her from her perch.

"Nay, can't let ye do that, Miss. Now, come with me." He pulled her along as Elias leapt up the ladder onto the quarterdeck.

"You'll pay for this!" she screamed at him. "My father is an admiral in the Royal Navy!"

Ignoring her, Elias continued shouting orders to the men below.

Mr. Ballard dragged her carefully down a ladder, then through a short, dark hallway lit intermittently by lanterns, before nudging her inside a small cabin. After gathering up scattered belongings lying atop the cot, a single chair, and a table, he stuffed them in a trunk and kicked it into the corridor.

"Pleasant eve to you, Miss." Tipping his head, he closed the door, the lock snapping shut on the other side.

Charity sank to the cot and put her head in her hands.

"God, you must really hate me."

"Do you think I wanted to kidnap her?" Elias removed his baldric and weapons and laid them on his desk.

"Seems to me you was havin' a bit of fun." Josiah followed him into his cabin, along with Ballard, his quartermaster, and Gage the ship's surgeon, all three of his friends obviously curious about their new guest. Gage went for the bottle of rum housed in Elias' cupboard.

Sighing, Elias sat back on the top of his desk and crossed arms over his chest. "The foolhardy woman wouldn't listen to reason."

"Whose reason? Yours or hers?" Ballard snickered and tugged on his neckerchief.

"Any reason at all," Elias returned. "In any event, she's alive and free, which wouldn't be the case if she'd remained in Kingston."

"Though I doubt she sees it that way, Captain." Gage poured himself a glass of rum and tossed it to the back of his throat. "The alive part perhaps," he choked out as the liquor no doubt burned going down.

Cringing as his friend poured himself another, Elias added, "I'll set her free once we set sail."

Josiah only grunted.

The brig teetered over a wavelet, creaking and groaning and sending ribbons of light over the bulkhead from the lantern above.

"'Tis a good thing most of the crew are of the Godly persuasion, Captain. She's a comely one, that one." Ballard plopped into a chair and motioned for Gage to pour him a drink.

"Aye, though there's a few men I intend to keep an eye on." Elias stared at his friend. Ballard being chief among them. "Either way, she'll be safer here than in Kingston or on the last ship she sailed on."

Josiah grunted again.

"You have something to say, my friend?" Elias raised brows toward the black giant who was both his friend and his first mate, but the man remained silent, as was his way. Except of course when he had wisdom to impart. On that rare occasion, 'twas best to listen to every word for fear of losing valuable advice. Something Elias could not say of most people.

Gage handed Ballard a mug. "Word in town is the woman stole a horse."

Ballard sipped his rum and cocked a brow. "And you paid double the fee to release her."

Elias chuckled. "How swift the wings of gossip fly."

"Truth isn't gossip." Gage lifted the bottle toward Elias, but he put up a palm and bit back his burning desire to join his men in a drink. He'd not had a sip since he'd returned to his senses three years past, and he intended to continue his sobriety, though he oft wondered if his cravings would ever diminish.

Gage's hand was already shaking as he set the bottle on Elias' desk. Hopefully there would be no injuries tonight that would require his surgical skills.

"Why is the lady traveling alone on the Spanish Main?" Ballard crossed legs at his knees and lit a cheroot from the lantern on Elias' desk. "Not exactly a safe haven for her gender."

Elias shoved a hand through his hair. "I'm not entirely sure she's been forthright with me. Something about a broken engagement and an angry relation in pursuit." He only hoped that during the week it would take to sail to Barbados, he'd get to know the lovely Miss Westcott and mayhap discover why there was such anger and fear in those lustrous honey-colored eyes.

"Most fortunate she happened upon *you*, then, wasn't it?" Ballard winked.

"If you mean to imply I encouraged the lady, you are mistaken. And it wasn't luck. It was God looking out for her. If only she'd recognize it and accept the help." *Any* help. Yet God had put her in Elias' hands, and he didn't intend to let the Almighty down.

"Takes some o' us longer to see the hand o' God at work." Josiah shifted his gaze to Gage, but the surgeon stared hazily out the stern windows where lights flickered in the distance from town.

Ballard puffed on his cheroot. "But you *do* have a penchant for beautiful women, Elias. There's no denying it."

"There's no denying any man does. But I no longer look merely at the outward appearance."

"What else is there to look at?" Gage chuckled and downed the remainder of his drink.

Elias frowned and decided 'twas best to change the subject. "Josiah, did you get the new bosun, Nelson, settled?"

Josiah shrugged. "Took off after you did, Cap'n. I showed him his berth and then he was gone. Said he had business t' attend in town before we set sail."

Gage turned from the window and set down his cup. "Gentlemen." He rose. "I shall relieve you of my company, for, I daresay, I hear the siren's call from shore."

And just like the sirens of old, the wenches Gage frequented would end up leading him to his death.

Elias bit back his disapproval, knowing it would do no good. He allowed his men their freedom as long as they performed their duties and obeyed his rules while at sea. Still, he would love to stop his friend from wenching and drinking, both of which were the ruin of a man. Yet until God opened Gage's eyes, pointing out the man's faults would do more harm than good. Yes, Elias was first and foremost a preacher, and he loved opening people to the truth, seeing that light in their eyes when they realized there was a God who created them and loved them, who died for them so they could spend eternity with Him. But Elias was also—when necessity called—a merchant and a privateer should his country need him. Hence, he manned his ship with the most skilled sailors he could find, some Godly men, some not, knowing that the influence of the former on the latter was of utmost importance.

Gage was one of the latter. A man who reminded Elias of himself just three years past. Even now as the surgeon straightened his coat and bid them adieu, Elias could see the hopelessness in his eyes.

Then there was Matthew Ballard, the state of his soul unclear to Elias. He spoke all the right words, but he seemed more in love with money and women than God.

After his men left, Elias blew out his lantern and lay down on his bunk, one hand behind his head, trying desperately to empty his mind. But his thoughts filled with Miss Westcott.

Should he go see her? Nay, she would still be angry at him. And rightly so. 'Twas the first time he'd been reduced to kidnapping a woman, but it couldn't be helped. If he would have done so with his sister Caleigh three years ago, her life would never have been ruined.

Charles Gregson, Lord Villemont, entered the printer's shop, two of his men on his heels, and removed his gloves ever so slowly. Slowly because it helped calm his nerves, bound tight ever since he'd anchored at Kingston and found the *Enmity* undergoing repairs and Lady Villemont nowhere to be found. He'd sent his men out to question the drunken flotsam inhabiting the uncivilized port town, but all they'd returned with were tales of a man carrying a wench over his shoulder onto a ship. Not an uncommon occurrence, according to the locals. Surely Lady Villemont wouldn't be involved in such improper antics. But then again, she *had* murdered his brother.

He drew a deep breath, stifling the pain of that last thought. Poor Herbert. He didn't deserve to die so young. Not at the hands of a fluff-headed harpy. Herbert had told Charles more than once that the woman was mad—the reason he'd kept her locked up at home. But Charles hadn't thought she was dangerous. If he had, he'd have been there to save his brother—like Herbert had saved Charles all those years during their childhood from their father's violent cruelty.

Charles' throat clogged with emotion. He cleared it and tapped his cane on the floor.

The printer looked up from his work and approached, wiping soiled hands on his apron. His brows lifted as his gaze took in Charles' blue silk French coat embroidered with satin floral motifs. Apparently he rarely entertained people of class.

"I'm Lord Villemont," Charles began. "Was there a message left for me, perhaps by a sailor recently come to town?" He'd discovered that the local newspaper, if one could call it that, was only printed every fortnight. Hence in all likelihood, if one of the sailors aboard the *Enmity* had seen the reward poster in Nassau and recognized Lady Villemont on the ship, he certainly would have left word at the most logical place. In lieu of a proper postal system, the inhabitants of this squalid town had informed his men that letters were passed through the printer, who charged a penny a post.

"Ah, yes, milord." The man started one way, then turned to go the other way, all the while mumbling to himself. He returned within seconds and handed Lord Villemont a piece of folded parchment.

Taking it, Charles broke the seal.

"He didn't know how to write." The printer pointed toward the script. "So I wrote it for him."

"Thank you." Lord Villemont turned from the annoying man, snapped his fingers, and one of his men handed the printer a shilling as Charles read:

*Your Lordship,*
*Lady Villemont goes by the name Charity Westcott and is now sailing on the Restoration under Captain Elias Dutton, bound for Barbados. My name is Nelson and I be sailing with him as his bosun sos you can find me when you catch us.*
*Your humble servant,*
*Marcus Nelson*

Good lad, this Nelson. Good lad. He folded the paper and slid it in his pocket as he limped from the shop and adjusted his periwig. Placing his tricorn back atop his head, he slid on his gloves and waited for his men to flank him. "Find out all you can about a ship called *Restoration* and a Captain Elias Dutton, then meet me on board in two hours." He gazed up at the sun halfway to its zenith in the sky. If the ship had set sail that morning, they'd still have time to give chase.

# Chapter 13

Charity stood at the railing of yet another ship and gazed over the glittering fan of turquoise spreading to the horizon. Though her father was an admiral in the Royal Navy, she'd never been fond of sailing. Not like her sister Faith who talked of naught but wind and wave and knew the name of every sail on her father's flagship. For Charity, there was something daunting about being confined on a boat no larger than a home, surrounded by dangerous waters, trapped, imprisoned. Mayhap that was why she hated it so. She'd been locked up in a house for the past two years, and all she wanted now was to be free.

A blast of warm, salty wind wafted around her, loosening curls from pins and cooling the perspiration on her neck. Bracing her feet on the shifting deck, she closed her eyes and pretended she was a bird soaring over these gorgeous seas, not subject to wind or current or the desires of man, but free to go where she pleased, when she pleased.

And for that brief moment with the setting sun warming her eyelids, all was well with the world.

But Elias' first mate, a large Negro with a beaming grin, barked an order to the men in the tops that gave her a start. Sailors' bare feet pounded over the deck and loosened ropes from belaying pins.

She kept her face forward, too embarrassed to look any of them in the eye after she'd demanded they rescue her from their captain the night before. Even so, most had smiled warmly at her when she'd first come above. Only a few had stared inappropriately. And though she was livid with Elias, she had to admit she felt much safer aboard a ship that he captained.

After a restless night, a man who introduced himself as Leggy—odd since he was missing one leg below the knee—brought her a boiled egg and toast for breakfast. And coffee! Such delicious coffee she'd not had since leaving Portsmouth. Famished, she ate every last bite of food and completely drained her mug. Though the door remained unlocked, and Leggy had told her she was free to roam the ship, she'd remained in her cabin most of the day, too angry to face Elias and too weary of facing the lecherous gazes of yet another crew. But late in the day, the heat and boredom conquered her stubborn will, and she crept down the hall and up a ladder, following the sunshine. Thankfully, Elias was not on deck.

Now, as she attempted to balance on the heaving ship, it occurred to her that she'd kept her breakfast down. Which put her in her fourth or fifth month. Already, when she disrobed, the swell of life at her belly brought a smile to her lips. But it wouldn't have the same effect on others when they noticed it on an unwed woman. Where she would spend her lying-in and how she would conceal it from the world, she hadn't considered yet. Her family would offer to take her in, of course, but she wouldn't dare put them in danger.

She drew a deep breath as the ship bucked and misted her with salty spray. *One day at a time, Charity. One day at a time.* First things first, extricate herself from the clutches of this pretend preacher, who must be working for Charles, for no one was this kind to a stranger unless they wanted something in return. She'd once believed in kindness, naïve as she was. She'd once believed that some people were willing to sacrifice for others, expecting nothing in return. After all, she had been that way most of her life. But then she had married Lord Villemont. And he had laughed at her innocence—

And taught her the truth.

*There are no good in people,* he would say, *just a desire for wealth, success, and pleasure. If being kind to someone aids in acquiring those delights, then so be it.*

And this from a man who went to church religiously and oft quoted Scripture. Charity thought to ask him why the Bible spoke of loving one's neighbor as oneself, but decided it wouldn't be worth the repercussions.

"Good day, Miss." A man appeared beside her, giving her a start. "Forgive me, I didn't mean to frighten you." His smile was genuine on a pleasant-enough face with a straight nose and serious eyes. Brown curly hair loosened from a ribbon tied behind him and fluttered in the wind. "Matthew Ballard at your service, quartermaster on the *Restoration*."

She recognized him as one of the men who'd approached Elias when they'd come aboard last night. "Miss Westcott," she replied, encouraged by the man's apparent education. "And if you are truly at my service, can you free me from the madman who captains this ship?"

His lips lifted slightly, then lowered to a frown. "In truth, I am appalled at the manner in which you were brought aboard," he said with all sincerity as he straightened his fine cambric waistcoat. "'Tis most untoward for a lady to be treated thus."

"Indeed?" She studied him with a huff. "And yet you sail with the man who performs such atrocities with impunity."

"A necessity for the time being." He squeezed the bridge of his nose, and Charity wondered if she'd found an ally aboard the ship.

"Does Mr. Dut—the Captain—make a habit of kidnapping ladies?"

He chuckled and glanced over the sea. "I believe you are the first, Miss Westcott. At least since I've been sailing with him."

"'Tis unclear whether I should be happy or sad at that news." She frowned as a blast of wind gusted over her, whipping hair against her neck. "How long have you been sailing under Mr. Dutton? You don't appear ... you don't seem ..."

"Like an uncultured sailor?" He laughed. "My father was a gentleman, Miss, my mother the daughter of a baron. They owned a large estate in Northhamptonshire, just outside Brackley."

"Owned?"

"Yes, they are passed now."

"I'm sorry to hear that." Charity well knew the grief of losing a parent. "What of the estate?"

"It fell to me, their oldest. I hired a trustworthy overseer and went to sea. Too many memories there, I'm afraid." He drew a deep breath, though Charity sensed no sorrow within it. Nor in his eyes as they gazed out to sea. How odd that a man of land and wealth would subject himself to a dangerous life at sea.

"And how did you come to meet Mr. Dutton?" she asked.

She knew before he opened his mouth to answer that Elias stood behind her, for Mr. Ballard stiffened, put on a tight grin, and offered no reply.

"Back to your post, Mr. Ballard," Elias commanded. "The sails need trimming." He'd expected the man would seek out Miss Westcott's company. He just hadn't expected he'd do it so soon.

Mr. Ballard bid her good day and sped off while Elias leaned one arm on the railing a good yard from where she stood.

Egad, but it was good to see her here on deck with her cinnamon curls dancing about her neck, her maroon skirts fluttering in the wind, and those thick lashes brushing over sun-kissed cheeks. He'd feared she would remain in her cabin the entire week. Yet when he'd come above, he could not deny the leap of his heart at the sight of her.

"Have I grown horns that you stand so far off?" she said curtly without looking his way.

"I fear those fists of yours, Miss Westcott. My back still suffers from the thrashing they gave me."

She gave a ladylike snort. "I doubt that, Mr. Dutton."

"At the very least," he said. "I fear you may attempt to toss me overboard."

"If only I had the strength to do so," she murmured, and he believed she meant it.

"I hope you'll see in time that I merely wished to save your life." He inched toward her.

"Do you always go about saving people who do not wish to be saved?"

"Of course." He smiled, though she still refused to look his way. "'Tis my job as a preacher."

"Preacher, vapors!" she spat out. "Do you find me such a dolt?"

He chuckled. "I would never permit myself to think such a thing."

"I know you are working for my br—Charles."

Elias closed his eyes for a second. Oh, how the woman's words scrambled his mind! "I know not this brcharles, and I work only for God."

She narrowed her eyes at him. "You are truly the captain of this ship?"

"Brig, and aye."

"You could have simply told me that when you extended your invitation."

"Would you have come with me then?"

"No." The bite in her tone made him smile.

Sails thundered above as the brig plunged into the trough of a wave, and he moved closer to place a hand on her back to steady her. She leapt away as if he had the ague.

He leaned his elbows on the railing. "Leggy informed me you ate your food this morning. Mayhap you are growing accustomed to the sway of the sea? If so, I invite you to dine with me and my officers tonight. Rarely does such a lovely guest grace our table."

"Suddenly I am your *guest*?" she quipped.

"Of course. You are free to roam anywhere you like on the brig."

"You mean prison."

He glanced over the churning sea. "I'm sorry you see it as such."

"Not only a prison, Sir, but you have ruined my reputation by placing me on a ship full of men without a proper companion."

He growled inwardly. "And it wasn't ruined when we shared a cabin as man and wife?"

He enjoyed the blush blossoming on her cheeks as she glanced around and gestured for him to lower his voice.

"If 'tis your reputation that concerns you," he added, "it would have been ruined far more if you had stayed in Kingston alone."

"What is it you want from me, Mr. Dutton?"

Elias breathed out a sigh. "Why are you always asking me that?"

"Whatever Charles is paying you, I'm sure my father can match it." She bit her lip. "Or double it."

"No one is paying me, I assure you." Elias glanced toward the horizon where a dark haze rose to obscure the beauty of the setting sun. "Does your mistrust stem from me being a preacher or a man?"

"Both."

"In truth, Miss Westcott, my only wish is to take you to Charles Towne and deliver you to your family unscathed. Is that so hard to believe?"

"Yes."

Sails snapped above, drawing his gaze. "Reef topsails!" he shouted to Josiah, then waited for the man to repeat the orders before he faced Miss Westcott again. "Has no one ever done a kindness to you and not expected anything in return?"

Drawing a deep breath, she seemed to ponder the question before uttering a definitive "No."

Elias' heart crumbled. What had happened to this poor lady to make her so bitter, so angry and distrusting? Whatever it was, he longed to heal all her wounds, or better yet, point her to the One who could. "Then allow me to be the first," he said, longing to ease a strand of riotous hair behind her ear. "And in the process prove to you that there is still good in the world."

The brig rose up a swell and she gripped the railing. "It seems I have no choice."

"What say you to a truce, Miss Westcott?"

"I say 'tis a ludicrous notion since you have already won the war."

"Merely a battle." He grinned, inching his hand closer to hers on the railing.

He finally got a tiny smile out of her. "What exactly are your terms, Captain?"

Elias fingered the cross hanging around his neck. "I shall promise never to kidnap you again."

Shielding her eyes, she gazed at him with suspicion. "Even after we arrive in Barbados?"

If he hadn't convinced her of his sincerity by then, he was a far worse preacher than he thought. "You have my word."

"Very well, truce." She lifted her hand to shake his, and he relished the opportunity to encase her small, soft hand in his. But she quickly pulled it back.

She may have agreed to a truce, but she obviously wasn't done fighting. "Now that we are friends again—"

"Again? Were we ever?"

"Well, we were husband and wife for nearly three days."

"True." She flattened her lips and gazed out to sea, giving him a chance to admire the way the setting sun cast streaks of golden glitter on her face and through her hair.

"Tell me about your family in Charles Towne. Your father is an admiral?"

"Yes, Rear-Admiral Henry Westcott. A good one too. In fact, he'd have you strung up by your toes if he knew you'd kidnapped me."

"Mayhap I won't take you to Charles Towne, after all." His chuckle garnered another smile out of her. "And your sisters?"

"All younger. Faith, who loves the sea and sailing, Hope, who loves parties, and Grace, who is much like you, pious and self-righteous."

"Ouch." He cringed at the insult. "And I try so hard not to be either." Regardless, he could tell from her tone and the affectionate look in her eyes that she loved her sisters.

"How long since you have seen them?"

"They left Portsmouth four months ago. I miss them terribly." She swallowed and looked away.

"Why did you not go with them?"

"I was…engaged at the time."

"Surely they left you with a relative, your mother?" For no one would leave a single lady to her own devices.

"My mother is dead." Wind spun her hair into a frenzy as she lowered her gaze to the choppy sea. "Five years past."

"I'm sorry." Elias laid his hand atop hers.

Jerking hers away, her jaw stiffened. "Mother was taken from us far too young, and with Father away so much, my sisters and I had to run things. Honestly, I have few happy memories of my childhood. Our governess often took to her cups and stole money that should have gone to our needs."

Elias leaned on the railing and stared down at the water dashing against the hull. He'd love nothing more than to take the lady in his arms and offer what comfort he could. He'd had quite a different childhood—two parents who adored him, plenty of siblings to love and grow up with, a good education, all his needs met, and a home full of love and laughter. Not only did this lady have none of that—save the siblings—but her family had abandoned her. Why?

"I'm sorry, Miss Westcott. You are here now. Safe and on your way to rejoin your family. All will be well, you'll see."

She turned her face away. "Forgive me. I overspoke. I don't know why I'm telling my kidnapper such intimacies."

"Not your fault, Miss. 'Tis a benefit of my vocation— luring people to spill their secrets."

"Cap'n!" one of the sailors hailed him from the quarterdeck.

Elias nodded toward the lady. "I shall relieve you of my company for now, Miss Westcott. I'll have Leggy escort you to supper at eight bells." Before she could protest, he marched away, a smile on his face at the possibility of seeing her again so soon.

# Chapter 14

A knock rapped on her cabin door, and Charity opened it to Elias, wearing a rather sultry grin on his face. Oddly, she began to mutter like a silly schoolgirl, quickly shifting her gaze away from his thickly-muscled frame attired in a cambric shirt and a damask waistcoat with silver braid. Black breeches led down to equally black leather boots. His hair was neatly combed and tied behind, his chin bore the barest hint of stubble as if his attempt to shave had faltered, and those crisp sea-blue eyes looked at her with such wisdom and care.

And suddenly she wished for a fresh gown and a lady's maid to pin up her hair in a proper style. *Vapors!* What was she thinking? Yesterday this man hoisted her over his shoulder like a sack of grain and stole her against her will!

"I thought you would send one of your men to escort me." She forced a tone of nonchalance.

"After our engaging conversation on deck today, I longed for the honor." He proffered his elbow.

"Engaging? Is that what you'd call it?" She refused to take his arm and swept past him into the hall, still regretting disclosing so much about her past to this man.

"Indeed. You are a fascinating woman, Miss Westcott."

Charity couldn't remember ever being called thus. "Obviously you haven't met many women." She made her way down the narrow corridor, lit by flickering lanterns attached to the bulkhead.

"Too many, I'm afraid. Of the wrong kind."

Surprised by his comment, she halted and stared up at him. Had he grown taller or was it being confined in such a tiny space that made him seem so large? "Why, Preacher, I'm stunned to hear you say so."

He gestured for her to proceed. "There are many things about me which might shock you, Miss Westcott."

She doubted it, but against her will, she found her curiosity piqued. Still, the only thing she *should* be curious about was whether this man worked for her brother-in-law. Which was the main reason she'd lowered her claws and agreed to be friendly. If she played the nice mermaid, perhaps he'd let down his guard, and she could slip away once they anchored in Barbados.

Elias' cabin was elegantly and tastefully decorated. She'd expected a preacher's cabin to be sparse, dull, housing a single chair, and a worn table on which perched a candle and an old Bible. On the contrary, this cabin boasted oil paintings and tapestries on the bulkheads, a lush Turkish carpet on the floor, cupboards nailed to the wall, filled with tins of coffee and tea, books ranging from mathematics to navigation to poetry, along with various bottles, statues, and trinkets. A teakwood trunk guarded the foot of a bunk that was neatly made with a dark purple coverlet. Two lanterns framed the stern windows, their light joining the flickering candles atop the table from which rose five men from their seats as she entered.

The scent of fish, onions, and potatoes swirled beneath her nose from various bowls and platters already on the table.

Introductions were made as Elias led her to a chair on the right of his at the head of the table. She'd already met Mr. Ballard, was surprised to see Mr. Nelson from the *Enmity*, was warmed by the large Negro Josiah's smile, and was greeted with the lift of a glass by Mr. Evan Gage, a handsome man with light hair and a kind face. A lad no more than fifteen—a Mr. Wilcox—sat to his left and blushed as she acknowledged him.

Elias took his seat, announced grace, and proceeded to thank God for the food in the most sincere, informal tone she'd ever heard.

Unnerved by the intimate conversation with God, she accepted Mr. Gage's offer to pour her some wine.

"Do tell me, gentlemen, are you all preachers like Mr. Dutton?" She began the conversation as platters of food were passed, though she already knew the answer.

As she suspected, laughter ensued.

"Nay, Miss," Mr. Ballard replied, dipping his head toward Elias. "The Captain is the only *holy* man on board."

Was it her or did she detect a hint of disdain in Mr. Ballard's voice?

"There is none holy but God," Elias offered.

Amused by the tension between the two men, Charity served herself some sea pie. At least that's what the men were calling the buttery pastry filled with chunks of fish and vegetables.

Mr. Gage plucked a soft tack from a platter and gestured toward the large Negro. "However one might assume Josiah is a preacher as well by the way he carries that Bible around as if it could shield him from musket fire."

Josiah only smiled and patted his waistcoat. "It may do that one day. But it isn't the full Bible yet."

At her perplexed look, Elias explained, "Josiah is copying the Holy Scriptures word for word onto parchment."

First of all, Charity had never eaten a meal with a Negro. Her father never had slaves, nor had Lord Villemont, though she knew of a few acquaintances who had. Still, they would never think to dine with them, slave or not. Secondly, while many of the commoners in England were illiterate, apparently this Negro not only spoke well but could write.

"Josiah, that seems quite an enormous task. Whatever possessed you to embark upon it?" she asked.

"To learn, Miss. It's the best way for me to learn the Scriptures and keep them wit' me at all times."

She stared at him, baffled.

He finished a spoonful of rice. "The Captain's Father, Rowan Dutton, rescued me from slavery off a merchant ship." His voice was as deep and smooth as his smile, and she instantly felt at ease in his presence. "I was only nine at the time. Sailed wit' the Captain's father for years before I joined his son." He smiled at Elias. "Elias taught me to read and write and even promoted me from seaman to first mate."

Elias popped a slice of papaya into his mouth. "You deserved it. I've never seen anyone work so hard and learn so quickly." He gripped Josiah's shoulder, and Charity was surprised at the affection stretching between them. She'd grown up in a world where bloodline and wealth meant everything. Here on the ship—at least under Elias' rule—neither seemed to matter.

"And just how does a preacher come to captain a ship?" she asked Elias. "Shouldn't you be on land saving souls from hell?"

"Are there no souls to save at sea?" Elias winked at her then bit into a biscuit. Behind him a starry sky dipped in and out of view with each sway of the ship.

"I'd say we've seen plenty of dark souls at sea," Mr. Ballard offered as he served himself another helping of sea pie.

"'Tis true," Elias said. "And more on land. This way I can reach both." He passed the decanter of wine but didn't pour any in his glass.

Mr. Gage happily took it and refilled his.

Charity sipped her own wine and then bit into her soft tack, thankful it wasn't the hard biscuit they'd served on board the *Enmity*. In fact, for shipboard food, everything was delicious. Or mayhap 'twas because she finally had an appetite.

She turned toward the young lad who had already devoured his plateful of food and was helping himself to seconds. "And what is it you do on board, Mr. Wilcox?"

"Call me Eddy, Miss. Everyone does. I'm a topman," he said proudly, giving her a boyish grin. "I furl and unfurl sail on the foretop."

"Oh, my. How exciting and dangerous for such a young lad."

"He's also my apprentice," Gage said, glancing at Eddy fondly. "I'm the surgeon aboard the *Restoration*."

Part of Charity was glad to know there was a doctor aboard. Another part wondered what type of surgeon he could be as he poured himself yet another glass of wine.

"He's the smartest lad I ever met." Gage slapped the boy on the back, causing him to blush. "He'll make a fine ship's surgeon someday."

The boy gazed up at Mr. Gage with the affection of a son to a father, and Charity couldn't help but smile.

The ever-present rush of water against the hull, coupled with the groan of wood, provided the music for their evening meal as plates, bowls, and candlesticks inched back and forth over the table in a dance as formal as any ball.

Still, an odd chill scraped over Charity. Not the first time that night, she looked up to find Mr. Nelson's eyes locked upon her, assessing, appraising, she couldn't be sure. "Mr. Nelson. I remember you from the *Enmity*. How did you come to be on Mr. Dutton's ship?"

He quickly averted his gaze. "As ye know, Miss, the *Enmity* were badly damaged, an' I needed the work."

"And Mr. Dutton was kind enough to take you on, of course." She hated the admiration rising within her for the man who seemed to go out of his way to help others.

"And you, Miss Westcott?" Mr. Gage grabbed his glass and sat back in the chair, a teasing grin on his face. "What brings you on board our fair brig?"

He knew very well what, or rather *who*, had brought her on board. Obviously he'd consumed too much wine. Either way, she should thank him for the reminder, for it instantly doused her rising esteem for Elias. "I was kidnapped, as you all know."

Not one of them expressed an ounce of shame or indignation. In fact, they all chuckled. Even Mr. Ballard, who'd earlier seemed sympathetic to her plight.

Josiah helped himself to more sweet potatoes.

Furious, Charity addressed the Negro. "Have you not transcribed that part of the Scriptures which say that stealing someone against their will is wrong?"

Josiah shrugged. "If the captain kidnapped you, he did it for your good."

Mr. Gage loosened his cravat. "Before you were kidnapped by our illustrious captain"—he raised his glass toward Elias and smiled—"what brought you to the Caribbean, Miss Westcott?"

"I'm on my way home to Charles Towne, Carolina."

"Ah, Charles Towne, I know it well. Charming little post."

"I've never been. I do hope it is somewhat civilized."

Mr. Gage offered no comment as he twirled a finger around the rim of his glass, seemingly mesmerized with the liquor within.

"Far more civilized than Kingston," Elias said with a grin.

Mr. Ballard lit a cheroot from a candle and took a puff. "But why travel alone, Miss Westcott? 'Tis not only dangerous but unseemly for a lady."

"My companion and I were separated."

Elias' brows shot up. "Indeed? Run off by the man chasing you, no doubt?"

She glared at him, noting the playful spark in his eyes. "No *doubt*. However—" she lifted a hand just as Gage seemed ready to ask another question. "I don't wish to discuss it."

The men took the hint and went on to talk about ships, weather, crew members not doing their jobs, rigging that needed repairing and other topics which bored Charity. It gave her a chance, however, to enjoy her food and steal glances at Elias as he spoke with his men, authoritatively, confidently, yet with a camaraderie she'd not seen in a man of authority.

Wine was passed and Charity poured a tiny bit more into her cup, while Elias refused it yet again. She huffed to herself. No doubt 'twas a sin for such a pious man to drink. Although that had never stopped her husband.

Mr. Gage, however, helped himself to yet another glass. His fourth? She'd lost count.

"Confound it all! 'Tis a shame there hasn't been any good wars of late," Gage slurred as he slammed his glass on the table, startling Charity. "Most unfortunate to be sailing under one of the best privateers ever to grace these waters and have no way to use his skills."

"What do you need with a fortune, Gage?" Mr. Ballard chuckled. "To line other men's pockets at gaming tables?"

"You forget yourself, Ballard," Gage stuttered out with an angry glare.

The young lad tossed down his fork. "Mr. Gage don't need no money anyway. His father is a wealthy man."

"Ah, yes." Ballard puffed on his cheroot. "We all know your father procured your commission in the Royal Navy to sober you up and make a man of you."

"And what, pray tell, will aid you in that regard?" Gage retorted.

Nelson chuckled, along with the lad.

"Now, now, gentlemen," Elias said. "There's a lady present."

Nelson let out a belch and rubbed his belly. "Word is, Cap'n Dutton, ye won a fair amount of prizes when ye had papers to attack Spanish ships."

Elias pushed back his plate. "God was with us. Besides, we may have the chance again if the rumblings of war coming from Europe are true."

"Indeed?" Charity said. "Preacher *and* privateer? What an enigma you are, *Captain*."

"Aye," Nelson growled. "A good war would certainly fill our pouches."

"And kill innocent people," she added.

Elias smiled at her. Was it the wine or was he more handsome here in his element with his men around him, the candlelight glimmering over his face, and a backdrop of moonlit waves shimmering through the stern windows behind him?

Nay, most likely the wine.

Shoving his chair back, Gage rose, raised his glass, and offered a toast. "To privateering!"

But before others could join in, the deck canted, sending him stumbling backward. With arms flailing and wine sloshing over the rim of his cup, he landed smack on the deck.

Charity gasped. The men burst into laughter.

"Forgive us, Miss Westcott. We aren't accustomed to entertaining ladies." Elias gave her an apologetic look as he rose to help Gage to his feet. "Have a care, Gage. There is no one to repair you should you injure yourself."

"Surely this man is not your *only* surgeon?" Charity asked, disgusted by the display.

"Hard to believe at the moment, but yes, Gage is quite good at fixing the injured. In truth, one of the best." Elias returned him to his seat, where the man wobbled before placing his elbows on the table. "Trained with the surgeon on HMS *Prelude* under Captain Markham," Elias added.

Mr. Ballard snorted. "A midshipman who preferred to be a surgeon. Bah! Another stain on your family's reputation, Mr. Gage."

The *surgeon* attempted to get up again, but instead poured himself more wine.

Charity suddenly felt sorry for him. She could certainly relate to being an embarrassment to her family. "I've heard my father speak of Captain Markham. How is it you are no longer in the Navy, Mr. Gage?"

"He deserted." Ballard snorted.

"He did not!" Eddy protested. "He fell overboard."

Mr. Gage raised his glass in the air. "More like took a midnight swim."

"Oh, my." Charity pressed a hand to her stomach. "They'll kill you if they find you."

"I'm well aware, Miss." Gage smiled at her and sipped his wine.

"We do our best to steer clear of the Royal Navy." Elias winked at her.

If Charity's father could see her now—dining with a deserting, drunken surgeon and an ex-slave who fancied himself a scribe. Not to mention Mr. Nelson, who kept staring at her as if she were dessert, and Mr. Ballard who, by all accounts, should be home managing his vast estate rather than flitting about the Caribbean on a ship that rarely made a profit, it would seem. At least not during wartime.

And then there was Elias Dutton, preacher, privateer, merchant, rescuer of women and lost souls.

If she didn't know better, she'd think she'd joined a troupe of tragic actors. "Forgive me gentlemen. 'Tis been an ... well, an interesting evening, but I'm rather tired." She was. Mayhap 'twas her full belly, the wine, the gentle sway of the ship. Or all three.

"Pleasure, Miss." Each man rose as she stood.

"I'll escort you." Elias started for the door, but one of the paintings hanging beside the bookshelves caught her eye. "What is *this*, Captain?" She teased and moved closer to examine it. "'Tis a portrait of you!" She laughed. "I do remember something in the Bible about vanity." She glanced back at him "Aren't preachers supposed to be humble?"

Chuckles emanated from the table.

"Everyone is supposed to be humble." He reached her side, his look of annoyance fading as he stared at the painting. "My mother painted it, if you must know."

"Ah, the talented L.M, famous pirate painter." Ballard's voice blared from the table, his tone more sarcastic than complimentary.

Charity lowered her gaze to the signature. "Your mother is the pirate painter, L.M.?" Yet now that she studied the portrait in more detail, she saw the brush strokes, vibrancy of color, and realism for which the pirate painter was known.

"Do you know of her?" Elias asked proudly.

"I've seen many of her paintings back in Portsmouth. She's quite good," Charity had to admit, though she hated to offer her kidnapper's mother a compliment. Nevertheless, L.M. had captured her son perfectly, the wisdom, kindness and slight sorrow in his eyes, his confident stance, his easy smile, and his powerful presence.

Elias grasped hands behind his back. "She is at that. We are very proud of her."

Turning, Charity bid her dinner companions goodnight once again and proceeded into the hallway, angry that every little thing she learned about this man only endeared him to her more.

"You have quite an interesting crew, Mr. Dutton," she said as they walked down the narrow corridor. "For a preacher, that is. I doubt they are much help in your proselytizing."

Chuckling, he halted before her cabin. "I need no help but God's in that regard. And as I said before, I surround myself with those who have lost their way and need someone to guide them back."

The ship creaked over a wave, tilting the hallway as lantern light speared his strong jaw. "Is that what you are doing with me? Do you feel I have lost my way?" If he said yes, he'd be right, for she'd felt lost for a long, long time.

"You tell me. *Have* you lost your way?"

"You're the preacher."

"I am also a man. And I can be a friend, a good one, should you find yourself in need."

She *did* need a friend. Desperately. But she wasn't foolish enough to seek friendship with a man. She should go inside her cabin. She should thank Elias and bid him goodnight. Instead, she raised a coy brow. "Why do you not drink spirits, Mr. Dutton? Are those who drink them going to hell?"

He chuckled. "Gads, Miss, but you seem overly obsessed with eternal damnation."

She frowned. 'Twas true, she supposed, because there was no doubt in her mind that's where she was going.

The ship tilted and he steadied her with a touch to her elbow. "I have naught against them, Miss. But they have caused me too much trouble in the past to be entertained again."

"This past you speak of intrigues me."

"*You* intrigue me, Miss Westcott." He rubbed a thumb down her cheek. She should be frightened by such an intimate touch. She should dash into her cabin and slam the door in his face. But instead of terror, she felt the oddest sensation ripple through her. Not altogether unpleasant. She lifted her gaze to his as he continued caressing her cheek, sliding his finger down her jaw, then fingering a lock of her hair as if it were made of silk.

Still nothing but care, concern, even admiration glimmered in his eyes. No lust, no hatred or ill intent. His breath swept over her, warm and spicy. His presence, strong and comforting, filled the air.

Heart racing, she inched back from him. She must change the subject, break this strange spell between them. "Vapors, intriguing?" She laughed. "Of course I'm intriguing, I'm the only woman on boar—"

Elias' lips touched hers.

A shard of heat spiraled down to her toes. Along with a jolt of alarm—her one thought to run for safety. But Elias' lips weren't hard, demanding, punishing. They didn't pry her lips apart and take what wasn't given. Nay, they barely pressed on hers—the kiss of a feather—before they lifted, hovering over her mouth as if awaiting further invitation. His breath wafted over her cheeks in warm waves, his right hand tenderly cupped the back of her head, waiting...waiting...

Against all reason, she moved her lips forward until they touched his again, the slightest of touches, but that's all it took for him to take her in his arms and deepen the kiss. Still 'twasn't an angry kiss or vicious or fierce. It was closeness and intimacy and care... But her mind began a fearful spin when she realized she was trapped in his arms. She couldn't breathe, couldn't move. Panic took hold as memories possessed her.

"No!" Shrieking, she shoved from him, holding her hand to her mouth. He gaped at her, stunned, as she pushed him back, darted into her cabin, and slammed the door.

Leaning against it, she slid to the floor, ignoring his apologies from the other side, and sobbed.

# Chapter 15

Sometime in the middle of the night, Charity woke with a start, still sitting on the floor with her back pressed against the door. Memories of Elias' kiss rose, and she touched her lips, heart reeling, fingers trembling. She'd never been kissed so tenderly before, so lovingly. Lord Villemont's kisses had been rough, determined, savage, as if he were conquering her in battle.

But Elias' kiss ... she had no words. It awoke something within her that was anything but fear. And that scared her most of all. Vapors! Why had she granted him such liberties? Why had she not been terrified at his touch? Surely it was her indulgence in wine.

Or mayhap just her stupidity. She'd been gullible and trusting her entire life. She'd always believed people when they told her things. She'd believed everything Lord Villemont had said—how much he loved her, how he'd always be there for her, to cherish her and provide for her and protect her. And she'd fallen in love with him. Far too easily. Wanting so desperately to leave home and have a man's affection and admiration—a man who didn't love the sea more than he loved her. A man who wouldn't sail off on his ship every chance he got. Like her father.

The ship swayed, and the timbers groaned as if they were tired of life. She could relate. She pressed a hand on her belly. "If not for you, little one," she whispered, "if not for you." Streams of glimmering moonlight filtered through the porthole and waved over the bulkheads and deck, providing the only light in the gloomy cabin. Shadows slunk from every corner, reviving memories of a time when Lord Villemont had locked her in the cellar for questioning his decision in front of a guest. No amount of pleading, screaming, or pounding on the door had set her free. After the first day without water, her voice abandoned her. The second day, the darkness had come to life—specters from hell forming from the black mist, trying to drag her to the underworld. She began to believe they would succeed. But then Lord Villemont released her, brought her water and bread and ordered a hot bath to be drawn. He even looked slightly apologetic when he'd said "I hope you've learned a lesson, Charity. You know I hate punishing you."

Indeed. She *had* learned, for she'd never contradicted him again.

Closing her eyes to the misty demons, Charity drew her knees up and hugged herself. "Sing a song of sixpence, a pocket full of rye," she half-hummed, half-sang. "...they sent for the king's doctor, who sewed it up again ..." Over and over she sang until her heart settled and her breathing calmed and sometime after that, the creaks of the ship faded into the background.

A bold ray of morning sun shifted over her shoes and reflected off a brass button into her eyes. She opened them to watch it oscillate, joined by other glittering beams, in a dance welcoming the new day. Prying her forehead from her knees, she dared to glance over her cabin, relieved to find the demons had retreated for the night.

But they'd be back. They always came back.

An hour later, after she'd washed her face, did her best to press the wrinkles from her skirts, and pinned up her hair, Elias knocked on the door. She knew it was him before he said a word, before he begged for a moment of her time.

"I have a headache, Mr. Dutton. Perhaps later."

To which he hesitated for a moment before informing her he would send Leggy with some tea. It was several minutes before she heard him march away. Minutes in which she wanted to fling open the door. If only to see him, to see that look in his eyes that made her feel so safe and cherished.

But she was a fool. A gullible, naïve fool. And before she faced Elias again, she needed time to remind herself of that, to patch the breach he'd made in the fortress around her heart.

As promised, Leggy arrived with tea and biscuits with mango jam. Four hours after that, he returned with salted pork and sliced bananas and an invitation from Elias to come on deck and enjoy the fresh air.

To which she refused.

When a knock sounded on her door two hours after that, she finally felt strong enough to face Elias and flung it open to see Mr. Ballard instead. A pleasant smile graced his lips as he dipped his head. "Miss Westcott, forgive me, but the captain informs me you are ill, and I thought perhaps I could help."

My, but the man dressed well for a sailor. Clean shaven, freshly pressed shirt, waistcoat, and breeches. The fine fabric and embroidered trim was evidence enough that he came from money. Add to that his bearing and manners, and she could well imagine him a gentleman of an estate.

"I don't see how you could help, Mr. Ballard, though I thank you for your kindness."

"Perhaps I can escort you above?"

She wanted to tell him should she wish to go on deck, she needed no escort, but "A sail! A sail!" echoed down the hallway from the tops, and her heart coiled into a ball. There were many ships sailing the Caribbean. Simply because one was nearby didn't mean it was a pirate, or worse, her brother-in-law, did it? Besides, how would Charles know whether she had left Nassau at all and if she had, on what ship? Nevertheless, she suddenly felt the need to find out.

"I would love to go on deck, Mr. Ballard." She closed her door, and with ever so slight a touch on his arm, allowed him to lead her above.

The sun hung over the horizon—a sphere of brilliant gold and coral—causing Charity to squint as Mr. Ballard led her to the railing, all the while trying to keep her balance on the galloping deck. A deck that seemed much more wobbly than before. She knew why when she glanced over the sea. A cauldron of foam-capped swells advanced on the ship from an eastern horizon clogged with dark clouds.

But it was the ship off their starboard beam that drew her attention.

"'Tis a restless sea today, Miss Westcott, but if you hold fast to the railing, you should have no trouble," Mr. Ballard assured her, placing his hand atop hers as if demonstrating.

"Thank you." She tugged hers away.

"Mr. Ballard, relieve Kannes at the wheel!" Elias' voice bellowed over the deck, causing her heart to skip.

Mr. Ballard's upper lip twitched before it dipped in a frown. "I must away to my duties, but would be happy to escort you back to your cabin when you desire."

"Thank you, Mr. Ballard," she shouted into the wind, but didn't look his way. She couldn't. All she could see were bloated orange sails perched atop a ship in the distance.

And her heart plummeted into the trough of a wave along with the brig.

*How did Charles find me?*

Elias was the biggest cad on the planet. Still fuming at himself for his behavior last night, he stood on the quarterdeck, feet spread, arms crossed over his chest, commanding his men through rough seas while he attempted to command his heart through equally turbulent waters.

He knew Miss Westcott was fearful of men's touches. It was one of the things he admired about her. Her timidity revealed that she was chaste and pure. A quality he *must* have in any woman he courted. Not that they were courting, but oh, my...that kiss. So sweet, pure, hesitant, innocent, stirring him like no other. But blast it all! 'Twas precisely because they had no understanding—yet—that he shouldn't have taken liberties.

She must think him a lecherous swine, and he couldn't blame her. He longed to beg her forgiveness, but it was late in the afternoon watch and she'd yet to emerge from her cabin. The last thing he wanted to do was frighten her by continually banging on her door.

"A sail! A sail!" the shout blared from the tops.

Elias plucked his scope from his belt and leveled it on the horizon even before Josiah could reply "Where away?"

The direction came swift, and Elias swept the glass toward the horizon off their starboard quarter. Indeed, a ship, a merchantman to be exact, keeping pace with the *Restoration* on her starboard flank.

He focused the spyglass, hoping to make out her colors, but she was too far. No matter. If she had ill intentions, she'd soon discover she picked the wrong prey. Lowering the scope, Elias' gaze landed on Mr. Nelson standing at the bow, glass to his eye as well. Odd that a bosun would carry a telescope. Odder still, the hungry grin that overtook his face as he snapped the glass shut and returned to his duties. As if he recognized the merchantman.

Elias was about to shout for his attention when a flap of maroon skirts directed his gaze to Charity coming on deck on the arm of none other than Mr. Ballard.

Against his will, jealousy prickled his skin as his gaze followed them to the railing.

Josiah approached. "The merchantman that follows, Cap'n. Your orders?"

"Steady as she goes. We'll keep an eye on her for now, Josiah." He took in the rising swells and darkening skies. "In the meantime, reef topsails."

"Aye, Cap'n." Josiah turned to shout orders to the crew.

"Mr. Ballard," Elias shouted. "Relieve Kannes at the wheel!"

Ballard shot him a scathing look before he turned to say something to Charity.

But she didn't seem to be paying attention, her gaze locked on the merchantman.

Leaping up the quarterdeck ladder, Ballard took the wheel.

"And how fares Miss Westcott today?" Elias asked him, forcing down his jealousy.

"Well, Captain. She was most anxious for me to escort her above."

*She was?* Elias' insides boiled. Only on Mr. Ballard's arm, apparently. Perhaps Elias had been wrong about her. Perhaps she sought after the wealth and status a preacher could never provide. If so, 'twas best he discovered the truth now before he lost more of his heart to the little mermaid.

Bracing *that* heart, along with his boots on the deck, he glanced at the black clouds bubbling atop the eastern horizon. Confound it all! He grimaced. A storm would only delay him further in getting to his sister. He hated not knowing whether she was safe, not knowing whether those cullions had done more than damage property. "Josiah, strike topsail yards!"

The first mate fired orders to the crew as Elias turned to Ballard. "Keep our bow toward the swells."

"Yes, Captain. What of the storm?" Ballard tightened his grip on the wheel.

"Veer south southeast. Two points before the starboard beam. We'll sail around her. Besides, 'tis not a large one from the looks of it."

The brig turned to starboard, sending sails flapping, and deck canting, and Elias' gaze landed on Charity once again—hair blowing in the wind, hands gripping the railing, and eyes remaining on the merchantman.

Odd. Yet when he raised his scope again, the ship veered on the same tack as the *Restoration*.

Whoever it was, they were following them.

The slam of the front door reverberated through the house, the hollow stomp of shoes up the stairway, the drunken bellowing, the curses aimed at an inept staff and equally inept wife. Charity's lungs turned to ice. Her heart rammed against her ribs, seeking escape. He was home. And he was drunk.

She sprang to sit in her bed. Furniture formed ominous shadows in the darkness, lit by a milky shaft of moonlight slinking through the windows.

Tossing off her coverlet, she froze, unsure what to do. Would he come in or would he merely go to his own chamber? Should she hide? Terror numbed her. Her legs wouldn't move. She listened for the creak of the floor outside her door and waited...waited ... trying to still breathing that was so loud, she feared it would give her away.

The floor in the hallway creaked. *Pass by. Please pass by!* She closed her eyes to pray, pray for mercy, pray for help! *God, please!*

The door swung open. Lord Villemont stumbled in, the very vision of the devil himself, spewing curses on fiery noxious breath and tearing off his coat and vest as he went. "Come here, wife. Perform your duties."

Charity laid back on the bed and closed her eyes. God hadn't answered her prayer. He never answered her prayer. She was all alone.

*The maid was in the garden, hanging out the clothes...*

Harsh hands gripped her shoulders. Brandy-saturated breath drowned her. *When down came a blackbird that pecked off her nose...sing a song of sixpence...* Slowly, as Villemont grunted like a wild pig above her, she drifted off to a place where normally there was naught but sunshine and bubbling creeks and flower-filled fields—her special hideaway of happy endings.

But this time there was only darkness and fog. *Icy* fog. It pierced her nightgown and snaked around her body until she shivered uncontrollably. She hugged herself, touching moisture, drawing her gaze down. Blood stained the bottom half of her nightgown and dripped onto the cold ground. *So much blood. No! Help! Someone, help!* She dashed forward through the mist, shoving it aside as she went. It only grew thicker and colder, surrounding her like a death shroud.

She was in hell. That must be it. She darted forward. Her bare foot struck a rock, and she stumbled and fell to the hard dirt. Pain sped through her toes and ankle. Fog parted, the ground shook, and a large oval stone rose from the dirt. Words formed on it. *Beloved Cassia.* Clutching her stomach, Charity bent over and wept. *No! No! No!* Other tombstones rose around her. A mound of fresh dirt formed before one of them. Words written by an invisible hand scrolled across the hard stone.

*Lord Herbert Villemont*
*Man of God. Man of honor.*
*Born Sixteen-hundred eighty-five*
*Laid to rest in the Year of our Lord,*
*Seventeen-hundred eighteen*
*Murdered by his vicious wife.*

"It was an accident! It was an accident!"

The dirt shifted, lifted and rose as if pushed from beneath. Charles Villemont's face formed in the dirt. His mouth opened. "I'll find you and hang you!"

Charity leapt from the cot and landed on the floor with a thud. *The floor*—the deck of a ship. The creak and whine and gush of water confirming it. She remained there, palms on the stained wood, taking deep breaths to calm her thrashing heart. Just a dream. They were coming more frequent now, more terrifying. Would they eventually drive her completely mad and she'd be imprisoned in one of those gruesome asylums?

Struggling to rise, Charity lit a lantern with a trembling hand. Nay. She would not allow Lord Villemont to have the last word, to finish the torture he started. She'd rather die.

Panic forced her gaze down to her chemise. No blood. Pressing a hand on her rounded belly, she breathed a heavy sigh. "You are safe, precious one." A tear slid down her cheek. Wiping it away, she glanced out the porthole. Still dark. Hugging herself, she leaned against the bulkhead, unable to stop her body from shaking. She needed air. She needed to get out of this tiny cabin where memories seemed free to torment her.

Quickly dressing, she made her way above to stand at the railing. One sailor manned the wheel, while two others stood watch. None of them paid her any mind. Good. Gusts of salty wind blasted over her as the ship rose and plunged over inky swell after inky swell—unusually large swells which forced her to keep a tight grip on the rail and her shoes firm on the deck. A quarter moon frowned down at her, casting diamonds upon the black sea...out of her reach...always out of her reach, taunting her with light and happiness that would never be hers.

Was Charles still following them? Darkness denied her the answer. Mayhap 'twas seeing his ship that had caused her nightmare. She'd recognized those unique orange sails from the tour he'd given her and Lord Villemont of the vessel just after their wedding. Charles was always investing in one thing or another, and the merchantman had been one of his new enterprises.

But if it really was him and Elias was in his employ, why hadn't he hailed him? Why hadn't he brought the *Restoration* to a halt and allowed Charles to board? It made no sense. Mayhap she'd been wrong. But what other motive could he have for his kindness?

A curse drifted down from above, and she peered up into the few sails that were unfurled in the heavy winds. *Wait.* Someone was up there. She spotted the outline of a man moving among the shadows. A cloud parted and a blink of moonlight shone on the main topmast. *Nelson.* At least it looked like Nelson. But what was he doing in the yards by himself at night? The fore-watchman must have heard him too, for he glanced aloft, but a cloud stole the light and Nelson was gone.

Returning her gaze to the sea, Charity braced herself as another blast of wind tossed her unbound hair behind her.

"Good evening, Miss Westcott." The voice was soft, so as not to startle, but with the characteristic depth and strength of Elias.

Vapors, but she wasn't quite ready to face him yet.

His hand appeared on the railing beside hers. Twice the size of hers and all blistered and rough.

"What brings you above at such an hour?" he asked.

"I couldn't sleep."

"Another nightmare?"

A spear of moonlight revealed the cut of his strong jaw and his lips...those lips...

She looked away.

He leaned on the railing and smiled. "You had them when we were married."

She laughed. It felt good. "Don't allow the crew to hear you, or 'twill seal the ruin of my already dubious reputation."

"Yet if we *were* married, there'd be no need for worry."

Shock buzzed through her. Was he asking for her hand? "Yet, we are *not* married, Sir." She snapped her gaze to his, but it landed on his lips again. *Vapors!*

He must have noticed, for he grew serious and glanced out to sea. "Please forgive me for taking advantage of you the other night. If you'll allow a personal admission, I have a weakness for beautiful women."

She huffed. "The curse of most men, I would think."

"Indeed, but my weakness came at a great cost to me and my family."

"This illusive past of yours, Captain? I cannot imagine it."

"That pleases me, for I am a new man now. Thank God, He is in the business of not only forgiveness but restoration."

*Ah, of course...the name of his ship.*

Charity frowned. Perhaps God restored others. Just not her. "Yet this new man kissed me without an understanding." She teased.

"I didn't say I was perfect." His grin lowered. "You are a chaste lady under my protection, and I took advantage of you."

*Chaste?* She held back laughter even as she wondered at his sincerity. Yet naught but honesty shone from his expression as he stared out to sea, the wind whipping his hair behind him, his shoulders stiff, jaw tight as if he bore the burdens of the world. The man baffled her. Was he friend or foe?

"Something concerns you, Captain?"

"Yes, my sister's welfare."

The ship bucked, and she gripped the railing tighter. "That trouble you spoke of with the family business."

"'Tis much more than that. But we shall be there soon."

She wanted to ask more, but he kept staring into the darkness. "Do you seek the ship that followed us today?"

He looked at her curiously. "Nay. However, you seemed overly interested in it earlier. Does it concern you?"

Perhaps 'twas the strong wind singing through the rigging, the concert of rushing water and creaking wood, that created an enchanted atmosphere that made her want to tell him, to confide in this man who seemed to have the answers for everything.

"I fear 'tis my fiancé's brother." She gauged his response, waiting for guilt to line his face.

But, instead, he seemed shocked. "Bah! The man would travel so far, at such danger and cost? What does he hope to accomplish? He can't drag you back to England against your will. He can't force you to marry his brother. It makes no sense."

"You don't know him. His family is powerful. They are worth a fortune and bear a title as well. And a mere admiral's daughter has brought irreparable shame to their name. So, yes, he can very well kidnap me and bring me home. Kidnapping me was quite easy for you, was it not?"

He frowned. "I was trying to protect you."

"As he is trying to protect his family."

The ship galloped over a wave. He pressed a hand to her back to steady her as a salty mist showered over them. "Be that as it may, it seems a bit extreme. What does he plan to do with you back in England?"

She thought to move from beneath his touch, but the strength and comfort radiating over her back kept her in place. "No doubt convince me of my error. Purchase my devotion with trinkets and baubles."

"And can your devotion be bought?"

At one time, long ago, her answer would have been yes. Now, she was not so foolish. "Nay. I care not for such things."

This seemed to please him immensely. "What a brave lady you are, Miss Westcott. Yet one thing still confuses me. Why did you not run to the protection of your ward? Or your family before they left?"

Charity bit her lip, chastising herself for opening the door to this conversation. "Things grew worse after my family left." That much was true. "And my ward, my Aunt Bernice, being in her dotage and possessing little wealth and no placement in society, couldn't protect me against such a well-positioned family and their threats." It would have been true, if she *had* an Aunt Bernice.

"Threats?" Elias rubbed the back of his neck. "Over a broken engagement? I've never heard of such a perverted obsession."

Charity groaned inwardly. What to do...what to do...to get herself out of this tangled web of lies? She raised her chin. "Engagements, as you know, Sir, are taken quite seriously, almost as binding as a marriage itself."

"Indeed. But people *do* break them on occasion. 'Tis not worthy of being hunted like a criminal."

"As I said, you don't know my fiancé's family." The ship rose over a wave, and Charity took the opportunity to release the railing and stumble backward in hopes of diverting the conversation.

Elias caught her in his arms. "I'm sorry this happened to you, Miss Westcott."

She knew from his tone he meant it. His eyes met hers as he gently placed her hands back on the railing, covering them with his own. And she found she couldn't look away from the care burning within them. Wind tossed hair into his face, and he snapped it away. "Until I deliver you safely to your father, I hope you'll consider me your protector."

Overcome with an emotion she'd rather not name, she faced the sea. "'Tis hardly proper, Captain. I'm already risking enough of my reputation. Besides—"

"I know, I know, you don't want my protection. Another thing I lo—admire about you. Your independence."

Charity could have sworn he'd almost said loved. But that couldn't be. Nor did she want it to be. *No! No! No! Charity, don't be stupid. Don't fall for another man's lies.*

No matter how handsome and kind and honorable he seemed. No matter that he made her feel safe—something she hadn't felt in a very long time.

But it was all a delusion.

Her plan to be friendly with Elias appeared to be backfiring, allowing traitorous feelings to form that were anything but good for her safety. And her sanity.

Wind struck them, swishing past her ears so loud, she couldn't hear anything. The ship leapt in the air, then dropped, and Elias gripped her elbow and leaned toward her.

"Never fear, Miss Westcott. 'Tis but a small storm. On our present course, it will pass us by."

But it didn't pass them by. Nor was it small. More than once during the night, Charity was nearly tossed from her cot as wind and wave pounded against the hull and thunder shook the ship.

At dawn, a crewman tossed her ropes and ordered her to tie herself to her cot. But, instead, she went above, wanting to determine the extent of the storm for herself and hoping beyond hope they'd lost Charles among the waves.

But upon seeing the massive foam-crested swells curling above the ship, the black cauldron of swirling clouds, and white-hot forks of lightning scouring the sky, she realized she might lose more than Charles.

She might lose her life.

# Chapter 16

Elias' mind and heart were still reeling from his pleasant conversation with Charity when Josiah nudged him from his semi-sleep haze. "Cap'n, the storm worsen, and we can't raise storm and stunsails. You're needed above."

That's when Elias noticed it wasn't just his mind that was reeling, but the entire brig as well. "Confound it all!" He sprang from his bed. "I'll be up in a minute."

Water dripped from Josiah's floppy hat as he shoved it on his head and darted off.

Elias all but leapt into his breeches, flung a shirt over his head, and donned his oil-slicked coat. Grabbing a rope from his trunk, he lifted a quick prayer for safety, then marched down the companionway, halting at Miss Westcott's cabin with the intent of ordering her to tie herself to her cot. But when he swung open the door, she was gone.

Of course.

He found the brave woman above decks, gripping the capstan, with Josiah hovering over her.

Wind punched Elias. He stumbled to the side as the brig yawed to port. Rain flung pellets at him from dark skies, stinging his skin. Bracing on the slanted deck, he charged toward Charity.

"Get below, Miss Westcott. That's an order!"

Josiah wiped water from his eyes. "I been tellin' her the same thing, but she won't move."

Clinging to the capstan, her knuckles white, strands of saturated hair flailing about her face, she gazed up at him with terror-streaked eyes. He desperately wanted to take her in his arms, reassure her all would be well. But he hadn't time for her defiance.

"Hank, Ross!" He shouted to two passing sailors. "Take the woman below and tie her to her cot!" Then spinning on his heels, Elias made for the quarterdeck, Josiah on his heels, thankful the wind drowned out the woman's protests.

Thunder exploded, shaking the brig, and Elias glanced aloft. "Report!" he shouted at Josiah over the din of the storm. "Wait. Why are the topgallants still up and the yards and masts on the fore? By all that is holy, what have you been doing?" He retreated across the main deck toward Nelson, who stared up at the sails as if he were seeing a ghost.

"Nelson, haul in foretopsails, lower topgallant yards, strike the mast! Up stunsail! Now!"

Josiah appeared beside him. "Somethin's wrong wit' the foretop rigging, Cap'n. We lost control of the foresails and yards."

"Wrong? What the devil do you mean, *wrong*?"

A wave crashed over them, nearly sweeping Elias off his feet. Water cascaded off Nelson's hat and coat, but he remained staring aloft. For the love of … Elias followed his gaze to men precariously balancing on yards and in shrouds.

"Gedding is up there inspectin' it now," Josiah shouted over the wind.

Thunder roared again, and the brig pitched to starboard, thrusting the port railing toward the sky. All three men lost their footing in a mad rush of seawater, tumbling uncontrollably over the deck. Elias dragged his hands over the sodden wood, seeking anything to grab onto. Seawater flooded his mouth. Lightning flickered gray over the morbid scene. And just when he thought he'd be swept out to sea, the brig leveled. Reaching up, he grabbed the railing and hauled himself to stand, breath heaving, and water dripping from his clothes. A quick account of the deck revealed Josiah and Nelson were still on board.

Despite nearly being tossed into the raging sea, the storm wasn't the worst he'd encountered. Far from it. If he could raise and lower the appropriate sails, the *Restoration* would be able to lie to and survive the storm without being sent too far off course. But without control over the foresails, the brig could broach and capsize.

"Nelson!" He shouted for the bosun, and this time the rain-soaked man looked his way. "Lower main topgallant and topsail."

"Mr. Ballard," he shouted up to the helm. "Hold her four points to the wind!"

"Aye, aye, Captain!"

"With me." Elias gestured for Josiah to follow him below.

Back in his cabin, hair dripping over a chart and bottles and pens tumbling over the map, he found what he was looking for. "There. We'll seek shelter on that island. 'Tis close, and if I remember, it has a natural harbor."

"Aye, Cap'n. We been there before."

"When the storm passes, we'll fix our rigging and be on our way." *Scads!* He raked back his wet hair. Of all the luck. 'Twould seem something or *someone* seemed determined to keep him from saving his sister.

The brig seesawed, and Josiah gripped the desk for support, his dark eyes meeting Elias', missing the usual peaceful assurance that followed the large Negro around.

Gedding burst into the room, carrying a bundle of frayed lines in his hands. "Cap'n. The rigging. Someone cut straight through it."

The ship shot into the air like sparks from a fire. Tightening her grip on the table, Charity's legs and arms burned from trying to avoid being tossed around the cabin like a sack of grain. The table and cot were the only two things bolted down, and she took turns clinging to one or the other.

The men who had dragged her here on the captain's orders had given her a rope with which to tie herself to something solid, but she didn't want to be trapped should the ship capsize. *God forbid.* Alarm zipped through her at the thought of water gushing through the doorway so hard she wouldn't be able to escape. Though it would be a fitting punishment for her crime. A wave pounded on the porthole as lightning painted everything in morbid gray. Charity pressed a shaky hand on her belly. Not a fitting punishment for her baby. An innocent who had committed no sin.

The storm roared, hammering the hull with watery fists. Charity lost her grip and tumbled over the deck. Her head hit the bulkhead just as the floor tilted the other way, shoving her into the cot.

Enough! 'Twas as if Lord Villemont had resurrected in the form of a storm, intent on beating her to death from the grave. She would not allow it. She'd rather face him above with sea and wind than remain helpless in this tiny prison.

Grabbing her rope, she stumbled out the door, and struck the hall bulkhead. *Hard.* Dazed, she managed to climb the ladder up to the main deck, only losing her grip on the rungs twice.

Elias, Josiah, and Mr. Ballard stood on the quarterdeck, lashed by ropes to railings and binnacle, eyes on storm and sails, and shouting orders to a crew doing their best to keep the ship afloat.

Yet the storm seemed no worse than when she'd been on deck before. In fact, it seemed to have quieted a bit. She started for the capstan, arms raised at her side for balance, when something fell from the sky.

*Splat!* A man landed on the deck nigh two feet in front of her. *The young lad, Eddy!* Blood pooled beneath him, instantly washed away by rain and wave.

Charity screamed.

She didn't know how Elias got to her so fast, but his arms engulfed her and forced her back from the horrific sight.

"'Tis Eddy! Eddy!" She freed herself from his grip and darted for the young man, falling to her knees before him.

Water soaked through her skirts. Thunder pounded the sky with its displeasure.

"Hicks! Ross! Bring him below." Elias shouted, prying Charity up. "And find Gage!"

The men hoisted Eddy by his feet and hands and carried him below. A wave slammed over the deck, wiping away his blood as if it had never happened.

Still gripping her, Elias spouted orders and chastised the men, in particular Nelson. "Why wasn't he lashed to the mast?"

Nelson shook his head, his eyes hollow, water streaming down his face

The men returned from below. "Cap'n, Gage be in no condition t' help Eddy."

She felt Elias stiffen against her. Wind whipped hair in her face. Lightning flashed silver spikes across the charcoal sky as the deck raised on one end. Grabbing the capstan with one hand, Elias tightened his grip on her with the other.

Josiah charged toward the bow where sailors struggled with tangled lines. Mr. Ballard shouted from the wheel. "Captain, where do I point her?"

"I'll help him." Charity turned to look up at Elias, his face just inches from hers. Water beaded on his lashes and matted his hair to his head. She could see the conflict in his eyes. "Allow me to do *something*."

"Do you know doctoring?" he shouted above the wind.

"A bit." What was one lie among so many? Besides, she'd doctored herself plenty.

He nodded and released her to one of his men.

Charity regretted her decision the minute she stepped onto the gun deck and was led to a far corner where a lantern oscillated above Eddy's still form lying atop a table. Blood trickled beneath his head and dripped onto the floor, while Gage stood staring at his friend with a look of sheer panic on his face.

The sailor who'd escorted her, a Mr. Ross, gripped the surgeon's shoulders. "Mr. Gage. Mr. Gage! The lady's here t' help."

Gage slowly lifted his eyes to her, blinked a couple of times as if he weren't sure what he was seeing, then stared back at Eddy.

Charity rolled up her sleeves. She'd seen blood before. Lots of it. Mostly her own. "I'll need clean rags, water, if you have any, rum, and Mr. Gage's surgery bag."

Relief lifted the man's expression as he nodded and sped off.

The ship jerked. The deck tilted, and Mr. Gage stumbled. Charity blocked his fall with her body, and was rewarded with a cloud of alcohol that stole her breath. She shoved him to stand. "Mr. Gage. You must sober up and help Eddy. Please tell me what to do."

The sailor returned, arms loaded with a black bag, cloths, and a pitcher from which water sloshed over the rim. His nervous gaze landed on Eddy. "He didn't fall from too high. He's goin' to be okay, ain't he, doc?"

Gage didn't answer.

Gripping the surgeon, Charity shook him. "What do I do, Mr. Gage?"

He rubbed his eyes, then blinked as if trying to focus. "Press rags over the wound on his head. Hard."

Grabbing the clean cloths from Ross, Charity circled the table and nearly slipped in a pool of blood. "Help me turn him on his side."

Placing the other items on a chair, Ross took Eddy's shoulder, lifted him, and positioned him on his right side where they could get a clear view of the wound.

Blood oozed from a matted patch of hair on the back of his head. Gulping down nausea, Charity covered it with rags and held them as firmly as she could.

The ship bucked, and Gage wobbled and plopped into a chair against the bulkhead, dropping his head into his hands.

Blood soaked through the rags. Terror soaked through Charity.

"Now what, Doctor?" she shouted. "Sober up. We need you!"

Gage struggled to rise. "I must examine the wound." Teetering around the table, he leaned toward Eddy as Charity removed the blood-soaked rags.

"Can't see if the skull is injured. But we must stitch the wound." He held his hands before him, trembling as much as the ship around them. "You're going to have to do it, Miss."

"Me?" Charity's heart cinched. "I can't."

"You'll have to, Missss Westcott." He slurred out the words, his eyes flitting over her as if he couldn't quite see where she was.

She snapped her gaze back to Eddy. "Will he live?"

"Not if we don't close that wound."

"We?" Charity huffed.

"I can help." Ross approached with more rags.

Charity took them and covered the wound again. "Find a needle and twine in Gage's bag. And rum." He handed her a bottle. Uncorking it, she poured it over the wound, then onto the rag, her mind numb, her heart tight, and her breath coming hard.

She could hear Gage instructing Ross how to thread the needle, his voice uneasy and distant, but all she could see was the inch long gash on the back of Eddy's head and the blood bubbling from it like a fountain.

What in God's name was she doing? The room spun, and she closed her eyes for a moment. She was going to be sick.

The ship veered again, the deck slanted, and waves thundered against the hull. But from the sound of the water, it seemed they were slowing. She hoped that was a good sign.

Ross handed her the needle. She turned to ask Gage how to proceed, but the surgeon stumbled to the corner and emptied his stomach. Bile rose in her throat as she exchanged a glance of terror with Ross.

"Hold the lantern for me, will you?"

He nodded, eyes wide, and sweat dotting his forehead.

Charity bit her lip. How hard could it be? Just like sewing a quilt, right? *While sitting atop a galloping horse.* Except this was human flesh. And a life that depended on her.

Holding that flesh together, she slid the needle through.

Ross' eyes rolled back in his head, and he wilted before her eyes. Charity grabbed the lantern before he toppled to the deck. Beyond him, Mr. Gage was still heaving in the corner.

Setting the lantern on the table, Charity took a deep breath, along with a minute to gather herself.

She had to do this and do it well, or Eddy would die.

"Let go the anchor!" Elias shouted, and Josiah repeated the order, adding specifics for the anchor crew. Despite heavy wind and high seas *and torn rigging,* Elias had found the island and navigated the ship into its small harbor. They'd be safe until the storm passed, at which time they could effect repairs.

Too busy preventing the ship from capsizing, he'd had no time to consider who would have sabotaged the rigging and why. Now, as the wind lessened and brig settled into a rocking motion instead of seesawing, his fury rose.

But before he took action, he must check on Eddy.

Leaving Josiah in command, Elias leapt down a hatch, scrambled down a ladder to the gun room, and followed lantern light to a sight he'd never expected to see.

Ross and Gage slumped on the deck and Miss Charity Westcott stitching a hole in Eddy's head.

All by herself.

Her hair had dried into honeyed corkscrews tumbling to her waist, blood stained her gown, and she bit her bottom lip as her eyes remained intent on her task. Elias could only stand there, dripping on the deck, not wanting to disturb her, admiration burgeoning at the lady's courage.

Finally, she slid the final loop through, knotted the twine, cut it with a knife, and placed a clean rag over the wound.

Releasing a breath, her shoulders slumped, and she started to sink to the ground. In two steps, Elias caught her by the waist and led her to sit on a barrel. She stared up at him, numbly. "I didn't hear you come in."

"You stitched Eddy up."

She stared off into space. "As you can see, I was the only one who could."

Circling the table, Elias examined the wound, smiled at the haphazard stitches, then began mopping the blood on the table. "Excellent work. It will hold."

"Will it?" She lifted droopy eyes to his. "I hope so. My first."

"I see Ross was of no use." He thumbed toward the man lying in a heap on the deck.

"He tried." She attempted a smile. "The storm?"

"We are safe, anchored near an island."

Gage moaned from the corner and started to rise.

Elias thought to help him but changed his mind. "Besotted clodpole."

"I'm sorry," Gage muttered and wiped his mouth. "How is he?" He staggered to the table and gripped the edges.

Charity also stood. "The bleeding is stopped and the wound is stitched, though I'm not sure I did it right." She dipped a clean rag in water and laid it on Eddy's forehead. "Why isn't he awake?"

Gage stared at his friend then hung his head, his expression folding in agony. "He may never wake." Despair broke his voice. "Only time will tell. He's concussed from the fall. There's no way to know how much damage his brain endured."

Elias wanted to throttle the man for his intemperance, for putting young Eddy at risk, but from the look in Gage's eyes, he knew the man was already suffering his just dues.

"We will pray for him. You, me, and Miss Westcott," Elias said, noting the upsweep of Charity's brow.

"I don't pray anymore," she mumbled.

"It doesn't matter." Withdrawing his wooden cross from beneath his shirt, Elias bowed his head and offered a simple prayer for complete healing and protection for Eddy, at the end of which both Gage and Miss Westcott added, "Amen."

Now, Eddy was in the best hands of all—God's.

Assured that Eddy would be properly attended, Charity went back to her cabin, more exhausted than she ever remembered being. The wind still howled through the rigging, the rain still tapped on the deck, and the waves still slapped the hull, but to a much lesser degree. Relief swept through her that they were near land and safe from the storm. Too tired to undress, she fell onto her cot and thought of Elias' prayer for Eddy's healing. She'd never heard the likes of such a prayer. Did God even heal today? Yet Elias' words and tone were full of confidence that God not only did, but that He delighted in doing so.

She rubbed her temples where a headache formed. The odor of sweat and blood and Gage's vomit rose to bite her nose. Oh, how she longed for a bath. And a new gown. For now, she longed for sleep. But it remained elusive—just out of her reach, as usual. Instead, her thoughts filled with blood and Lord Villemont and lost babies, and she left her bed before the nightmares possessed her.

Wind wailed a mournful song through the rigging above, sending a chill through her. She didn't want to be alone. Not tonight. Slipping out her door, she crept down the companionway, hoping to find Elias awake. A strip of lantern light shimmered from beneath his door. She smiled. The irony of her seeking out a man's company was not lost on her. In truth, it nearly sent her rushing back to her cabin. But then voices reached her, and she eased beside the door that was slightly ajar.

"I was much like you, Gage," Elias said.

"I can't hardly credit it, Captain."

"'Tis true. I wasted two years of my life in the bottom of a bottle."

From Gage's silence, Charity assumed he was as shocked as she.

"'Tis the devil's trap, this vile brew," Elias continued. "Lured in by a promise of escape from troubles, false confidence, and fleeting euphoria, a man soon finds himself adrift on a fool's sea with nary a paddle to reach land."

"I can't stop," Gage breathed out with a moan. "It takes away the pain."

"Does it truly? Or doesn't it make it worse in the end?"

Gage chuckled. "Indeed. Until I have another drink."

Silence, save for the creak of wood and the song of wind settled on them before Gage continued. "I've had everything most men crave, family, wealth, opportunity, and I've squandered them all away. Shamed my family."

"As did I. But 'tis not too late, my friend," Elias said.

"I nearly killed him." Gage's voice cracked. "Poor Eddy."

"Perhaps, but God sent Miss Westcott to your rescue." Not a hint of sarcasm tainted Elias' voice.

God sent *her*? She nearly laughed.

"But what about next time?" Gage groaned. "I don't believe I will be able to resist a drink."

"You can't on your own strength. But God can help you. Turn to Him. He helped me, and He will help you as well."

Turning, Charity made her way back to her cabin. She didn't want to hear that God helped people, that He gave them strength to endure temptation, strength to overcome trials. For He had never done that for her.

Angry at herself for seeking out Elias, she slammed her cabin door shut.

She had no need of anyone. Not Elias. And certainly not his God.

# Chapter 17

Against her will—yet again—Elias lifted Charity into his arms from the boat and waded through the water to shore. Once he set her down, she thanked him and started down the beach, stumbling as her legs grew accustomed to solid land.

"Don't wander far, Miss Westcott." Was all he said, and she was glad she couldn't see the expression on his face, which she was sure was one of kindness. She was also glad he didn't force her to stay and converse with him, for the man had appeared on deck that morning looking like a pirate god with his black leather breeches and waistcoat and wild hair blowing in the wind—a man that was anything but a mealy-mouthed preacher. He'd saved a ship from pirates, rescued her from hanging, and now had brought his entire crew safely through a storm. Was there nothing he couldn't do? As if that weren't enough, he seemed to really care about others, extending mercy to those who didn't deserve it.

Like Gage.

*Land!* She focused her thoughts elsewhere. How wonderful to be walking on something that wasn't constantly heaving. Despite her wobbling legs, she made her way down shore, dismayed when Mr. Ballard appeared at her side.

Vapors, but the man wouldn't leave her alone. Just that morning, he'd come by her cabin with an old gown he'd found stuffed in a chest in the hold. Though he apologized for the base-born fabric and style, Charity was more than happy to rid herself of her bloodstained skirts. Even if she *did* look like a scullery maid. 'Twas kind of the man, and she found naught to dissuade her from his obvious advances. Two years prior, she would have welcomed interest from a man with such a vast estate, gentlemanly manners, and noble blood—albeit distant noble blood. But she was not the same innocent she once was. Her zeal for wealth, title, and escape from her father's house had cost her dearly.

Besides, Mr. Ballard's presence and pleasant conversation left her cold. So unlike Elias. Which made the preacher a danger to her. She glanced at him and found his glare locked on her and Mr. Ballard. Best to keep the captain at a safe distance, and what better way than to entertain Mr. Ballard?

"May I accompany you down shore, Miss Westcott?" He loosened his cravat and smiled.

"By all means, Mr. Ballard. By all means."

But she didn't miss the spiteful glance he cast over his shoulder toward Elias.

Grumbling to himself, Nelson plunged into the jungle in search of firewood. What a numbhead he was. As soon as he'd seen Lord Villemont's ship, he'd had come up with the plan to hack through the rigging—secretly of course—in an attempt to slow the *Restoration* down and hinder her steering. That way Villemont had a better chance to overtake them.

He slapped a mosquito on his arm and picked up a piece of wood. The sooner Nelson handed Miss Westcott over to Villemont, the sooner he'd have his reward. And the sooner he could get off this preacher's brig, invest in land somewhere, and never take another order from no one.

But he hadn't counted on the storm hitting them straight on. Devil's blood! He'd almost cost them all their lives. He had to be more careful from here on out. More cunning, smarter. Patient. Not one of his best qualities. After all, he'd left word in Kingston that they were heading to Barbados.

Once they landed, if Captain Dutton took the lady to his sister's home, Nelson only needed to meet up with Villemont and lead him there. Problem was, he didn't know the sister's married name nor the location of the estate. But he knew just who would disclose such information.

He picked up another chunk of wood and smiled. Serves that preacher right for falling for a murderess! Lud! Soon she'll be swinging from a gibbet and ole Nelson will be counting his coins.

No wonder the Scriptures say that jealousy is as cruel as the grave. Elias fisted his hands and stared after Ballard and Miss Westcott.

"Most of the men are ashore, Cap'n," Josiah stepped beside him. "Wit' enough supplies to last the night. 'Cept those repairin' the riggin'."

"Thank you, Josiah." Elias tore his gaze from Charity and glanced at the *Restoration* bobbing in the turquoise waters of the tiny inlet. What a masterful vessel. He rarely got such a view of her as the rising sun warmed her with a blanket of gold. Nearly surrounding the brig, palms and ficus sprang from creamy sands and waved in the strong breeze left over from yesterday's squall. Sodden sand and the drip-drop of water from leaves in the jungle behind him provided further evidence of the storm's passing.

To his left, Gage and a few sailors were erecting a shelter of bamboo and palm leaves over Eddy, who, thanks be to God, was breathing steady now. Though he hadn't yet woken.

"What you gonna do about the torn riggin'?"

"Seems we have a traitor on board. Though I can't imagine why anyone would put the brig at risk."

Josiah only grunted.

Elias eyed him. "Are we of the same mind?"

The black man shrugged. "He's the only new crew member."

*Nelson.* Elias glanced down shore where he'd seen the man disappear. Leaves parted and he reappeared with an armload of wood, oddly casting a sideways glance at Charity before proceeding toward camp. "If it *was* him, I can't figure out his motive." A breeze whirled around them, stirring sand at their feet and causing palm fronds to sing.

"Post extra guards on the brig tonight," Elias said. "We can't afford for this to happen again. And, blast it all!" He shifted his boots in the sand. "I need those repairs done quickly. I fear each day puts my sister in more danger."

"Aye, Cap'n. And I'll keep a weather eye on Nelson just in case."

Elias released a sigh and crossed arms over his chest, unaware he was staring at Charity and Ballard again until Josiah said, "The lady has a hold on you."

"Aye. Nay." Elias snorted. "I don't know. One minute she's kind and engaging, the next she makes it quite clear she loathes that I'm a preacher, that I don't drink, and as far as I can tell, that I want to protect her." *Baffling woman.* "Now she seems quite taken with Mr. Ballard." He glanced their way again. "Bah! Where did he find that gown?" More importantly, why hadn't Elias thought to search for one in the hold? Regardless, he never thought any woman could be so stunning in such common attire—simple homespun that only enhanced her natural beauty.

Josiah chuckled. "Why, I never thought I'd see you jealous, Cap'n."

"I don't think I've ever been." Elias smiled. "The woman drives me mad."

"Perhaps a good kind o' mad, Cap'n?" Morning sun beamed off Josiah's white teeth and twinkled in his eye.

Elias chuckled. "She certainly intrigues me. But after what happened with Rachel, I must find a woman who'll make my family proud."

"There are many Godly women who'll make your family proud."

"Aye, I've met quite a few. But none who heat my blood like this one."

"Ah. It's passion you want."

Elias glanced at his friend. "Is that so wrong?"

"No. God created it for our pleasure. Wit'in boundaries o' course." Josiah closed his eyes to the warming sun. "But this lady... are you sure, Cap'n? She don't seem too Godly to me."

Elias glanced her way again. "Something happened to her to make her turn away from Him. She won't say. But at least I know she's not lying to me about her faith." Lying, he would never tolerate. "In truth, I don't know what to do. I want to help her, but she won't allow me."

"People have to know they need help before they ask for it. God is a gentleman. He never forces hisself on anyone. He just makes the offer and waits 'til they accept. You do the same with Miss Westcott. If it's meant to be, it'll be."

Elias rubbed the back of his neck. "How did you get so wise, my friend?"

"Traveling so many years wit' your father. And more importantly"—he patted his vest pocket—"learning these Holy Words."

Begging off with a need for privacy, Charity finally relieved herself of Mr. Ballard's company. It took him a minute to fully understand her meaning, but he finally sped off, sporting a blush.

Pushing aside leaves the size of men's hips, she entered another world...one so different from anything she'd seen back home. Lush green plants and vines of all shapes and sizes—quite large by comparison with England's flora—surrounded her in a maze as tightly wound as a ball of yarn. Birds in every imaginable color flitted from branch to branch above her, singing happy tunes. The ground was soft and mushy, and the air was saturated with the scent of earthy loam and life. She drew in a deep breath and inched forward, digging through greenery.

One glance over her shoulder told her Elias remained in deep conversation with Josiah while the rest of the crew set up camp or picked fruit from trees. Elias had informed her that, for her safety and propriety, she'd have to return to the ship to sleep. Hence, she wanted to spend as much time as possible free from the confining walls of her cabin.

She didn't plan to go far, perhaps seek out a creek or pond to wash in. All the while exploring this fascinating world. Although, as she passed a rather large lizard with a streak of red on his head staring at her from his perch on a trunk, she wondered if that was a good idea.

As the sun rose higher, perspiration slid down her neck and back. Despite air so thick, it choked her, she relished being alone, away from all the men on the ship and away from the way Elias made her insides twist and turn in a most pleasurable way.

The trickling sound of water drew her to the right. Shoving through foliage, she pushed a final leaf aside and a small creek appeared. A ray of sunshine forced its way through the canopy and lit the water in a ribbon of sparkling silver as it splashed happily over mossy rocks, winding its way through the jungle.

Dropping to her knees, Charity scooped mouthful after mouthful to her lips, until, finally satisfied, she sat back and breathed a huge sigh. What she wouldn't give to strip off her clothes and sit in the creek, though it seemed only a few feet deep at most. But she couldn't be sure someone wouldn't wander by. So, she did her best to splash water over her face and neck, then removed her shoes and stockings and dipped her feet in the swirling brook.

Nothing had ever felt so good. At least not until she unpinned her bun, hiked up her skirts, and dipped her hair in the water. She could almost feel the sweat and salt leech from each strand and float away down the creek. Afterward, she squeezed her hair dry and used her fingers as a comb, chuckling at how far she'd fallen.

From the daughter of a British Admiral to the wife of a viscount to a destitute maid traveling about the Spanish Main—on a preacher's ship, of all things! And bathing in a creek! Without benefit of even a brush or comb. Or mirror! What she must look like. She lowered onto a large rock, fighting back despair. Every single dream she'd ever had as a child had been trampled—over and over until not a spark of life remained. Not only that, but she'd ended up in a far worse situation than when she'd started—her life crushed beyond recognition and shoved so deep in the mud she would never find her way out.

She would ask God why—if she thought He cared.

Her sisters came to mind, and a longing welled within her to see them again. Especially Hope, to whom she owed the greatest of apologies. If her suspicions were correct, something horrible had happened between Hope and Lord Villemont, something unimaginable, something Charity had refused to believe. But now something she realized must be true.

Would it be a happy reunion? Even if her father was there? Or would he—being a man trained to follow rules—berate her and turn her over to the authorities? Could she even risk seeing him? Yet, what choice did she have? She needed money to travel north and start a printing shop—money to care for her and her child until Charity could start making a profit.

Something moved to her right, and she leapt off the boulder. A hairy leg appeared from under a leaf, followed by seven more as a spider as big as her hand skittered across the clearing. Heart pounding, she glanced up where the sun's rays speared the jungle from the west. How long had she been there? *Vapors!* Brushing off her skirts, she started back the way she'd come. She hadn't traveled that far. All she need do is follow the sounds of the waves back to shore.

But there were no sounds of waves. Only the warble and buzz of the jungle. A different warble and buzz than she'd heard before—from different birds and different insects as shadows crept from behind trees with the fading light. After what seemed like an hour, with darkness encroaching and no shore in sight, fear sliced through her.

"Elias!" she shouted. "Elias!" Surely the island wasn't very large, and he would hear her and come running. That's what he loved to do, wasn't it? Rescue her. And though she hated herself for needing him again, she found terror a powerful motivator.

Something large scampered across the trail. Screaming, she darted forward, waving her arms, and ran straight into a jumble of sticky threads. A spider web. Ugg! She screeched and batted the hideous fibers from her face and hair.

A deep guttural growl rumbled through the jungle.

Breath in her throat, she dove into a tangle of greenery, barreling away from the sound, and emerged into a small clearing. She halted and listened for the sound of waves. But all she heard were footsteps, dozens of footsteps. Lights dotted the dark jungle, growing larger. *Thank God.*

"I'm here! Over here!" she shouted.

Ten dark-skinned men wearing nothing but loincloths and brandishing lit torches and spears stepped into the clearing.

# Chapter 18

"**Y**ou let her traipse into the jungle *alone?*" Elias speared a hand through his hair and took up a pace before Ballard. "I assumed you were with her, protecting her." Elias had rowed out to the brig to assist with the repairs and hadn't noticed when Ballard returned to camp. In truth, he'd been so jealous, he'd kept his gaze from wandering down the beach, knowing if he saw Miss Westcott conversing and laughing with Ballard, it would only cause him further distress. Besides, he was focused on the task at hand and especially on keeping an eye on Nelson as he managed the repairs.

Ballard frowned. "She had to use the necessary. What should I have done?"

"Waited for her." Elias growled. "Gone after her when she didn't return."

"I thought … I got distracted searching for fruit with Leggy." The muscles in Ballard's jaw bunched as he gazed toward the jungle where she'd disappeared. "I didn't realize … I didn't know you wanted me to watch over her."

"Of course I—" Elias started to shout, but then halted his pace, along with his tongue. The blame was all his. Charity was under his protection, and he hadn't handed off the responsibility to anyone else.

Josiah groaned. "I shoulda seen her gone, Cap'n." He'd been the first one to notice and promptly shouted from shore until he got Elias' attention.

"'Tis only been a few hours." Ballard plucked his sword from the sand where he'd thrust it earlier. "She might be right around the bend. I'll go check." And off he dashed, kicking up sand as he went.

*Foolish lady.* She had no idea the dangers lurking in these tropical jungles. "Gather a search party," Elias ordered Josiah. "Five men. Tell them to arm themselves and bring water and lanterns."

Within minutes, Ballard returned empty handed and joined the group just as they forged into the jungle, Elias at the lead.

*Dear God, please keep her safe and help me to find her.*

Too terrified to think, to speak, or even breathe, Charity stumbled down the trail, following—or rather, being pulled—by the native in front of her. Rough rope scraped her wrists, paining her with each yank, while the tip of a spear prompted her forward from behind. Branches and leaves slapped her face and neck and tore the cheap fabric of her gown. *Captured by natives!* 'Twas too horrifying to believe. Too horrifying to wrap her mind around. Surely God was punishing her for killing her husband. For taking matters into her own hands when He wouldn't help her during the years she'd cried out to him.

Or mayhap, He just hated her.

Her feet ached, scratches covered her arms beneath torn sleeves, and her heart felt like a frozen chunk in her chest. Elias had no idea where she was, where to look for her, or what happened. Why hadn't he warned her there were natives about? Most likely because she hadn't given him the chance. Most likely because she didn't want to rely on him for anything. Nay, she wanted to rely on herself—the only person she could truly count on. Yet apparently she couldn't be trusted either.

The natives, who'd been silent during the trek, now chattered excitedly, laughing one minute, and arguing the next. They quickened the pace, dragging her along. Her wrists and legs burned. Her feet throbbed. Her mind grew numb with fear. And just when she thought she would faint, flickering lights appeared ahead, and they dragged her into a large clearing. She blinked to clear her spinning vision. A dozen different-sized thatched huts spread along the bed of a creek, while a giant fire pit stood in the center of the clearing, around which several bare-breasted women cooked over iron pots. Torches flickered from atop poles, casting light on the naked children running to and fro as men of all ages greeted the returning party. All eyes locked on Charity. She tried to swallow, but couldn't get past the lump of terror in her throat.

What now? Were they going to ravish her? Marry her off to one of these men? Force her into slavery, or ... God forbid, cook and eat her? She stared at brew bubbling in an iron pot and her heart vaulted. If only she hadn't listened to the horrific tales of cannibalism and torture that had made their way to Portsmouth.

Before she could faint, she was pulled through the village to stand before one of the larger huts. A man emerged who must be the chief due to the number of feathers and shells tied in his long black hair. Only the gray streaking the strands and the lines on his face indicated his age, for he assessed her with youthful eyes filled with a wisdom she didn't expect.

Unfortunately, he seemed pleased with what he saw, for a slow grin overtook his mouth, revealing teeth that had been shaved to points. He questioned the men who'd caught her. Their replies started a rather animated and passionate discussion involving nearly the entire tribe, reminding Charity of the haggling she'd witnessed at street markets on the lower east side of Portsmouth. Only this time, apparently, she was the item being auctioned.

*This can't be happening.* She couldn't breathe. *Inhale...exhale...come on, Charity!* Gagging at the odors of sweat, blood, and a bitter meaty scent filling her lungs, she dove into her song, her safe place...

*The maid was in the garden*
*Hanging out the clothes...*

The men continued to quibble, including a few of the women, who forced their way to the front and pointed at Charity as if she'd committed adultery with their husbands.

Finally, one of the men who'd captured her stepped forward, silenced the mob with a wave of his hand, and proceeded to give a speech that must have made sense to the chief, for he nodded his approval. Which only sent the rest of them into another bout of ardent squabbling.

The chief quieted them down with a shout that surely must have been heard on the other side of the island. The man who'd spoken grabbed Charity and dragged her away as two women chased after him, shouting what surely was obscenities. Dread sank her already deflated stomach as she realized she would either become this man's meal. Or worse.

His wife.

She couldn't feel her arms anymore. Numbness crept across her shoulders and down her back, and she wished it would invade her heart. Why, when no matter how hard she tried, she always ended up under the power of a man? The native pinched her arm tighter, and Charity tugged on his grip and raised her foot to kick him, but he leapt aside and only tightened his grasp. She punched his shoulder. He didn't flinch. She was about to punch it again when he released her arm and grabbed her hair instead.

The women behind them laughed.

Pain spiked her scalp, leaving her powerless to do naught but follow him.

He passed the fire pit. Nay, not his meal. Which meant the alternative. Wrists raw, body aching, heart thundering, Charity closed her eyes.

*They sent for the king's doctor*
*Who sewed it on again*
*He sewed it on so neatly...*

A voice filtered past her song to light upon her last speak of hope—a voice speaking English. Her would-be-husband halted and loosened his grip on her hair. Shouts and footsteps ensued. Charity opened her eyes to see several natives pointing spears at the dark jungle.

The leaves moved and in marched Elias, hands in the air, and a smile on his face.

"Greetings, my friends," Elias said in the Arawak native tongue as he searched the crowd nervously. *There.* There she was. Charity, her hair in the grip of the chief's eldest son, Hadalak, if Elias remembered his name. "I come in the name of my God, Yahweh."

When he'd found the barefooted footprints alongside the mark of woman's small shoe, he'd felt a bit of relief. At least she'd not been bitten by a poisonous frog or gored by a wild boar. However, he also knew what the Arawak did to women prisoners, especially white women, and time was of the utmost importance. His men at his heels, Elias had rushed after them, lifting up an urgent prayer that these particular natives would remember him from his visit last year.

Apparently his prayer was answered as the natives lowered their spears, and Elias found himself instantly assailed by respectful greetings from all around. Bowing men parted the way for him, women reached to touch his clothes, while little children circled around him, laughing and playing.

Leaves shuffled and Elias' men shoved through the foliage behind him, but the Indians paid them no mind as

Elias approached Hadalak and gestured toward Charity. He said something in the Arawak language that essentially meant "this is my woman" to which the man's eyes narrowed and his jaw tightened. Elias stood his ground, not yet looking at Charity, but praying silently for God to reveal His strength through Elias' eyes to this young native.

Releasing her hair, Hadalak backed away and crossed arms over his chest, none too pleased at the turn of events. Only then did Elias face Charity. Her hair a tousled mess, her eyes glazed with shock and terror, she simply stared up at him as if she were seeing a ghost.

"You came," she mumbled out.

Smiling, he took her hand in his, felt her quivering and instead wrapped his arm around her shoulders. When he turned around, the *cacique,* or chief, stood before him, extending his welcome with a subservient bow. Then gesturing for Elias to follow him, he led him to the center of camp and motioned for Elias to take the honored seat beside him on a wooden stool.

Elias gave Charity his most reassuring look, instructing her to sit at his feet as was the custom of the wives of spiritual leaders. Thankfully, she complied without the argument he expected. But then again, surely she was beyond terrified by now. Oh, how he longed to comfort her, but that would have to wait until they were alone. And out of danger. If he knew one thing about these Indians, 'twas that it only took one wrong move, one wrong answer, and their reverent fear of him would dissipate with the balmy breeze. In truth, he couldn't blame them. Most white men had done naught but lie and enslave their people.

The chief's wives surrounded Elias—a good sign—while much to his father's dismay, Sulamet leapt into Elias' lap. The chief chastised his son, but Elias told him all was well. In truth, he was most pleased to see the seven—now eight—year-old lad so healthy and strong. He tickled him, eliciting a giggle, then released him back to his mother as he scanned the mob for any sign of hostility. A few talked amongst themselves, others gazed at him as if waiting for a word of wisdom, some nugget of truth to hold onto, or mayhap a miracle as he had done before. But he was more interested in whether they still followed the Son of God he'd told them about last year—the great Creator's Son who sacrificed His life for them. As he glanced over their eager faces, his spirit quickened. What he wouldn't give to remain with them a week or more to instruct them further and encourage their faith. But he had his sister to think of…and more importantly at the moment, the poor lady huddled beside his leg.

He'd never seen Charity so complacent. *And quiet.* She surveyed the scene beneath lowered lashes, her chest rising and falling, her tremble evident to all. 'Twas shock, to be sure. He must get her back to the ship post-haste. Rising, he drew her up beside him and faced the cacique, intending to offer his apologies for his short stay, when the chief also stood, gestured toward Elias and addressed his people. With every word he spoke, Elias' gut wrenched tighter and tighter.

# Chapter 19

Outside the invisible fortress Charity had erected around herself was the intriguing vision of a native encampment, complete with dark-skinned men and bare-breasted women decorated with shells, feathers, and bones. All of them chattered in an unknown tongue as the fire crackled and spit into the starry sky, and the smell of roast meat and yams and corn sizzled beneath her nose. A moment ago, she'd been about to be ravished by one of the natives, bound once again to an abusive man...powerless, enslaved. Yet now, she had somehow conjured Elias from the jungle. He couldn't be here, of course. That didn't make any sense. Nor did the way the natives almost worshiped him. Nay, more like revered or ... *feared*. But that also was ludicrous. She was probably in the Indian's hut right now, enduring hell. But in her mind, she was next to Elias as he sat on a stone beside the chief, his thick boot shielding her side, his hand gripping hers—a bulwark of strength and protection— chatting away in the natives' language as if he'd been speaking it all his life.

What a wonderful dream! She'd try and stay as long as she could. Or mayhap, if she were lucky, she'd never wake up again.

She *did* wake up, though, when Elias pulled her to her feet and seemed ready to leave. But then the chief said something, and Charity felt Elias stiffen beside her before he lowered her back down. When he finally looked at her, 'twas with blue eyes pouring peace and safety straight into hers, his features melting with concern. "You are safe now, Charity." He gave her hand a squeeze as if to affirm his words. "We must stay awhile, but I'll have you back to the brig in no time."

She could only stare up at him and ask. "How...how are you here?" Before he could answer, a commotion among the Indians drew his attention to his men standing at the edge of the clearing—Josiah, Mr. Ballard, and two more sailors. Ballard's eyes met hers, and he started for her only to be stopped by a fence of spear tips.

"Back to the shore, gentlemen," Elias said. "We will join you there."

"But, Cap'n," Josiah protested, his brow dark and beading with sweat.

"Now." Elias' tone brooked no argument. Grunting, the men disappeared into the greenery.

Charity's fear returned. Now 'twas just Elias against *all* these Indians. Did he know what he was doing?

Yet, as the natives relaxed and everyone in the village settled into an evening of eating, talking among themselves, and listening to every word Elias spoke, she had to admit that he did. He knew precisely what he was doing.

Women worked over the fire, and bowls were passed, along with gourds of water and chunks of some kind of hard bread Charity had never tasted before. *Cassava*, she was told it was called.

Elias handed her a platter of meat and offered her a smile that held such promise, tears burned in her eyes. She took a piece, oddly finding her fear subsiding and her trust rising for this man who waltzed into a camp of savages, speaking their language and commanding their respect.

Hours passed, and although Charity's stomach felt like one of the iron pots over the fire, she forced herself to sample the food, some of which she recognized, some of which she was afraid to ask what it was. She shifted her gaze between the ground by her skirts and Elias, her anchor of strength, her rope of safety among this sea of unknown dangers. He kept a firm grip on her hand and gave it an occasional squeeze, and she resisted the urge to lay her head upon his knee, to feel the warmth and strength therein.

Despite the dozens of eyes she felt raking over her body, she tried to avoid looking at the faces of the Indians and the bare breasts of the women. Heat flushed her at their lack of modesty, but she never once caught Elias staring at them, which is more than she could say of his men before they'd left.

Elias consumed his meal with gusto, conversing with his host and a few others nearby. Women brought their children to him, and he laid hands on each one and prayed for them in their native language, always ending it with the name of Jesus. A word, a Name, she well recognized.

"I don't understand," she asked him when the natives' attention was elsewhere. "Do you know these people? How are they so kind to you?"

"I'm a missionary, remember?" He winked and took a bite of what looked like roasted bat.

The yams in her stomach soured.

"You see that little boy?" He pointed to the child who'd leapt into his lap earlier. "God used me to raise him from the dead last year."

Charity choked on her cassava bread. "What?"

"I came here to preach the gospel, but they had already heard it from other missionaries, men who brought weapons along with Bibles. They intended to roast me alive. Not a pleasant prospect, I assure you,"—he added with a smile—"when the chief's son was bit by a poisonous spider and died. I told them my God could revive him, and they allowed me to pray for him."

"And he came back to life?"

"Does that shock you? Jesus and his disciples brought people back to life."

"But that was only for them, for a short time."

He grinned, firelight twinkling in his eyes. "'Twould seem I've proven otherwise, eh?"

Yet how could she deny it? If it hadn't happened, these people would not be treating him with such reverence. They weren't treating *her* with reverence, or at least looking at her with reverence. That, coupled with an uneasiness she sensed in Elias, caused her dread to return. "How long must we stay?"

"The night."

"Nay." She would not survive a night of such terror. "I couldn't possibly..." Her breath caught. "I—"

"You must," Elias said without looking at her as the chief began speaking to him.

That night began when, after the meal and festivities, one of the natives escorted Elias and Charity to a small hut near the center of the village. Once inside, and with the cloth flap closed, only a sliver of moonlight filtering through a hole in the roof provided any light. Enough to see that one large hammock swung from a post in the center, upon which two blankets laid.

Charity hugged herself.

"Are you all right, Charity?"

He'd never used her Christian name before, and the sound of it on his lips brought her more pleasure than she cared to admit.

"I have no idea."

He moved closer, perhaps to embrace her for comfort. But she couldn't. She wanted to feel his arms around her so desperately. She needed to feel safe, cared for, protected. But to depend on this man would be the worst thing of all. Especially the way her emotions whirled with feelings for him she could no longer deny. She stepped back.

He halted. "I'm sorry we are forced to spend the night together yet again, but their belief that you are my wife is the only thing that saved you."

"Thank you," was all she could manage. Though she owed him much more.

She heard his boots shuffle in the dirt, saw his shadow move, sensed him smiling as he said, "This is the second time in days we've been married. Mayhap God is trying to tell us something?"

His voice teased, and she responded in kind. "Don't get your hopes up, Mr. Dutton."

"Will you at least call me Elias? Since we must share this hammock?"

She swallowed and glanced at the tiny cloth tied between two poles. "The name I will agree to. The hammock, absolutely not."

He shrugged. "Then you and the bugs shall be very happy."

A shiver coursed through her, and she glanced down at the shadowy ground. "Surely a gentleman should offer to sleep on the floor?"

"There are poisonous spiders on this island, my little mermaid. I doubt you'd want to face the Arawak without me in the morning."

The thought crossed her mind that she really didn't want to face much of anything without this man. But she shoved it aside. "I can't believe you risked your life to tell these people the gospel."

"*Preacher.*" He chuckled.

Indeed, but not like any she'd known. Not like any *man* she'd known.

Wind rustled the flap door and brought a swirl of dust into the hut. Elias pushed the animal skin aside and peered outside. "So, Miss Westcott, associating with a preacher definitely has its advantages, no?"

She smiled. "More than I had anticipated." Light from the fire accentuated the strong lines of his face, the stubble on his jaw, and the intensity in his eyes as he surveyed the surroundings. Was he worried for their safety? She hugged herself. "Thank you for coming after me." Though she still could not fathom why.

He closed the flap. "I wish you hadn't wandered off."

"I hadn't planned on it."

"Easy to get lost in these jungles. I should have warned you."

His shadow moved to the hammock and crawled inside. "Join me, Charity. I promise to behave."

She hesitated, a battle raging between emotions and reason, fear and faith, desperate need and overwhelming terror. In the end, she realized if this man intended her harm, he'd had plenty of chances. Besides, she could already hear the bugs skittering across the dirt floor. Moving toward him, she grabbed his hand and awkwardly climbed into the hammock and slid beside him with her back against his chest. Immediately the sides folded in and pressed them together so tight his warmth seeped into her from a body as solid as the ship he sailed upon. Keeping her arms low over her belly—lest he feel the babe growing there—she breathed in the unique scent of him, wood smoke and loamy musk, the effect oddly calming.

She'd never been in a man's arms when she wasn't afraid. She'd never slept so close to a man either. Lord Villemont had always left as soon as he was done with her. Now, as this man, *this preacher*, drew an arm around her like a fortress, a small part of her heart began to soften, to yearn for possibilities...love...safety...a future and a hope.

But that scared her most of all.

The comfortable silence stretching between them—like a couple long accustomed to being in each other's arms—also unnerved her. She must speak, talk, get her mind off the heady sensation of him.

"You didn't seem the least bit afraid marching into this hostile native village," she said. "Nor did you display fear in the storm, nor when facing the pirates. Is there anything you fear, Mr...Elias?"

His answer came swift and serious. "Not protecting those I love."

Not the answer she expected. Several minutes passed in which only the crackle of the fire, distant voices, and the buzz of insects filled the silence.

"I can't sleep," she finally said.

"I admit to having difficulty myself."

"You realize what is left of my reputation is forever ruined."

"Never fear, the Arawak are not prone to spreading rumors." He chuckled.

"Tell me stories, Elias. What of this mysterious past of yours? What events shaped such an enigma of a man?"

"Enigma, is it?" His laughter rumbled through his chest and rippled over her back like a warm wave. "If I tell you, it may disparage your good opinion of me."

She doubted it. "Test me."

He released a heavy sigh and proceeded to tell her what a great childhood he had, raised by Godly parents who were missionaries and privateers like him.

"My father, Rowan Dutton, was a pirate."

Charity smiled. "An evil one?"

"Is there any other kind?"

"That explains your ability to battle at sea."

"Aye, he taught me well."

Amazing. A preacher trained by a pirate. "Pray tell, what turned him from his vile ways?"

"God and my mother, Morgan."

"The lady who paints? She sounds like a remarkable lady."

He laughed again. "You wouldn't believe me if I told you. Let's just say she's a very different lady from a *very* different place."

Charity almost said she'd love to meet her someday, but that would presume things she couldn't afford to be presumed.

Elias shifted, swinging the hammock, and she got the impression he was having as much trouble being close to her as she was him.

"So, is that the extent of your disparaging past? Your father was a pirate." Vapors. God forbid he should ever discover hers.

"If only that were true." He sighed, his warm breath wafting over her neck and causing a tingle down her spine. "Nay, like the prodigal son, I drifted away from the things I knew were right, from God Himself and"—he hesitated, and she sensed a deep sorrow come over him—"I became a pirate for a short time. Two years, in fact."

Astonishment swept through Charity, and she turned slightly and looked up, hoping to see his expression. "I can hardly believe it, *Preacher*."

He must have heard the teasing in her voice for he responded, "You don't find it appalling?"

"Nay. Shocking, exciting, perhaps. But not appalling. Unless you ravished women, of course, or stole from the poor."

"Neither. I did have *some* scruples." He brushed hair from her face, and warmth flooded her at his tender touch. "You are a remarkable woman, Charity."

Her huff of disbelief only caused him to squeeze her tighter. "'Tis true."

Feelings of being worthy of such a man, of being cherished like he was doing now, swelled her heart to near bursting. But his admiration was based on a lie. A lie among many, that if he knew of them would cause him to hate her. "You don't know me, Elias." She tried to push away from him, to put distance between them, but the more she moved, the closer the hammock pressed them together.

"Then enlighten me. Tell me, who is this Charity Westcott?"

She faced away from him and felt the wooden cross he always wore press against her back. A further reminder of the vast difference between them. "I wish to hear more of your tale first."

He rubbed her arm. "Very well. I finally came to my senses, thank God. But I had done so much damage, caused my parents so much pain and worry. I longed to make it up to them. They always wanted to see me as happily married as they were, so I vowed to find a Godly woman they would approve of and marry her." He paused, and she sensed his angst fill the air around them. "Miss Rachel Channing." He spit out her name with both sorrow and spite. "I thought she was someone she was not. She presented herself as a God-fearing, kindhearted, pure lady who loved children and wanted to live her life serving God and others."

*A woman.* Charity should have known. Emotions roiled. One she recognized as jealousy and quickly dismissed. The other...guilt, for what was she presenting herself as to this man?

"Rachel sought after wealth and title," he continued. "She discovered that my great uncle Merrick is the Earl of Clarendon, and assumed since we had connections at Court and holdings in the West Indies that we were wealthy."

"And you are not?"

"Nay."

"Yet you throw away ten pounds on releasing a foolish woman from prison."

She sensed him smile. "Not a waste. What money my family has and what we acquire, we give to those in need."

Charity stared into the darkness, pondering his words. If what he said was true, she'd never met such a man, nor such a family. "What happened to Rachel?"

"We were to be married the next day." He gave a sorrowful laugh. "She not only left me but she stole valuable jewelry from my mother, among which was a ruby heart amulet very important to my father."

*Vapors!* Any woman who turned down this man's proposal was a fluff-headed harpy who hadn't the sense of an ox. Anger seared through Charity toward this woman who had caused Elias so much pain. "I'm so sorry, Elias."

"I should have seen it. She was beautiful, charming, and quite convincing. But in the end, nothing but a liar. I can tolerate many things, but never a lie."

Charity cringed. And she'd been doing naught but offering them to him on a silver platter. Just like Rachel. The thought invoked a sorrow so deep, she felt the pain in her gut. Rachel had broken this strong, honorable man who, by all accounts, was unbreakable.

And Charity was following in her footsteps.

She swallowed a lump of burning regret and thought to leave the hammock at once, remove her vile polluted self from so pure a man before she soiled him with her sin and broke his heart. But she sensed there was more to the story. "Did you get the jewelry back?"

"I did. But at a huge cost."

Charity felt the beat of his heart against her back, his warm breath on her neck, his pain leech through his skin onto her, adding to her own.

Outside, a bird sang a sad tune as if it were listening to the melancholy tale.

Elias pulled out his wooden cross and Charity couldn't help but turn to stare at it as he fingered it in the moonlight.

"My younger sister Caleigh adored Rachel like an older sister. They'd spent hours together choosing fabrics for new gowns and hats from the millinery, making plans for the wedding. When Rachel disappeared with the jewels, Caleigh ran after her. She found her on the ship on which she'd bought passage back to England. In her urgency to hide, Rachel disobeyed the captain and boarded early without permission, and when Caleigh chased her onto the main deck, one of ropes on the pulley broke and a crate fell to the deck. It hit her." He paused, his voice cracking. "She lost her leg."

*Oh, my.* Tears burned behind Charity's eyes as she strained to see his face. "Did she survive?"

"Aye. But what kind of life will she have now?" He rubbed his thumb over the cross. "I made this from that broken crate. 'Tis a constant reminder of my stupidity and gullibility. A reminder to always follow God and to always protect those I love with every ounce of my strength."

Which explained his desperate need to protect Charity. "Surely you can't blame yourself. 'Twas an accident."

"If I hadn't brought the thief home," he ground out with more anger than she'd ever heard from him, "made her one of my family, she never would have stolen the jewels, and my sister never would have been on that ship. Aye, I blame myself completely."

Charity struggled to sit, nearly tipping them over. How could this noble, God-fearing man blame himself? He had no power over that crate falling. But there was Someone who did. Anger raged through her. Groaning, she untangled her legs from the hammock, swung them over the side, and leapt to the floor. "Where was your God?" she shouted, facing him, hands on her hips. "Shouldn't He have protected your sister? Why did He allow such a tragedy to happen to an innocent woman? That's Who you should blame. Not yourself!"

Instantly regretting whatever he said to cause Charity to leave... to cause her so much anger, Elias slid from the hammock and approached her, slowly, as one would a wild tiger.

"God? What had He to do with any of it?" he said softly. "'Twas completely a consequence of my own actions that led to the disaster. Why are people always so quick to blame God for every mishap?"

"Because He has the power to protect us and to change things if He wants. Isn't that what your *precious* Bible says?"

"Indeed, God *is* all powerful, but He gave us free will to make our own choices, good or bad. Suffering the repercussions of our bad decisions is simply part of that."

"Then explain to me why your sister suffers for something that was not her fault?"

Elias could barely make out her shadow lingering against the wall of the hut. But he didn't need to see her expression to realize her fury. He could hear it in her voice, sense it in the air heating between them—a fury directed not at him, but at God Himself.

He took another step toward her, unsure of how to answer.

"What happened to her anyway?" she spat out.

"She is recovered and well. Though I fear she will be a spinster the remainder of her life." Pain twisted his gut at the thought. "No man vies for the hand of a crippled woman."

"How sad." Charity leaned against the hut as if too weak to stand, and Elias longed to take her in his arms. But he remained still, cautious, sensing her need to talk.

"If someone makes a bad choice in ignorance," she said, "and then cries out to God for help, shouldn't He answer? How long does He allow someone to suffer for a mistake they were not even aware they made?"

"Of course God answers prayer. If we are sincerely repentant, He will always turn our errors out for good. Plus, He will provide a way out in time."

To this, she snorted, and he thought he heard a sob escape her lips.

Still, Elias sensed a weakening in her, a chance to discover her past, to help her move beyond the anger and pain. "What happened to you, Charity? Does this mistake concern your fiancé?"

His answer came in the form of a palpable silence, made all the more distinct by the sounds of night birds, insects, and the wind whistling through trees outside the hut.

Pushing from the wall, she strode past him, hugging herself. "He had wealth, title. He provided an escape from my father's house, an entry into society…things I thought I wanted. Things I thought would make me happy."

"He struck you, didn't he?"

Seconds passed as she continued walking, her skirts rustling.

"Yes," she finally said.

Elias raked back his hair, shoving down his anger. "Thank God you didn't marry him."

Again silence, followed by a sorrowful sigh. "He was a God-fearing man, always reading his Bible, attending church. He and the bishop of our diocese were good friends."

Elias flattened his lips, restraining a growl. So that's why she hated preachers. Like so many people, she'd encountered a hypocrite and assumed all men of God were the same. "Your fiancé may have been religious, but that doesn't mean he was God-fearing." *Just like Rachel.*

"He read me many things from the Bible," she continued as if she hadn't heard him. "How women should be submissive, honoring, obedient to their husbands."

"People twist God's words all the time for their selfish needs. Why did you continue the engagement for so long?"

She stopped her pacing, her back to him. "He begged my forgiveness over and over, promised it would never happen again."

"He hit you more than once?" Fury raged through Elias, tightening every muscle, until he felt like punching something. *Or someone.* "Did you not have an escort when you were together? How could he get away with it?"

Coughing, she stepped farther into the shadows on the other side of the hammock. "My aunt...uh...she was often ill, and our only lady's maid had to tend to her needs. We had no butler or footmen, so my fiancé used his own as escorts. Paid by him."

Elias could still not imagine that a servant would tolerate such a thing, no matter how much he was paid. "And you never told the constable?"

"To what end? My further punishment? He and my fiancé were also friends. *Good* friends." Her tone stung with spite.

"Did your aunt know of this?"

"Yes, but what could she do? He threatened to ruin her as well."

Elias rubbed his temples. Something wasn't right. An inconsistency that needled the edges of his reason. A fiancé who beat his intended, servants who looked the other way...and this lady—this independent, stubborn lady—who tolerated it for some unfathomable reason. This man, whoever he was, could not have been *that* powerful. She was holding something back. But what?

*Secrets.* So many secrets. He had another of his own that, in the intimacy growing between them, she deserved to know.

Still hugging herself, she wove around the hammock toward him. "God is punishing me, Elias. I made a mistake, and He's never going to forgive me or offer His help."

"That's not true."

"I prayed and prayed and prayed, but He never answered." Her voice was hollow, wooden, and he thought he saw the glimmer of a tear slide down her cheek in the moonlight.

"Seems He did. For you are safe now, Charity." He reached for her, but she wiped her face and backed away.

"I will not let this man's brother near you," he said.

"That is not up to you."

He wanted to tell her that he'd like it to be, if she allowed it, but he sensed 'twas not the right time. "Mayhap, we should get some sleep." He climbed into the hammock once again and held out his hand, surprised when she allowed him to assist her back beside him.

She nestled against his chest, and he caressed her cheek. "Sleep, my little mermaid."

"I'm not sure I want to," she replied. "For that's when the nightmares come."

Elias ground his teeth together. How could anyone harm such an innocent lady? "He can't touch you here." He squeezed her close, and within minutes, he felt her body relax and heard her breathing deepen.

Yet there was no chance of sleep for Elias. Not with this enchanting woman in his arms, with her sweet smell, her soft skin, and the little whimpers drifting from her lips. Especially not now that he knew so much more about her. Her sad story touched a deep place in his heart, igniting a burning desire to protect her forever.

So, he spent the long hours of the night holding her and praying—praying for her to come back to God, for her fiancé to pay for what he'd done, and for God's peace and joy to fill her. He prayed until he heard someone stoking the fire and rattling pots for breakfast, and dawn slipped golden fingers in between the slats of their hut.

Charity squirmed beside him. His body reacted. Lifting his hand ever so slowly, he stroked her hair and smiled, watching her stir and her eyelids flutter, waving a forest of black against her cheeks.

She pried her eyes open and gazed up at him. Instead of the fear he expected to see, affection glimmered in them, warming him head to toe.

"Good morning, Mr. Dutton," she said.

"Good morning, mermaid. Now that we've spent the night in each other's arms, I should do the right thing and marry you."

# Chapter 20

*Marriage.* Elias' half-taunting proposal flirted with Charity all through the afternoon as they trekked back to shore. It continued its dalliance as they rowed out to the *Restoration*—repaired, with cargo reloaded and ready to go. And even now, it invaded her heart as she stood at the railing, gazing over turquoise waters glistening in the noonday sun. Men raised sails, and soon wind glutted them in a thunderous snap. Trade winds blasted her with warmth and life, and the foamy water gurgled against the hull as they weighed anchor and left the small island for the open seas.

Why didn't the idea of marriage completely and utterly terrorize her? Make her vomit profusely and run as far as she could in the opposite direction? *Because it was marriage to Elias.* This Godly, honorable, caring, self-giving man who seemed almost like a god himself, able to conquer any foe and overcome any problem. Though they'd slept pressed so close together she'd felt his blood pulsing through his veins, he'd made no attempt to take advantage of her, not a single inappropriate touch during the nights they'd spent together. Perhaps he was an angel sent to minister to her as the Bible said angels did, or even possibly…love her. But that would mean God actually cared enough to send one.

She gripped the railing and silently chastised herself. Hadn't she thought the same thing of Lord Villemont? Well, nearly the same thing. Her father had warned her of her starry-eyed dreams more than once. Mayhap she still harbored a bit of that gullible young girl, her head filled with flighty romantic notions. Even after all she'd endured. Yet, hadn't she seen signs, warnings when she and Lord Villemont had been courting? Episodes of temper, impatience, his reprimands for the tiniest infractions. There were none of those with Elias.

But how could she ever trust herself? *Or* any man. In truth, she never wanted to marry again.

Then why did she suddenly find such delight in the idea?

A fantasy, a young maiden's dream, was all it was. But she was no maiden. She was a murderer and—she pressed a hand over her belly—and she had another life to consider. The most important one of all. The evidence of which would soon reveal itself, proving to Elias that she was either a trollop or a liar.

Both of which he would abhor.

Truth was, she wanted to be neither of those things. She wanted to be chaste, pure, Godly, honest, honorable—a woman good enough to gain the love of such a man. But once again, her reason was not grounded in reality...in the way things worked in this world.

The ship jerked and the deck tilted, and she held on, remembering Elias' story of his past. *A pirate!* Smiling, she turned and glanced at him standing on the quarterdeck issuing orders to his men—feet spread, hair tossed by the breeze, sword winking at her from his hip—and she could well believe he'd made a good pirate. How does one change from a thief to a man of integrity? All the more reason *not* to trust him. For now, she would enjoy the next few days in his company, cherish every moment, implanting it in her memory for those lonely years ahead when she was on the run from the law or settled to a life of isolation with her child.

Yet one speck of hope lit her sorrow as she remained on deck nigh two hours later—no other ship was in sight. Which meant her dear brother-in-law had lost them in the storm. Thank God for storms, though she doubted the Almighty had sent it for her benefit. Perhaps, she was finally free of Charles.

She felt free, indeed, as Elias escorted her to dinner that evening. He made no mention of their intimate conversation the night before, though she'd admit to a slight blush when she'd first opened the door to his knock. He stood tall and strong and smelled of the sea and wind with a slight hint of lye. That and his smooth jaw and fresh attire put a smile on her face as she realized he'd made an attempt to clean and dress appropriately for her. Entering the cabin on his arm with nary a twinge of fear at his touch, she nodded at the officers rising to their feet on her behalf. Though 'twas just more of the same romantic fantasy to be escorted to supper by this preacher-pirate, treated like a princess, protected, and, dare she say, cared for, she vowed to enjoy every minute of it.

Once all were seated and the blessing was said, the men dove into their food with the usual gusto, and Charity asked Gage about Eddy.

More reserved than usual, the surgeon smiled at her from his seat at her left. "He is well, Miss. Woke up this morning and appears lucid, thank God." He cleared his throat and glanced down at his food. "I never had the chance to thank you for your help. What you did was very brave."

"You mean since you were too besotted to hold a knife?" Mr. Ballard chuckled. "Had to have poor Ross and a young miss do your work for you."

The table exploded in snickers.

Charity laid a hand on Mr. Gage's. "I was happy to help. And I'm more than pleased to hear Eddy is well."

He nodded his appreciation and when Charity looked up, she found Elias smiling at her.

"Your hard work, Miss, and God's healing," Josiah interjected, helping himself to a slice of boiled pork.

Nelson snorted.

Mr. Ballard scooped rice into his mouth. "Nevertheless, quite heroic, Miss Westcott, quite heroic in my eyes. As was your time captured by natives. I was most concerned for your welfare. What a horrifying experience."

"I will admit to being quite terrified, Sir. That was, until El—the captain appeared." Her affectionate glance with Elias apparently did not go unnoticed by Ballard, for he added, "Yet, if the captain had warned you not to venture into the jungle in the first place, you could have been spared the horror."

"I take full blame for that, Mr. Ballard." She gave him a tight smile. "I'm a foolish woman at times."

"I can hardly credit that, Miss." Ballard dipped his head toward her with a grin.

"Ballard's right." Elias sat back in his chair. "I should have warned you as well as assigned a man to watch over you."

Charity waved a hand through the air. "But it worked out in the end, did it not? Let us move onto happier topics."

Gage poured himself more wine but sipped it sparingly.

While Charity consumed her meal—more famished than she'd been in months—the men spoke of Barbados. More than once, she caught Josiah studying her with curiosity, Ballard with desire, and Nelson with a look akin to greed. But 'twas Elias' gaze she sought out most of all and in particular, the knowing glances they shared which bespoke of familiarity and mutual admiration. And something else...

Something that caused warmth to flood her heart. Lord Villemont had never looked at her like that.

"Of course since you will be busy dealing with this nasty business of your sister's, Captain," Ballard said. "I shall be happy to escort Miss Westcott about town. You'd love

Bridgetown, Miss. It has a quaint wildness to it that is so different from Portsmouth."

Elias frowned. "That is up to Miss Westcott." He glanced her way. "But she is welcome in my sister's home."

"Where be that home, Cap'n?" Nelson asked, rubbing a sleeve over his long, pointy nose. "Far from town?"

"Not too far. Which reminds me, Nelson. I don't expect to be setting sail for at least a fortnight. You might wish to find work on another ship. There's plenty of labor for a good sailor in Bridgetown."

Grunting, Nelson dropped his gaze to his food.

"May I ask what the pressing business is with your sister?" Charity found herself suddenly curious whether 'twas the same sister who'd lost her leg. Yet, hadn't he said this sister was with child?

Elias finished his mouthful and washed it down with a sip of water, his expression tightening. "'Tis a long, complicated story, but suffice it to say that she is being harassed by a few of the more powerful plantation owners on Barbados."

"Harassed?" Gage asked.

"Entire fields of sugarcane burned, workers threatened to the point of leaving her employ, horses and livestock stolen." Elias released a heavy sigh. "And she is about to give birth to their first child."

Beneath the table, Charity laid a hand on her belly. "How terrifying for her. Did her husband not leave a responsible overseer in charge?"

"He did, yes, but the man was severely injured and sent to hospital."

Ballard poured himself more wine. "What do these plantation owners want?"

"The land, the power. My sister's estate is quite small compared to the major plantations that occupy Barbados."

"Then why do they want it?" Charity asked.

The ship rose over a swell, shifting platters and cups across the table and sending Gage's undrunk wine dribbling over the rim of his glass.

Candlelight flickered over Elias' grim expression. "They hate our family name. They loathe that we are preachers to pirates, that we are against slavery..." He shrugged. "Many reasons. Oh, and they hate that part of our land is used for an orphanage when it could be put to a more productive use."

Charity shook her head at such ridiculous motives for violence. "Can't you go to the general assembly?"

"They *are* the general assembly." Elias lifted a brow.

Ballard snorted and lit a cheroot in a candle. "Then how can you possibly fight them?"

Elias sat back in his chair and fingered his cross through the fabric of his shirt. "Precisely why my brother-in-law left. My Uncle Alex and his wife Juliana are in London, along with my parents, for my sister Emmaline's wedding. Uncle Alex is the son of Edmund Merrick, Earl of Clarendon, who has powerful ties with the King—a King who is, shall we say, in Merrick's debt. They hope to procure a Royal Dictum ordering these men to cease their hostilities at once."

Charity nearly dropped her fork. She had no idea the earl Elias was related to was the Earl of Clarendon. Everyone in England had heard of the notorious pirate, Edmund Merrick, who eventually reformed and became a missionary to the pirates. Tales of his exploits, both before and after his conversion, along with his romance with Lady Charlisse Bristol, who herself became a pirate of sorts, were the fodder for many fascinating conversations around dinner tables.

Elias was definitely well-placed in society, yet it seemed of no consequence to him, his only concern for the safety of his sister, the protection of his family, and the salvation of souls. A sudden longing rose within her to have such a brother, to have been raised with a champion who would have stood up for her and protected her. Come to her aid when Villemont...*Vapors!* There she went again, dreaming things that could never be.

"I see why you are in such a hurry to reach your sister," she remarked, noting Josiah's eyes locked upon her. Instead of shifting her gaze away, she stared back at the large Negro.

He smiled. "You do realize, Miss, that the Cap'n's family gives most o' their money to the poor."

She could only stare at him in confusion. "So I have heard, Josiah," she replied curtly, as Elias cast his friend a bewildered look.

Gage loosened his cravat. "So, you expect to run off these villains, Captain?"

"If need be. I'm hoping my very presence will dissuade them. However, if they see fit to attack again, I will happily engage."

"God is taking care o' her, Cap'n," Josiah said. "You have nothing to fear."

"Indeed Josiah. I believe that too. But the sooner I arrive, the better."

Later that evening, unable to sleep, Charity stood at the railing once again. She was growing quite fond of the warm tropical breezes, so different from chilly Portsmouth evenings. She was also growing fond of the ever-changing beauty of the Caribbean. No scene was ever the same. Tonight, with barely a sliver of a moon and the black sky dusted with glittering stars, the sea looked like a giant pool of ink, frosted in dribbles of foamy milk. She drew a deep breath and thought of Elias—no doubt the reason for her sleeplessness. The preacher had escorted her to her cabin after dinner, planted a kiss on her hand, and ran a thumb down her cheek before heading back to his cabin. Such a gentleman. Such a wonderful man. She had two more days to enjoy his company. Then she would leave him forever. 'Twas for the best. She'd rather remember Elias as he was today—looking at her with such affection and admiration—than face his hatred when he discovered the truth.

She pondered her dinner companions: Josiah's questions, Nelson's nervousness, and Ballard's flirtations. Odd men, all. And Gage. Not drinking as much, yet so sullen. Had Elias finally gotten to him?

The preacher *did* have a way about him, a kind, calming and nonjudgmental way. She smiled.

A breeze swirled about her, tickling her neck, and she closed her eyes and gripped the railing tighter as the brig leapt over a wave.

"Hello, Miss Westcott."

Startled, she opened her eyes, her heart galloping.

"Forgive me. I didn't mean to frighten you." Ballard held out a hand, and when she didn't take it, he gripped the railing instead.

Charity settled her breath. "Tis so hard to hear someone coming with all the wind and waves."

"It is. I should have thought."

"'Tis all right, Mr. Ballard. What can I do for you?" She hoped nothing. The man was pleasant enough and in possession of manners, but she longed to be alone.

"I thought you might enjoy company." He glanced over the sea. "'Tis beautiful this time of night."

"Yes, and peaceful."

He leaned one arm on the railing and turned to face her. Lantern light from the mainmast accentuated his thick eyebrows, sharp eyes, and almost regal expression. "You have been through more harrowing events than most women endure in a lifetime. I admire your courage."

"Thank you, Mr. Ballard. But I can't own up to possessing courage through most of it. I am grateful for the captain continually coming to my rescue." She nearly laughed at her own words, such a contrast from only a few days ago. Yet so much had happened since then.

"He does have a penchant for women in distress. Do not presume you are the first." He chuckled. "Why, he sails across the Caribbean rescuing fair maidens all the time."

A spire of foolish jealousy took root, even as her reason shook it off. Elias was free to do as he pleased. She'd be out of his life soon enough. "Yet he is unmarried. Odd."

"Preachers, missionaries. 'Tis a hard life for any woman. Not many would agree to it."

"Why do you dislike him so?"

His eyes widened. "Dislike? Nay." Belying his statement, he narrowed his eyes and stared at the horizon. Moments passed in which he seemed conflicted about what to say. Finally he faced her. "I informed you that my parents are dead."

She nodded.

"What I didn't tell you was that Elias converted them." His lips tightened. "Converted may not be the right term. They were already church-going, good people. But this change in them." He shook his head. "I've never seen them so passionate about God. Mad with their desire to serve Him! Went off to be missionaries in Guiana." His eyes locked on hers. "They were butchered during a native uprising." The words spilled from his lips devoid of all emotion, save one.

Anger.

"I'm so sorry," was all Charity could think to say as both sorrow and fear coiled within her. Sorrow for this man's incredible loss, and fear that he blamed Elias. "A tragedy, Sir. But they made their own choice, did they not?" Even as she said it, her own choices rose to taunt her. "Surely, you cannot fault Elias."

He gave a forced smile. "Have you not noticed? He has a way of destroying the lives of anyone close to him." Without permission, he took her hand in his. "I would hate to see you lured into a life that would make you unhappy."

She snagged her hand back. "What, pray tell, makes you think I'm being lured into anything."

"Then you have no understanding with the Captain?"

"Certainly not," she said before she realized where it would lead... to a huge smile on Mr. Ballard's face and him inching closer to her.

"That pleases me more than I can say, Miss Westcott."

"I don't see why." She looked away, hoping to dissuade him.

"Do you not? I have much to offer a lady like you. Much you deserve."

"You know nothing of what I deserve, Mr. Ballard."

"I wish you would call me Matthew."

"Yet one's wishes are not often realized." She hated to be rude, but there was no way around it. Turning, she started to leave when he grabbed her arm. *Tight.*

# Chapter 21

It took every ounce of Elias' will to keep from revealing himself as he hid among the shadows beneath the foredeck. Especially when Ballard grabbed Charity's arm so insistently. But he wanted to see how Charity would respond. In the darkness and unable to hear their exchange, Elias couldn't be sure she hadn't invited Ballard's touch. She certainly had allowed him to hold her hand just moments before.

Relief loosened the knot in his gut as she jerked from the man's grip. His quartermaster's interest in Charity could not to be denied. What might possibly *be* denied was whether she returned it. The man had land, wealth, and a noble bloodline. Everything a woman could want. In truth, Elias wouldn't blame her for at least considering a courtship with Ballard.

But he *had* to know—after all they'd been through, after all they'd shared—were title and wealth more important to her? He could not bring—*would* not bring—another Rachel into his family's life. Another liar who would destroy them. Even so, guilt rose. He hated spying on Charity. Yet he couldn't stop the smile forming on his lips as she backed away from Ballard.

Sliding along the foredeck, Elias stuck to the shadows, hoping to overhear their conversation, but the wind allowed only a few words to speed past his ears.

"... apologies, Mr. Ballard. Perhaps... misunderstood ... kind gentleman..."

"Then you prefer the penniless preacher, after all?" Ballard fumed, lifting his chin in the air.

"How dare you?" Grabbing her skirts, Charity marched across the deck and down the companionway, leaving Ballard to utter a rather foul curse atop an ungentlemanly growl.

Elias leapt down the companionway, ensured Charity's door was secure, and then made his way to his cabin. Josiah stood examining the ledger that listed goods in the hold they'd picked up in Kingston to be sold when they reached Barbados.

"Did you learn what you hoped?" His friend looked up from the documents.

"I did."

"And what exactly be that?"

"That I'm going to marry Miss Charity Westcott."

Growling, Josiah tossed down the quill pen and rounded the desk.

Elias gaped at his friend. "How now? Why such a reaction?"

"Cap'n, I don't like it. This lady, she's hidin' somethin'. I feels it."

"I know you have the gift of discernment, my friend, but you're wrong this time." Elias strode to the windows and gazed upon the dark seas, trying to control his temper. "I just witnessed her rejection of Ballard's advance, proving she has no desire for fortune, land, or title. Also, have you ever seen a lady who doesn't complain about poor food, no proper toilet, and only a simple maid's gown to wear? And she loves her family. You know how important that is to me."

He spun to face his friend. "I'll grant you, her opinion of God is in error, but at least it is an *honest* opinion—one that can be changed over time. And she's brave. Traveling across the pond alone, or with one lady's maid? I've not seen such courage among most men I know." Elias exhaled and gripped the back of his chair. If anything, spouting all of Charity's good qualities only made him love her more.

Josiah, however, didn't seem convinced as he crossed beefy arms over his chest and gave Elias a look of reprimand. "Yet you truly know nothin' about her, Cap'n. You've yet to meet her family."

"Aye, good point. I'll do so when I sail her home after Duncan arrives with the King's script. But I've never been more sure of a lady's character before, Josiah. You have naught to fear. I'm no longer the foolish lad I used to be."

A woman's laughter jarred Charity awake. Wind fluttered the gauze curtains of her bedchamber window, and she tossed off her quilt, slipped from her bed, and lowered the window pane. Outside, a single street lantern lit the road, shifting golden beams over the cultured gardens of Hemsley House. No one was in sight. No gentlemen and certainly no ladies at this hour. She lit a candle and glanced at the clock atop the mantle. Three in the morning. She was hearing things. "Or mayhap 'twas you, little one, stirring and waking your mother." She caressed her swollen belly beneath her nightgown and smiled. "Just another five months and you'll be here."

*Wait.* There it was again. A woman's flirtatious giggle. Followed by a man's laughter. *Lord Villemont.* Flinging on a robe, Charity took the candle and inched down the hallway toward her husband's bedchamber, knowing what she would find before she pushed open the door.

A half-naked woman in his bed.

She should turn around and leave. She should pretend she never saw a thing. She knew he wasn't faithful. She knew he had mistresses about town. But what she couldn't tolerate was him bringing them into her home, beneath her roof, especially when she was carrying his child!

"How dare you bring a whore into our house!" the words escaped her lips, too angry to consider the repercussions.

Those repercussions came hard and swift. Leaping from atop the trollop, his face a bloated mottle of fury, he shoved into his breeches and dragged her back to her chamber.

*Pain, pain, so much pain!* Strike after strike came down upon her as she cowered on the floor, arms shielding her womb, protecting her babe. The stench of brandy and hatred flooded her, prickling her skin like a thousand needles. Thrusting his face into hers, he pulled her up by her hair. "Never enter my chamber again without my permission! And I will bring whom I wish into *my* house." He slapped her face, punched her belly, and tossed her onto the bed before storming out and slamming the door.

Curling in a ball, Charity sobbed and sobbed until she had no tears left. A sharp pain speared her belly. Then another. And another. Spasms of agony more intense than anything she'd ever felt wracked through her.

Blood gushed from between her legs. *Oh, God. No! No!*

Breath heaving, she leapt from the bunk. *Bunk? Thank God!* Creaks and groans and splashes met her ears. The brig. Elias' brig. Safe. She slumped to the deck, arms around her womb and listened to the blood pound in her ears.

She'd lost her precious Cassia that night. Held the babe who was no bigger than a small teapot in her hand…kissed her…and with Sophie's help, laid her to rest at dawn at the back end of the estate.

The next morning, Lord Villemont begged her forgiveness. 'Twas the only time he'd expressed convincing remorse, though he'd oft borne silent shame after a particularly vicious beating.

Rising, Charity struck flint to steel and lit her lantern, glad when the light chased the shadows, along with the memories, back into the corners. Sleep would not visit her again this night. She rubbed her belly. "But I didn't let him harm you, little one."

Glancing down, she started to smile when a spot of blood blossomed on her chemise.

"Mr. Ballard, a moment of yer time, if I may?" Nelson sidled up to the pretentious clod on the quarterdeck.

"What is it, man?"

The quartermaster's superior manner and easy dismissal of those beneath him never failed to grate on Nelson. Sure, the man owned land and had wealth, but did that make him any better than Nelson? Besides, Nelson intended to remedy his situation soon. Sooner if he could get Ballard's help. Nelson was no string-brained fool. He'd not missed the animosity Ballard held toward Captain Dutton, nor the fact— as was the word about the brig—that Miss Westcott chose the Captain over Ballard.

Nelson scanned the surroundings to ensure no one was listening. "How would you like to cause Captain Dutton a bit of pain?"

Ballard snorted and adjusted his neckerchief. "What on earth are you talking about?"

"Listen, I knows ye don't harbor no affection for the man. I heard about yer parents and then about Miss Westcott."

Ballard's eyes narrowed. "Only a fool listens to rumors."

"I heard she turned ye away." Nelson withheld a laugh.

Ballard's face reddened. "Then you heard wrong! 'Twas I who denied her. An admiral's daughter? Posh! She's too far beneath my station. Now, what is it you want? I have duties to perform."

"What if I told ye I knows a way t' have Miss Westcott taken away from the Captain, break his heart as he's broken yers?"

Ballard shot him a fiery gaze. "I would say you'd better intend the lady no harm."

"No harm from me, Sir, I assure ye." He leaned closer to Ballard's ear. "All I needs is for ye t' tell me the location o' the Cap'n's sister's plantation." Nelson had been unable to determine even the lady's married name, otherwise, he could inquire around town for the information he needed. But that would delay his reward. And chances were, Lord Charles Villemont was already in Barbados waiting for him.

# Chapter 22

O f the three harbors Charity had sailed into since arriving in the Caribbean, Kingston was still by far the most gorgeous, yet Carlisle Bay definitely came in a close second. She hadn't thought 'twas possible for water to become a deeper, more vibrant shade of turquoise than what she'd already seen. But there it was, purling against the *Restoration*'s hull, ribbons of sapphire blue and emerald green, capped in sparkling sunlit diamonds. As they entered the narrow bay, the smells of the city swept over her: smoked meat, horses, tar, wood, and a hint of fragrant flowers. The sounds of bells clanging, horses clomping, wagons squealing, and people chattering soon followed. Several docks jutted into the water where ships—from tiny dories to a large East Indiamen—rocked in the incoming waves.

However beautiful the scenery, it did naught to cheer the dour mood shrouding her ever since she awoke and realized that, after today, she would never see Elias again. Forcing down her sorrow, and the tears that came with it, she'd dressed, pinned up her unruly hair, and went to stand on the deck as he and his men navigated the ship into the bay. No longer concerned with hiding her interest in him, she watched his every move, the way he balanced on the deck with ease, the breadth of his shoulders beneath his shirt, the strength and tenor of his voice shouting orders, and the smiles he offered those standing nearby. A sword blinked at his side, and she wondered why he wore it. Perhaps he expected trouble at his sister's plantation straightaway. Such a gallant rescuer, this brave, wondrous man—every woman's dream of a chivalrous knight. Someday he would find a lady worthy of him.

It just wouldn't be her.

An hour later, with sails furled, anchor tossed, and nearly everyone brought ashore, Charity took Elias' outstretched hand and allowed him to assist her onto the wobbling dock. He gazed at her oddly for a moment, no doubt feeling the tremble in her hand as she tugged it back. Her throat burned and tears threatened to fill her eyes at the thought of bidding him farewell. Nay, she couldn't do it. Not without becoming a puddle at his feet. So, when he turned to speak to Ballard, she clutched her skirts and darted down the wharf, hoping he wouldn't notice.

The thump of his boots gave chase. His grip on her arm halted her.

"Where are you going?" Stark blue eyes met hers, unusual uncertainty flooding them. "Why are you crying?" He lowered his grip to squeeze her hand.

She turned her face away. "I'm not crying. Why would I be crying?" She waved her other hand in the air. "And, if you must know, I'm going to find passage to Charles Towne." Jerking yet again from his grip, she started forward.

"If *I* must know." Elias groaned and appeared beside her. "Aren't we past being mere acquaintances and keeping secrets?"

When she didn't answer, he continued, "Woman, why do you insist on romping around dangerous cities on your own? Every port we land in sends you off on a dangerous adventure."

Charity wove around a group of sailors and headed toward what looked like the dock master's shed. "Because I am not part of your family and have no right to impose on your sister."

"Ah, that's it." He raked his hair back and sighed. "Forgive me. I thought you understood you were welcome. Ballard, Josiah, and Gage are imposing, why shouldn't you?" He smiled, that boyish mischievous smile of his that did funny things to her insides. "Charity, you know you wouldn't be imposing. Rose will adore you, I'm sure. Besides, there's someone I want you to meet."

"I must get to Charles Towne." She continued forward, but he stepped in front of her, all six-foot-plus of him—a shield of manhood, protection, and care so strong it began to crumble her defenses.

"And I intend to take you there just as soon as I ensure my sister's safety. Besides, you have no money, little mermaid. And I'm not giving you any." He arched a single brow above a devilish grin. "Come." He proffered his arm. "Our carriage awaits, milady. If I know my sister, she will prepare a feast to celebrate our arrival. If that doesn't entice you, mayhap a hot bath, clean attire, and a proper bed will." Sunlight twinkled in his eyes.

Charity felt her resolve weaken. She glanced from the coach Ballard and Gage waited beside back to Elias' expectant smile. To willingly spend more time with this man—knowing she must leave him—was akin to tearing out one's heart, tying it to an anchor, and casting it into the sea. Her stomach rumbled, and she knew she must nourish her wee one soon. And although she'd found no further blood on her chemise, she didn't want to risk harming her babe with another frightening journey so soon. She needed rest. She needed peace. Her child came first.

"Very well, I will join you, but on one condition."

"Anything."

"You lend me money to travel to Charles Towne—money I *will* repay—and do not take me yourself. You have enough to deal with here."

"I can't promise that." He took her hand and pressed it in the crook of his elbow.

"You said anything!"

"A woman traveling alone is a target. Are you so anxious to be rid of me?" He led her toward the coach.

She didn't answer. Instead, she took her place in the carriage beside him, facing Ballard, who refused to look at her, Gage, who smiled, and Josiah, who stared out the window.

Elias tapped the roof, and the driver snapped the reigns. Charity busied herself glancing out the window at the mobs crowding the streets of Bridgetown. Shops, taverns, and boarding houses in every color of the rainbow sped past as they rumbled down the narrow avenue. Soon, large buildings gave way to smaller ones spread farther apart, until finally naught but lush greenery filled the window. Barely a breeze entered the coach, bringing with it the heavy scent of earth and tropical flowers.

Charity dabbed the perspiration on her neck as Ballard and Gage began a heated argument about whether the large tree they passed was a Spanish Cedar or Kapok.

She sensed Elias tense beside her. He shifted in his seat, glanced out the window, then back inside the carriage, before finally leaning toward her. "I fear there's something you don't know about me, Charity, that might shock you."

She nearly laughed at the irony. "I can't imagine."

"It will destroy any good opinion you have of me."

"Nothing could do that."

Chuckling, he took her hand. "Baffling little mermaid. You say something kind like that but then do all in your power to leave me."

She looked away. "I'm most anxious to see my family."

"I understand. And you will."

The passage grew bumpy, jostling the carriage back and forth, making further conversation difficult, though Elias continued to squeeze her hand as if afraid whatever secret he held would cause her to bolt. Against her better judgment, she allowed his touch, much to the dismay of Mr. Ballard, who cast them disdainful glances.

Sunlight speared the carriage, and Charity leaned her head out the window for a better view. Trees lined a dirt road from which manicured lawns extended on either side, while in the distance a two-story white house rose out of the jungle. Within minutes, they halted before the doorway, and Elias leapt out and assisted her from the coach.

"What a lovely estate." Begonia and gardenia bushes surrounded a grand two-story home, complete with pillars supporting a portico that wrapped around the front and sides. Fields of sugar cane extended from the left as far as the eye could see, while an orchestra of birds, accompanied by the chattering of some kind of animal, joined the crash of waves in the distance.

A comely woman with hair of spun-gold emerged from the house, followed by a bevy of servants. Upon seeing Elias, she waddled forward, hand on her back, doing her best to navigate the stairs, all the while gleefully exclaiming, "Elias! Elias!"

The pirate-preacher dashed toward her and took her in his arms, laughing and showering her with kisses. "Look at you! I've never seen you so fat!"

She slapped his arm. "Any day now, brother. Any day, and you shall be an uncle."

Charity couldn't help but smile at the exchange.

Elias led his sister down the rest of the steps. "Miss Charity Westcott, may I introduce my sister, Rose Bennet."

"A pleasure, Miss Westcott." The lovely woman smiled. "How utterly delightful! My brother brings home a lady. Pray tell, Elias, where on earth did you find such a beauty?" She winked at Charity.

*Beauty?* The lady was clearly mad. With no comb, brush, bath, or decent attire in months. Charity knew she looked like a washerwoman from a hovel.

Elias gestured toward his friends. "And you remember Mr. Gage, Mr. Ballard, and Josiah."

"I do, gentlemen. Welcome! Please come in. You must be exhausted from your journey. Banes," she addressed a man in a butler's livery behind her. "Tell Mrs. Woodhouse we are to have a party tonight, a feast and dancing." She clapped her hands together. "I haven't had a party since before Duncan left."

"Have you heard from him?" Elias asked.

"His last post said he should be home by Christmas." She leaned against him. "I'm so glad you are here, Elias. I'm sorry you had to miss Emmaline's wedding."

Elias extended one arm for Charity and one for his sister and led them up the stairs. "I saw she was happy and that was all I needed. You know I will always come when you call, dear sister."

Two ornately-carved mahogany doors opened, and Charity entered a marble tiled foyer with a curved stairway to the right and double-arched openings on the left that led to galleries overlooking the gardens. A bronze chandelier hung overhead, its light joined by flickering sconces lining the walls. A man and two women dressed in service attire hurried forward.

"Winston, will you show these gentlemen to their rooms? And Miss Westcott, I hope my brother has been treating you well." She cast a look of censure his way. "I can't wait to hear how you came to be on his brig."

Charity exchanged a look with Elias that must have conveyed more than friendship, for Rose smiled even wider. "Now I am even *more* anxious to hear the tale." She scanned the foyer, then glanced out the door toward the coach. "But have you no luggage, Miss Westcott?"

"A long story, Mrs. Bennet," Charity said.

"Please call me Rose." She drew an arm through Charity's. "I've got just the room for you. Mable and Sally will draw you a hot bath, and I'll have some clothing sent up." She leaned back and studied Charity. "Yes, indeed. My gowns should fit you nicely."

Charity liked this woman already. Her kindness and generosity reminded Charity of her sister Grace.

Two maids approached, dipped curtsies at Charity, and started leading her up the stairs when she glanced at Elias to ensure he was still pleased to have her here. But his focus was down a hall beyond the foyer. Odd, he seemed quite agitated about something. "Where is he?" he turned to ask Rose.

Before she could answer, the patter of little feet echoed down the hallway, and a young boy no older than three ambled into the room and leapt into Elias' waiting arms.

Charity could only stare astounded at the love and affection passing between them—the way Elias kissed him over and over and then held him back to examine every inch of him as if to ensure he bore no injuries. *Vapors*, were those tears in the preacher's eyes?

The boy, equally excited, kept hugging Elias. But it was the words that proceeded out of the lad's mouth that sent Charity's mind tumbling down a dark hole. "Papa! Papa! Home!"

# Chapter 23

Elias didn't have a chance to explain to Charity before the maids whisked her upstairs. He did, however, have time to see the horror on her face before she turned to leave. *Horror!* But what did he expect? The revelation he had a son 'twas not only a shock, but spoke to a lack of character on his part that he was sure a lady like her wouldn't tolerate.

Which was why he hadn't told her, why he wanted her to see that he was a different man now. He longed to run after her, but the lad in his arms needed him more at the moment.

As much as Elias needed him. Two months was far too long to spend apart from his son. Kneeling, he tousled the boy's dark hair and drew in his sweet, innocent scent.

"She doesn't know," Rose said, staring after Charity.

Elias gazed up at his sister. "I should have told her, I know. But she tends to run away. *A lot.* And I didn't want to give her more reason."

"But there's obviously an understanding between you."

"Nothing spoken yet." Elias scooped Edmund up in his arms and kissed the lad again. "I didn't want to ask for a formal courtship until she knew the truth."

Rose put a hand on her hip. "Really, Elias, could you not have thought of a better way to inform her?" She shook her head. "You always were so theatrical."

"Horses? Papa?" Edmund asked, saving Elias from yet another lecture from his sister.

Rose rubbed the boy's back. "He's been asking to go riding for weeks."

"Yes, of course, Edmund." Elias squeezed him. "Just as soon as I'm settled." He'd been taking the boy for horse rides ever since the lad could sit without falling. 'Twas one of the special things they did together as father and son.

Rose led them down a hall and through a door into the parlor. "Forgive me, but I need to sit." She slid onto a flowered settee and rang a bell.

Setting the boy down, Elias sat across from her. "'Tis I who should apologize. How are you feeling?"

"Good...well." Plucking a fan from the table, she opened it and swept it over a face that looked much too pink to be a mere healthy glow.

"We should leave you to rest, Rose." Elias took his son's hand and started to rise.

"You will do no such thing!" She swatted him playfully with her fan.

A maid entered with a tray of tea.

"Biscuits! Biscuits!" Edmund squealed and reached for one, and Elias drew him into his lap before he sent the platter crashing to the floor.

"Thank you, Mrs. Woodhouse." Rose poured tea and handed Edmund a biscuit, which the boy immediately chomped into. "I must hear more about Miss Westcott. Though I fear you've ruined whatever is between you. Women hate to be lied to, Elias."

"Men too." He took the cup she handed him. "And I didn't lie. I simply omitted the truth." He cringed at the ridiculous statement. "She's a decent lady, Rose. Kind, honorable, pure. She's been through a very difficult time."

"And of course you came to the rescue." She smiled and leaned to touch his hand. "You don't have to be everyone's hero, you know."

"I don't?" He winked at her.

"Papa is a hero." Edmund grabbed another biscuit, crumbs flying from his mouth.

"No more after that, Edmund." Elias set him down and the boy ran off, half a biscuit hanging from his mouth. Rose and Elias laughed.

"You love her." Rose's declaration shifted his attention back to her.

Elias huffed. Rose, always the intuitive one. "I do. I want to marry her."

"But you have yet to ask her."

"Nay. She keeps trying to run away from me." He chuckled.

"Hmm. I can see where that would give you pause." Rose's eyes twinkled. "Yet she's here, isn't she?"

"Indeed. And I thank God for that. Now, if she'll only understand."

"If she loves you, she will."

Elias nodded, unusual uncertainty brewing in his gut. "However, more importantly." He reached to take her hand in his. "What news of your troubles here?"

Rose sipped her tea and gazed at Edmund playing with a fringed cord attached to the curtains. "More sugarcane burned, one of our mills destroyed, and two horses stolen last week. Oh, my." Eyes widening, she set down her cup with a *clang*. "I nearly forgot. Caleb is here!"

Elias could hardly believe it. His cousin, his good friend, the lad he'd grown up with—the two of them engaging in all sorts of boyish mischief together. Caleb was Alex and Juliana's son and grandson to Edmund Merrick, in line to be the Earl of Clarendon someday. "I thought he was chasing Barbary pirates off the coast of Africa? When did he arrive?"

"Two days ago. He's already had one altercation with the vigilantes. He and Banes chased them off. Though my butler was none too happy about engaging in such violence."

Elias chuckled, trying to picture the proper Englishman wielding a sword.

"Pirates!" Edmund dashed toward them, grabbed a spoon from the tray, and thrust it before him.

Rose and Elias both chuckled. "Guess it runs in the family," she said.

"But is he here?" Elias glanced out the doorway.

"Nay. He had business in town, something to do with his ship. But he'll be here tonight."

"Good. I look forward to catching up. In the meantime, I should gather the men and make my presence known as soon as possible."

"Not today, Elias. You must rest. Tonight we shall celebrate your safe arrival. There's plenty of time tomorrow to save the world."

Elias smiled. "You know me too well, sister dear."

Rose winced and pressed a hand on her stomach.

"What is it?" Rising, he knelt by her side. "The babe?"

"'Tis nothing. I get these pains now and then."

"You've endured far too much stress, Rose." He kissed her hand. "But you have naught to fear now. You are not alone anymore."

"God has always been with me, Elias."

"Indeed. And now He has brought me to you as well."

"Yes, he has." Smiling, she tugged on a strand of his hair. "Just look at you. Hair a mess, shirt wrinkled. No wonder the lady ran upstairs."

"I beg your pardon, *milady*, but I have been at sea." He stood and raised a brow.

"Indeed, you look the part of a pirate."

Edmund dashed through the room, spoon waving before him. "Papa Pirate! Papa Pirate!"

Rose laughed. "Your son gives you away. Now, go rest, bathe, and afterward, when you fetch Miss Westcott for the party, explain things to her. From the way she looked at you, she deserves the truth."

He nodded. "But first, I must take this lad on my horse."

"Yay! Yay! Papa!" Abandoning piracy, Edmund dashed into Elias' arms.

He welcomed the boy in a tight embrace. Oh, how he'd missed him.

Now, if only Charity would grow to love him too.

A hot bath never felt so marvelous. Charity couldn't even remember the last bath she'd had. Months ago, back at Hemsley House in Portsmouth. She'd been spoiled living in the luxury Lord Villemont provided, a prison of gowns, jewels, and delicacies. He'd denied her nothing, save love, happiness, and safety. Funny how no amount of luxury made up for the lack of those three things.

Yet, now as the layers of salt and grime washed from her skin and hair, her thoughts were consumed with Elias. *And his son!* A plethora of battling emotions stormed through her—betrayal that he'd withheld such vital information, shock, of course, and, if she admitted it, pain at the deception. Yet stronger than all of those was the way her heart swelled at the look on the child's face as he ran to his father and the way Elias absorbed him in his arms as if the boy were all that mattered in the world.

Now she found herself more than curious as to the identity of his mother, and what had caused the pious preacher to defy his God and produce a child out of wedlock. Indeed, just when she thought she had this man figured out, he never failed to surprise her.

"Miss...Miss..." The maid's voice burst into her musings, bringing Charity's gaze up to the young lady standing beside the tub with a towel in hand. "You best get dressed, Miss. They'll be expectin' you downstairs soon."

Charity smiled. She hadn't heard the girl enter. And though she'd been the same maid who helped her undress and who'd organized filling her tub with warm water, she'd rushed off so quickly Charity hadn't had time to thank her.

"I took yer things down to be washed, Miss, but...but there's blood on..." The girl bit her lip.

"My chemise, yes. Nothing to worry about. I doubt I'll need them back, Miss...forgive me, what was your name?"

"Mable. Miss Mable." She curtsied.

Gripping the sides of the porcelain tub, Charity rose and stepped out into the waiting towel, careful to keep her back to the maid, as she had when Mable had helped her undress. The girl scrambled to the bed where she'd laid out a fresh chemise, petticoats, stockings, and a lavender silk skirt with brocaded multicolor flowers, double-ruffled sleeves, and a matching bodice, all trimmed in metallic lace. So thoughtful of Rose to send up such a lovely gown. And to put Charity in such an elegant bedchamber. Rich mahogany furniture filled the large space, including a desk, chest of drawers, bed, and dressing table. Books lined shelves against the wall, while a door opened to a balcony on the other side of the bed where waves of maroon, lemon, and peach drifted inside from the setting sun.

Mable held up the chemise, and Charity finished drying and dropped the towel. When she'd married Lord Villemont and he'd presented her with her very own lady's maid, she'd relished having someone help her dress, style her hair, and rush to satisfy her every need. It seemed a luxury only the wealthy could afford and a sign she had finally made it. Yet, the past few months, she'd grown accustomed to fending for herself on the various ships she'd sailed upon. And she rather enjoyed the independence, save for being forced to abandon her stays.

Mable flung the chemise over Charity's neck, chattering on about how the gown belonged to her mistress and how she knew it would fit Charity because they had the same figure before Rose had blossomed with child and...

The woman stopped in mid-sentence, her eyes locked on Charity's belly. *Vapors!* Charity had been far too concerned about the scars on her back to realize that, unclad, her condition was all too obvious.

Red blossomed up the poor girl's face as she attempted to continue her conversation—this time stuttering. Still, she managed to assist Charity in donning her petticoats, stays, bodice, and finally, skirt, all the while never ceasing to talk, even when she worked on Charity's hair, pinning it up in a bouquet of curls.

"If tha'll be all, Miss, I must be going." Mable started for the door, refusing to look at Charity.

"Thank you, Mable. I trust in your discretion as a lady's maid."

"Yes, Miss. None of my business, Miss." And off she ran, closing the door behind her.

Charity should leave. Right now before they discovered her secret and threw her out. She could find Josiah and ask him to drive her into town. 'Twas obvious he didn't trust her and wanted her far away from Elias.

She didn't have time to ponder her predicament when a knock sounded on the door. Perhaps 'twas Mable forgetting something, but it wasn't Mable. It was Elias...

Not the Elias who captained *The Restoration*, with his leather breeches, loose white shirt, baldric, and boots, but Elias looking as if he were an earl himself. Black velvet breeches tightened over muscular legs, a gray silk embroidered waistcoat peeked at her from beneath a dark coat with gold metallic trim. A silk cravat bubbled from his neck, above which glistened a smooth jaw and hair neatly combed and tied behind him. But it was his smile that melted her heart, along with the look of utter delight sparkling in his eyes when he saw her.

And if Charity weren't so distraught at the moment, she'd fall into his arms.

"I expect you have some questions for me," he said, looking rather sheepish for a hero.

Charity stepped back. "'Tis none of my business."

He scanned her and shook his head. "I didn't think it was possible you could be more beautiful."

Oddly, Charity felt a blush rising.

"The lad is Rachel's." He leaned on the door frame and released a sigh.

"Not yours?"

"Nay, he's mine. At least that's what she said when a year after she left me, she sailed back into my life with a babe in her arms."

"So he *could* be yours."

He swallowed. "Yes. 'Twas an indiscretion, a moment of weakness, a foolish mistake from a young man in love who intended to marry the lady."

She could only stare at him, at the sorrow lining his face, the shame filling his eyes.

"What you must think of me." He lowered his chin.

"She gave up her child?" Charity could not conceive of such a thing. "What kind of woman gives up her baby?"

"I imagine the boy would have interfered with her plans to marry fortune and title."

"And she's not seen him since?"

He stared at her as if confused by her line of questioning. "I'm sorry I didn't tell you before. I should have."

"You owe me nothing, Elias."

"Ah, but I do." He took a step toward her. "I had hoped we had an understanding."

She, too, had hoped. But in another life, another time, another world, perhaps. Not this one. She fought back tears and gripped the bedpost for support. "Why didn't you tell me?"

"I was afraid to lose you." He reached for her hand, caressing it gently, tentatively. She didn't want him to stop. She longed to tell him that she had no right to judge him when she'd done far worse. In fact, his human frailty only endeared him to her more. But saying that would encourage the feelings between them, mayhap even embolden Elias to ask for *that* understanding—a courtship she could not accept. This was her chance to dissuade him, the perfect reason to reject his advances and demand he take her back to town.

He stepped even closer. Looming above her by at least a foot, the strength of his presence undoing her, his natural scent, unfettered by cologne, tingling her senses. "Tell me I have not lost you, Charity." He reached up to caress her cheek just as the pitter-patter of little feet drummed down the hallway, and Elias' son darted toward him, grinning. "Papa!"

Elias scooped him into his arms. A woman, who surely must be the lad's nanny, came barreling after him, her rotund figure preventing any further speed. "Sorry, Sir, he got away from me again."

"Not to worry, Mrs. Norsen," Elias said. "I know what a handful this little pirate can be." He tickled the boy, eliciting giggles and squirms.

"I'm a pirate, Papa?" the boy asked.

"You'll always be my little pirate." Elias kissed him on the cheek.

The boy pointed toward Charity. "Is she my mama?"

# Chapter 24

"This is Miss Charity Westcott, Edmund. Charity, Master Edmund Dutton."

Charity smiled. "Pleased to meet you Master Dutton."

The lad giggled and squirmed in Elias' arms, then much to his surprise, held out both hands toward Charity. Elias started to force the boy back, when Charity reached and took the boy in her arms, snuggling him against her chest.

"You're such a big boy, Edmund. How old are you now, nearly ten?" She winked at Elias.

Edmund smiled proudly and held up three fingers. "Papa says I'm a man, not a boy."

"Indeed you are." She drew him close and kissed his forehead. "And just as handsome as your father."

Elias blinked and stared at the exchange in wonder. Edmund had never taken to any woman so quickly. Especially not a stranger. It had taken Mrs. Norsen a full month before the boy would allow her to embrace him. Yet here he was nestled against Charity's bosom, fingering one of those delicious chocolate curls dangling about her neck.

"Are you coming to the party?" the boy asked. "I like your name."

"Only if you are coming as well." She set him down and brushed a lock of hair from his face.

Elias turned to the waiting nanny, her face still red with exertion. "We'll take him down, Mrs. Norsen. I'll bring him up in an hour for his bedtime."

"Very well, Sir." She leaned toward Edmund. "You be a good boy." Her scolding tone belied the grin on her lips before she scurried off.

Edmund straightened his shoulders, slid one of his little hands into Elias' and the other into Charity's, and proceeded to lead them down the hall to the top of the stairwell, where sounds of an orchestra rose. Charity cast a smile toward Elias that melted everything within him as they walked, like a family, down the stairs and into a ballroom where a few guests had arrived early.

A small orchestra consisting of two violins, a harpsichord, flute, cello, and trumpet tuned in the far corner while servants in crisp liveries passed around trays with drinks in crystal glasses.

Mr. and Mrs. Dodd, who owned the plantation across the island, ran up to him, exclaiming their excitement at seeing him again. Mr. Dodd, tall and lanky, made some snide remark as was his way, while Mrs. Dodd, ever the cheerful saint, expressed her utter joy at seeing such a lovely lady at Elias' side. Several others joined them with happy greetings and well wishes.

Each time Elias introduced Charity, he couldn't help but admire the polite and mannerly way in which she addressed them and answered their questions, all the while including Edmund in the conversation.

What a treasure! If 'twas possible for Elias to love this lady more, his heart would burst. She had accepted his indiscretion with incredible grace, forgiving him, it would seem, even for his deception. Then, as if that weren't charitable enough, she'd embraced Edmund, displaying such love and affection he'd not thought possible from a stranger. Would she never cease to amaze him...this mermaid he'd swept from the sea?

Rose entered into the room, looking rather flushed and uncomfortable, but still a beauty in her green satin gown trimmed in Mechlin lace. Her face lit up upon seeing Elias, and she headed toward him.

"Brother dear, I thought I only dreamt of your arrival. 'Tis so good to see you. And looking quite dashing, I might add." Her eyes twinkled mischievously as she glanced at Charity.

"I am here till you toss me out, sister." Elias took her arm and led her to a row of chairs pushed against the wall. "Pray do not tax yourself. I wish you hadn't thrown such an affair on my behalf."

"'Tis nothing. Merely thirty or so close friends, all anxious to see you. Besides, I've been so bored without Duncan. Oh, my. Why is it so hot in here?" Withdrawing a handkerchief, she dabbed her neck and glanced at the open doors leading to the veranda. "Mayhap the evening will soon usher in a breeze."

"I'm sure it will." Elias smiled, though it didn't feel overly warm to him.

Charity took Edmund's hand in hers. "Come, Edmund, let's find your aunt something cool to drink." And off they went to the refreshment table at the other end of the room as if they'd known each other forever.

Rose's gaze followed them before she turned and smiled at Elias. "The boy has taken to her."

"Indeed. Quite amazing." Elias rubbed the back of his neck, then glanced over the large ballroom. Polished parquet floors led to carved wainscoting rising up the walls below floral wallpaper. Tapestries and paintings—some of them, his mother's—decorated the walls, while bas-relief cherubs and garlands embellished the ceiling from which hung three chandeliers. Chairs and tables had been pushed to the sides to allow room for dancing. "You've kept the estate well in Duncan's absence, Rose. 'Tis a lovely party."

Gage and Ballard emerged from the growing crowd and stopped before him, extending their greetings to his sister.

"What a lovely party, Mrs. Bennett." Ballard adjusted his cravat and glanced over the room. "'Tis been quite a while since I've had the pleasure of such an affair."

"You are welcome here anytime, Mr. Ballard. And you as well, Mr. Gage."

Gage, distracted by a group of young ladies standing in the corner, finally faced Rose, a blush on his face. "You are most kind."

Ballard adjusted his cravat yet again and eyed the front doors as if expecting someone.

"Relax, Ballard," Elias said. "Take the night off. Dance with a comely lady. Dance with a bevy of them. In fact, there's one looking at you now." He nodded toward the same group Gage had noticed before—four ladies giggling and peeking at the gentlemen from behind fluttering fans.

"Yes, Captain." Ballard's smile seemed forced, and the twitch at his right eye gave Elias pause. "But first the refreshments." Ballard pointed toward the table lined with all manner of drinks and food. "Shall we, Gage?"

Gage licked his lips, his eyes holding a hesitancy, as he followed Ballard into the crowd.

Elias sat beside his sister. "Where is Josiah?"

She cleared her throat and tilted her head to the left where Elias found his first mate, donned in his finest, talking with Ruth, one of the women who assisted in the orphanage. He grinned at the way the woman lowered her lashes and smiled at something Josiah had said.

"When did this happen?"

"Last time you were here. But you were too busy to notice, I suppose." Plucking out her fan, Rose swept it over her heated skin. "She's a Godly woman, Elias. She'll make Josiah a good wife."

"I'm happy for him." Now if he could only get his own love life settled.

Charity returned, a glass in one hand and Edmund holding the other.

"I hope melon punch is acceptable, Mrs. Bennet." She handed it to Rose.

"Please call me Rose, and yes, 'tis my favorite. Thank you."

Edmund slid onto Elias' lap. "Papa, can you teach me how to dance?"

"What's this?" Elias wiped crumbs from atop his son's lips.

Charity shrugged. "Somehow a piece of cake leapt off the table into Edmund's mouth."

Edmund giggled.

Elias squeezed the boy and shared a smile with Charity. "I must speak to that cake at once and tell it to stop jumping at our guests!"

"I'm not a guest. I live here, Papa!"

"Indeed you do, young man."

Various couples streamed toward them to greet him and his sister and thank them for the invitation: the Mackens, Franks, Paulsons...all good people and friends. But as soon as the band began to play a *gavotte*, they excused themselves to line the floor.

Charity must have noticed the forlorn look on Rose's face because she said, "You must miss your husband so. Is he often away?"

"Nay. Not often. And yes, I do miss him terribly." She sipped her drink, smiled, and tipped her head to something behind Charity.

Charity followed her gaze to a group of ladies across the room staring at Elias. "Seems you have admirers, Captain," she teased him.

Elias glanced toward them, sending the ladies into a flurry of chatter, waves, and fluttering fans. Bah! "The Chesterfield daughters. Egad! Have they not been married off yet?" He glanced down at his son. He'd thought the lad would be a deterrent to highborn families from allowing their daughters even a glance his way. But that had not been the case.

"Oh, you poor man, so many women admirers," Charity quipped.

"Jealous?" He winked.

Rose sighed. "I daresay, Elias, they are not going to give up on you until you *are* married." She cast a quick glance at Charity, which he was glad Charity didn't see.

"Papa, can we dance with Miss Charity?" Edmund tugged on his coat.

"Why, thank you, Edmund," Charity said with a sigh of impatience. "Finally someone has asked me to dance."

Grinning, Elias led Charity and Edmund to a far corner away from the main dancers, where they mimicked their moves as a threesome—an awkward threesome. But a rather delightful threesome, all laughing and enjoying the moment.

Several people came up to meet the new young lady, while thankfully Elias' admirers had given up and were otherwise engaged.

Finally, when Edmund could no longer keep his eyes open, Elias called a footman to carry the lad up to Mrs. Norsen.

Now he had Charity all to himself. If he could but find the time and the right moment, he intended to ask for her hand.

Charity was living a dream. A dream she'd not had since she was a little girl. A dream of romance and love and passion. In the arms of this magnificent man, gliding over the floor to the music of Bach, Handel, Corelli, and Rameau, candlelight shimmering over them like falling stars, and his eyes intent on hers, she never wanted to leave. 'Twas an impossible, beautiful dream meant for princesses and pious ladies. Certainly not broken, lying murderesses.

Yet she felt like none of those horrid things tonight. Tonight she felt adored and cherished and even good and kind and pure—at least that's what she saw reflected in Elias' eyes.

And she could stare at his image of her forever.

In this case, forever would last only one night.

But she would remember this night forever.

"I've never seen you smile so much, Miss Westcott," Elias said as he took her hand and led her in the minuet.

Charity blushed. "I give myself away."

"If by that you mean you are happy in my arms, I'm thankful you can no longer hide it."

"No longer?" She smiled as they parted and twirled around. "You are quite sure of yourself." She realized she was flirting with him, so unlike her. Yet it seemed so natural with this man.

He stepped toward her, and they touched hands then parted quickly. "With you, Miss, I fear I am never sure."

Charity wheeled around the couple behind them, then met Elias again. "You dance quite well for a preacher-pirate."

"Neither occupation preclude good breeding, Miss."

"As I have discovered."

He swept her past another couple, and she was surprised to see Mr. Gage with one of Elias' lady admirers. "Mr. Gage seems to be enjoying himself."

He followed her gaze and smiled. "And last I spoke to him, I smelled no alcohol on his breath."

"Perhaps your sermons are having some effect on him, after all."

They touched right hands, then left hands, and spun around.

"If only they would penetrate your heart as well," Elias said in passing.

"Why, whatever do you mean, Sir? I don't take to drink."

He smiled, but they parted again, preventing his response.

Good. She didn't want to talk about God or her past or anything serious tonight. She wanted only to remember how it felt to float over the dance floor, the envy of every lady in the room, how gentle Elias' touch was on her hand, the deep tenor of his voice, and his blue eyes exuding affection and admiration.

They met again, hands grazing. "Edmund is quite taken with you."

"I'm quite taken with him. He's a charming boy."

"He doesn't warm to most people so quickly." Elias turned around and faced her again. "You are good with children."

"I love children." Her voice held more sorrow than she wanted, so she started to add, "They are—"

A woman screeched, halting some of the dancers as a man in sailor attire, armed with pistol and sword dashed into the room, four men at his heels. He whisked away strands of coal-black hair from his face and searched the crowd. Upon spotting Elias, he charged toward him.

"Elias."

He held out his hand, and Elias gripped his arm in return. "Caleb. I heard you were in town. Thank you for coming to my sister's aid."

"Of course. We are family. If I had known of her troubles, I'd have been here sooner. But there is an urgent matter at hand." He spared a glance toward Charity.

"Mr. Caleb Hyde, may I present Miss Charity Westcott."

The handsome man bowed slightly, took her hand, and placed a kiss upon it. "A pleasure."

"Hyde, as in the earl of Clarendon?" she asked. "Captain Edmund Merrick Hyde?"

"My grandfather, Miss. Do you know him?"

"Nay, I've not had the pleasure." Charity had never been introduced to an earl's grandson. Especially not one as famous as the great earl Edmund Merrick turned pirate. But she hadn't time to ask him any further questions.

"Time is of the essence, Elias. I need your help. Do you have men here?"

"Aye." Elias glanced across the room. "I'll gather them and meet you outside."

"Miss, if you'll excuse me." Mr. Hyde dipped his head. Gripping the hilt of his sword, he left the room, leaving a trail of swooning women in his path.

Charity put her hand on Elias' arm. "What is it?"

"I suspect trouble from those trying to drive us from the land." He searched the crowd then faced her with a smile. "Naught to alarm yourself over. Enjoy the rest of the party, and I shall see you tomorrow." Then planting a kiss on her cheek, he sped off, interrupting Gage's dance and Josiah's flirtations as he went.

Enjoy the party without him? Unlikely. Yet as she watched him dash out the door, many of the guests buzzing in speculation, she knew what she had to do. *Leave.* Leave while she could, leave with her treasure chest full of memories from such a wonderful night. She was a fool for staying as long as she had. But when Edmund had run into her bedchamber and the three of them descended the stairs to the party, she couldn't tear herself away from the dream of having such a family.

If only for an hour…or two.

Still, how cruel and selfish of her to keep up the charade when Elias made his intentions obvious. He would ask for permission to court her, of that she was sure.

If only she could say yes.

She wove through the crowd, her plan to first seek out Rose to thank her for her kindness, and then head to the stables to find a groomsman to drive her into town.

But Rose didn't look too well. Perched on the same chair where Charity had left her, face pale, eyes wide, she bent over, gripping her waist. No one around her seemed to notice her discomfort, not even the two ladies who stood by her side chattering away.

Dropping to her knees, Charity grabbed her hand. "Rose, what's the matter?"

The lady clawed at Charity's arm, eyes burning with pain. "Please, help me."

# Chapter 25

"What news?" Sliding his foot in the stirrup, Elias swung onto the back of a chestnut gelding and took the reins from the groomsman. Beside him, Caleb's steed pawed the ground in anticipation.

"Vigilantes spotted on the eastern boundary. Carrying torches. We think they intend to set fire to the barn full of recently harvested sugarcane ready to be transported to the mill."

Elias nodded and glanced at Ballard, Gage, and Josiah, fully armed, mounted on horses behind them. Gage and Josiah looked a little more than nervous on their frisky horses. Elias smiled. Most sailors hadn't opportunities to perfect their equestrian skills.

Behind his men, ten more were mounted and ready to go, some workers from his sister's estate and others from Caleb's ship.

Caleb stared off into the night, his black hair blowing behind him. "We fended off a band of them last night, shot two and ran a sword through one. I thought that would stop them, but apparently they need another lesson."

"Then let's teach them one, shall we?" Elias raised his brow.

Grinning, Caleb nudged his horse, and they charged into the night.

An hour later, shirt dampened with sweat, Elias raised his sword to fend off his opponent's latest attack. Moonlight shimmered off the advancing blade, making it easy for Elias to knock it to the side. Metal on metal chimed through the night air, along with grunts and groans, and the stomp of boots in mud. Beside him, Caleb swept his blade in low and sliced his adversary's leg. Howling, the man fell to the ground.

They had come upon the band of miscreants just yards from the barn. Though they were outnumbered two to one, Caleb's expertise in battle, along with Elias' skill with the sword, had encouraged their men to make quick work of the villains.

Several had already abandoned the fight.

The man who now attacked Elias, upon seeing his companion fall, tossed his blade to the ground and darted into the darkness.

Another man picked up the sword and swung it at Elias. He leapt out of the way just in time and pivoted to slice his blade across the man's arm.

Caleb knocked a new attacker over the head with the hilt of his sword, then turned to face another, while in the distance, Ballard, Gage, Josiah and the rest of the men shouted and grunted as they battled the remaining scoundrels.

The smell of sweat, blood, and, oddly, night jasmine filled Elias' nose as he rushed his opponent, sword swirling aloft and then cleaving down with a hissing sound. The man met his blade, the eerie chime echoing into the night. Back and forth they parried until Elias nicked the villain's belly and knocked his sword from his hand. Eyes wide, the fellow took off faster than his wide girth should allow.

Caleb plucked out his pistol and pointed it at his opponent's head. Trembling, hands raised, the man fell to his knees. "Don't kill me! Please...don't kill me!"

The rest of the vigilantes, seeing their leader cowering before Caleb, fled into the night.

Grabbing ahold of the man's collar, Caleb jerked him to stand, then spun him around and kicked him in the behind. "Take a message to your benefactors. Any man who dares attack Bennett land again will have an appointment with the devil."

The man stumbled across the field, never looking back, and disappeared into the jungle.

Panting, Caleb wiped a sleeve over his forehead. "That should put them off until Duncan arrives with the King's command."

"Indeed." Elias smiled and clapped him on the back. "A pleasure to fight by your side."

"'Twas fun, wasn't it?" Caleb grinned.

Gage approached, splatters of blood on his shirt, and Elias gripped his shoulder. "Good fighting for a surgeon."

Grinning, Gage flipped his knife in the air and caught it by the hilt. "Who says a surgeon's only skill with a knife is on the operating table?"

Elias searched the men and found Josiah sheathing his sword. "Where's Ballard?"

Gage shrugged. "He was just here, Captain."

After ensuring all their enemies had fled, Caleb and Elias mounted their horses and led their battle-weary men back to the estate. Aside from some minor cuts and bruises, no one was hurt badly, thank God. Except Ballard had disappeared. Odd. Perhaps the man was a coward and ran back to the house.

Moonlight banded the sugar fields in silver while a breeze cooled the sweat on Elias' arms and neck.

"I hated that I wasn't here when Rose needed me," he said to Caleb riding beside him.

"You were at your sister's wedding in London, correct?"

Elias nodded.

"Then 'tis no need for remorse. God is with Rose, and He sent me as well."

"How did you even know to come?"

"I didn't. Just a feeling, something in my spirit. I expect that was God." Caleb chuckled.

Elias nudged his horse around a large rock. "But I should have been here. I knew she was with child and all alone."

"'Tis her husband's and God's charge, not yours. You aren't God's appointed champion of the world, you know."

Elias grimaced. Hadn't his sister just told him the same thing? "Nay, but He made me defender of my family."

"He did?" Caleb smiled. "You must be quite powerful and resourceful for Him to charge you with such a responsibility."

Frowning at the man's sarcasm, Elias withdrew his cross from beneath his shirt, barely making it out in the dim light. "After I behaved the fool and ruined my sister's life, how could God do any less?"

"You speak of Caleigh?"

Elias nodded, but couldn't bring himself to say her name. The cry of a nighthawk rose to accompany the stomp of horses' hooves in mud and the distant waves crashing ashore.

Caleb gave an incredulous snort. "You blame yourself? She lost her leg because she foolishly ran after that woman … what was her name?"

"Rachel." A sour taste filled Elias' mouth. "And 'twas me who brought *that woman* into my home long enough for her to pretend to befriend Caleigh."

"Caleigh chased after Rachel of her own volition. Against your parents' orders."

"She was young and vulnerable, and with all her sisters away, desperate for a friend her own age."

Caleb turned the horse onto the Bennett driveway leading to the stables. "You carry a huge burden on your shoulders, Elias."

"Can you deny I ruined her life?"

"Indeed, I can. I recently saw her in Charles Towne. She seemed quite happy. In fact, your mother says she has so many suitors she cannot choose."

Bah! That couldn't be true. What gentleman would court a woman who couldn't walk, who would *never* walk. Not many he knew. "I don't believe you."

Caleb laughed. "Begad, Sir. Are you calling the son of a pirate, the grandson of a pirate, a liar?"

Elias smiled. "I wouldn't dare. I've just seen your skill with the sword."

"Wise man."

They arrived at the stables, and Elias dismissed the men who had injuries to Gage's care.

"You should have your surgeon attend to that as well." Caleb pointed to a cut on Elias' arm.

"'Tis nothing." Elias hesitated. Part of him wanted to run back to Charity, part of him needed to continue his discussion with Caleb, needed to sort out his thoughts. His friend had always been a good listener and someone Elias trusted.

Caleb must have sensed his need. "Walk with me, Elias."

Together they strolled through the gardens in silence, listening to the chirp of katydids drifting atop orchestra music from the house.

Stopping by a stone fountain, Caleb faced Elias. A dark cloud swallowed up the moon, hiding his expression. "Did it ever occur to you that mayhap 'twas God's will Caleigh lost her leg?"

"Nay!" Elias growled. "Never let it be said God would ordain such a thing."

"Have you spent much time with your sister since the accident?"

Thunder rumbled across the sky.

Elias glanced up and sighed. "'Tis difficult to see her pain, knowing I am the cause."

"You and you alone are the cause, is that it?" Picking up a stone, Caleb tossed it into a bush. "No allowance for her own free will or God's plan? She's become a different person after the accident, Elias. Kinder, more charitable, considerate. And if I had to guess, closer to God." He chuckled and speared a hand through his hair. "You must admit she used to be a bit of a spoiled chit."

Against the angst churning in his gut, Elias smiled his agreement as the sweet scent of rain filled the air.

"Elias, you cannot take all the blame for her accident on yourself, nor burden yourself with the protection of your siblings. First, you must consider that our enemy lurks about like a lion seeking whom he may devour. Next, that the free will of others plays an enormous part in life's events. And lastly, we never know the plan and purpose of God. His ways are so far beyond our understanding."

Rain drops splattered on the stone fountain, splashing Elias' arms, but they did naught to cool his anger. "I cannot believe the ultimate plan of God was to cripple my sister for life."

"It may not have been, but seems He used it for her good anyway. Even if you were partially to blame, what if it *was* His will? What if God saw the accident as the only way to get Caleigh to turn to Him? Is her leg worth more than her eternal soul?"

Elias rubbed the back of his neck and gazed at the house. Music, laughter, and light spilled from windows and blended with the darkness beyond. So much like life where light and dark melded so close together 'twas impossible to distinguish one from the other. Thunder growled again as the raindrops grew heavier, tapping on the dirt and leaves, and pummeling his head and shoulders.

Caleb stood his ground, unaffected by the storm. "A year ago," he began, raising his voice over the din. "I found myself imprisoned on a Spanish Merchant Ship by my own foolishness. I knew I shouldn't have gone to Porto Bello. I heard God's warning loud and clear, but in my stubborn arrogance, I thought I could stop my sister from marrying Don Garcia del Bosque. I failed to trust God and took matters into my own hands. Instead of saving my sister, I was captured and imprisoned on a ship heading for Spain."

"I never knew this. What happened?"

"God in his mercy sent a pirate to the rescue." Caleb chuckled. "Quite an entertaining pirate, I might add. A Captain Poole. He plundered the Spanish merchantman, rescued me from the hold, and set sail. Soon after, a squall rose so violent it threated the ship and all on board. I felt God leading me to command the waves to be still in the name of Jesus."

Elias stared at him in wonderment. "What happened?"

"The seas calmed, of course, and all the pirates on board witnessed the hand of God."

"Amazing." Elias never grew tired of stories of God's power. "What did they do?"

"Fearful and anxious to be rid of me, they set me on the nearest island instead of kill me for refusing to join them. So, you see my friend, those men would have never heard about God without my foolishness. He used my mistake for good in the end."

Elias nodded. "'Tis a good story with a happy ending. Not all are that fortunate."

"All God's endings are happy if we wait for them."

Elias gripped his friend's arm. "You have given me much to think about, Caleb."

"Good." Caleb thumbed toward the house and started walking. "Let's get out of this rain and find that beauty of yours. I'd like to get to know her better."

Elias fell in step beside him. "Do you take me for a fool? I'm not letting you anywhere near her."

They both laughed and started up the stairs…when a blood-curdling scream blared from the house.

Charity paced before Rose's bedchamber, nervously wringing her hands and wincing every time the poor woman screamed. Next to her in the hallway huddled a group of housemaids, anxious for news of the new arrival—though their faces portrayed more fear than excitement. Indeed, birthing was akin to battle for women. Many didn't survive. Nor did their children. And though Charity had never pushed a full-grown babe from her womb, she had delivered a wee one, not yet big enough to survive. Wiping tears from her eyes at the memory, she continued pacing. She couldn't even think about that now. Wouldn't think about it. Suddenly she wished she was on speaking terms with God so she could lift up a prayer.

The midwife had arrived an hour ago, a seemingly competent older woman who had immediately dismissed Charity as being a maiden and hence, unable to assist. If she only knew.

But with each howl of agony, Charity longed to enter the room and help in any way she could. The poor woman's husband was not even here, nor Elias, gone off to defend the estate. "God protect him," she whispered a prayer, hoping mayhap God would have mercy on her and listen for once. "And God save Rose and her babe," she added just in case.

The door flung open and a maid poked out her head. "Harriet," she addressed one of the servants. "More water and clean cloths."

"How is she?" Charity asked, straining to peer into the room but seeing only the midwife's large frame looming over the bed.

Terror sparked in the young lady's eyes before she closed the door.

Charity swallowed, her heart sprinting, her hands moist from perspiration.

A groan, grunt, and then a wall-shattering howl blared from the chamber, chilling Charity to the bone. Unable to stand by another second, she shoved the door open and dashed inside.

*Blood...blood...so much blood!* And Rose a wilted flower deflated on her pillow, her face white, her eyes mere slits as if all her energy had escaped her. A tiny form lay still in the midwife's hands.

It wasn't moving.

Charity drew a deep breath to calm herself, to think...think...think...but nearly choked on the metallic smell of blood mixed with tallow from the candle that flickered from the nightstand. Rose's lady's maid fell to the floor sobbing, while the midwife wrapped the baby—a boy—in a clean cloth.

"My baby." Rose raised a hand toward her child, the smile on her face indicating she didn't yet know his fate.

Forcing back tears, Charity knelt by her bed and took her hand in hers. Cold, so cold, Charity attempted to warm it between hers.

"Charity," Rose breathed out. "Where is my son?"

Charity glanced at the midwife. Sorrow claimed her chubby features as she shook her head to affirm the worst.

"Your son is in heaven, Rose. Where all angels belong."

Rose's eyes widened as if she refused to believe the words. Her forehead wrinkled. Her breath came hard and fast. Tears flooded her eyes. "No! No! No!" she wailed in agony, squeezing Charity's hand. "No! This can't be. Let me see him."

The midwife made no attempt to hand over the babe.

"I *will* see my son!" Rose attempted to rise but then fell back.

A servant entered with a pitcher of water and cloths, halting at the sight. The lady's maid continued sobbing on the floor.

Taking charge, Charity stood and pointed at the weeping maid. "Please take her out of here!" she ordered the servant, and as the girl dragged the maid from the room, Charity took the child from the midwife and placed him gently in Rose's arms.

"Oh, my poor baby, my poor baby!" Moving aside the cloth, Rose examined his tiny, still body, tears pouring down her cheeks onto the babe's head.

Charity could no longer stop her own tears. Her knees quivered and it took all her strength not to topple to the floor at the sight. *So many memories—horrid, horrid memories.* She knew this pain intimately, felt it gnaw open a gaping wound in her gut that had never healed.

Rose leaned to kiss her child then suddenly snapped her gaze to Charity. "You must pray for him, Charity. You must pray and he will live."

"What are you talking about?" Charity shook her head. Panic stormed through her, and she feared the worst. *Anguish was driving Rose mad.* "I can't pray. God doesn't listen to me. I'm sorry."

"You must. Please!" Sniffing, Rose wiped tears from her face with the back of her hand. "It is *you.* It has to be you."

Ignoring them, the midwife started gathering the blood-soaked cloths scattered around the bed.

Charity backed away. "We should wait for Elias. Or I will gladly call someone else to pray."

"Nay, it must be you. Please! You must hurry." Rose gazed down at her son.

Numbness crept up Charity's legs. *What am I to do?*

*When the pie was opened*
*The birds began to sing*

*Wasn't that a dainty dish*
*To set before the King...*

She couldn't let this sweet woman down. Not when she
had hope, even if it was misplaced hope. What Charity
wouldn't have given to have had someone pray over her lost
child. If only to bring comfort.

"Very well." On wobbling legs, Charity approached the
bed, knelt beside it, placed her hands on the babe, and bowed
her head. She had no idea how to pray such a prayer. All of
Elias' recent prayers filled her mind. She would pray like he
did, like God was really there, and He actually cared. "Father
God, please revive this child."

What else could she say? She searched her mind for things
she'd read in the Bible. Hadn't the disciples merely
commanded a person to rise? "Be healed, come to life, rise,
in the name of Jesus," she added. Tears trickled down her
cheeks, dripped off her jaw onto the coverlet. The boy didn't
move. Lying her head on the bed, she broke down and
sobbed.

The door slammed open, and Charity looked up to see
Elias, bloodstains on his shirt, water dripping from his hair,
and a look of terror on his face. His gaze passed from her to
his sister to the babe.

The child coughed.

# Chapter 26

E lias rubbed his eyes, unsure whether he was seeing things clearly. He wouldn't normally have burst into the middle of a birthing, but the maids outside the door were wailing so hysterically, he feared the worst. After he assured himself his sister was alive, his eyes landed on Charity, hands on the babe, praying for it to rise. Had he heard her correctly?

The baby coughed, gurgled, and began to wiggle. Shouting with glee, Rose scooped up her child while Charity struggled to her feet, stumbled, and backed away from the bed, hand on her chest.

A large woman who must be the midwife stared in horror before she dashed out of the room, screaming as if she'd seen a ghost.

"My son! My son!" Rose exclaimed, gesturing for Elias to enter. "He's alive. God raised him, Elias!"

Mind spinning, Elias closed the door ever so slowly and approached. Avoiding the bloody sheets, he sat on the bed beside his sister.

Nestled within a blanket, the infant squirmed and whimpered as she unwrapped him and checked all his toes and fingers before swaddling him tight again. "Meet Malcom, my son." Rose smiled.

"He's beautiful, Rose."

She glanced over at Charity who had retreated into the shadows by the armoire. "Thank you, Charity."

"I didn't…didn't…he was stillborn."

"Yes." Rose kissed his forehead. "But God told me He would use you to heal him."

Rising, Elias moved slowly toward Charity. Shock screamed from her eyes as she stared at the babe as if looking at a ghost. He reached for her hand, and only when he gripped it, did she finally look his way.

"God used your prayer to save this child, Charity. He answered you." This was precisely what he'd been praying for, for God to make Himself known to her…to show her that He loved her. *Thank you, Father.*

But his words didn't bring her the comfort he hoped. Instead, she threw a hand to her mouth and ran from the room weeping.

A half-moon spiraled white light around Charity, transforming pools into silver and droplets on leaves into glittering diamonds. She hugged herself and continued sloshing through the soaked gardens behind the estate, realizing she was ruining the beautiful silk embroidered shoes Rose had so graciously lent her. Guilt piled atop her dismay, but it was too late to replace them with her own shoes. She hadn't even returned to her room, knowing Elias would probably seek her there. She had to be alone. She needed to think. But her mind, along with her heart, was careening this way and that, emotions whirling—pain, shock, elation, fear, anger. So many, she couldn't latch onto any one of them in the hope of regaining her sanity. So, she'd spent the past hour among the night owls, insects, and frogs, the distant sound of waves, and a sky so lustrous with stars, she wondered how she could ever have thought there was no God.

But she had. She'd been battling the idea for years. Her father believed, her sisters—well, most of them—believed, but had *she* truly believed He was real? That His Son had died for her? Or had she just spoken the words everyone expected?

What few crumbs of faith she possessed, Lord Villemont had then stolen. Until tonight. Until she felt God's mighty power rush through her hands, extend through her fingertips in spires of tingling heat, and breathe life into that small babe.

The voices that rose to taunt her afterward—telling her 'twas naught but a coincidence, that the infant had been alive the entire time—she dismissed immediately as lies from the pit of hell. Of all people, she knew exactly what a stillborn babe looked like.

And that baby had been dead for over five minutes.

Which only meant one thing. There was a God, and He answered prayers.

*Even* hers.

Water splashed and footsteps approached, and a giant shadow headed her way. Clutching her skirts, she was about to run when Josiah stepped into a sliver of moonlight.

"Josiah, you frightened me." She caught her breath.

"Forgive me, Miss. I saw someone movin' from my window an' thought mebbe was one o' those villains come to attack again."

She spotted the bandage on his arm. "You're hurt."

"It be nothin' miss. They fared much worse."

Charity smiled, picturing Elias wielding a sword and pistol. No doubt the men had not expected such fierce and well-skilled opposition.

"I heard what you did wit' the babe," Josiah said, his voice as deep and dark as his skin. His immense frame engulfed hers as if she were but a skiff drifting beside a Ship of the Line. Yet, she bore no fear. A peace clung to him she could not explain. A peace she hadn't felt in years, if ever.

At her silence, he added. "The news is all over the house, Miss."

"I did nothing."

"Not what I'm hearin'. I would think you'd be happy, but I sense a sorrow about you."

"I am happy the baby is alive and well." She lowered her chin and sighed. "I'm just confused and, I suppose, angry." She knew he wouldn't understand, so she excused herself and started walking away.

He appeared at her side, keeping her pace, silent, waiting...

And she found herself longing to ask him the question burning on her heart—ask this ex-slave, this wise man who carried Scripture in his pocket. She shouldn't. He was first and foremost Elias' man. But something about him...his silence, his patience, dare she say, the care she felt emanating from him...lured it out of her.

"There was another baby once," she said. "One God did not spare."

He continued walking by her side, saying nothing.

Anger raged within her, and she stopped and stared up at him. "Why didn't God save her? Why save this one and not the other? Don't misunderstand, I'm happy for Rose." She rubbed her temples. "Never mind. I don't know what I'm saying, forgive me." She started on her way, but he halted her with a touch.

"Not all prayers get answered the way we wants, Miss."

"Some don't get answered at all," she retorted. "Or perhaps only good people's prayers get answered."

He laughed. "God's no respecter o' persons, Miss. As long as you are His child and sincere in your prayer, He hears and answers."

"Then I must not be *His* child."

"If you've received the sacrifice of His Son, Jesus, on your behalf, then you are His child. He adopted you in His family."

A breeze stirred her damp curls, bringing with it the spicy scent of rain, moist earth, and the sea. She sighed. "Then I suppose God is a harsh Father, ready to punish for every mistake, every infraction." Just like her own father had been.

"Aye, He's a father, an' sometimes He has to discipline His children to get them back on the right path. But the Scripture says"—he patted his pocket—"His mercies are new every morn." His white teeth gleamed in the moonlight. "He forgives an' blesses us when we don't deserve it."

Charity huffed. She had yet to experience either. "Why, then, when we pray and pray and pray, do things get worse and worse?"

"We's all got choices in life, Miss. One choice leads us down a certain path, which leads us down another path that mebbe God hadn't planned on. Then He's got to change things up, try to help us out o' where we're at. But if we won't listen to him an' keep makin' bad choices, what can He do? Or mebbe someone else's bad choice affects us, or maybe the devil hisself attacked an' plundered us. This world be fallen, Miss."

"But God still could have saved the child I'm talking about."

"How do you know He didn't?"

Confusion joined fury in a vicious brew in her stomach. "I buried her myself," she spat with more spite than intended. "I buried her myself." This time, the words spilled out on a sob as tears trickled down her cheeks, and she felt all strength abandon her.

She must have wobbled, for he grabbed her arm and held her in place. "Her body. Not her soul or spirit. Miss. That baby be now in Heaven wit' God. An' believe me, there's no better place to be. Who knows what tragedies she woulda suffered if she stayed here."

Stunned, Charity had never considered that. No doubt her precious Cassia would have grown up unloved and abused by her own father.

Releasing her, Josiah plucked a handkerchief from his pocket and handed it to her. "There's so much we don't know an' so much we can't see goin' on around us. Our lives are but a drop o' water in the sea." With more tenderness than she thought possible from such large hands, Josiah touched a drop of rain dangling from a leaf. "All you can do is follow God the best you can an' trust He loves you."

"Thank you, Josiah." She dabbed her eyes. "I see why Elias relies on you so much."

He grunted. "Now, you best get inside, Miss. It's not safe out at night."

Up in her chamber, Charity disrobed and slid beneath the coverlet, feeling no better for her chat with Josiah. In fact, she was more confused and distraught than ever. No matter how hard she tried, the vision of Rose's dead son haunted her. One minute he lay there, lifeless and blue, the next she saw her own baby girl, smaller but just as still and quiet. Dead—her grave a cold, dreary place for all eternity.

In a fitful state, she drifted in and out of consciousness, feeling tears soak her pillow.

Memories paraded through her thoughts—faces, moments in time, words and warnings. Her father's disapproval of Lord Villemont...

"The man is not right for you, Charity. There's something about him that disturbs me, but I will give my blessing if this is what you want."

Her sisters warnings, particularly Grace's. "He's not a Godly man, Charity. He's all show and pomp."

But he *was* a Godly man. At least that's what Charity had thought. He could recite the Bible, he attended church regularly, and he prayed the most eloquent prayers she'd ever heard.

She'd stood there, hands on her hips, facing her disapproving family, determined to marry him, despite the gnawing in her own gut. Lord Villemont was the most charming man she'd ever met, kind, loyal, wise, and he had fortune and title. What more could a lady want? What other way to escape the mediocre, lonely life of an Admiral's daughter and elevate her station?

A collage of cruel beatings and verbal beratings twisted her thoughts. He had changed so quickly after the wedding.

*You worthless cow. Can't even manage a house like a lady should.*

*Where has your beauty run off to? Did I not marry the prettiest lady in Portsmouth, yet you have aged ten years in the past month. Scads! You disgust me!*

A strike to the face, a shove that sent her toppling into a table, a slap, a chokehold about her neck, brandy tossed in her face, a torn gown, a broken arm, black eye...

A lost child...

A door opened. Outside, the sun shone bright and clear, and the air was fresh. Inside was darkness, stale odor, and hate. A pouch of money appeared in her hand. A man made entirely of light filled the doorway, gesturing her forward.

She could leave. She could be free! But wait. If she left, she'd disgrace her family, she'd lose her title and fortune. She'd be nothing but a poor admiral's daughter again.

She hesitated. The door shut.

Darkness consumed her. Lord Villemont's squealy laughter scraped down her spine. Like an executioner's drum, his footsteps approached.

Another door opened. The light beckoned. "Come, come, I will keep you safe," the voice said, the kindest, most loving voice she'd ever heard. She must go. She could leave. But no...

The door slammed shut.

Darkness again. Her sister Hope screaming for help.

"Where are you, Hope? Where are you? I'm coming." Charity groped through the thick blackness.

Lord Villemont laughed. His sharp slap stung her face. She tumbled backward and landed on the floor as Hope's weeping faded.

Steam from the teapot rose to mingle with the afternoon sun streaming through the windows of her parlor. Charity ran a hand over her belly and smiled, then checked the rest of her attire, making sure there were no rips or stains or wrinkles which would embarrass his Lordship in front of his guests.

Then he stood before her, dressed in his usual glimmer and fluff, a pistol at his hip. Why? Ah, yes, that's right. He was assisting the constable on a legal matter. She remained still, as was required, while his dark eyes assessed her for some unknown infraction. The stench of brandy surrounding him didn't bode well for his mood. Charity swallowed the bitter taste in her throat as everything shifted into the slow motion of a horrifying nightmare...

The grate of carriage wheels outside the window, the scent of tea and brandy, Lord Villemont angry about something...

She couldn't make out his words. He struck her face. She fell backward onto the settee. He slapped her again, his ring slicing her lip. Clutching her hair, he dragged her up. She struggled to be free.

He drew back his fist to punch her in the stomach.

*No! Not my baby! Not again!* She grabbed the gun, cocked it, and pointed it at him. It trembled in her hand.

He laughed. "You pathetic little whore." He charged her, gripped the weapon, and tried to yank it from her hands.

*POP!*

Charity's eyes snapped open. She flung off the covers, heart racing, breath panting, and damp with perspiration.

Threads of bright light wove through a crack in the curtains. She breathed a ragged sigh and brushed hair from her face.

Sobbing, she slid off the bed and dropped to knees. She'd suspected what Villemont had done to her sister Hope. She knew something was terribly wrong from the look on her sisters' faces, the whispers behind her back. When she confronted him, he denied it, said they were jealous that she'd found a man of title and wealth while they were but spinsters. But she knew. Tears spilled over her lashes. And she'd done nothing. *Stupid, stupid woman!*

God had warned her not to marry Lord Villemont, through her family, through her own instincts. But she had not listened. Then after she was married, God had opened doors for her to escape. Yes, as the memories flooded back, there'd been at least three times when she had the money and means to leave and return to her family—two before they moved across the pond to Charles Towne, and one afterward. But she had stayed. At first for the title and fortune, the respect— things that in retrospect now seemed so unimportant. Then, she'd stayed because everyone loved Lord Villemont, a pillar of Portsmouth society, and leaving him would bring irreparable shame to family. Besides, he kept promising never to strike her again, that things would get better between them. And like a fool, she believed him.

However the final reason she stayed trumped all the others. He threatened to hunt her down and kill her if she left him.

So she stayed, instead of trusting God.

Josiah was right. God had been trying to rescue her all along, but she had kept making the wrong choices, thwarting His plans. And in the end, she'd blamed Him for it.

Charity fell to the floor in a heap as deep, gut-wrenching sorrow consumed her in wave after wave until she could hardly breathe. "I'm so sorry, Lord. I'm so sorry. I've made a muck of things. If I had only listened to You. If I'd only believed."

Silence invaded the room, so deafening it seemed to swallow her whole. She pushed from the floor and wiped her face, gazing upward. "Father, please help me." Would God hear her? Would He care? Or was it too late for her?

Warmth encased her. Not the warmth offered by the sun, a roaring fire, or a thick quilt. But a warmth that bloomed deep within her. It radiated through her belly, her chest, then out every limb.

*I've always loved you, daughter. All is forgiven.*

Her heart leapt as she heard the words clearly in her spirit.

*Now, my child, you must go tell Elias the truth.*

# Chapter 27

"Mr. Ballard, Sir. May I speak with you?"

Ignoring the young maid's voice behind him, Ballard continued out the front door of the Bennett manor, nodding at the butler holding the door open as he went. He hadn't time to deal with whatever minor issue the staff had and hoped she'd go away.

But she didn't go away. She dashed down the front steps after him as he took the reins of a horse from the groomsman.

"Mr. Ballard, a word, Sir?"

Huffing, he faced her. "Miss, I fear I'm quite late for an appointment. Is it urgent?" Yet he couldn't imagine what the woman could possibly say that would be of import to him. At least not as important as his meeting with Nelson in town— one that he'd arranged last night. Word was this Charles Gregson, Lord Villemont, had arrived in Bridgetown, and he and Nelson were waiting for Ballard's directions to Bennett manor. Why? They wouldn't disclose the specifics, only to say that Elias Dutton would suffer.

And that was enough for Ballard.

"Beggin' your pardon, Sir, but yes, I think it's urgent. It's about Miss Charity and Mr. Dutton."

The horse snorted and pawed the ground. Ballard slid on his gloves, studying the maid. "Do tell."

"The truth is I 'aven't known who to tell, but I see you're a good friend of Mr. Dutton an'—"

"Tell what, Miss? And hurry with it."

"It's Miss Charity. You see I 'elped with 'er dressing nigh' afore last and she ..." The maid glanced down.

"Out with it!" Ballard grabbed the pommel and swung onto his horse.

"She's with child, Sir."

Ballard nearly lost his balance. The horse bucked, and he quickly tightened the reins lest the animal toss him to the ground.

He stared down at the young woman. "Are you sure?"

"Aye, Sir. I recognize the condition from when Mrs. Bennett was in the same way."

*Interesting. Very interesting.* Ballard smiled. Whatever Nelson and Villemont had planned, it couldn't be as delicious as this. However, since Elias had departed early that morning, and no one knew when he would return, Ballard might as well join forces with Nelson and Villemont and cause even more damage.

"Thank you, Miss. You can be sure I will handle the situation with the utmost care."

After rising and donning a fresh gown—chosen from among the many Rose had deposited in the wardrobe— Charity all but floated down the stairs toward the dining hall. She couldn't explain it, but she felt different, as if a huge weight had been wrenched from her shoulders and tossed into the sea. She couldn't wait to tell Elias about her newfound faith and her talk with God. Well...at least some of it.

Apparently everyone had already eaten, for there was no one in the dining hall save a footman and a maid ready to serve her. A balmy breeze wafted in through open French doors, where she spotted the sun high in the sky, shimmering light on waving palms and flitting birds. Shame heated her at how long she'd slept.

Though she was anxious to speak with Elias and check on Rose and the baby, the scents of fresh papaya, bananas, eggs, and sausage lured her to at least sit for a moment and enjoy a small bit of the delicious-smelling food, along with a cup of Jamaican coffee. That bit turned into an entire plateful as she found her appetite nearly insatiable.

Even the footman's brows lifted at the amount of food she consumed, but when she inquired after Elias, he informed her Mr. Dutton had left early that morn to meet the master in town and then attend the Assembly meeting.

"Mr. Bennett has arrived home?" she asked the tall, light-haired man.

"Indeed, Miss. We received word his ship arrived just before dawn."

With that happy news in hand, Charity sought out Rose, but the housekeeper told her she and the babe were sleeping. So Charity wandered around the house, admiring the teak and Spanish cedar furniture, coral tiles covering the floors, marble statues of angels, and painted vases filled with freshly picked flowers, all the while enjoying the cool breezes that swept through the house from all directions. She ended up in the parlor near the front entrance where she spotted paintings of various pirates hanging on the wall—all done by the elusive *LM*—Elias' mother. She smiled. Finally, as the sun sank toward the horizon, she strolled through the garden, stopping to gaze at the endless fields of sugar cane waving in the breeze—a sea of lustrous green—and breathed in the air scented by sweet flowers, earthy loam, and the sea. What a beautiful place to live.

If only that were possible...

But she knew it wasn't. God had ordered her to tell Elias the truth. And she must do so. She must, for once, follow His will and not her own. Though Elias might be able to forgive her delicate condition because of his own indiscretion, he would never forgive her for all her lies. She couldn't blame him. After Rachel, he needed a woman he could trust. And Charity had proven she was not that woman.

After she told him her sordid tale, she would leave this beautiful place and make her way to Charles Towne—if Elias would even allow a murderess to go free. However, she imagined he'd be glad to be rid of her when he discovered the truth. At least she wouldn't slink away in the middle of the night, leaving him forever wondering why. This way, 'twould be her heart, and her heart alone, that would forever split into a thousand pieces.

The wail of a newborn brought her back to the house. She found Rose in her bedchamber sitting by an open window, swaddled babe in her arms, and an angelic look on her face. Though the maid had told Charity that Rose was accepting visitors, she hesitated at the door, unsure whether to intrude, but Rose looked up and smiled. "Charity, dearest, come in."

Charity rushed to her side. "You must be so thrilled your husband is on his way home!"

Rose's eyes twinkled. "I cannot wait to see him." She glanced lovingly at her baby. "And I cannot wait for him to see his son. He, along with Elias and Caleb, should have already delivered the king's letter to the Assembly by now. Hopefully that will stop all this madness."

"Let us pray so." Charity slid onto the window seat beside her.

"Perhaps I should ask *you* to pray for that." Rose smiled, then reached for Charity's hand. "How can I thank you for saving my son?"

"You know as well as I that I had naught to do with that."

"You were obedient to the voice of God. And for that, I owe you all."

Charity lowered her chin. 'Twas she who owed these people everything.

"Would you like to hold him?" Rose asked.

Delight lifted Charity's gaze. She swallowed, feeling suddenly overwhelmed with conflicting emotions. The last baby she'd held had been the lifeless body of her daughter. Would she lose control, weep incessantly, and embarrass herself? "Yes, I'd love to."

Carefully, Rose transferred the babe into Charity's arms. He squirmed and made sucking noises with his perfectly-shaped pink lips. Smiling, she held him close and dared to touch his cheek. *So soft!* He opened his eyes ever so slightly and stared at her...and unable to help it anymore, tears blurred her vision. "He's perfect."

Rose allowed Charity to hold him for nearly an hour before he grew hungry. Yet when Charity started to leave to give her privacy, Rose insisted she stay. Settling down onto a cushioned chair, Charity could hardly believe the lady found her company enjoyable. Yet several hours passed in which they laughed and chatted about all manner of topics. Charity had never had a true friend. Though she'd grown up with three sisters, they'd spent most of their childhood squabbling. This precious woman before her was the friend Charity had always hoped for, longed for, but had never been allowed to have after she married Lord Villemont.

Boot steps stomped down the hall and a rather handsome man with brown wavy hair, a strong jaw, thick eyebrows, and serious eyes appeared in the doorway.

Rose nearly leapt from her seat. "Duncan!"

He sped toward his wife and knelt by her side, caressing her cheek, before he stared down at his son, emotion flooding his eyes.

Charity slipped quietly from the room, halting in the doorway for the briefest of seconds to watch the exchange, unable to pull herself away from the love pouring between the couple as they rejoiced over their son.

Would she ever know love like that? Would she ever have a family of her own—a man who would love her child and give her more?

After Villemont, she vowed never to take a chance. But then came Elias. His love gave her hope that maybe...maybe her dreams could come true after all.

She wandered down the hall, rubbing her temples where a headache brewed. Mayhap she didn't have to tell him about Villemont, her marriage, his death at her hand. After all, it seemed her brother-in-law had given up the chase, and it was quite possible no one sought her in the colonies.

If she told Elias only about the child and then vowed never to lie to him again, would that satisfy God. What good would it do, anyway, to tell Elias everything? Nothing would be gained, and it would only cause him pain.

*Except you would be disobeying God.*

Two hours later, Charity, decked in her evening attire, waited in the library. A servant had delivered a note to her chamber asking her to meet Elias privately before the evening meal. For what purpose, her imagination took flight. Yet each time she allowed her heart to swell with possibility, her hopes were quickly deflated by the fact that she *must* tell him the truth. The thought of exposing her true nature, revealing her dark heart to this honorable man, made her queasy.

She paced before the fireplace, realizing she'd never repented for certain unmentionable acts. "Father God, I am truly sorry for killing my husband. 'Twas an accident, as You know."

But *was* she truly sorry? Hadn't she rejoiced in his death? That joy had long since faded, replaced only today by a rising sorrow for the man. If he hadn't been a true follower of Christ, he was not in a very nice place at the moment. And despite all his cruelty to her, she didn't want that end for him. Or anyone.

"Yes, I *am* truly sorry, Father. If I had only done as You asked, it would have never happened."

Turning, she paced in the other direction as an unusual sense of love and acceptance bubbled up within her. *God?* She nearly giggled with joy. Could God truly forgive such a horrid sin? Yet she could not deny His presence filling her heart and the warmth tingling down her as if God, Himself, were embracing her.

"You look lovely." Elias' baritone voice drew her gaze to the door where he stood smiling at her as if she were pirate treasure. Dressed in a suit of black velvet with a fine cambric shirt, tall Hessian boots, and his chestnut-colored hair slicked back into a tie, she could only stare as he strode toward her, all man and strength and honor.

She felt a blush rising. Averting her gaze she fingered the books on the shelf. "I hear you have yet again saved the day."

"To which brave feat do you refer? The thwarting of vigilantes last night or standing with Duncan before the Assembly today?"

"Both." She turned and clasped her hands before her, suddenly nervous.

He started toward her, a half smile on his face and his eyes beaming with affection. "You flatter me, my little mermaid. I had little to do with either success."

"I doubt that, Preacher. You have much to do with a good many things."

He stopped, shifted his feet uncomfortably and looked away. Was he embarrassed by her flattery? How utterly charming.

She swept past him, brushing his arm and inhaling a whiff of his scent. No cologne for this man, just a fresh earthy scent that was uniquely him. She sashayed around a chair and table, fingered a lamp, and then nonchalantly examined a tapestry hanging above the mantel—playing the coquette, if only to settle her nerves. However, she found she rather enjoyed the romantic dalliance.

And by the grin on his face as she glanced his way, he was enjoying it too. Is this what it felt like to be courted by a real gentleman? Loved, sought after, cherished—a wondrous adventure awaiting them both as they plumbed the depths of each other's souls, discovering common dreams and hopes that forged a bond of eternity.

*Vapors!* What was she thinking? Silly, silly woman! Would she never learn?

He moved to stand beside her.

She strolled to the far window where a night breeze stirred maroon curtains. "What is it you wish to speak to me about, Elias? I must admit I'm quite famished and anxious for dinner." Her stomach felt like a tangled ball of wire.

"If you'd stop running from me for a moment, I'll be glad to tell you."

She turned around and bumped into him. They both laughed.

He took her hands in his, rubbing her fingers with his thumbs. "Tell me, Charity, after last night's miracle with the babe, have you made peace with God?"

"I have. He and I had a long conversation last night."

His eyes couldn't have sparkled brighter. "Pray tell, what did you discuss?"

"Oh, Elias, 'twas so wonderful." She squeezed his hands. "I blamed God for everything, when in truth, I had made many of my own choices. In fact, He revealed to me how He'd never left me and every time I called upon Him, He provided a way of escape. But I was too foolish to take them."

Smiling, Elias slid a finger down her jaw, sending heat fluttering through her. "And me, I'm just as foolish. I blamed myself entirely for Caleigh's accident, without considering God's sovereignty and people's choices." He chuckled. "You blamed God for everything and I blamed only myself. Quite a pair we are!"

She smiled. "Things are not so black and white, are they?"

"Indeed. God is on His throne, but this world is ruled by Satan. As long as that is true, evil will abound."

Charity stared up at him, shifting her eyes between his, longing for this moment to never end...knowing it would when she told him the truth. "Elias, I must tell—"

He placed a finger on her lips to silence her, then lifted her hand for a kiss. "Let me speak first." He drew a deep breath. "Charity, I've never known such an enchanting, exquisite woman. You are kind, generous, forgiving, pure, and proper. You don't seek after status or fortune, and you love children. How can I do anything but that which my heart begs me to do. I love you, Charity. Will you do me the honor of accepting a courtship between us? With every intention of making it permanent." Expectant hope reigned in his smile.

Her heart nearly exploded in her chest. How could such a magnificent man love *her*? She was none of those things he said. But she could become them, couldn't she? With God's help. "Oh, Elias." Sobs of joy cluttered in her throat as a tear spilled down her cheeks.

*Tell him.*

"You don't know everything about me, Elias."

"I know enough, my little mermaid." He brushed a lock of her hair behind her ear. "I can bear it no longer, have mercy and give me your answer." Releasing her hands, he reached around his neck, pulled his cross over his head, and handed it to her.

More tears spilled. "I can't take this, Elias. 'Tis too special to you."

He shook his head. "I no longer need it. In my pride, I tried to take the place of God. I want you to have it." He closed her fingers around it. "To remind you that God loves you. And that I love you."

She took it, holding it against her bosom. When she looked up, his lips met hers, and the world around her faded into an ecstasy of light and hope, love and protection. *Ah, to belong to this man!*

He wrapped his arms around her and squeezed her against his chest, exploring her mouth with his, gently, lovingly, causing pleasurable ripples down to her toes. She could get lost in him, in the tender way he touched her as if she were precious and fragile, in the shelter of his arms, the safety, the love...she hadn't thought such feelings possible.

He groaned and pressed her even closer.

"Ah, how touching." Ballard's voice broke the trance, sending Charity pushing from Elias.

"Have you no decency, Ballard? 'Twas a private moment." Elias took a stance in front of her.

"So I see."

"We have just agreed to a courtship. There was nothing improper."

"Improper! Lud!" Ballard laughed so hard, he pressed a hand on his belly. "I'll tell you what is improper. A preacher courting a woman carrying a bastard child."

Charity's blood turned cold.

Fists at his side, Elias charged toward him. "I'll call you to swords for such a lie!"

Ballard merely shrugged, his tone conciliatory. "The maid told me. She saw Miss Westcott's condition with her own eyes. I thought I should warn you, Captain, before you made a tragic mistake. I know how you value truth and purity in women."

Elias swept his gaze toward her, inquisitive eyes, searching eyes...waiting...waiting for her to deny the accusation.

Her stomach sank like a millstone. All hope drained from her heart, leaving naught but a cracked shell. "'Tis the truth, Elias. I should have told you."

He shifted his boots on the carpet, shoved a hand through his hair, all the while gaping at her as if she were the Kraken rising from the sea. "Villemont's child?"

She nodded, watching the admiration, the love of only a moment ago spill from his eyes, replaced by shock, confusion, and finally fury. Growling, he marched to the bookcase and punched the poor defenseless tomes lining the shelves.

Smiling, Ballard slipped out. *The snake.*

Anger temporarily shoved aside Charity's shame. "Why are you so furious when you did the same thing? It's all right for you, but not for me?"

He spun around. "That's not it. You lied to me."

She had, but not about this. "I simply didn't tell you. As you simply didn't tell me about Edmund."

His jaw flexed. His eyes narrowed. "I waited until you knew about Edmund before asking for a courtship. When were you planning on telling me?"

"Tonight." A tremble overtook her and she hugged herself, shame returning. "I'm so sorry, Elias. I've been trying to tell you. I just...I didn't want to ruin the moment." God had told her to tell him... but she'd delayed, she'd hesitated, once again not trusting Him.

Elias released a huge breath and slowly approached her. The lines on his face faded along with the rage in his eyes. "You're right. We both made the same mistake." He took her hands and stared at her belly. "But a babe?" He shook his head.

"Aye, four months now." She followed his gaze to the life growing within her. "I understand if you wish to withdraw your offer." 'Twould be the best thing. Then she could leave without having to tell him the rest. As it was, she could hardly bear the loss of admiration in his eyes.

Releasing her hands, he backed away, lips tight. "I'll admit 'tis a surprise I wasn't expecting."

"I understand." She held out the cross to him, forcing back tears, ready to dash out as soon as he took it.

He didn't take it. "Please Charity, I can't tolerate any more lies. Nothing Rachel told me was the truth. Even her affections for me were a lie."

A single tear spilled over her lashes. "You know mine are not, Elias. I love you. I will always love you." She would give him that. Mayhap it would comfort him in the days to come.

"I need time to think." His moist eyes found hers, and her heart shriveled at the pain in them. He pushed her hands, bearing the cross, back to her bosom. "Keep the cross. I'm not withdrawing my offer." He gave a sad smile, then pulled her into an embrace. "No more lies, Charity. No more lies."

There, pressed against his firm chest, his scent flooding her nose, Charity could no longer hold back the torrent of tears. He understood! He wasn't withdrawing the offer. Was it possible she could have a life with this man?

"Charity what is the matter? Shhh. Shhh." He rubbed her back and planted a kiss on her head. "'Tis alright now. No need to cry."

Horses neighed outside, the front door crashed open, and voices echoed through the foyer.

Nudging her back, Elias opened a wooden box on the desk and withdrew a pistol. "Stay here," he said before heading out the door.

But a voice...a familiar voice bade Charity follow him. Clutching the cross, she crept out behind him, surprised to see a group of men filling the foyer. She spotted Ballard and, oddly, Nelson among them. Her pulse hitched.

But 'twas the man who hobbled to the front who caused her heart to stop.

Her brother-in-law, Charles Gregson, Lord Villemont.

# Chapter 28

"What's the meaning of this?" Though Elias spotted Ballard and Nelson among the mob of intruders, he kept his pistol raised at the six men he didn't recognize. All of them well armed. One of them, a light-haired man donned in fine satin, limped toward the front, cane pounding on the tile, haughty brow lifted, as if he were the king of England himself.

Charity's footsteps sounded behind Elias. Blast the woman's disobedience! Motioning her to come no closer, he took a stance in front of her. "Ballard, Nelson, Explain yourselves! Who are these men?"

Duncan charged into the foyer, musket leveled on the men. "Indeed, what are you doing in my home?"

Wearing a superior grin, the light-haired leader peeked around Elias at Charity. "I'm here to arrest a fugitive, Mr. ... Mr..."

"Duncan Bennet, the owner of this estate. And you are?" Two footmen appeared behind Duncan, also armed.

This seemed to bear no effect on the light-haired man. "You may address me as Lord Villemont."

Elias gulped. *This* was the man who courted Charity, who beat her? Fury took over reason. He charged him. The man's eyes widened, but before he or his men could react, Elias slugged him across the jaw. His Lordship stumbled backward, cane and arms flailing, nearly knocking over

Ballard, while his men cocked pistols and leveled them at Elias.

One of them poked Elias in the chest with the barrel and attempted to push him back.

He didn't budge. Instead, he cast Lord Villemont a scathing look. "Come to beat her some more? Is that it? Couldn't find another defenseless woman to torture?"

Gage and Josiah dashed into the foyer, pistols in hand, and stood on either side of Elias.

Outside the open front door, a thick blackness ruled the night, and Elias was tempted to shove these vile specters back into the sludge from whence they came.

"Is that what she told you? Pshaw!" Villemont rose to his full height, withdrew a handkerchief, and wiped blood from his lip. "Touch me again, Sir, and you will pay."

Ballard grinned as if enjoying the proceedings, while Nelson crossed arms over his chest, looking bored. The rest of the men kept their weapons raised and their determined eyes pinned on Elias and Duncan.

Duncan cocked his musket. "Get out of my home, or you'll be the one who pays, *milord*!"

"I will be happy to leave once you hand over the lady." Villemont gestured behind Elias.

Elias finally glanced at her. What he saw brought him no comfort. Lips trembling, face white, she gripped the stair post for support and refused to meet his gaze. He faced forward again. "And why would we do that?"

"Because she is a fugitive and I'm bringing her back to England to stand trial."

"For what crime?"

"Murder."

Elias chuckled. "Then you have the wrong lady. She has been with me for the past two weeks."

"I agree, Sir. 'Tis why I've been chasing you." Villemont sighed in exasperation as if Elias were an ignorant dolt. "Do you wonder why she allied herself so easily to a stranger? I was in Nassau about to capture her when she convinced you to take her aboard that merchantman."

A breeze swept in and stirred the candlelit sconces on the wall, casting eerie shadows on the floor and sending a chill over Elias. The hairs on the back of his neck stiffened as he remembered the desperation and fear he'd seen in her eyes. But nay. Couldn't be. He gazed back at her. She melted in a heap of skirts on the bottom tread of the stairs.

Outside a monkey howled.

"Ah." Villemont chuckled. "You believe she loves you!"

Nelson and Ballard snickered, joined by grunts of amusement from the other men.

"She convinced my brother of that as well." Villemont said with spite. "Before she shot him in the heart."

Pieces of a very demented puzzle came together in Elias' mind, causing his heart to fold in on itself. "And who exactly is your brother?"

Villemont's dark eyes speared to a point. "The late, Herbert Gregson, Lord Villemont. Her husband."

Elias' stomach turned to ash. He snapped his gaze to Charity, but she refused to meet it.

The tick-tock of a clock hanging on the wall penetrated the ensuing silence. *Tick-tock tick-tock tick tock*...counting down the final minutes of his happiness.

"Ah, of course. You didn't know." Villemont's tone was taunting. "She wouldn't have disclosed her dark heart for fear of not getting what she needed from you."

Josiah groaned. Gage turned to stare at Charity.

So did Elias. "Tell me this isn't true. Tell me he's lying, and I will force these men to leave at once."

She lifted her tear stained face to his. "He speaks the truth," she said numbly.

Elias might have been gouged by an anchor for the pain that stabbed his entire body. Gage cursed and lowered his pistol.

Ballard grinned.

"Hand her over." Villemont limped forward, tapping his cane on the tiles.

Elias blinked. He couldn't think...couldn't breathe...couldn't move. *This can't be happening! Not again!*

Gesturing for his men to lower their weapons, Duncan came to his rescue and stepped before the lady, mermaid, vixen...liar, whoever she was. "Pray, milord," he addressed Villemont. "Night is upon us. You cannot set sail until morning. Allow her to remain here tonight."

"So she can escape?" Villemont snorted.

"Post a man at her chamber door and one outside her window, a regiment of men if you desire. No need for hostility." He glanced at Elias, but Elias was having trouble breathing.

Duncan gave Villemont a forced smile. "'Twas merely a misunderstanding. And to make amends, I insist you join us for a meal and spend the night. Surely, you are famished and exhausted from such an arduous journey. My cook is known for her delicacies."

Lord Villemont's men licked their lips, eyes sparking to life. His Lordship, on the other hand, took a moment as he gazed around suspiciously, eyes flaring at Charity, fingering his chin, before finally conceding. "Very well. I thank you for your hospitality. Lower your weapons, you oafs!" He shouted to his men.

Duncan quickly ordered one of his men to escort Charity upstairs, while Villemont sent three of his behind them.

Elias' blood turned to razors in his veins, slicing their way to his heart. He heard the men assist Charity to her feet, heard her sobbing. But he couldn't bring himself to look at her.

He just stood there, the room hazy around him, the air heavy with sorrow, until finally servants entered to escort the guests to their rooms. Still Elias remained, as if in a dream, waiting to wake up.

Ballard's defiant snort did the trick as the man turned to leave, Nelson beside him.

"Why, Ballard?" Elias asked.

Spinning around, Ballard smirked. "Do you think I wanted to sail with the likes of you? Do you think I enjoyed lowering my station and taking orders from the man who murdered my parents?"

"What?" Elias' head spun. "I didn't..." Shifting his stance, he squeezed the bridge of his nose. He *had* convinced them to become missionaries. But the choice had been theirs in the end. He sighed and shook his head at the irony. Just like Elias had blamed himself, and Charity had blamed God, Ballard blamed Elias. Wasn't it just like human nature to want someone to blame for life's tragedies? Someone on whom to enact revenge.

*Stupid, stupid!* Elias cursed himself. How could he have been so naïve? "And you Nelson?" he asked. "I took you on my ship, befriended you."

"Sorry, Cap'n. Nothin' personal. I was after the forty-pound reward." He shook the pouch at his belt.

Of course. Elias hung his head. More betrayals, more deceptions.

He hoped they were at an end, for he didn't think he could take any more.

Toppling to the floor in a heap, Charity buried her head in her skirts and wept. Her chamber door slammed shut, and she heard the men who were to guard her settle outside against the wall.

"Oh, God, why? Why?" she wailed. "All is lost." She'd lost everything. Her freedom, her life, but worst of all, she'd lost Elias. Not only lost *him* but lost his love as well. He hated her. And she didn't blame him one bit. He'd never looked at her once as they led her away. In fact, after he realized the truth, he never looked at her at all. Once again just when happiness and love seemed a possibility...within her reach, her husband stole them away, torturing her from his grave, sending his brother to exact the punishment he would have given her for the rest of her life had he lived. She could almost hear him snickering. "You thought you'd escape me? Pish! My dear. You are mine forever!"

Indeed. She rose and wiped her face, trying to settle her convulsing body. Clutching Elias' cross to her chest, she gazed at the moonlight taunting her with freedom through her window. She should have accepted her fate with Lord Villemont, waited for God to show her a way of escape, offered no resistance. Then she wouldn't be a murderer, and she wouldn't have taunted—no, tortured—herself with a life she could never have. And her heart wouldn't now be crushed so badly, she doubted it could ever be put together again. Yet *all* of her bad choices...*all* of them had led her here. To this moment of agony. Even her last foolish choice to not tell Elias the entire truth, though God had asked her to.

Would things have ended differently if she had? Sighing, she lifted the cross and kissed it. One of her tears spilled onto the wood, christening it with her love...only causing more tears to flow. She might have been able to bear losing him, but she couldn't bear his scorn.

She moved to the window and leaned on the frame, gazing upward at the black sky sprinkled with silver beads. "Father, I'm so sorry. Once again, I took matters into my own hands and didn't trust You. Now, I'm to be trapped, imprisoned, living or dying at the behest of others. Oh, please help me."

Fear clutched her heart so tight, she felt it would shrivel away. What would happen to her baby? She ran a hand over her rounded belly. Would they wait for her birth before they hanged her? Would they take him away from her, put him in an orphanage where he wouldn't receive love or care or even enough food?

Tears flowed again and she crumbled into a ball on the floor.

Sometime in the night, the latch on her door clicked and someone stepped inside. Too light-footed to be Elias—as Charity first hoped—the footsteps tapped over the carpet. Pushing from the floor, Charity squinted in the darkness. Skirts swished. The scent of lavender wafted over her, and Rose touched her arm.

"Charity, dearest. Get up."

"Rose what are you doing? You should be abed."

"And let my friend suffer a most horrid fate? Never." She moved to the open door and peered into the hallway, then gestured for Charity to follow.

*Friend?* Despite her agony, Charity warmed at the title as she struggled to rise.

In the hallway, three guards sat beside the door, their heads slumped on their chests.

"What have you done?" Charity whispered.

Rose waved a hand through the air. "Oh, don't worry about them. My lady's maid slipped them some ale with a bit of laudanum in it. Well, quite a lot actually." She smiled and pulled Charity along the dark hallway. "I have a horse saddled and ready to go. You can ride, can't you?" She glanced at Charity over her shoulder, but didn't wait for a reply before she continued. "There's a ship waiting for you called the *Respite*. 'Tis my father's ship."

"Ship?"

"Yes, my father has many of them. He used to be a pirate, you know."

Rose halted at the front door and opened it ever so slowly, then led Charity outside. Moonlight turned Rose's night robe into creamy milk flowing in the breeze as the precious lady gripped Charity's hand.

"The captain will take you to Charles Towne. There's extra clothes, undergarments, pins, hairbrush, oh, and some money in the saddlebag."

Emotion burned in Charity's throat. "How can you help a murderess?"

Rose drew her into a tight embrace. "You are no murderer, Charity. That much I know."

Charity glanced at the footman holding the horse's reins, then back at Rose. She handed her the cross. "Please return this to Elias. Tell him…tell him…"

"I know." Rose nodded. "I will."

Giving her friend one last hug, Charity allowed the footman to assist her onto the horse. Then snapping the reins, she sped down the palm-lined entrance, never to see Elias again.

*Torture!* Surely this was what hell was like. Endless agony with no relief in sight. Elias sank to the couch and dropped his head in his hands. An ache throbbed behind his temples, adding to the wrenching pain in his gut. He smelled of horses and sweat and anger, and more than anything he wanted to charge into Charity's bedchamber and demand an explanation. Instead, he had mounted one of Duncan's prize horses and ridden the poor mare as hard as he could over fields, up hills, then raced through thicketed jungle trails until both man and beast were covered with sweat and sores.

It hadn't done any good. Elias was still as distraught and furious as he'd been when he first discovered Charity's treachery. *Treachery, indeed! Murdered her husband?* Punching to his feet, he marched to the window where darkness still clung to the estate like a demon of gloom. He refused to believe it! Could he really be that stupid, falling for the lies of *two* women? Both who pretended to love him only for what they could get from him?

*No! No! No!* Growling, he fisted hands at his waist and circled a game table and chairs. He'd seen the signs with Rachel, hints of deception she quickly covered up with flirtations. But Charity. She'd never faltered in her charade. Not once. He passed the buffet, lined with bottles of brandy and port and licked his lips. Of all nights, surely this night he deserved a drink. Beams of moonlight wove red ribbons in the dark liquor, enticing him, luring him, as he reached ever so slowly for it.

Nay! He snapped his hand back and continued on. Like so many others, the liquor pretended to be his friend at first, only to crush him in the end.

*Lies and Betrayal!* Elias pounded his fists on the wall. And him the biggest fool of all. Why? Because he still loved her. She'd lied to him about *everything* ever since they'd met. But for the life of him, he could not shove her from his heart.

He plopped down into a chair and groaned. "Why, God, Why? I was going to marry her."

A breeze stirred the curtains, shifting moonlight over the table. But no answer came.

Instead, a vision of Charity swinging from a rope—the same vision that had haunted him all night—emblazoned across his eyes. Charity would hang for her crime. Of that Elias had no doubt. Regardless of her guilt, wealth and influence often weighted the scales of justice.

How could he allow that to happen to the woman he loved? He had to put aside his own pain, his own sorrow, and think of her. If only he could hear her explanation. Surely she hadn't meant to kill her husband? If he could but hear her deny it from her own lips…then, maybe then, he would set her free.

The only problem? The three muscled oafs guarding her.

"Is it right to even think of freeing her?" He groaned and jumped to his feet. "What do I do, Father? Give me a sign."

Footsteps pounded in the hallway, and he jerked his hand to the pistol stuffed in his breeches.

Caleb, Josiah, and Gage walked into the room.

"Figured we'd find you here," Caleb said, approaching Elias.

"Go away. I want to be alone."

"Can't do that, Cap'n." Josiah's huge shadow moved to the window as Gage took up a stance by the door.

Caleb gripped Elias' arm. "We thought you might need some assistance."

"For what?" Elias couldn't make out his expression in the darkness, though he had a good idea what he meant.

"I think you know," Caleb responded.

"Don't let them take her, Captain," Gage said. "I like the lady. She was always nice to me."

Elias sighed. Yes, she had been. In fact, she'd been remarkable in every way. *Except in telling the truth.* "I can't ask you to be complicit in anything unlawful."

"Unlawful?" Caleb chuckled. "All we are offering is to knock unconscious three intruders."

Elias smiled, the first smile in hours. "Gentlemen, I believe we are of the same mind."

Charity nudged the horse forward, hoping he knew his way into town. Of course, there was only one road, but this particular road was surrounded—both sides and over the top—by a web of leaves so thick, she felt packed tight in a coffin. Not a very comforting analogy at the moment. Darkness as heavy as ink prevented her from seeing more than a foot in front of her. Still the horse plodded on, despite the croaks and chirps and buzz and the occasional growl emanating from the jungle.

Accompanied by her constant sobbing. Would she ever run out of tears?

Every inch down the road brought her closer to freedom...

And farther away from Elias.

Another choice in life. Like the many she'd had before—the many in which she'd chosen poorly. Down this road or down that road. Turn left or turn right. Marry this man or another man, get on a ship with her family or stay in Portsmouth, grab her husband's pistol or let it be. Come or go, leave or stay. And now her final decision—freedom or death. Even though she'd never really consulted God on her decisions, she realized that He had tried to guide her down the right path all along.

But what *was* the right path now?

Swiping tears from her face, she gazed up, hoping to catch a glimmer of moonlight through the canopy. "Father, what would you have me do? What is Your will?"

She hoped it wasn't prison, for she'd spent her entire life in a prison of sorts. And this final one would be the worst of all.

*Go back, my daughter.*

"What? Was that You, Father?" Couldn't be. Surely God wouldn't want her to hang.

*Go back.*

She tugged on the reins and the horse stopped. Insects buzzed around her in air as thick as the jungle. Perspiration slid down her neck. *She recognized that voice!* She'd heard it before during her darkest nights when, after Villemont had beaten and ravished her, she'd lain in her bed and cried out to die. The voice had simply said, *I love you.*

At the time, she'd thought it was her imagination, her mind going mad with grief and sorrow. But, no. The voice was always soft, the words always short, and the feeling afterward, always one of peace.

She smiled as a sob rose in her throat. God wanted her to go back. Back to prison, back to death, back to losing her child and everything she feared the most.

"I can't." She hung her head as an owl hooted and the horse pawed the sodden earth. "How can you ask that of me?"

A breeze came out of nowhere and wafted around her, cooling her skin, and gently brushing her hair as if God were lovingly caressing her, silently telling her all would be well.

And she knew. She had to obey God. This time, she had to do the hard thing and trust Him.

With a slight kick to the horse's flank, she tugged the reins and turned the beast around.

# Chapter 29

"She's missing?" Villemont raged across the foyer, his cane banging his displeasure on the tile floor. "What mischief is this? I trusted you!" Halting, he pointed his cane at Elias and then shifted it to Duncan. "You helped her escape. Both of you!"

"We did no such thing!" Elias feigned indignation and gripped the pommel of his sword. "I resent the implication, milord."

"As do I," Duncan added, brows raised. "I assure you, we are as shocked as you."

"Humph." Red-faced, Villemont tugged on his cravat as if it were choking him. Sunlight streamed through the beveled windows on either side of the front door as servants could be heard in the background preparing the dining hall for breakfast.

"You posted three armed men at her door and two beneath her window," Elias said. "Surely if there was a scuffle or shots were fired, you would have heard it since your chamber was beside hers. Do your men say we attacked them, knocked them unconscious with nary a struggle?" Elias shared a glance with Duncan and then with Gage, Josiah, and Caleb standing by his side, weapons at the ready.

In truth, they *had* dashed upstairs with the intent on doing just that, but they'd found the guards asleep, the door ajar, and Charity gone.

Sorrow so deep it threatened to undo him had pressed on Elias, and he chastised himself for not coming sooner. Now, if these buffoons delayed him further, he would never see her again. And the gaping hole forming in his gut told him he would suffer that loss forever.

But at least she would be free. Of that, he was grateful.

It hadn't taken long to determine the culprit. Rose had never been good at telling lies or keeping secrets. Yet when she returned his cross along with Charity's last words of love, Elias felt unworthy of the mud caking the bottom of his boots. Charity loved him. And he had allowed her to be led away without making a move to stop it or even asking her to explain. She had lied to him about her identity and her husband's death to protect herself and her babe. He could understand that. But why continue the deception after they'd grown so close? When he could have helped her. Unless...she truly *had* murdered her husband. Rose insisted there had to be another explanation, and his sister's instincts in these matters were far better than his. She had been one of the most adamant opponents of his engagement to Rachel.

But Elias could neither hear Charity's explanation nor protect her from these men intent on seeing her hang. It was too late. She was gone.

Villemont's groan brought Elias to the present. The man's eyes narrowed as he glared at his men who stood to the side, gazing down at the floor. "I'm no fool. 'Tis obvious you drugged them."

"Again, milord, your accusations are without proof and completely unfounded. I am a preacher, as is Caleb Hyde." Elias gestured to his right. "Grandson of Edmund Merrick Hyde, Lord Clarendon. Mayhap you've heard of him?" He waited for a reaction but only saw Villemont's eyebrow twitch. "We do not lie," Elias concluded.

"Preachers! Swounds!" Villemont spit out. "Crooks, the whole lot of you." He waved his cane through the air and nearly stumbled. Righting himself, he leaned on it and assessed the five of them—Elias, Duncan, Josiah, Gage, and Caleb—all of whom, if Elias had to admit, looked rather formidable fully armed and dressed more like pirates than gentlemen.

They'd been about to leave in search of Charity when Villemont emerged from his room, gathered his men, and went to retrieve his prize.

Now, if they could just avoid a bloody altercation.

And if Villemont and his men would leave...

Then Elias could seek out Charity before she did something foolish—like set sail unescorted on a ship full of lusty miscreants. Even if she did as she was told and sailed on the *Respite*, there was no guarantee of her safety.

Villemont gazed back at his men, then faced forward again, his jaw working, his eyes hard. He must have determined he would lose the fight because he growled and then uttered, "Then let's be off! We have a murderess to catch!" He gestured toward the door with his cane, then flashed Elias one more searing glance. "Our business is not finished, Sir."

Elias gave a mock bow. "I shall await its conclusion with great enthusiasm, milord."

Caleb chuckled as Villemont and his men headed for the door. The butler opened it and stood to the side, and just when Elias thought he was free of them, they all stopped suddenly at the threshold.

Gripping the hilt of his sword, Elias anticipated the man's change of heart and impending battle when...

Miss Charity Westcott strolled into the foyer with all the grace and dignity of royalty—chin high and regal smile on her face as if she were attending a ball.

Gaping at her, the men parted the way as she sashayed forward.

Elias' heart leapt into this throat.

"Gentlemen," she addressed everyone, her eyes grazing over Elias, a sorrow he'd never seen before tinting their lustrous honey color. "Charles." She nodded toward Villemont, who continued to stare at her in disbelief. "I understand you've been looking for me."

With an inhuman growl, Villemont clutched her arm so tight she screeched.

Elias drew his sword, the chime echoing through the foyer. He leveled it at Villemont's chest before the rest of the man's hired reprobates could cock their pistols. "Let her go!"

"Pshaw! Again? Never!" Villemont faced her. "I have you now, you murdering shrew!"

Elias pressed the tip of his blade to the man's chest. Villemont winced and eyed him with spite.

Charity shook her head. "No, Elias. Leave him be. I will go with him." Such love and peace poured from her eyes, he could only stare at her, astounded.

Villemont laughed. "Yes, you will, my dear. And you'll hang for your crime."

"If God wills it," she returned with confidence.

What had happened to the mermaid vixen who fought so vehemently for her freedom? Who'd repeatedly risked her life rather than be beholden to anyone?

Elias kept his sword aimed at Villemont's heart. "I will run you through, milord, before you even voice the order to kill me."

"I'd listen to him if I were you," Caleb said from behind Elias. "The man is quite good with the blade."

Josiah grunted, and out of the corner of his eye, Elias saw Duncan take a position to the left of the mob, pistol raised.

Still Villemont remained, one hand clutching Charity, the other gripping his cane, his eyes pools of hatred. His men shifted nervously, weapons waving over Elias and the others. Their six men to his five. Good odds since Elias had Caleb and Josiah on his side.

*Tick tock...tick tock...* that blasted clock chimed Elias' doom once again. Outside, the melody of birds and rustle of leaves trilled a happy tune, so at odds with the tension inside where raised weapons formed a maniacal web of death.

Elias knew they could take them. And from the look in Caleb's and Duncan's eyes, they agreed. Blood would be shed. But in the end, Charity would be free. He would not allow her to be taken by this man. He must protect her at all costs! At any cost. Hadn't he sworn to do so with all those he loved?

She raised her moist eyes to his, desperate, pleading. Yet not with a pleading to rescue her.

But a pleading to let her go.

"What is it going to be, Dutton?" Villemont sneered. "Will you put your life and the lives of your men at risk? And for what? This vixen?" He shook her until she cried out in pain.

Elias pressed the tip of his blade. A spot of blood appeared on Villemont's silk waistcoat. He glanced at it briefly then huffed. "Kill me if you wish. My men are under orders to take her back with or without me. They have a reward awaiting them I'm sure they'd not wish to forfeit." He smiled.

"Elias. Please. Let me go." Charity swallowed. "I killed my husband. I did. 'Twas an accident." She turned to Villemont. "You must know that, Charles. I never meant to—"

Releasing his cane, Lord Villemont slapped her across the face.

Elias lowered his sword and barreled into him, knocking him away from Charity. Villemont stumbled backward, a look of horror on his face, before he toppled to the ground. Jumping on the swine, Elias did what he'd been wanting to do since he met the man yesterday. He beat him, fist after fist, across the jaw.

Villemont's men shouted and cursed. A pistol fired. But Elias couldn't stop. All he could think about was Charity, the abuse she had endured at the hands of this man's brother, and that he, now, wanted to continue that abuse by seeing her hang.

Shouts filled the room. A sword chimed. Another pistol cracked the air.

Strong hands that must be Josiah's yanked Elias from Villemont's body and hauled him back.

Panting, he wiped his mouth with his sleeve just as Charity flew into his arms.

*Ah, sweet life! To feel her again. To embrace her and protect her!* Cupping her face in his hands, he nudged her back to look up at him, caressing her skin, drinking in the scent of her.

"I won't let them take you, Charity."

"Nay, Elias." She stepped back, and the room grew cold. Tears filled her eyes. "Justice must be served. I must have a trial. 'Tis God's will."

The sting of gun smoke bit his nose. Villemont's men shifted all their pistols onto him. One glance told him none of his men were hurt.

Caleb gripped his arm. "Elias. She's right. You must trust God with her fate."

Groaning, Villemont rose, blood dripping from his nose. He hobbled toward them, and before Elias could react, he dragged Charity beside him once again.

Caleb yanked Elias, drawing his gaze, and shaking his head as if to say, "let it be."

Elias tore from his grip and shoved a hand through his hair. His sword lay at his feet, ready to retrieve and continue the fight. How could he allow the woman he loved to die when it was within his power to save her?

*Leave her in My hands...*

*Nay!* He groaned. *Father, No! How can I?*

Yet hadn't both Caleb and Rose told Elias he must learn to rely on God—to do his best, do what God commands, and then trust Him for the rest?

Despite every urge within Elias, he knew this was one of those times. Blast it all! This was one of those times.

Yet his fingers ached to slice Lord Villemont in half, dispatch the rest of these blackguards, and run away with Charity to the ends of the earth... to keep her safe and to love her the rest of her days.

"Enough of this!" Villemont dragged a sleeve over his nose and yanked Charity toward the door. He snapped his fingers for his men to follow. Backing away, they kept eyes on Elias, pistols raised.

Elias followed them outside, shoving his way toward Charity. "A moment with the lady," he told, rather than asked, Villemont.

The man spun on his heel, studied Elias, then snorted in disdain. "A moment is all you'll get."

For the second time in twenty-four hours, Elias pulled his cross over his head and handed it to Miss Charity Westcott.

She shook her head, a tear glistening down her cheek. "I can't."

He grabbed her hand, placed the cross inside, and closed it again. "I love you, Charity."

Villemont's men chuckled as Villemont grunted in disgust and hauled her toward the waiting carriage.

She glanced over her shoulder. "I'm so sorry, Elias. For everything," she said before Villemont assisted her inside. The last vision he had of her before the carriage ambled away was her sweet face in the window, mouthing the words. *I love you.*

Elias dropped to his knees and growled in agony.

# Chapter 30

One of Villemont's lackeys opened the cabin door, and Charles shoved Charity inside. She gripped the edge of a table to keep from falling, then looked up to find Sophie running toward her, arms wide.

*Sophie!*

"Oh, my dear, my dear!" The woman embraced her so hard, they both nearly fell backward. "Are you all ri'? I were so worried for you."

"Yes, I'm all right, Sophie." Charity hugged her back, feeling an urge to shout with glee at the woman's presence, but unable to lure any joy out of her despair.

"Touching," Villemont spat, leaning against the door frame. "No doubt the maid was complicit in your crime."

Releasing Sophie, Charity faced Charles. "Leave her out of it! She had naught to do with anything."

"Humph. We shall let a court decide. In the meantime, get used to seeing these four walls. You'll be imprisoned here the entire voyage back to Portsmouth."

"But you've allowed me out, milord." Stepping forward, Sophie wrung her hands together.

"You, I can tolerate. But this"—he gestured toward Charity with a snarl—"Why upset an otherwise pleasant voyage with the sight of her?"

He continued to stare her up and down, his cold eyes like those of a serpent ready to strike, and Charity remembered all the times they had laughed together at dinner parties. He'd always treated her with kindness, welcoming her into the family, though she was but the daughter of an admiral. But because his loyalty and love for his brother had been more than evident, she'd kept silent about her husband's cruelty. Now, she saw she'd been right to do so. At least she'd made one wise decision.

His eyes moistened as if he saw his brother in her eyes. Then clearing his throat, he turned and marched away. The door slammed and locked shut from the outside, and Charity sank onto the only chair in the room.

She wanted to cry, but couldn't. Instead, she turned to Sophie, dear, sweet Sophie, who stared at her with concern.

"I'm so sorry he found you, milady." She knelt before Charity and took both her hands. "I were prayin' and prayin' for him to never catch you."

"Thank you, Sophie. 'Tis I who should apologize. Look what I've got you mixed up in." Charity stood and took the three steps to the other side of the cabin, longing to pound on the bulkhead, scream at the top of her lungs, cry herself into blissful oblivion. "Pray, how did you get on Charles' ship?"

"He caught me at Nassau, milady," Sophie squeaked out.

Charity turned to face her as guilt clambered atop her sorrow.

Sophie shook her head. "I didn't tell him nothin', milady. Besides, I didn't know where you were. But he kept insistin' I mi' be useful in findin' you." Tears rolled down her chubby, red cheeks.

Charity hugged her. "Sophie, sweet Sophie. This is all my fault. He's kept you imprisoned in this cabin the entire time?"

"It weren't too bad, milady. They fed me well and allowed me on deck durin' the day. Some of the sailors been nice to me. And Lord Villemont...I can't get used to callin' him that, after wha' happened..."—she gave Charity a look of horror—"told me he'd take me back to England when all this were done."

"I'm thankful he's been kind to you. 'Tis just me he hates."

"Nay, milady. Once he gets to know you. Once he hears wha' happened."

"I don't believe he's in a listening mood, nor an understanding one." Easing an arm around Sophie, she drew her close. "At least you will be safe once we arrive home."

"But where 'ave you been, milady? Wha' happened to you in Nassau?"

"A long story." Charity finally found a smile as she pressed fingers against Elias' cross beneath her bodice. "And it would seem we have plenty of time for me to share every detail."

As it turned out, it took several hours to relay her adventures to Sophie. The maid sat on the edge of the bunk, gazing up at Charity as she paced and recalled her every move since last they'd seen one another on board the *Neptune*. Gasps of shock, exclamations of glee, tears, and even a little laughter provided Charity the impetus to continue. Sophie was particularly happy that Charity had made peace with God.

"Tha's what I were prayin' for, milady." Sophie wiped a tear from her eye.

Charity stopped and studied the woman. She'd never considered that Sophie prayed for her. Reaching out, she squeezed the maid's hand. "Your prayers worked. Thank you, Sophie."

Charity tried to avoid talking overmuch about Elias, for fear she'd melt into a weeping blob of uselessness from which she'd never recover. But 'twas impossible not to speak of him and all his courageous deeds, rescuing her from all manner of dangers and peril of her own making. She *did* cry.

A little. And every time she did, Sophie drew her down to sit beside her and hugged her until she calmed.

Now, as the maid snored from the tiny bunk, Charity sat in the chair and envied Sophie's peaceful sleep. With no window, she had no way to gauge whether 'twas night or day, though she knew by the water roaring against the hull and the teeter-tottering of the deck, the ship had set sail hours ago. No food or water had been brought, and the oil in the lantern was running out.

Finally it sputtered and choked its last breath, and a black shroud dropped on Charity. Despair set in. Agonizing despair. Terror gnawed at her soul. Had she done the right thing? She ran a hand over her belly as renewed tears filled her eyes. "Oh, my poor baby. Will I ever see you? Will I ever hold you? Or will they whisk you away before I've had a chance, and then lead me to the noose? Oh, God." She dropped her head in her hands. "I did what You said. Now, what is to become of us?"

Yet as she sat there, her sobs rising to compete with the creak and groan of the ship and rush of water, she heard one simple word loud and clear. And that word was …

*Trust.*

Tugging out Elias' cross, she cradled it in her hands. *Trust.* "All right, Father. I will try."

The next week crawled by like a snake through molasses. And despite all efforts to the contrary, Charity's faith oft abandoned her, stealing all her hope with it. During those darkest moments, when her body convulsed with grief and terror, she would pull out Elias' cross and hold it to her bosom. It became dearer to her than life itself—a lifeline, reminding her of God's sacrifice for her, Elias' love, and the truth that everyone had their own cross to bear if they were to be called children of God. Just feeling the sturdy wood in her hands brought comfort and settled her spirit enough to hear God's voice within, reassuring her all was well.

Once again, Charity didn't know what she would do without Sophie's uplifting manner and encouraging words. Though Charity was not permitted above, Sophie brought back tales of the sun, sea, and sailors, along with the scent of salty brine that Charity had grown to love so much. The maid even requested that they pray together three times a day for God to rescue them, to free Charity, and to keep the babe in her womb safe and healthy. Charity treasured those times, for they never failed to feed her dwindling hope.

Other times, however, in the long reaches of the night, doubt taunted her, accusing God of being unfaithful and uncaring. She knew it wasn't true. But it took all her strength—and much of God's, she imagined—to cling to the robe of her divine Savior and believe He would turn around, take pity on her, and come to her aid.

She also prayed for Elias. She had broken his heart and destroyed his life just like Rachel. He deserved so much better. And as hard as it was, she prayed for God to send him the perfect woman.

On one such long night, while Sophie's snores competed with the creak of wood, Charity held Elias' cross close to her bosom and prayed for him, sobbing and moaning and pleading for his happiness. Sometime near what must be dawn—due to the sounds of movement on the deck above— pain shot through her womb so intense, she cried out and woke Sophie.

"I'm goin' to tell his lordship about the babe," Sophie announced as she donned her gown. "They aren't feedin' you well, and it's bad for the wee one."

"Please don't, Sophie. I don't want him to steal my child." Pressing a hand to her belly, Charity rose. "Besides, I'm feeling better now."

"If you go to prison, he'll get the babe anyway, soon as it's born." Sophie stuffed hair inside her mobcap. "This way, least you'll get decent food, and the babe won't be stillborn."

Charity hadn't the strength to stop the maid as she banged on the door until the guard opened it, then dashed out. Blowing out a ragged sigh, she decided 'twas best to get dressed for the inevitable meeting with Charles. One she was not looking forward to.

Five minutes later, still light-headed and with a dull throb wracking her womb, she hadn't made much progress.

She attempted to slip her arm through one side of her bodice when the lock jangled, the door slammed open, and in hobbled Charles. Her bare breasts nearly exposed beneath a sheer chemise, she shrieked and turned her back to him.

The back that was marked with scars from her husband's cigar.

Charles Gregson, Lord Villemont, stopped in mid-stride, his fury instantly extinguished by the sight of dozens of burn marks on Charity's back—perfectly circular pink scars that curdled her skin like holes in Swiss cheese.

Charity screeched. "I beg you to leave, milord, until I am dressed."

"Of course," Charles mumbled out, still wincing at the sight as he slipped from the cabin and shut the door. He stood there staring at the oak for several minutes, his mind in chaos, his emotions trampled. He stood there until that silly maid ambled down the companionway, carrying the pitcher of water she'd requested for her mistress, along with a plate of dried biscuits.

"Milord?" She gazed at him inquisitively.

He coughed and straightened his cravat. "I'll send a man to escort Lady Villemont to my cabin in an hour. Make sure she is ready." Then leaning on his cane, he marched as quickly as he could away from the confusing scene.

Confusing, indeed. In truth, confusion had surrounded him, knotting both his thoughts and feelings, ever since the morning at the Bennett estate when he'd caught Charity. Or rather, when she had *willingly* surrendered to a fate that would surely end in her death.

Ignoring the greetings of passing sailors, Charles mounted a ladder and made his way down another hall to his cabin. He closed the door behind him and leaned back onto the hard wood, wishing he could close out the tormenting thoughts afflicting his mind.

He'd always prided himself on understanding the human psyche—what made people do what they did. But that morning, as he'd watched Charity sacrifice herself for no reason he could fathom, he found himself utterly and completely baffled. In addition, 'twas clear to all present that Mr. Dutton and his men could easily defeat the toads Charles had hired. Forsooth, he could see the fury in the man's eyes, could almost taste his desire to do him harm. *Had* tasted it, in fact. Charles rubbed his jaw, still sore from the man's assault, and made his way to a table where he poured a glass of brandy.

Why hadn't Mr. Dutton defeated him and taken Charity for himself? 'Twas the second question that had haunted him since they'd set sail.

And now, the babe. His brother's child growing in that witch's womb! He tossed the brandy to the back of his throat and let out a foul curse. Mayhap 'twas not even his brother's. Herbert had always said Charity was naught but a trollop. However, on the chance she carried his niece or nephew, Charles proceeded to summon his cabin boy and ordered him to bring two meals forthwith. Then dropping into a chair, he poured himself another drink, and waited for his sister-in-law.

By the time she arrived, Charles was on his third glass of Brandy, and feeling rather relaxed. *And* audacious. "Ah, here comes my brother's murderer!" He greeted her as his man escorted her inside. "Do come in and have a seat." He nodded for the man to leave them, and the door slammed shut.

Charity stood, chin up, staring straight at him. "You wanted to see me."

"I wouldn't exactly use the word *want*."

The savory scents from two plates of eggs, sausage, rice, bananas, and fresh coffee drew her gaze to the table where his cabin boy had placed the meals.

"For you, my dear." Charles gave a tight smile. "Help yourself. Your maid informs me we aren't feeding you enough. At least not for two."

"I wish she hadn't told you." She swallowed and placed a hand on her belly.

Strands of brown hair dangled about her neck, a rather lustrous, creamy neck, framed by a lace-embroidered gold bodice that led down to emerald satin skirts. Even with wrinkled attire and shadows beneath her red, swollen eyes, she was a comely woman. Charles had never questioned his brother's attraction. Only why he had married so far beneath him.

"Why do you wish she hadn't told me?" He sneered as the deck tilted slightly, and she stumbled. "Because the babe isn't Herbert's?"

"How dare you?" Chest heaving, her eyes became slits. "Unlike your brother, I was always faithful in our marriage."

"Hmm." He eyed her. "Do sit and eat." He gestured toward a chair beside the table.

"I'm not hungry." She slid onto the chair anyway and pursed her lips. "What do you intend to do with my child?"

Setting down his drink, Charles rose, but the room spun, and he quickly sat back down. Footsteps pounded above, along with the snap of sails shifting in the wind. The deck tilted, and Charles rubbed his temples, seeking clarity...seeking answers. "Why did you surrender to me, Charity? When you were clearly free."

"You wouldn't believe me if I told you."

"I insist." He gazed up at her.

"God told me to."

With an unavoidable chuckle, Charles poured himself more brandy. "Indeed? God speaks to harlot murderesses?"

"Amazing, isn't it?" She gave a curt smile. "In truth, Char—Lord Villemont, I have learned much about God these past weeks. I have learned that no matter the circumstances, He never leaves us, and we must trust Him to see us through and make good of it in the end."

"Humph. Was God making good of it for my brother the day you shot him?" He sipped his drink, his anger returning.

"God cannot help those who refuse His help."

"What foolishness is this? Herbert was a pious man, an honorable man!" He slammed down his drink.

She returned his gaze with one that was oddly calm. "Pious, perhaps. But he didn't know God."

Rising, he hobbled toward her and shoved his glass in her face. Brandy sloshed over the side—a waste of good liquor on this tramp. "What right does a heartless murderer have to judge anyone's faith? My brother attended church whenever the doors opened. He could recite every prayer from the Book of Common Prayers. How many men can claim the same?"

To her credit, she didn't cower beneath his temper. She merely sat, back straight, staring into the cabin. "Never again. Never will I allow you or any man to cause me to live in fear." Her words were soft, yet defiant, and he sensed a strength in them he'd not known she possessed.

Charles stepped back, and she gazed up at him. "Knowing God has naught to do with those things."

"Pshaw!" He stumbled back to the table and set down his glass. Enough Brandy. 'Twas making him soft and ignorant, for deep in the recesses of his mind, the woman's words began to make sense. Memories of his brother drinking to excess, gambling, and womanizing rose to taunt Charles' defense of him. And his temper! A vicious, explosive temper that sent everyone in its path scrambling for cover.

Shaking off the memories, Charles snorted. "And what of your lover, this Mr. Dutton? Seems his affection for you wasn't enough to cause him to risk his life."

"He is *not* my lover. However, I would wager to guess that Eli—Mr. Dutton also decided to trust God and do the right thing."

Charles turned to face her, laughing. "The right thing in sentencing the woman he loves to the noose, *that* right thing?"

"If need be. God is bigger than the noose, milord. But if 'tis the noose that ends my life, He will be ready to receive me into a place far better than this."

Her confident tone, the odd peace shining in her eyes, set him aback. 'Twas as if she believed every word she spoke.

Charles suddenly felt the need to sit for fear of falling. He'd never seen the likes of such devotion to an invisible God. Not in word or ritual. But in the heart. A devotion that sent one to one's death if need be, rather than deny allegiance.

Closing his eyes for a moment, he rubbed his forehead and listened to the swish of water against the hull and whistle of wind in the sails above.

"My brother is the one who scarred your back," he finally said, opening his eyes. A ray of sunlight shifted over Charity from the porthole as if pointing him to the truth.

She swallowed, looked down, and nodded.

"What else?" When she hesitated, he added, "The truth. I wish to know."

"He beat me repeatedly. I lost our first child due to his abuse."

Though Charles longed to deny it, to defend his brother's honor, he knew he must finally admit the truth of her words. "I suspected," he mumbled, then wished he hadn't.

"What?" She looked at him, anger sparking in her eyes.

"Herbert always had a violent tendency. So much anger in him from Father... just boiling beneath the surface."

"Why didn't you do something, help me, help him?!" She stood and walked to look out the porthole, her face a mask of anger and pain.

"Do you know what my brother meant to me, *witch*?"

She bristled at the title, but replied. "I know you loved him."

"Did you know I'd be dead without him? Ah, yes. I can see he never told you." Charles leaned back in his chair and sighed. "My father was a cruel man. He hated Herbert and me, made it quite plain he wanted naught to do with either of us. But you know boys. We seemed to always get in his way. Punishments came swift and hard. Beatings, starvation, banished to the barn on cold winter nights."

Charity faced him. "What of your mother?"

"She could do naught to stop him. 'Twas probably why she died so young." He choked back pain at the memory. "Regardless, when Father over-drank and was in a rage about something, he would have the carriage hitched, and he'd drive it like a madman over our estate for hours." Pain pinched his leg and he reached down to rub it. "On one such night, Herbert and I had escaped while our nanny slept, and we were climbing trees, pretending to be infantrymen spying on the French. I fell from a particularly high branch onto the dirt pathway just as Father's carriage turned the corner, heading straight for me."

He hesitated, picturing the hooves pounding his way, flinging mud into the air. He remembered the terror. "I was too stunned to move. 'Twas Herbert who leapt from the tree and pulled me to safety. At least most of me. One of the horses trampled my leg." He sighed. "Did Father see me? I'll never know. But if Herbert had not risked his life to pull me out of its path, more than my leg would have been crushed."

He looked up at her and found her eyes moist with tears.

"So you see, I owed him everything. Still do."

"Which is why you crossed an ocean to find me. For him," she said softly.

"Yes."

She approached and stopped before him. "I don't blame you, Charles. But you must know one thing. Your brother was going to beat me, beat my unborn child. I couldn't lose another baby. So I grabbed his gun... he tried to take it from me." She shook her head, tears trickling down her cheeks. "Still, you are right. If not for me, your brother would be alive."

She knelt by his side and gazed up at him. "I am sorry, Charles. I'm sorry you suffered such a cruel childhood. I am so sorry for what I've done. I deserve whatever punishment is coming to me." She lowered her chin.

Yes, she did. And he'd see to it she got it. Yet—he shifted in his seat—where was the anger of only a moment ago? It seemed to drip from him like the tears now sliding off this woman's chin into her lap.

Deep down, he'd known his brother was hurting Charity. Yet he'd done nothing. Tried to deny it. Kept it hidden because of a debt he felt he owed. Didn't that make him as much to blame for Herbert's death as this woman? Mayhap more.

Shame swamped him. What of this God of hers? Not the God of the liturgy, the rituals, or even the church. But a real God who waved at him from her eyes, smiling and luring and offering unconditional love... something Charles had never known.

And suddenly, he found himself wanting to know more about this God.

Charity rose and started for the door. "If that is all, milord, I'm not feeling well."

"Nay, that is not all." He spoke more sternly than intended as he struggled to stand.

She stiffened, awaiting his wrath.

"You have endured enough at my brother's hand."

Ever so slowly, she turned to face him, confusion clouding her expression.

Grabbing his cane, he limped toward her. "There's been far too much suffering, wouldn't you agree?"

"What are you saying, milord?"

# Chapter 31

Charles Towne harbor looked exactly like Charity's sisters had described it. Gorgeous, sunlit waters gushing through a narrow inlet into the sea from two mighty rivers that divided and cradled the magnificent outpost—a walled outpost, complete with gun turrets and drawbridges. Though, as they sailed closer, it appeared the town had spilled outside its original walls.

Charity could hardly believe it! She would soon be reunited with her family. A family she had not appreciated when she'd been growing up, but one she now realized she'd been fortunate to have. Even her father, with his cold, harsh demeanor, had always provided for them and ensured their safety. And he had never once hit Charity. Or any of them. Indeed, she was even excited to see him, though he was most likely out to sea.

The best part about coming home was that she would never have to leave. Another thing she could hardly believe—she was finally free! After her talk with Charles that night over a week past, he'd informed her that he forgave her and planned on turning the ship around to take her home. At first she hadn't believed him. Surely 'twas another of his cruel jokes intended to torture her—a common trait of his brother's.

But after she'd been brought back to her cabin, two things happened which sparked her hope. One, the door was not locked, freeing her to roam the ship. And two, she both heard and felt the ship turn around in the pounding of feet above, shouts, thundering of sails, and tilting of the deck.

In the days that followed, she and Sophie ate like queens, and Charles often called her into his cabin for discussions. They spoke of many things, but mostly he wished to discuss God—this God who was both Father and Friend and who continually surprised her beyond her wildest dreams. In the wee hours of the night during one of their long discussions, Charles bowed knees and head and submitted himself to God through His son Jesus. And Charity finally realized why God had told her to return and surrender...why He had told Elias to stand down.

'Twas for the soul of Charles Gregson, Lord Villemont.

Ah, the lengths God went to save a single soul! That He had used her and Elias' obedience to do so warmed her to her toes, and she thanked Him that she had obeyed and been able to witness a soul snatched from darkness and brought into the light. If she hadn't trusted God, who knows what would have happened to Charles?

But now she knew that God was indeed in control and that He always had a plan. If she would but listen! And then trust.

Sophie looped her arm through Charity's as the ship canted over a wavelet. Smells of tar and fish and pine filled her nose—different scents than the Caribbean—as they neared the docks.

"'Tis cold, Milady." Sophie shivered. "I though' Charles Towne were warmer than England."

"Not in the winter. We are but a week past Christmas." Charity glanced toward shore where workers decked in heavy coats, hats, and scarves hauled goods to and from the wharves.

At least a dozen ships were anchored in the bay and several more tied to pilings at the end of piers jutting far into the water. Bells clanged, birds squawked, water sloshed, and she could even hear the click-clack of carriage wheels in the distance.

Charity could hardly contain her excitement.

"Do you think your family will accept me, milady?" Sophie said, biting her lip.

Charity drew her close. "Of course they will. They will love you as I do." However, whether her family would understand Charity's part in her husband's death, or—she placed a hand over her womb—that she carried his child, she had no idea. The last thing she wished was to bring further shame to them.

Thank God the child seemed well again. In fact, she could have sworn she'd felt him kick that morning. If only she had someone to share it with, a man who loved her and who would love her child.

*Elias.*

She pressed a finger over the cross beneath her bodice. Though she'd tried to avoid thinking of him, he consumed her thoughts day and night. She had a feeling that would be the case for quite some time. At first, she intended to seek him out after she got settled, tell him the good news about Charles, and that she accepted his courtship if he still wanted her. But then she realized how selfish she was being. Elias would be much better off without her. If she stayed out of his life, he would soon forget her and meet another lady, a chaste woman who'd never been married... one who wasn't carrying another man's child.

And who hadn't murdered her husband.

'Twas for the best. Though her many tears spent during the long nights spoke otherwise.

"Wha' will you do in Charles Towne, milady, now tha' you are free. Start your printin' business as you always hoped?"

"You know me too well, Sophie. I'm not one to sit idly around. And with this wee one"—she gazed down smiling—

"I'm not likely to attract many suitors." Not that any man could ever compare with Elias. "Nay, Sophie, God has given me a better idea." She gazed over the multicolored roofs peeking at her above the walls surrounding Charles Towne. "With His help, I want to open a home where women who are being beaten by their husbands can find shelter—women who have nowhere else to turn."

Sophie sniffed, her eyes moistening. "Oh, milady, wha' a grand idea!"

After the sails were furled, yards struck, and the anchor tossed, a boat was lowered to take them to shore. Standing there with the brisk wind slicing through her, Charity turned to face Charles, a man she'd grown oddly fond of these past few weeks.

"My man will bring you to shore and hire a carriage to take you home." His once cold eyes now held a warmth that made her return his smile. An icy breeze skimmed his short light hair and caused him to tuck his scarf tighter around his neck.

Charity took his hands in hers. "How can I ever thank you, Charles?"

Sighing, he glanced over the bay. "There is no need. We both have suffered much. And now, thanks to you, I have hope for the future."

"You must promise to return and meet your niece," she said.

"Niece, eh? I wouldn't miss it."

She squeezed his hands. "God be with you, Charles."

"And with you, milady." He bowed to kiss her hand.

An hour later Charity and Sophie stood shivering before a red house on Hassel Street.

"This must be it, Sophie. There aren't any other red houses on this street." Charity glanced down the row of homes on either side.

Light beamed through windows, but no sounds came from within. And no footman had appeared when the carriage ambled into the driveway. Odd.

"I don't know why I'm so nervous," Charity said, teeth chattering. Finally, she raised her hand and lifted the brass door knocker, her heart all but stopping in her chest.

Moments later, the door opened to Edwin's stodgy, angular face. *Yes, the right place!*

"Edwin!" Charity couldn't help but leap into his arms, hugging him. "'Tis me, Charity."

Stumbling backward, he pushed from her and stared, jowls quivering and shock streaking across his eyes. "Miss Charity!" he finally exclaimed. "How? What? Oh, my." He withdrew a handkerchief, mopped his brow, and lowered to a chair against the wall. "My nerves."

Charity tugged Sophie inside and shut the door, only then noticing the cases, trunks, and portmanteaus stacked in the corner of the foyer.

"Faith! Hope! Grace!" She shouted up the stairway as she removed her cloak and gloves and set them on the banister. Nothing.

Distant laughter lured her down the hallway to the back parlor, Sophie hurrying behind her. As she neared the room, male and female voices, along with the crackle of a fire met her ears. *Male?* Definitely not her father's voice.

Drawing a deep breath, she entered the room.

Her sister Faith, red hair spilling to her waist in a fiery waterfall, stood by the fireplace caressing the jaw of a rather handsome man in a suit of black velvet. *Caressing? Faith?* The woman who had written off men years ago? Charity's gaze shifted to Hope, her blonde hair pinned up in a bounty of curls, sitting on the sofa beside a man who looked at her as if she were more precious than gold. And as if that wasn't proof enough that Charity had gone mad, she spotted Grace, the dark-haired beauty leaning over what appeared to be charts, beside a man who looked very much like a pirate!

Charity couldn't move. She could only stand there and stare at the three women she loved most in the world, talking, laughing, and enjoying their male companions. So much for Faith's bold declaration before they left Portsmouth that they would all either be stuck in unloving marriages or end up spinsters! Yet here they were, seemingly happy and loved. Charity began to cry.

"Can I help you, Miss?" the voice came from behind as a Negro woman nudged beside her, carrying tea service on a tray.

Charity was about to respond when squeals and shouts warned her of the coming onslaught as her sisters bombarded from all sides.

"Charity! Charity! I can't believe you're here!"

"How did you...? Where...?"

"Oh, praise be to God! Just, look at you! Thank goodness you are well."

Overcome with emotion, tears dribbled down Charity's cheeks as she folded into their loving embraces. Finally, they backed away to look at her, while the three men stood in the background, smiling.

"So this be the wayward sister." After setting down the tea, the Negro woman placed hands on her rounded hips and smiled. "I told you the good Lord would fix thin's, didn't I?"

"You did at that, Molly," Hope chimed. "Molly, meet our sister, Charity. Charity, this is our cook, Molly."

"Pleased t' meet you." Molly's grin couldn't have been brighter. "These girls have missed you terribly."

"Thank you, Molly. It's good to be home." Charity glanced over her sisters, still not believing her eyes. "Oh, I almost forgot." Turning, she dragged Sophie forward. "This is Sophie, my lady's maid."

"Welcome, Sophie," Faith said, and her sisters joined in with their warm greetings.

Sophie smiled, even as a blush reddened her cheeks.

"Bless your heart, Sophie," Molly exclaimed. "You came all the way from England wit' Charity?" Molly took her arm. "Come on, now. I'll get you settled in a nice warm room. You look as tired as I feel."

"That's all right, Molly," Charity said. "Sophie's welcome to stay with us."

"I don't mind, milady," Sophie said. "Enjoy your sisters. Truth is, I *am* cold and tired."

"Then I'll see you later." Charity smiled as Molly led her from the room.

Faith grabbed Charity's hand and squeezed it. "You look well, Charity. When did you arrive in Charles Towne?"

"Only an hour ago."

"You must be beyond exhaustion. Please sit." Grace led her to the sofa, and Charity sank onto the soft cushions. She ran her hands over the floral print, so familiar, so full of memories. And she was suddenly glad Father had insisted they bring some of their things with them in the move.

When she glanced up, everyone was staring at her. *Smiling.* Even the three handsome men standing before the fire. She took a minute to gather her emotions as she studied the well-appointed parlor. Chiseled stone made up the fireplace surrounding flames that sizzled and crackled and filled the room with warmth. A garland made of evergreen intertwined with holly, pine cones, and berries was strung over the mantle, matching the ones around the windows decorated for Christmas. Two sofas framed a table in the center of the room, while beyond stood an old oak desk, a gaming table and chairs, and a pianoforte. Brocade curtains hung around two windows through which Charity saw a garden sparse in the grip of winter.

Dabbing her eyes, she gazed at her sisters' loving smiles. "Why are you all staring at me?"

Grace poured her a cup of tea and handed it to her. "Because we cannot believe you are here."

"Do tell us what happened," Hope said, her blue eyes sparkling with excitement. "I cannot wait another moment."

"I will." Charity sipped the warm liquid, savoring the lemony ginger taste, and wrapped her cold hands around the cup. "But first you must introduce me to these handsome gentlemen."

The man in the fine velvet suit stepped forward, and Faith took his arm, smiling up at him. "This is my husband, Dajon Waite."

"Husband?" Setting down her tea, Charity leapt to her feet and dashed to congratulate the couple. She grabbed Dajon's hand. "Oh, my. Pleased to meet any man able to capture Faith's heart."

Dajon shared a knowing glance with Faith. "'Twas a formidable feat, I'll grant you."

Everyone laughed.

Hope sashayed forward. "Made all the harder when Faith became a pirate."

Charity couldn't help but chuckle. "Indeed?" She gave Faith a look of reprimand. "I had my suspicions about you, sister dear."

Grace slid onto a chair and reached up to hold the dark-haired pirate's hand. "She was about to be hanged when Dajon saved her."

Charity gasped and shook her head. "I see I have missed much."

Hope moved to stand beside the third man, a light-haired gentleman in plain attire, bearing a kind face and a confidence about him that put Charity at ease. "This is

Nathaniel Mason. But our story is rather boring compared to Faith's."

Grace laughed. "If you call about to be sold as a slave on St. Kitts boring. Or surviving a hurricane at sea only to be stranded on an island."

Hope shrugged. "'Twas not so bad when Nathaniel was there." She gazed up at him.

Nathaniel drew her hand up for a kiss. "You nearly killed me multiple times, if I recall, kitten."

"Oh, pah." Hope pouted. "I didn't mean to. Besides, you're a survivor, Nathaniel Mason."

He slid a finger over her jaw and smiled. "I'd have to be to marry you."

Charity stared at the happy couple, overjoyed that Hope had found a man strong enough to tame her. She hadn't the best reputation back in Portsmouth, and Charity had always feared she would end up in a far worse situation than Charity's.

*Wait.* "Did you say marry?"

Hope lifted her hand, and firelight sparkled over the ring on her finger. "We are to be wed in the spring!"

"I'm so happy for you, Hope." Charity hugged her and greeted Nathaniel.

"And now." Charity raised a brow and turned to Grace. "Out with it, sister. Do tell me you haven't married this pirate?"

The dark-haired man acted indignant. "*Zut alors!* I am no pirate, Madam," he spoke in a French accent. "Though I admit I'm related to one. *Mais,* I beg you, do not say such a thing or *ma cherie* may change her mind." He winked at Grace.

She smiled up at him and squeezed his hand. "Never, *monsieur.*"

Faith gestured toward the man. "Meet Monsieur Rafe Dubois. He kidnapped Grace in order to sell her to a Spanish

Don who wanted revenge on Papa." She said the words with a yawn as if it were an everyday occurrence, causing them all to laugh.

Charity's head spun. "I can't wait to hear every detail! I thought to come home to three sisters, but now I am blessed to have three brothers as well."

"Three brothers."—Dajon arched a brow and gripped the hilt of his service sword— "who will protect you from whoever is chasing you."

Charity's throat burned with emotion even as confusion tripped her mind. "How did you—"

"Which brings us to you," Hope said. "What on earth are you doing here? We thought you were—"

"On your way to Portsmouth for trial!" Admiral Henry Westcott marched into the room with the authority of his station, dressed in his uniform blues, and wearing his usual scowl.

At first he merely stared at her, the only indication of emotion the shifting of his jaw. Charity's insides cringed, awaiting his castigation. But then the oddest thing happened. Tears blurred his eyes, and he seemed to be trying to say something, but choked in the process. Finally, he ran for her and surrounded her with beefy arms.

"Charity, my child, my precious child." He rubbed her head, loosening hair from her pins.

Stunned, Charity stiffened, waiting for the joke to end, the shouting to start. But then he nudged her back to examine her. "You look well! I was so worried. We feared for your life."

"You did?"

Faith intervened. "We heard your husband was dead, Charity."

"Indeed." Her father released her. "At first, word was he died in a duel, and I sailed quickly from my post along the African coast to Portsmouth to bring you home."

Charity swallowed, bracing for a flood of shame. "But when you got there, you heard a different tale."

"We heard you'd killed your husband," Grace said, holding Rafe's hand, yet the usual judgment was missing from her voice.

"And that you'd fled," Hope added.

Charity stared at them all. Why weren't they angry, ashamed of her, disgusted? Why wasn't her father ordering her to turn herself in?

Instead, pulling out a pipe, the Admiral moved to the fire to light it. "Hence, I set sail immediately for Charles Towne, thinking you surely would come here first." He puffed until rings of smoke shot from the top of his pipe. Somehow, she had missed seeing him enjoy his pipe, missed smelling the sweet, woodsy scent.

"Dear one." He looked at her, sorrow in his eyes, then glanced at her sisters. "I've not been the best father to you girls, and I'm sorry for it."

Charity's legs turned to pudding. She lowered to the sofa, staring at the man who never apologized for anything.

"Can you forgive me, Charity?"

"Of course, Papa." She fought back tears, tried to rise, but found she couldn't. "I must admit"—she glanced at her sisters—"we were not the easiest daughters to raise."

Dajon coughed, while Monsieur Dubois and Mr. Mason chuckled.

Charity fingered the rim of her tea cup. "I'm sorry. The news of what I…what happened to my husband must have upset you all."

"Upset? Nay." Faith glanced at Hope. "The scoundrel deserved what he got."

Charity's gaze locked with Hope's, seeking the anger she deserved. Or at the very least, the pain and sorrow of loss. But she found none of those. "Hope, we must talk. I owe you the deepest of apologies."

"You owe me nothing." The sweetest smile graced her lips. "But I would love to talk."

"Regardless," Grace interjected, breaking the sudden dour mood. "We were terribly worried about you."

"In truth,"—Charity lifted her teacup—"I intended to sail here right away but—"

"Your brother-in-law found you," her father interjected.

Confusion spun eddies in Charity's mind. "How do you know that?"

Footsteps pounded in the hallway, drawing all eyes.

"*I* told them." Elias entered the room, his blue eyes latching upon her.

# Chapter 32

Elias stared at the woman he loved more than anyone in the world, the woman he thought was surely in the middle of the Atlantic by now, locked in some cabin or worse—chained in the hold. When he'd entered the house after helping Lucas settle the horses, he thought he'd heard her sweet voice drifting down the hall, teasing him cruelly. Thinking he was going mad, he'd shaken it from his head, but it rose again, louder and clearer as he approached the parlor.

Now, as he rubbed his eyes and gazed at her again, he saw it was no trick. She was here! Sitting on the sofa, eyes wide, mouth open, looking a bit tired and bedraggled, but more beautiful than he remembered.

A thousand questions chased each other through his mind as the teacup slid from her hands and dropped to the carpet by her feet, liquid spilling. Slowly she rose, staring at him in wonderment. "I'm seeing things. You're not here."

He started for her. "I assure you, my little mermaid, I am."

Hope giggled.

Wobbling, Charity raised a hand to her forehead, but he wrapped an arm around her waist before she fell. "See, I'm quite real." Leaning, he kissed her cheek, wanting to kiss more...wanting to absorb her in his arms, but feeling too many eyes upon them.

She glanced up at him, eyes moist with shock and joy and love. "How...?"

"We were planning to sail to England tomorrow for your trial." Grace tucked an errant strand of hair into her bun. "Father intended to hire the best barrister he could."

"He did?" Charity shifted her gaze to her father as if confounded by the idea.

Elias tapped her affectionately on the nose. "Praise be to God! How are you here in Charles Towne? Did you jump ship again and swim across the sea?"

Finally, she smiled. "I do believe my mermaid days are over. Nay. Charles brought me here, if you can believe it."

"Your brother-in-law?" Faith cocked her head. "The man who sailed across the sea to bring you back to hang, *that* Charles?"

"Yes." Charity's eyes twinkled with delight. "And you'll never guess, but he intends to tell the authorities back home that I didn't commit the crime. So I am free!" She glanced at all of them.

Not quite believing his ears, Elias shook his head as cheers shot into the room.

Grace clasped her hands together, beaming, while Hope and Faith hugged one another.

"Praise be to God," Nathaniel exclaimed. Dajon added his "Amen!", and Rafe began chattering in French.

Admiral Westcott remained by the fireplace, watching his children proudly.

Elias brushed a lock of Charity's hair behind her ear. "I don't understand. Why would he do that?"

"'Twas God who convinced him," Charity replied, staring up at Elias as if she didn't believe he was real. "'Tis a long, happy story. But you still haven't told me why you are here."

Hope sashayed over to Elias. "Imagine our surprise when Edwin announced that a man looking like a pirate was at our door informing us he was Charity's beau."

"And," Faith added, hand on her hip. "Telling us quite a tale about pirate attacks, storms, natives, and you running from the noose!"

Charity gazed up at him, confusion lining her forehead.

"I came to get their help." Elias ran a finger down her cheek, smiling. "I knew you had family here with the surname Westcott. 'Twas easy to find them."

Admiral Westcott placed a boot on the mantel step and grinned. "Ergo, the reason we were all setting sail on the morrow."

Grace smiled at Elias. "In just a few days, Elias has become part of the family."

"You have welcomed me warmly." Elias glanced over them all. "For that, I am most grateful."

"Now we see why 'twas so easy to do so." Hope gave a coy smile. "'Tis obvious Charity adores you."

*She does?* Elias glanced down at her and found a most adorable blush reddening her cheeks.

"Besides." Faith's brow rose. "Turns out Elias has much in common with our beaus. All of them are men of the sea. Nathaniel with his shipyard and merchant business, Dajon and my"—she glanced up at her husband and grinned—"well, whatever we do on the sea. And Rafe's"—she cleared her throat and chuckled—"*sailing* experience. You can imagine they've had much to discuss."

Rafe slapped Elias on the back. "*Certainement!* Part of the brotherhood of pirates, non?"

Elias laughed. "Not any more, my friend."

"*Oui,* I have changed my ways as well." He glanced back at Grace and smiled.

Admiral Westcott chuckled. "Good thing, or I'd have to arrest both of you."

"There is something else I must tell you." Charity swallowed and took a deep breath. "I am with child." She pressed a hand to her belly. "My husband's."

At first they all gaped at her, and Elias worried their reaction would put a damper on such a joyful reunion.

But finally, one by one, they all approached Charity and embraced her. "A child! Oh, my!"

"How wonderful! We shall have a little one running around the house!" Hope clapped her hands together.

Elias could swear he saw Admiral Westcott wipe a tear from his eyes. "I do hope 'tis a boy. Egad, I don't need any more daughters!"

Everyone laughed.

Charity glanced up at Elias with such love and promise, he thought he would burst.

Faith cleared her throat. "Let us give these two some privacy, shall we? Besides, we have unpacking to do."

"Oh!" Hope threw hands to her cheeks. "We must have Molly prepare a feast! You may have missed Christmas, but you haven't missed the feast of Epiphany. We will all go to church tomorrow and then come home to celebrate your homecoming with the greatest feast you've ever had."

"Wonderful idea," Grace said, rising.

Faith stopped before Charity and embraced her once again. "Finally, we are all home together. And this time to stay!"

Elias forced back his own tears at the happy scene as, one by one, everyone slipped from the room, leaving him alone with Charity. Silently he thanked God for delivering her from the noose, for bringing her here to him—so much more than he had prayed for! But wasn't that just like God? Yet he hadn't had time to prepare what he must ask her next, and he found a sudden nervousness tightening his heart. So much had happened since they first declared their love, so many lies exposed, so much heartache. Elias had not fought to save her from Charles, though it was within his power to do so. Did she understand why? Or had the few weeks at sea convinced her he could not be trusted with her heart?

No sooner did they all leave, than Charity did what she'd
been wanting to do ever since Elias had first appeared in the
doorway. She turned and fell into his embrace. Arms strong
and warm wrapped around her, squeezing tighter and tighter,
until she felt as if she would melt into him... become a part
of him and never leave. If only she could...

He laid his chin atop her head. "I still can't believe you're
here. And free of Villemont!" He rubbed her back. "He was
so intent on your punishment."

Charity drew in a deep breath of his scent—earth and
brine and a new scent, horses this time. "God. 'Twas God
who changed his heart."

Pushing back, she gazed up at him. "'Tis such a
miraculous story, Elias, and I can't wait to tell you. But for
now, I just want to stare at you." She squeezed his thick,
solid arms. "Feel you. Touch you." She reached up to rub his
jaw, rough like sand. And see the love pouring from his eyes.
"Elias, is it true? Am I free, and you are here? I never
thought I'd see you again."

"You didn't plan on seeking me out?" Pain tainted his
voice.

Turning, she moved to the fireplace, shaking her head.
"I'm not good enough for you, Elias. You deserve a real lady,
not a damaged one." She tugged out the cross and cradled it
in her hands.

His bootsteps thudded on the wooden floor toward her.
Taking her elbow, he turned her to face him, his gaze
dropping to the cross. "You still have it." He smiled.

Pulling it over her head, she handed it to him. "Of course.
'Twas all I had left of you." She placed it in his hand. "You
cannot know the strength it brought me, the hope it gave me
during my imprisonment on Charles' ship."

"I'm so glad," he said. "Seems God has used His cross to
free us both."

Before she could lower her hand, he grabbed it and placed the cross back inside, then gently closed her fingers over it.

"I lied to you, Elias." Tears burned her eyes. "I lied to you over and over. How can you ever trust me? Especially after what happened with Rachel." She looked down at the wood floor and his black boots standing there so firmly—just like the man, a bulwark of strength. "You cannot know how sorry I am."

"'Tis true, mermaid, you did spin quite a number of tales for my benefit." Oddly his voice carried no anger. "And I do hate being lied to." He huffed, placing hands at his waist.

Unable to bear his rejection, Charity turned to leave, but he snatched her hand and kept her in place. She lowered her eyes. Not wanting to see his expression when he told her he was glad she was well and safe, that he would have traveled to England to save her from the noose, but that anything that existed between them was over.

"And you *did* murder your husband." His tone bore the slightest hint of humor, and she couldn't imagine why.

"'Twas an accident. I hope you know that, Elias. He came at me—"

He pressed a finger on her lips. "No need. I don't have to hear it to believe you could never do such a thing."

She stared up at him.

"We are all so flawed, we humans." He cupped her jaw and caressed her cheek. "We make mistakes every day, and we will make many more in our lifetimes. Your intent was to save yourself and your child. How can I blame you for not trusting me or any man after what you endured?"

"'Tis no excuse, Elias."

"Nay, but it is a reason. Besides, how can I not forgive you when God has forgiven me of so much?"

A tiny speck of hope blossomed in Charity's heart. A heart that now sped up uncontrollably.

Elias knelt before her, his handsome face peering up into hers, his eyes full of expectation and a tinge of fear—something she couldn't recall ever seeing within them. "Charity, I love you. I promise I will never lie to you. I will never hurt you, physically or emotionally. And I will do all in my power to make you happy. Please do me the honor of marrying me."

Elation, disbelief, and overwhelming joy tingled over her entire body. Her mind reeled, her breath heightened. Dropping to her knees beside him, laughter bubbled from her lips as tears trickled down her cheeks. "Elias." She embraced him. "I'm so happy, I shall burst. Of course, I will marry you. Yes, yes, yes!" She covered his face with kisses then pushed back, sudden fear worming its way into her joy. "But the babe?" Had he forgotten?

He laid his hands on her belly. "I will love him or her as my own." A mischievous spark twinkled in his eyes. "On one condition."

Charity's stomach tightened. "What?"

"That we have many more." He cupped her chin affectionately and drew her lips to his.

# About the Author

AWARD WINNING AND BEST-SELLING AUTHOR, MARYLU TYNDALL dreamt of pirates and sea-faring adventures during her childhood days on Florida's Coast. With more than seventeen books published, she makes no excuses for the deep spiritual themes embedded within her romantic adventures. Her hope is that readers will not only be entertained but will be brought closer to the Creator who loves them beyond measure. In a culture that accepts the occult, wizards, zombies, and vampires without batting an eye, MaryLu hopes to show the awesome present and powerful acts of God in a dying world. A Christy award nominee, MaryLu makes her home with her husband, six children, two grandchildren, and several stray cats on the California coast.

If you enjoyed this book, one of the nicest ways to say "thank you" to an author and help them be able to continue writing is to leave a favorable review on Amazon! Barnes and Noble, Kobo, Itunes (And elsewhere, too!) I would appreciate it if you would take a moment to do so. Thanks so much!

Comments? Questions? I love hearing from my readers, so feel free to contact me via my website:

http://www.marylutyndall.com

Or email me at:

marylu_tyndall@yahoo.com

Follow me on:

FACEBOOK:
https://www.facebook.com/marylu.tyndall.author

TWITTER:
https://twitter.com/MaryLuTyndall

BLOG:
http://crossandcutlass.blogspot.com/

PINTEREST:
http://www.pinterest.com/mltyndall/

To hear news about special prices and new releases that only my subscribers receive, sign up for my newsletter on my website or blog! http://www.marylutyndall.com

# Other Books by MaryLu Tyndall

THE REDEMPTION

THE RELIANCE

THE RESTITUTION

THE RANSOM

THE RECKONING

THE FALCON AND THE SPARROW

THE RED SIREN

THE BLUE ENCHANTRESS

THE RAVEN SAINT

CHARLES TOWNE BELLES TRILOGY

SURRENDER THE HEART

SURRENDER THE NIGHT

SURRENDER THE DAWN

SURRENDER TO DESTINY TRILOGY

VEIL OF PEARLS

FORSAKEN DREAMS

ELUSIVE HOPE

ABANDONED MEMORIES

ESCAPE TO PARADISE TRILOGY

PEARLS FROM THE SEA DEVOTIONAL

CENTRAL PARK RENDEZVOUS

TEARS OF THE SEA

WESTWARD CHRISTMAS BRIDES